"Zuno's novel is a splendid historical epic with complex characters and richly drawn settings...An accomplished and stirring tale from a promising new author of historical fiction."

-Kirkus Reviews

"Zuno's enticing saga strikes an even balance between informative narrative and textured dialogue and even includes a sprinkling of humor...In all, this well-crafted blend of research, characterization, and moving story progression should appeal to those drawn to entertaining, believable, historical fiction."

-BlueInk

FREEDOM DUES

ISBN: 978-1-734-1652-1-0

Names: Zuno, Indra, 1970- author.
Title: Freedom Dues / Indra Zuno.
Description: San Diego : Spinning a Yarn Press, 2020.
Also available in audiobook format.

Identifiers: LCCN 2019916394 | ISBN 978-1-7341652-1-0 (paperback)
ISBN 978-1-7341652-2-7 (hardcover) | ISBN 978-1-7341652-0-3 (ebook)

Subjects: LCSH: Indentured servants--Fiction. | Liberty--Fiction.
Eighteenth century--Fiction. | Philadelphia (Pa.)--Fiction. |
Historical fiction.
BISAC: FICTION / Historical / General. | GSAFD: Historical fiction.

Classification: LCC PS3626.U56 F74 2020 (print)
LCC PS3626.U56 (ebook) | DDC 813/.6--dc23.

Spinning a Yarn Press
4075 Park Blvd., Suite 102-148
San Diego, CA 92103

FREEDOM DUES

a novel

5/7/21

To Dupre,
who keeps us connected
come rain or shine or
pandemics. :)

INDRA ZUNO

May 2021

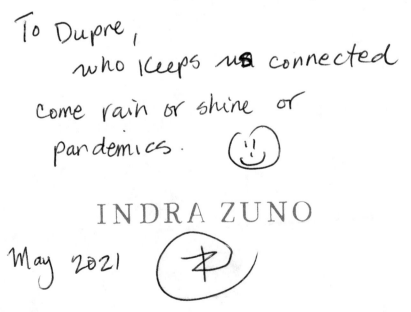

To my mother. Mami, I am beyond grateful for your unwavering support; without it, this book would not exist.

ACKNOWLEDGEMENTS

My UCLA creative writing instructors were extraordinarily generous with their wisdom and kindness. Steven Wolfson, you were my first teacher and my first editor, and you are my own personal Obi-Wan. Mark Sarvas, I could listen to your lectures till the end of time. Trebor Healey, I can't wait to hear your thoughts on three scenes that benefited from your class—you can't miss them! Robert Eversz, thank you for your detailed and thoughtful notes.

I once heard the opening statements at the awards ceremony of an association that recognizes editing in film, television, and documentaries: "…another year saving performers' careers." That's how I feel about my editors: Aaron Schlechter, Leslie Molnar, and Laurel Robinson.

Thank you to the crew of the *Lady Washington*, especially Johann Steinke, captain extraordinaire, and bosun Ryan Karakai, for sharing their knowledge with me.

I was honored to experience the annual Delaware Days with the Delaware tribe. Jim Rementer is a worthy guardian of the Delawares' language and traditions.

I was starstruck to meet Al Saguto, former master cordwainer at Colonial Williamsburg. But for Al and his apprentices, Mallie would have worn wooden clogs. The horror!

I was lucky to meet Harry Kyriakodis when he gave a lecture at the Historical Society of Pennsylvania. His book *Philadelphia's Lost Waterfront* was a wealth of information.

It has been a delight to correspond with Dauvit Horsbroch of the Scots Language Centre.

One of the highlights of this journey was visiting White's Tavern with the Belfast Pub Crawl led by Colin Brown.

The staff at the Ulster American Folk Park and the Ulster Folk Museum, and everyone I met in Belfast and Lisburn, was warm and welcoming.

Thank you to William Grow from the Fireman's Hall Museum in Philadelphia for taking the time to answer my emails.

David and Ginger Hildebrand, from the Colonial Music Institute, helped me more than they know.

Hattie Frederick graciously took time to teach me the basics of cribbage and reviewed a scene to confirm it was portrayed accurately.

Thank you to Jack Marietta, author of *Troubled Experiment: Crime and Justice in Pennsylvania, 1682–1800.* His book and answers to my questions were invaluable.

Thank you to Michael Horgan, from the California Blacksmith Association, and the blacksmiths at Los Encinos State Historic Park, for keeping history alive.

Ben LeVasseur, an expert in cedar shingles, helped me fix a scene that would have been implausible as originally written.

Thank you to my suffering friends who read the very rough first drafts: Adrian, Jason, Mark, and Paul. Your encouraging words truly put wind beneath my wings.

Thank you to my friends and family, who waited year after year as I posted updates and almost theres. You never grew tired of cheering me on.

Baby Cakes! Thank you, Yvette, for being my best friend.

I have no words to express how grateful I am to you, my Wolf, for your generosity of heart. May your moccasins always be dry, and your path clear of logs and briars.

PART ONE

CHAPTER ONE

July 6, 1729
London, Covent Garden

The small girl sat cross-legged with her back to the cracked window of the one-bedroom tenement apartment. A tortoiseshell cat brushed against her grimy and patched blue linen skirts, and she picked it up, brushing from its fur flakes of paint that the walls constantly shed. The cat nuzzled into the girl's milky-white cheek. A pink scar ran from the outer corner of her right eye to her chin. The girl watched in fascination as a young woman with auburn hair and freckles, wearing only a shift, raised her arms above her head while two other women placed a sort of hollow dome made of cork over her abdomen and secured it with twine. The girl giggled, a chirruping sound that, coupled with her slight frame, made her seem younger than her ten years. She nestled the cat in her skirts and smiled as it curled into a warm, purring puddle of fur.

The woman gestured impatiently at the petticoat, dress, and gloves that were laid out on the only bed in the room. "Get the clothes, Mallie."

The girl gently lifted the cat onto the floor, then jumped to her feet in one agile movement. She handed the clothes to the woman and sat on the edge of the bed.

"Off," the woman snapped.

"I wasn't going ter sleep on it," Mallie said softly. She plopped back down on the floor and returned the cat to her lap. "Lizzie!" she exclaimed when the woman was fully dressed. "Yer truly look as if yor childing!"

Lizzie pressed a velvet heart-shaped beauty patch on her right cheek, the sign of a married woman. "Who'll be me maidservant today?" She turned to one of the women who had attached her fake belly. "Winnet?"

"Yeah, it's me turn," said the woman.

"Mallie, get up," Lizzie said.

"Can't yer take Betsy?"

"Get up."

The cat meowed in complaint as it was lifted yet again, and Mallie kissed its head before setting it down. She stood up, reluctantly this time, then grabbed a basket covered with a linen rag. Winnet lit a candle and led the way three floors down through the narrow, windowless staircase, dark even in the middle of the day. They exited into shadows cast by leaning tenements rising on both sides of the alley, which in turn steered them to the street. On the sidewalk, they skirted a dead horse, and Mallie merged into the thick crowd of pedestrians, ahead of Lizzie and Winnet. When they reached Grace Church Street, Mallie stood aside to let them pass. Then she crossed the street and followed behind them, carefully avoiding piles of manure and stagnant puddles of rain and urine. Sulfurous coal smoke seemed to pour out of every building—the earthenware factories, blacksmiths' and glassblowers' shops, and houses—enveloping everything and everyone. A young shoeblack at a corner looked up from the boots he was shining and smiled.

"Mallie!"

Mallie waved happily and, without slowing down, pointed toward Lizzie. The shoeblack nodded knowingly and returned to his work. Always keeping her distance from Lizzie and Winnet, Mallie wove her way through members of the gentry, a milkmaid, a Jew selling oranges, a boy selling mousetraps, white and black beggars, and soldiers with wooden legs, all the way to the well-kept grounds of Drapers Gardens. A man holding a carved bamboo walking stick greeted Lizzie with a "Good morning, madam" as he tucked a silk handkerchief into his right coat pocket. At his side his black slave boy adjusted his bright-green turban. Mallie watched as Lizzie pretended to trip and allowed herself to land on her rump; if she had not known it was a ruse, she would have believed the fall was authentic. As Mallie expected, a crowd gathered around Lizzie like fish drawn to food sprinkled on the surface of a pond. Mallie was in charge of the fishing.

"Are yer hurt, m'lady?" Winnet inquired in an alarmed voice, faithfully playing her part. When the man with the bamboo walking stick hurried toward the incident, Mallie followed him into the crowd. She had begun to slither her slim fingers into his pocket when he whirled on her.

"Thief!" he cried, catching her wrist with his hand.

Mallie yelped in pain, his handkerchief still dangling from her fingers. He looked into her wide and desperate eyes and for a moment was confounded; one of her eyes was brown, the other green. As she tried to squirm free, her woolen cap slipped off to reveal a disheveled bun of jet-black hair. She'd been taught to keep quiet if she were caught, but this was the first time it had actually happened, and she couldn't help herself. "Lizzie, 'elp me!"

Winnet took off running. Lizzie's eyes flashed in anger and fear. Her face drained of all color when a man grabbed her right hand. "Madam, if you'll forgive me," he said, removing her glove. Upon seeing the *T* branded on her thumb, the man coolly announced, "Madam has been lettered."

The man clutching Mallie turned to his slave boy. "Fetch Constable Gardner."

Ireland
Province of Ulster
Borough of Lisburn

The teenage boy took one end of the pall, his brother took the other, and they draped it over the coffin, which rested on the box of a horse-drawn cart parked in front of the whitewashed stone cottage. The pall had arrived in Ireland with the boy's great-great-grandfather when thousands of Protestant Lowland Scots had settled in Ulster. Now, the funeral cloth would accompany his father to his final resting place. *Don't cry*, the boy told himself, his throat aching as he watched his mother and grandfather stand guard next to the coffin. Her expression was numb; the old man seemed angry. The boy swept his amber eyes over his family's small rented farm, over the crops that were withering just as they had the year before and the year before that. He walked to the front of the cart and stroked the horse's neck. The animal snorted, prompting him to glance toward another cart next to the cottage, the grass beneath it yellow. Their own mare had died months ago, as had their cow. He retrieved black cloaks from inside the cottage and handed them to those participating in the funeral procession. Then he started to make his way to the rear of the cottage.

"Blair, where're ye going?" his brother called after him.

"Tae the privy."

"Dinna tarry."

No sooner had Blair shut the door of the outhouse than he burst into tears. His Presbyterian pride mandated that he not carry on like the vulgar, barbarian papist Irish with their histrionics and hideous keening.

"Blair? Are ye awricht?"

Under any other circumstances, the sweet voice on the other side of the door would have made him smile, but this was the last person he wanted bearing witness to his tears. "Aye," he replied. He wiped his face dry with his sleeve and took a couple of deep breaths before stepping out. He removed his cap and combed his fingers through his deep-red hair, which gleamed even in the soft light of the overcast afternoon. No matter his mortification at being caught in a moment of weakness, Janet's emerald eyes were a balm. Her lips—which made him think of dog rose petals—were pressed tight with sorrow for him. How many times had he daydreamed he had won her affections, dreamed he had made her his wife? At fifteen they were too young to marry, but a few days prior he had finally mustered the courage and decided he would confess his love the next time he saw her. Then, the unexpected death of his father had upended everything.

"I'm verra glad ye're here," he said.

Janet smiled. "I'm yer friend. I'll always be here."

He caught his breath, wondering how much to read into her words. He pulled something from his breeches pocket. "I thought ye'd like this. It's from a kingfisher."

Janet held out her palm, and Blair placed a feather on it. She held it up between two fingers and twirled it; it shimmered with blue-green iridescent tones. "Is it mine tae keep?"

"If ye want it."

"I do want it."

A warm effervescence bubbled in his chest.

"Blair! We're waiting for ye!"

Blair winced. His brother was approaching, his dark-brown eyes stern.

"It's my fault, Ronald," Janet said. "I kept him."

"It's awricht, lass. We appreciate ye being here."

As the three walked to the front of the cottage, Blair glanced at his brother. Ronald was four years older, a full three inches taller, and treated his role as head of the household with the zeal of a herding dog. On the front door a rowan cross—to ward off witches, the evil eye, and evil spirits—swayed in the cold wind. Janet went indoors to join the rest of the women and help watch the children and prepare the food for the dredgy, the feast that would follow the burial. Blair raised his eyes to the gray clouds, so low they seemed within reach. *Please don't let it rain now*, he prayed. Everyone in Ulster knew that if you could see the hills, it was going to rain, and if you couldn't, it was already raining.

Blair grunted when he, Ronald, their uncle John, and five other men heaved the coffin onto their shoulders. Reverend McCracken took the lead, the pallbearers followed, then Blair's mother and aunt, then his grandfather and other male relatives, friends, and neighbors. They had barely started down the dirt lane when they found a wretched-looking woman standing by the side of the road, five barefoot and skinny children, none older than nine, clinging to her ragged skirts. She stretched a hand out toward Blair's mother as she walked past her. "Mrs. McKay," she said, "my bairns are hungry."

"Donia," Blair's mother replied, with sincere regret, "we have naught tae spare. We've been forced tae rent the common-use kist."

Hearing the beggar's name, Blair looked at her again. She had worked for his parents when linen was selling well. She and another five or six single and widowed women would sit with Blair's mother outside the cottage with their spinning wheels, hour after hour. Donia was almost unrecognizable in her deplorable condition. Her shoulders slumped, and she watched the procession pass with exhausted eyes. A quarter of an hour later, the mourners stopped, the pallbearers laid the coffin down, huffing, their faces flushed, and a jug of whiskey was passed around to everyone but Blair's mother and aunt.

"Would it make ye happy tae visit Donnybrook Fair in Dublin next year?" Ronald asked, handing Blair the jug after taking a gulp.

The gesture warmed Blair more than the whiskey itself. "Aye."

"I'll come with ye," said a voice at Blair's back. He turned and saw his cousin, a boy slightly older than himself.

"I'm sorry, Gilroy," Ronald replied. "This time we'd rather go by ourselves."

"Next time, then," Gilroy said, clearly disappointed.

Another eight mourners picked up the coffin. An hour and a half, seven stops, and two jugs of whiskey later, the procession reached the Lisburn Presbyterian Meeting House. The men entered the churchyard while Blair's aunt and mother stopped at the entrance. He took his mother's callused palm in his and held it to his chest for a moment.

"I'll see ye back home," Blair said. She nodded absent-mindedly. He looked as the two women walked away, glad that tradition prevented them from stepping into the church-yard. He stood next to his four siblings' graves, where a hole had been dug for his father. When Uncle John and Ronald removed the coffin's lid, Blair shuddered. During the two-day wake, when his father's body had been laid out on a table inside the cottage, many had touched it as a sign of respect and farewell, but Blair had avoided doing so.

"Blair," called his uncle, "come tae this side and help me take out yer father."

Blair tried to move, but his feet had turned to millstones, and he felt faint.

"I'll do it," Ronald said quickly.

The body, wrapped in a linen shroud, was secured with two lengths of rope and lowered into the ground without ceremony, and the whiskey was passed around one last time.

Blair's stomach dropped when his cottage came into view: Janet was by the fence, next to Gilroy, a harvest knot in her hand. Her cheeks were crimson as she studied the love token made with three oat panicles, the bottom portion of the stems braided together and then looped and fastened. As soon as she saw Blair approaching, she slipped it into her skirt pocket and looked at him expectantly. He breezed past her, ducked under the cottage's low thatching, and stepped inside. The cottage smelled of mutton, potato pancakes, turnips, thyme, and butter.

Ronald leaned into his ear and whispered, "Janet disna care for Gilroy."

"I dinna care for Janet," Blair snapped back.

The cottage was plain: a bedroom at one end, the loom room on the other, and all at once the kitchen, dining room, and sitting room in the middle, where Blair and Ronald slept. Blair noticed with relief that Janet did not sit with Gilroy but with her two older sisters, flanked by their mother and father. After eating, the children rushed outside to play, and Blair went around offering loose tobacco from a pouch, leaving Janet's father for last.

"Thank ye, lad," Janet's father said, looking up at him with sad, gray eyes as he tamped tobacco into his pipe.

"Yer welcome, Mr. Ferry." Blair kept his gaze firmly on the man but out of the corner of his eye saw Janet looking at him. When Ronald approached Janet's father with a spill to light his pipe with, her sisters sat up straight and smiled. Ronald winked at one of the girls and then, for good measure, winked at the other.

When Blair finished handing out tobacco, he sat next to his grandfather on the settle bed he shared with Ronald. In more prosperous times, there would have been lively conversation about a new breeding mare, or the best manure to use for crops. There would be lighthearted jokes about a girl who had given birth too soon after the nuptials: *no, the baby didna come early; the wedding came late.* There would be fiddles, pipes, and accordions, confirming that there was more mirth to be found at a Scot's funeral than an English wedding. That was all missing today, and the silence grated on Blair.

Finally, Uncle John spoke, addressing a neighbor. "Samuel, this might be a good time tae read the letter."

All eyes immediately focused on the man, who seemed uncharacteristically nervous. The man's wife, sitting next to him, brought one of his hands to her lips in a comforting gesture. He cleared his throat. "My brother Joseph arrived safely in Philadelphia. He sent this letter." He lowered his eyes to the paper. "*Dear Samuel, I account it my honor and duty tae give ye an account o' myself and my proceedings since I left ye. On the next Friday after we left Lisburn, we came on board the ship* Good Intent, *at the port o' Belfast, where we saw nine other ships also bound for the colonies. On the Wednesday following, we sailed for America.*" He paused, swallowed, and tried to continue, but his voice cracked. When Blair realized Samuel was about to break down in tears, he jumped to his feet.

"Do ye want me tae read it?" Blair asked. Samuel handed him the letter. Blair scanned the next line and tried to keep his voice as steady as possible. "*On the third day of our sail, our mother died and was interred in the raging ocean.*"

Everyone gasped. Those sitting or standing close to Samuel reached out and patted him on the shoulders, offering words of sympathy. Blair waited for everyone to settle down before resuming. "*Seven days later we lost sight o' Ireland. We were tossed at sea with storms, which caused our ship tae spring a leak. The ship's water pumps were kept at work many days and nights. We all suffered the most terrible seasickness and lost another five passengers, who had tae be put overboard. It pleased God tae bring us all safe tae Philadelphia after eight weeks at sea. I write these words before we make our way tae Donegal, the settlement founded by our very own people eighty miles west o' Philadelphia, where, by the blessing of God, we will prosper as farmers on our own piece o' land. I am yer dutiful brother, Joseph Shipboy."*

Blair handed the letter back, sat down, and took the pipe his grandfather offered. As he lit it, he sneaked a peek across the room. Gilroy sat on the floor next to Janet; she leaned toward him as he whispered in her ear. Blair felt as if he had swallowed a chunk of smoldering turf. He forced his attention back to Samuel.

"Will ye follow yer brother, Samuel?" Ronald asked.

"Maybe. Christy and I dinna want our bairns growing up slaves tae the English. The rents in Pennsylvania are said tae be small; there are no tithes tae pay, no county or parish taxes. All men are on a level, and it's a good poor man's country." Several heads nodded in understanding.

"I'll leave with ye."

Stunned, Blair turned to Ronald.

"I'll go tae Philadelphia," Ronald repeated.

"Ye canna leave!" Blair exclaimed.

"We both should leave. There's naught here for us."

Blair blinked in disbelief. "Ye would leave Ma?" He glanced at his mother; she was paying close attention to the exchange, but it was his aunt who spoke.

"Blair, darling, I agree with Ronald. I think—"

"Dinna encourage them," Uncle John said. "Blair and Ronald dinna have money for the passage; neither do ye, Samuel."

Blair raised his eyebrows at his brother; Ronald should know better. They had already been forced to sell their best farming tools, along with the family's two fiddles.

Janet's father pointed his pipe at Samuel. "As soon as ye abandon yer land, the Irish will invade it, just like they invaded yer brother's."

"We'll soon be evicted anyway," Samuel said. "We canna pay the rent."

"The Irish—" Blair's aunt stopped herself and stared down at her lap. "The Irish," she continued, her voice low, "are taking back what was theirs. We're on the land the English took from them." Blair looked around; some people seemed shocked, others indignant. "It's the truth," she whispered.

Blair, chewing furiously on the stem of his pipe, stared at her with concern. Maybe grief was driving her mad. He could feel his grandfather bristle at the words.

"This land was wasted for centuries on these leaderless, impoverished, ignorant papists." The old man's voice was hot with pride and whiskey. "They never accomplished anything but tae raise a few mud cabins, and nothing—"

Janet's father cut in. "We built these towns, and we've shed a lot o' blood defending them."

"And yet," Blair's aunt said, "to the Anglicans, we're little better than Catholics. Look at Bishop Hutchinson, using our money tae stuff his belly with oysters and claret while we canna pay our rents."

"*It's a lang gait that haes nae sindrins,*" Blair's grandfather said in the Scots language that only the elders still commanded. *Things will get better.*

Sick of the conversation, Blair got up and walked to the loom room, and sat at the loom where his father had taught him how to weave. The sight of piles of folded linen webs, nearly worthless now in the glutted market, filled him with hopelessness.

"Blair?"

He jumped. Janet had followed him and had shut the door behind her.

"May I keep ye company?"

"Ye may do as ye please."

She sat next to him; his heart pounded. They sat in silence for a while. Loud voices came through the door.

"Do ye want tae go tae America?" she asked. He thought for a moment. What if Ronald was right?

"Maybe."

"Please dinna go," she whispered. When he felt the warmth of her hand on his thigh, the room spun around him. He leaned his face into hers, pausing for a moment to gauge her reaction. She didn't pull away. He brought his mouth to hers, feeling her agitated breath, and pressed his lips against hers. Her hand clenched around his leg.

"Janet, yer father is calling for ye. Ye're going home."

Both jumped and pulled away from each other. Blair's grandfather was at the door.

"Thank ye, Mr. Eakins," the girl stammered.

Sad as he looked, the old man winked at Blair before shutting the door again.

"May I see ye tomorrow?" Blair asked.

"We're going tae Dunmurry tae visit my grandmother."

"Meet me in the morning the day after tomorrow at the castle ruins, then."

Her eyes sparkled. "Aye. Half past eleven."

London

A constable held Mallie by the arm and pushed through the crowd, behind a second constable and Lizzie. They trudged past coffeehouses, apothecaries, and inns, the shop signs hanging precariously above their heads. Finally, at a corner, they waited for a carriage to pass by, its metal wheels rattling over the cobblestones. They crossed the street, and the constable knocked on the door of the home of Sir Robert Baylis, the Lord Mayor of London. A maidservant let them in and led them to a hall outside the Lord Mayor's home office. There, they awaited their turn as he received the daily miscreants and complainants. Then it was their turn to be brought before him. He heard the victim's telling of the incident and, practically by rote, questioned the pickpockets. He did not even have to be shown the T on Lizzie's thumb to know she had been convicted of theft before: he remembered her. He ordered that the girls be sent to Newgate Prison and remain there while awaiting trial.

Two blocks before Newgate, even before it came into view, the putrid stench emanating from the bowels of the building crept into Mallie's nostrils. Upon reaching the gate, she raised her terrified eyes toward the spikes of the permanently raised portcullis, which hovered like fangs in a monster's jaw, a monster in constant need of human flesh. A roar of voices, yelling and fighting, reverberated from within. The constable knocked on a door, and the gatekeeper let them into the lodge. Mallie kept her eyes down and stood behind Lizzie, whose fake belly had been removed by one of the Lord Mayor's maids.

"Pickpockets," said one of the two constables delivering the girls.

The head turnkey—who had been drinking beer with the gatekeeper—eyed them with appetite. "I'd wager Covent Garden nuns."

"I ain't a whore," Mallie murmured.

"That's two shillings and six pence each for admission," the gatekeeper demanded.

"We don't 'ave money," Lizzie answered.

"To the condemned hold, then," the head turnkey said, standing up and grabbing a torch.

Terrified, Mallie kept close behind Lizzie as they followed the turnkey up a windowless staircase illuminated by torches on the walls. On the second floor, a gaoler stood guard outside a door with a small grated window. The hinges creaked as he swung the door open and let Mallie and Lizzie inside.

The cell was only about twice as large as the tenement room Mallie shared with Lizzie and Winnet, and the smell was a thicker version of what Mallie had picked up as they approached the prison. A single tiny window, too high for any of the inmates to see through, was the only source of light. Two women sat at a table below it; several others lay in bare wooden bunks along the walls covered only by the rags they wore. One was pregnant, a three-year-old boy curled up with her. In the corner, a woman with an eye patch was in the process of relieving herself in a pail. Lizzie sat on the blackened oak floor, her back against the stone wall. Mallie sat two feet away but began to inch closer after a couple of minutes.

"Lizzie, I'm sorry," she whispered. She yelped when Lizzie elbowed her in the ribs.

"Button it, you stupid, careless bitch."

Mallie brushed tears away, found an empty bunk, and curled up in a ball, shivering, terrified for herself and heartsick for her cat. She heard the door open, and she opened her eyes. A man carrying a pair of scissors and a bag walked in and approached the pregnant woman.

"I've come for yor hair," he said. The woman moved to a chair under the window, in quiet resignation, leaving her toddler asleep in her bunk. Mallie watched as the barber sliced off the woman's long hair, put it in the bag, and gave her some coins. Just then the toddler woke up and, finding himself alone in the bunk, burst into tears. His mother immediately went to him, but he was inconsolable. His wails mixed with the noises coming from all around: inmates arguing, laughing, or crying hysterically, gaolers yelling, and doors slamming shut. It all drilled into Mallie's ears like the ice pick she used on winter mornings to break the frozen layer in their bucket of wash water.

She spent the next few hours lying in her bunk, trying to shut out the racket, until she fell asleep.

A gaoler's voice startled her awake. "Time for sermon!" Several women—Lizzie among them—headed for the door.

"Yer 'aven't paid yor fees," the gaoler said, stopping her.

"I got no money."

The gaoler lifted her skirts. "Yer don't need money." Lizzie pulled away. "Yer don't need ter attend service either," the gaoler sniped before walking out.

Mallie was puzzled; Lizzie always carried some well-hidden money. Why claim she didn't have any? Why would she refuse to lie down with this man to get what she needed? He was no more disgusting than any other Mallie had seen her with. The door opened, and a woman in rags stepped inside and set down a bucket of water just to the side. She stepped outside for a moment and returned with a basket of stale bread and boiled pieces of meat, which she set down next to the water before leaving. The inmates clustered around like stray dogs, snatching up as many pieces of food as would fit in their hands before quickly stepping away. Around the bucket of water, one grimy pewter cup was impatiently being shared. Mallie squeezed between two women to try to reach the bread basket but was easily shoved aside. She tried again, only to have someone yank her skirts from behind. By the time she managed to reach the basket, there wasn't a crumb left. Someone tapped her shoulder, and when she turned, one of the inmates was offering the pewter cup, her wide, manic smile revealing broken and blackened teeth. Mallie took the cup, knelt next to the bucket of water, set the cup on the floor, and drank with her cupped hands. Then she went back to her bunk, her stomach growling.

"Take some."

Lizzie held out a piece of bread, her hand shivering from the cold. Mallie took the bread and scooted closer to the wall to make room for Lizzie. "I promise I'll do better from now on," she said, grateful for the bread and warm body, but most of all because it seemed Lizzie had forgiven her the clumsiness that had landed them in prison. At midnight the clanking of a bell jolted her awake. On the other side of the door, a bellman chanted three times:

> *All you that in the condemned hold do lie*
> *prepare you, for tomorrow you will die.*
> *Watch all, and pray, the hour is drawing near*
> *that you before th' Almighty must appear.*
> *Examine well yourselves, in time repent,*
> *that you may not t'eternal flames be sent;*
> *and when Saint Sepulcher's bell tomorrow tolls,*
> *The Lord have mercy on your souls.*

Mallie's heart slammed in her chest. "Lizzie!"

"Wot the 'ell do yer want now?"

"We won't 'ang, will we?"

"Not without a trial. Go ter sleep."

At six o'clock in the morning, the tenor bell at Saint Sepulchre-without-Newgate rang ominously, and shortly before seven, two gaolers came into the cell.

"It's collar day, wenches. Let's go," one of the gaolers said, rounding up four women and leading them out of the cell. Lizzie and the rest, except for the pregnant woman and Mallie, gathered around the second gaoler. Only to do what the others did, Mallie approached the gaoler, although she made sure to keep away from Lizzie.

"Get up!" the gaoler barked at the pregnant woman.

"I don't feel well at all," she said weakly.

"But the more alms yer make, the more food and gin and candles yer can buy from us," he said with exaggerated mock concern as he grabbed her by the arm and pulled her to her feet. He picked up her toddler and deposited him in her arms. "Little brats always make people feel generous."

Ah! Mallie thought. *He's picking people to go begging.* On execution days, prostitutes, pickpockets, and vendors gathered outside the prison to take advantage of the festive mood. Mallie and Lizzie had often been part of that crowd, and invariably there had been inmates begging at the prison gate. The gaoler took Mallie's chin in his hand and brought his nose much too close to hers. She stiffened.

"Those doe eyes of yours should loosen some purse strings." A whiff of decaying teeth floated from his mouth. The gaoler selected another two women but passed Lizzie over.

"I'll bring back money, I will," Mallie said, squeezing Lizzie's hand as she muttered a curse. The inmates followed the gaoler down the staircase to the first floor, where Mallie was chained by the wrist to another inmate, and the pregnant woman was chained to the fourth. They were led outside the gate, where women from other holds and about an equal number of male prisoners were already busy begging. Mallie watched as twelve men and four women, their hands tied in front of them, were loaded onto three open carts surrounded by armed cavalry and made to sit atop their own coffins. Once seated, a noose was draped around each of their necks, the length of the rope coiled on their laps. The ordinary, wearing his Geneva gown and white neckband, climbed into the lead cart and began to preach. The city marshal, the hangman and his assistants, and a troop of javelin men completed the convoy.

The townspeople who gathered to watch the spectacle bought fried sausages and muffins as they waited for things to get going. A woman held a stack of broadsides in one hand and waved one of the printed sheets with the other while braying, "The Ordinary of Newgate, his account of the behavior, confession, and dying words of the malefactors, who were executed at Tyburn, on Monday, the twenty-fourth of this instant March 1729! Two pence each!"

Determined to present Lizzie with several coins, Mallie chanted a line she had heard before: "Do, me worthy, tenderhearted Christians, remember the poor! Do, me worthy, tenderhearted—"

The piercing cant of a teenage girl standing to her right drowned out her small voice. "Me worthy heart, stow a copper in Edina's locker, for poor Edina 'as not 'ad a quid today!" Annoyed, Mallie studied the girl; every inch of her face was scarred by smallpox. The old woman chained to the girl yanked her wrist by its shackle.

"Ow!" the girl cried out. "That 'urt!"

"Why are yer even out 'ere?" the old woman asked. "Why haven't yer been transported?"

The girl rubbed her sore wrist. "I appealed me sentence. I'm waiting for an answer," she said sullenly.

When the caravan began to move, Mallie was so focused on the crowd of townspeople mocking the prisoners and pelting them with rotten vegetables as they followed behind the carts that she didn't notice a gaoler sidling up next to her. He pulled on a strand of hair that stuck out from under her cap, startling her.

"What a devilish good piece y'ar," he muttered, curling the strand around his finger. "Yer don't need to stand 'ere.

I'll move yer ter the Second Ward and give yer good bread and cheese every day, candles, gin if yer want it."

She froze, revolted. Suddenly, the pregnant woman let out a sharp cry, making Mallie jump and the gaoler release her hair. The toddler stared in puzzlement at the puddle his mother stood in. The gaoler, cursing, stepped away in disgust. The prison nurses were called, and they hurriedly escorted her, her toddler, and the inmate she was chained to back to the prison.

"If it's a girl, name 'er Edina like me. I was born 'ere too!" the girl scarred by smallpox yelled after them. She sighed. "Well, they can finally hang 'er." She looked at Mallie with amusement. "Yer better accept what the gaoler offered. He'll take what he wants whether yer give it or no."

Mallie watched the gaoler out of the corner of her eye, the girl's words filling her with dread. Suddenly something was placed in her outstretched palms: a wooden doll. She searched the crowd, but whoever had given it to her had already disappeared in the throng. She held the doll gingerly, afraid to soil the faded green lace and linen dress. With the back of a finger, she stroked its real human hair and its cheeks and mouth, which were quite rosier than her own. The gaoler glanced her way; she brought the doll behind her back with one hand while begging with the other. When he walked toward the opposite end of the line of inmates, she studied the doll again, marveling at it, delighted with her first and only toy.

One hour later Mallie was smiling to herself as she was led back to the hold, clutching a few farthings in her hand. Not as much as she had hoped for, but surely Lizzie would be pleased. Once she was back in the cell, however, Lizzie was nowhere to be seen, and when the turnkey locked the door at nine o'clock, she still hadn't returned.

"Yor friend paid ter be moved," one of the inmates informed Mallie.

"Moved where?"

"Ter the Second Ward."

So Lizzie did have money after all, Mallie realized. She hugged the doll to her chest, and her body trembled with every ragged, sobbing breath.

CHAPTER TWO

July 7, 1729

Blair glared with annoyance at his brother and Samuel walking next to him. He had wanted to keep his rendezvous with Janet a secret, but these two had been set on going to the Market House. They wanted to seek out ship captains' agents, who could always be found inducing people to leave for the colonies. When they reached Market Square, Blair looked toward the churchyard, just a few feet away. How could Ronald consider leaving the land where their father was buried?

"I'll see ye back home," he said as nonchalantly as possible.

"Where are ye going?" Ronald asked.

Blair's eyes unwittingly shifted for a second toward the castle ruins.

"I told ye Janet didna care for Gilroy!" Ronald laughed. He removed Blair's cap and tousled his hair. "At what time are ye meeting her?"

Blair swatted his brother's hand away. "Half an hour."

"Ye have plenty o' time. Come if ye want yer cap back."

Blair groaned and trudged along. It had been years since the Market House, where all of Lisburn's linen transactions took place, had been busy. The number of people there that day was half what it used to be, and most of them were not even there to sell or buy linen. A crowd near Blair, Ronald, and Samuel surrounded a well-dressed man who expounded on the wonders of the colonies. "Pennsylvania is a bonny country, with cows, sheep, horses, goats, deer, beavers, fish, and fowl. There's plenty of good land to be had, or you can receive good wages as a laborer, double or treble what you would receive here, or set up your own shop. A lass gets four shillings and sixpence a week for spinning linen."

Groups had formed around other men too, each who sang the praises of a different township in Pennsylvania or Delaware. Ronald and Samuel walked over to one of them, and Blair grudgingly followed. The man's clean white shirt, green waistcoat, and red frock coat and breeches gave him an air of respectability and prosperity.

"Ladies and gentlemen, my name is Neal Montgomery," he said. Blair scoffed. An Englishman, not to be trusted. "I wish to help you improve your circumstances," the agent continued. "I propose a voyage to America. A ship leaves Belfast in two days, bound for Philadelphia, a land that will provide you with all of life's necessities. The *King George* is a three-hundred-ton brig with eight carriage guns, three swivels, and small arms in proportion. I'll gladly endorse strong young men and women to Captain Nathaniel Stokes, an able and kind captain who hails from London."

At that moment, a loud rumbling burst on Blair's right. A man brought both hands over his stomach, embarrassed, and waited for his empty belly to settle. Blair studied the man's pale face and sharp cheekbones, knowing that soon, Ronald, his grandfather, his mother, and he would be forced to cut back on meals.

"Passengers will be divided into messes of five," the agent continued, "and each mess will be provided with beef, two and a half pounds of flour, and half a pound of plums, four days each week. Two days each week each mess will receive five pounds of pork, two pints and a half of peas, and one day two pounds and a half of fish and half a pound of butter. Every person will receive seven pounds of bread per week, and three pints of beer and two quarts of water per day."

Blair swept his gaze over the crowd. Eyes that had been hollow with hopelessness moments earlier now glimmered. Ronald seemed transported.

"How much is passage?" Samuel asked.

"Lad," Montgomery said to Blair, pointing at another agent, "ask that gentleman how much his captain charges."

Blair crossed his arms. "I'm no going tae America."

"I'll ask him, sir," Ronald offered, bounding to the agent and back. "Six pounds."

"My captain will charge five."

The crowd's budding hopes deflated with an audible groan.

"Not to worry," Montgomery said. "If you can't pay for passage, when you arrive you'll be bound to work for a kind master for a term of four years. He'll provide lodging, meat, and drink, and when your term expires, you'll receive freedom dues: two suits of clothes, one new and one used, one new ax, one grubbing hoe, and one weeding hoe. Prosperity awaits all kinds of tradesmen: bricklayers, shoemakers, tanners, bakers, smiths, joiners, bookkeepers, clerks, and even weavers."

At the word *weavers*, every man stood a little taller. Ronald nudged Blair in the ribs.

"Dinna do that," Blair said.

Montgomery addressed the women. "Lassies who are good seamstresses or cooks, who wash and iron and are good with children, will find good employment." The agent paused, allowing the promising news to seep into everyone's hearts and minds before finally opening the door of salvation. "Those wishing to go must meet me here Thursday at noon. We'll leave for Belfast, and the *King George* will sail the next day, weather permitting."

Ronald turned to Samuel. "Shall we go?"

The enthusiasm in Ronald's eyes made Blair's stomach turn. Samuel immediately answered, "Aye."

Blair planted himself in front of his brother, inches from his face. "Ye promised ye'd take me tae Donnybrook next year."

"Ye can't compare Donnybrook with Pennsylvania. Things were hard enough when Da was here. Do ye think we alone will manage tae save our land? Uncle John has his own land tae worry about." Ronald sneered. "*Our* land, *his* land. We *have* no land. I'll take the chance tae be a landlord one day, rather than be bound tae one till I die."

"Why then would ye encourage me tae woo Janet?"

"There'll be other girls in America; I'm yer only brother."

"I dinna want another—" A bell tolled, announcing noon. Blair gasped. "Ye made me late!" He took off running. As usual, several couples were lounging under the two huge elms on the grounds of the ruins of Lisburn Castle. Blair jogged from end to end of the overgrown gardens, passing still more couples, but Janet wasn't there. Thinking she might want to avoid being seen to prevent word getting back to her father, he looked in the ruins, but she was not there either. He returned to the entrance and waited another half hour. Furious at Ronald, but more at himself, he finally gave up and headed home. When he walked into his cottage, his brother was sitting at the dining table—and though their grandfather, mother, and aunt were also there, he stormed up to him, ready to blast him with reproaches. But before he could let his frustration explode, he noticed that his grandfather's nostrils were flaring, and his aunt and mother were each holding handkerchiefs, their eyes puffy and red.

"He's leaving with Samuel on Thursday," Blair's grandfather said bitterly.

Blair stared at his brother in disbelief. "What about yer American wake?" If Blair couldn't persuade him to stay, maybe the requisite week to say goodbye to friends and family would.

"I saw everyone at the dredgy," Ronald said calmly.

"What does Ma say?" Blair asked. He knelt at his mother's feet, looking at her questioningly.

"Blair," she said as tears streamed down her cheeks, "I'll be brokenhearted tae see both o' ye go, but ye're only fifteen and have been through two famines. Dinna wait for the next one, and the next. Believe me, they're coming."

Blair's grandfather slammed his hand on the table. "Ye dinna ken that!" After a long, shocked silence, the old man spoke again. "Will ye leave Janet?"

Before Blair could answer, his mother interjected. "Good-father, do ye truly think the English will ever recognize a Presbyterian wedding?" She looked earnestly at Blair. "I never told ye or Ronald this, but scarce a week after we were married, a pair o' men burst through that very door, and me and yer father were dragged tae an Anglican court and tried as fornicators. Was the worst day o' my life."

"Dinna tell them!" Blair's grandfather begged, but she continued.

"All our bairns were declared bastards."

Blair and Ronald looked at each other, stunned.

"It means nothing!" Blair's grandfather said, livid. "Ye both are Eakins proper, never forget that."

"They are," Blair's mother agreed. "And they deserve better. Blair, if ye marry Janet, ye'll always wonder when that day will come. Go find some good land and send for her. She'll wait."

Ronald looked at him and mouthed *please*. Blair could hardly think. He stood up, his legs stiff and his ears ringing. "I'm no abandoning Ma or Janet." He walked out of the cottage and slammed the door. Almost immediately the door opened and Ronald stepped outside.

"Blair, what else do ye—"

"Dinna talk tae me. Thanks tae ye, I have tae apologize tae Janet and hope she forgives me." Just as he stepped onto the road, he saw Janet's oldest sister running in his direction, a stricken look on her face. He rushed to meet her.

"Ye should come with me," the girl said, but she refused to answer when Blair asked what was wrong.

The two started up the road.

"What are ye doing?" Blair asked when Ronald caught up with them.

"I'm coming with ye."

Blair could not argue any further. Outside Janet's cottage her other sister sat quietly on a bench. Ronald remained outdoors while Blair went inside. Mr. Ferry was pacing, eyes fixed on the floor. When he looked up, the murderous glint in his eyes froze Blair on the spot.

"Is Janet awricht, Mr. Ferry?"

"Na, she's no awricht."

"What happened?"

As Janet's father formed the words, they seemed to make him gag. "She was raped."

The room lurched around Blair. His hand grasped the edge of a table, vertigo pulling him sideways, his breathing shallow and fast, his skin and scalp crackling with a sharp stinging.

"Where?"

"By the mill."

"Who?"

"She wilna say."

"*What?* Why?"

"She says he knocked her senseless. But I ken my daughter. She's no telling the truth." For the first time since walking in, Blair realized Mr. Ferry was looking at him with deep suspicion. "She's protecting someone."

"Mr. Ferry," Blair said, calmly meeting the man's smoldering gaze, "I was all morning with Ronald and Samuel. Ye may ask my brother; he's outside. And I'll die afore I hurt yer daughter."

Mr. Ferry's eyes shone with tears of rage, but his shoulders relaxed and the sharpness in his voice was no longer aimed at Blair. "I believe ye."

"Please, may I see her?"

Mr. Ferry opened the bedroom door a crack and whispered something. A moment later Blair was inside, Janet's mother quietly closing the door behind her. The girl lay under the covers, head on a pillow, eyes closed. Blair remained by the door for a full minute, squeezing his cap in his hands, eyes fixated on a vertical cut on Janet's swollen and bruised lower lip. She slowly opened one bloodshot eye; the other was a dark, ugly shade of purple, swollen shut. She stretched an arm toward him. He knelt next to the bed and gently took her cold hand.

"Ach, my dear lassie." He brought her hand to his cheek and closed his eyes.

"I'm so happy ye're here," she said, her voice weak and hoarse.

"I asked ye tae meet me."

"It's no yer fault."

They remained in silence for a long time, Blair holding her hand, his head resting on the bed. He finally raised his head and looked at her. "Tell me who did this."

"I dinna ken."

One look in her eyes and Blair knew her father was right. "Who was it?" he asked, his voice even.

"I dinna ken!"

"Was it Gilroy?" Simply uttering the name made Blair's insides curdle.

"No!"

Blair stared at the window. The more he thought about Gilroy, the more certain he felt. He got to his feet.

"Where are ye going?" Janet asked. When Blair's hand was on the doorknob, she finally blurted out, "I'll tell ye!"

Blair sat on a chair next to the bed. Tears gushed from her eyes. "It was one o' Bishop Hutchinson's clerks."

Blair blinked, unsure he had heard correctly. "Who?"

"One o' Bishop Hutchinson's clerks. He offered me a job in the bishop's kitchen if I yielded tae him. I told him no."

"Why are ye protecting him?"

"I'm protecting *my father*. I'm protecting *ye*."

Blair stared uncomprehendingly.

"I knew both o' ye would beat him tae within an inch of his life," Janet said. "Then ye'd rot in jail or hang. What would my family do without my father? What would I do without ye?"

Blair looked into her desperate eyes, admiration mingling with his fury.

"Please dinna tell my father."

Blair's chest heaved. He had to do *something*. "I could go tae Captain Spencer, but if I go on my own, yer father will find out."

Janet covered her face with her hands.

"Lass, think o' the harm he can do tae other girls if he's allowed tae go free."

"Fetch my mother. Only she can convince my father."

———

The horse grunted, unaccustomed to Mr. Ferry driving it at such a fast pace. In the box of the cart Blair ground his teeth as he seethed with rage. He looked up to find Ronald studying him with concern. The cart slowed as it pulled up to the pub where Captain Spencer usually had his dinner, but before it had even come to a full stop, Blair had jumped down. As soon as he opened the door, he spotted the captain, sitting at a table with two of his constables.

When the tavern keeper's son realized where Blair, Ronald, and Mr. Ferry were headed, he nervously stepped in front of them. "Mr. Ferry, ye shouldna bother them. I just put their food on the table."

Mr. Ferry placed a hand on the young man's shoulder. "They'll understand."

The captain and his men looked up with annoyance as Blair, Ronald, and Mr. Ferry approached. Mr. Ferry apologized for the intrusion and explained the situation. "Captain, please, ye must arrest the man." His hat trembled in his hands, but his voice was steady. The captain's nose twitched every time Mr. Ferry spoke, as if catching a whiff of something foul.

"Yer peasants mix the King's English with Scots so much, I can barely understand," he muttered.

Blair and Ronald looked at each other with loathing for the man. Mr. Ferry ignored the comment.

"Whom does she accuse?" the captain asked.

"One of Bishop Hutchinson's clerks," Mr. Ferry answered. The captain raised his eyebrows. "Is she sure?"

"Aye."

"I can't do anything. I suggest yer take better care of yor family. This is what happens when women are allowed ter attend fairs at unseasonable hours and become accustomed ter drinking and consorting with men."

An acrid heat gushed from the pit of Blair's stomach. He tried to take a step forward, but Ronald's arm blocked him.

"I'll go tae the high sheriff," Mr. Ferry said.

"My dear Mr. Ferry," the captain said, "Bishop Hutchinson's English clerk will never be prosecuted on account of an Irish girl."

Mr. Ferry's voice quivered, not from fear, but from rage. "She's no Irish, and she's only fifteen. Ye must have yer constables arrest him. It's yer duty."

"Don't tell me what my duty is, *autem prickear.*"

Blair, Ronald, and Mr. Ferry cringed at the curse words. A few patrons looked at the captain scornfully, but no one said anything. "Dissenters, papists, ye're all the same," the captain continued. "Get yor arse out of here, or I'll have me constables do it."

"I fought the papists at the Siege o' Derry when ye were but a wain," Mr. Ferry growled. "My first wife and daughter died o' the smallpox, and I survived on rats and tallow. Dinna ever again compare me tae papists."

"So ye're familiar with stoicism, Mr. Ferry. This is the time ter be stoic."

Mr. Ferry's lips trembled and his eyes glimmered with tears of fury. He walked toward the door, his movements slow and uncertain, like a sleepwalker who has opened his eyes to find himself in a dark, unfamiliar street. Blair stared at the captain insolently.

"I take it the girl is yor sweetheart," the captain said without sympathy. He stood up, and his constables rose with him. He lowered his voice. "Will she take yor family name, or will yer continue yor henpecked men's tradition of allowing yor wives ter keep their own?"

"We're no henpecked," Blair said, also in a low voice.

"Ronald, take yor carrotty-pated brother with yer."

Ronald grabbed Blair's arm, and Blair allowed his brother to guide him to the door. It had been a mistake to come to the authorities. But if the captain wouldn't handle things, Blair would. He would deal with the clerk himself. Crashing sounds and yelling at his back made him turn his head. The tavern keeper's son was on the floor as two patrons stood over him, kicking him. Blair, Ronald, and Mr. Ferry rushed back inside just as the tavern keeper placed himself between his son and his assailants and pleaded with them to stop. Captain Spencer and his constables approached the scene, looking exasperated, broken glass crunching under their boots.

"This here thief," exclaimed one of the attackers with a London dialect, pointing with the ivory tip of his cane, "tried to shortchange us."

The tavern keeper tilted his son's head back and wiped the blood off the young man's face with his apron. "My son wouldna try tae rob our patrons."

"A didna," the young man said, the blood in his mouth thickening his brogue. "It wis done in a mistak."

Blair watched in disbelief as Captain Spencer ordered his constables to take the young man to jail over his father's appeals. The tavern keeper stood just outside the open tavern door, staring after his son, shoulders heaving. Anger and impotence pulsated through the tavern. A couple of patrons walked over to the tavern keeper and talked to him in low, comforting voices. The captain turned to Blair, Ronald, and Mr. Ferry.

"And yer stay away from that clerk!" he snarled. "If anything happens ter him, I'll know who ter arrest."

July 9, 1729

Mallie and thirteen additional prisoners sat on wooden benches in the bail dock—the roofless patio of the Old Bailey courthouse—waiting to be tried. A bird had perched itself between two of the spikes protruding from the top of the wall that surrounded the bail dock, and Mallie looked at it longingly as it flew away. Raindrops made her blink, and she wrapped her arms as best she could around her doll. At least the courthouse was next door to the prison, so she had been spared the shame of a long walk in shackles. Lizzie was on the other side of the patio, ignoring her.

The first two men to be led into the courtroom were tried together for murder. In the space of twenty minutes, evidence was presented, the men were allowed to speak in their own defense, and the jury deliberated and returned their verdict. One man was acquitted; the other was found guilty of manslaughter and sentenced to be branded in the palm of his right hand. The next trial took ten minutes. A woman was found guilty of stealing a silver can and other pieces of silver plate and was sentenced to death. Mallie bit her nails, unable to make sense of the sentences or guess what she might expect for herself. A sudden and horrible screeching jarred her from her thoughts. Two guards were dragging a woman back from the courtroom to the bail dock.

"My curse and God's curse go with yer!" the woman screamed. "I would rather be hanged! Living in foreign parts is worse than a disgraceful death at home!" When the guards dumped her on the ground, she threw a few ineffective punches at them, and Mallie saw she was missing one hand.

"Transportation," someone muttered.

When Mallie's case was called, a cold chill ran down her back. She cradled her doll in her arms as she followed Lizzie into the large, high-ceilinged courtroom, her head barely clearing the bar where the accused were to stand. A crate was brought in for her to stand on while a court officer fidgeted with a rectangular mirror set on two tall legs on the bar. The officer tilted the mirror until it reflected light onto both Lizzie's and Mallie's face.

Six male jurors sat to the right of the bar, six to the left, the same twelve that would hear all of the day's cases. Court officers and privileged spectators looked on from balconies flanking both sides of the courtroom. Beyond the Doric columns holding up the upper floors, the yard was filled with observers from all walks of life. Mallie's heart dropped as she recognized, in the sitting area directly in front of her, the very man she and Lizzie had tried to rob and the constable who had arrested them. Eight justices were on the judges' bench along with the Lord Mayor and the recorder. The clerk read the indictment. The victim and the constable were placed under oath and told their version of events, after which the Lord Mayor asked them a few questions before turning to the accused.

"How do you respond, and do you have any friends to speak on your behalf?"

"I've no witnesses to call, m'lord," said Lizzie.

The judges looked at Mallie over their nosegays, imposing in their white wigs and black robes, like crows hovering over a mouse.

"I've no witnesses to call, m'lord," Mallie parroted. The Lord Mayor gave a brief summary of the case, and the jury disappeared to the deliberation room while Mallie and Lizzie waited where they stood. Barely five minutes had gone by when the jury returned with a verdict.

"Prisoners at the bar, you stand convicted of picking the pocket of David Lillo of a silk handkerchief. Have you anything to say?" the Lord Mayor asked.

"No, m'lord," replied both.

"Elizabeth Batt, for picking the pocket of David Lillo of a silk handkerchief and for having been branded before, you're found guilty of grand larceny and are hereby sentenced to death."

A sob escaped Lizzie's lips. Mallie shuddered. She was halfway down to her knees, determined to beg for her life, when her sentence was read.

"Malvina Ambrose, for picking the pocket of David Lillo of a silk handkerchief valued at ten pence, you're found guilty of petty larceny and are hereby sentenced to seven years' transportation to the American colonies."

Mallie blinked, relief and uncertainty pulling at her in opposite directions. *Transported where?* Back in the bail dock, the one-handed woman's words kept ringing in her ears: *I would rather be hanged. Living in foreign parts is worse than a disgraceful death at home.* The final prisoner was tried, and all inmates were led back to Newgate. When they reached the gate, they yielded to a cart exiting the prison. The cart stopped for a moment in front of Mallie, and she recoiled and screamed; it was full of corpses.

"Yer see?" observed a female inmate sarcastically. "Why fear the noose? The fever or starvation will have us all snug in a pit in the churchyard of Christchurch before the next collar day."

Mallie watched as the barber cut another woman's hair. He was gathering his things when she approached him timidly. "Sir, would yer…" Her voice trailed off.

"What?"

"Cut my hair?"

"Sit down, then."

Mallie held her doll in her lap while the barber tied her hair in a ponytail. The scissors made a dull scraping sound as they sliced through. The barber held the severed ponytail up and admired it. "A peruke maker will give good money."

Remembering the gaoler who had fingered her hair, Mallie pulled a lock to the tip of her nose. It was still too long. "Can ye shave it all?"

"If yer want."

She winced as the straight razor glided over her scalp. The barber wiped her head with a rag, and she flinched when she saw the lather laden with lice. She put on her grimy cap and approached Lizzie, who had been moved back to the condemned hold to await execution.

"Lizzie."

Lizzie stared straight ahead.

"Thank yer for not throwing me out on the street when me mum left," Mallie said. Lizzie rolled her eyes, but they gleamed with tears.

Mallie turned to keep herself from attempting to hug Lizzie, walked to the door, and slapped her palm on it three times. The gaoler on the other side opened the door and stuck his head in. Mallie held out some coins.

"I want ter go ter the Second Ward," she said, and immediately wished her voice had sounded more confident. But the gaoler happily took the coins and took her up one floor. She was surprised to see the Second Ward's door wide open and unguarded.

The gaoler said, "Yer can walk about, but ye'd better be back by nine." Just as he spoke, two male inmates nonchalantly walked past them and into the cell. She hesitantly stepped inside. Other than the moldy straw strewn on the filthy floor, and the fact that it was larger, Mallie could see no difference between this cell and the condemned hold. But she found what she was looking for: the girl who had been begging next to her.

"I remember yer," said the girl. "Yer look like a damned goblin."

Mallie went straight to business. "I 'eard yer say ye appealed yor sentence."

"Wot about it?"

"I was sentenced ter transportation. How do I appeal?"

"Yer write ter the Lord Mayor asking ter receive corporal punishment instead o' being transported. That's all."

"Which corporal punishment?" Mallie asked with suspicion.

"A whipping."

Mallie was well acquainted with a bucking paddle: first her mother and then Lizzie had wielded one with regularity and gusto. The fear she felt as she saw them coming at her was just as acute every single time, but the pain eventually subsided. She surely could withstand one single whipping. "Will yer write it for me?"

The girl snickered. "With the lovely handwriting I learned from me private tutor? A schoolmaster writes them for tuppence."

"I'll give yer a penny if yer take me ter 'im."

"Wot's yor name?"

"Mallie. Yor name is Edina."

The girl smiled. "Ye're a clever one." She guided Mallie to the first floor, to the men's Middle Ward. Several groups of men and women stood around or sat on the oaken floors, most of them stinking of gin. Snores rose from what seemed like slatternly piles of dirty laundry crumpled on bunks and a couple of men sprawled out on the floor. Edina approached a man sitting at a table and reading a newspaper by candlelight. Mallie stopped in her tracks when she spotted a male inmate sitting in a corner, his back propped against the wall, a woman straddling him, her skirts fanned out, grinding her hips. She looked away and brought the doll to her face, feeling safer behind it. Edina motioned with an impatient wave of the hand, and Mallie caught up.

"Schoolmaster," Edina said, and the man put his paper down and smiled pleasantly. "Mallie 'ere wants an appeal letter."

Blair sat with Janet on the bench by the front door of her cottage, choking on the words he had come to say. He had spent the night conjuring all manner of revenge fantasies, the image of Janet's rapist gutted like a lamb exquisitely satisfying, while Ronald snored softly next to him.

"I ken what ye're thinking of," Ronald had said at midnight when he woke up after his first sleep and found Blair staring into the ashes of the fireplace. "I would help if things were different."

Blair knew this to be true: his brother would have relished taking justice into his own hands.

"Dinna allow that bastard tae ruin yer future," Ronald had begged. "Ye'll hang."

An hour later, Ronald was deep in his second sleep, and Blair was in misery, dwelling on the same ideas over and over. As the night wore on, he felt trapped, helpless and hopeless, and he became so overwhelmed with anxiety that he wanted to throw up. In the morning, his grandfather had taken one look at him and read his thoughts. Blair had expected a barrage of incriminations, but the old man's defeated expression was much worse than anything he could have said. Blair had no words to explain how much it pained him to make this decision. It was cold comfort to see his mother's reaction: the line of her shoulders visibly relaxed as soon as he broke the news that he was leaving.

"Come with us, Ma," he had urged. She had chuckled sadly.

"I'm too old; I'll end up in the ocean like Samuel's mother. I'll stay here and watch over Janet for ye."

Now, Janet's good eye searched his face anxiously. Seeing her misshapen face made him want to throw away his plans and kill the clerk. But he would not allow that bastard to ruin *their* future. "I have tae get ye out o' here, lassie. I need tae find a good place tae build a good home for us. I'm leaving with Ronald. Tomorrow."

Tears gushed from Janet's eyes. Her shoulders shook, but she hardly made a sound.

"I wish ye could come with me, even without yer father's blessing. But I dinna ken where I'm going tae live, what I'm going tae do. I canna take care o' ye yet. I promise I'll return in four years. Promise ye'll wait for me." Blair held his breath.

She finally spoke, her voice still hoarse. "I promise."

CHAPTER THREE

As the horses picked up the pace and the cart lurched forward, Blair tightened his grip on the bag containing all of his earthly possessions. At his feet, on the box of the cart, lay a rolled-up tartan blanket fastened with twine. In the box of the cart, to his right, sat the agent Neal Montgomery; Samuel and Christy faced him, looking grim. He glanced at Ronald on his left and was bewildered—annoyed, even—by the enthusiasm illuminating his face. The previous evening their mother had given them fresh haircuts as she always had, by placing a bowl over their heads and cutting around the rim. As she worked on Blair, she talked about the feast she was already planning for his wedding. But when he later saw her putting the family Bible in Ronald's bag, his abdomen contracted painfully; she didn't expect to see them again.

They drove past green sloping fields striped with long webs of linen pegged to the grass, whitening under the sun. When they reached Shaw's Bridge, they came upon two girls who stood, waiting, though they were at least an arm's length apart. The driver pulled on the horses' reins, and the cart drew to a stop.

"You decided to come!" Montgomery said. Ronald immediately jumped up to help the girls climb and settle into the cart.

"My name is Ronald Eakins. What are yer names?" he asked cheerily.

"Aileen Stanehouse," replied the girl who had taken a spot beside him. Her strawberry lips framed her white teeth in a coquettish smile. The other girl, sitting next to Blair, remained quiet. Ronald asked again for her name.

"Jean Ó Súilleabháin," the girl said in a voice so quiet as to be almost inaudible. Ronald's smile vanished. He turned to Aileen and whispered, and they both snickered as Jean's timid blue eyes stared off into the distance. Blair stewed with resentment; of course his brother was sitting next to a pretty girl while he was stuck next to an Irish Catholic, and a Catholic whose name was similar to *Janet*, no less.

It was almost noon when two of Belfast's crumbling bastions came into view. Blair swept his gaze over meadows and failed oat fields. The cart dropped them off at Mill Gate, and they continued on foot, passing a row of relatively new, two-storied brick houses to their left. They walked past the ruins of Belfast Castle until they reached High Street, split down its middle by the Farset River, choked with animal entrails discarded by butchers. The wide street teemed with carriages, pedestrians, beggars, chimney sweeps, and stray dogs. Montgomery shepherded his group over one of the bridges spanning the Farset to a stationer's shop and went inside while everyone waited in the street.

"Can we see one?" Blair asked when the agent exited with twelve sheets of paper rolled into one cylinder. Everyone looked over Blair's shoulder at the preprinted indenture of servitude.

Belfast ff. These are to certify, that (name, residence, age, occupation) came before me one of His Majesty's Town Clerks, and Voluntarily made Oath that (he/she) this Deponent (is) not Married, nor Apprentice nor Covenant, or Contracted Servant to any Persons, nor listed Soldier or Sailor in His Majesty's Service, and (is) free and willing to serve (agent's name) or his Assigns ( ) Years in (place) His Majesty's Plantation in America, and that (he/she is) not persuaded, or enticed to do so, but that it is (his/her) own Voluntary Act.

(Signature of servant)
Jurat (date)
Coram me Town Clerk

They walked to Town Hall, where the indentures would be entered before the mayor of Belfast. After Montgomery paid one shilling per person, the clerk took two indentures and filled them out in Blair's name. Blair fixed his gaze on one particular line: *willing to serve William Rawle or Edward Horne or his Assigns 4 Years in Philadelphia, Pennsylvania.* He dejectedly signed his name on both sheets. The clerk threw one in a bundle to be filed later, and Blair watched with growing remorse as he handed the other to Montgomery. After every indenture had been entered, Montgomery led them to Whites Tavern, where he placed an order of stewed mutton chops for everyone, pints of beer for the men, and, following the tavern's rules, water for the women. Ronald discreetly pushed his beer mug toward Aileen, who sneaked a quick sip before putting it back on the table.

After eating, Montgomery brought the group to a shop with a blue-and-white-striped pole and a sign hanging above the door: "Rove not from pole to pole, but step in here, where nought excels the shaving but the beer." Behind the window hung pewter basins and a string of black teeth advertising barbering and teeth-pulling services. After the men were shaved, they were taken to a shop where everyone was given a bag and a blanket. Then, at a tailor's shop, each of them received a linen shirt, a pair of woolen breeches, a vest with tin buttons, a sea jacket, a woolen cap, and a pair of stockings; the women each received a petticoat, a shift, a jacket, and a pair of stockings. Last, all got new, cheap shoes.

At George's Quay they snaked their way through the crowds of dockmen, traders, merchants, and emigrants and climbed aboard a longboat, sharing it with one other man. Blair turned his eyes south and stared at the Long Bridge, intent on etching in his memory the twenty-one arches connecting the east and west shores of the River Lagan. The pilot took them into Belfast Lough, and over an hour later they reached Garmoyle Pool, where the *King George* rode at anchor.

"If there's something I ken about ships, it's that this one isn't three hundred ton like we were told, but closer tae eighty," the man who had taken the longboat along with Montgomery's group said sourly.

Montgomery kept a blank face. "Is it?" he asked in a flat voice. They all stepped onto a floating dock, then walked up the gangway and onto the brig's deck.

An unsmiling man approached them. "Mr. Montgomery, what did you bring me this time?"

"Captain Stokes. Only the best, as always."

The captain brazenly scrutinized everyone head to toe. The man couldn't be much older than Ronald, but his ashen eyes had a caustic streak that belied his age. When the captain turned to Ronald, Ronald didn't move or speak, but his hands formed tight fists behind his back. While Captain Stokes examined the rest, Blair looked around. A few deckhands, several no more than boys, played cards or dice in the shade cast by the jolly boat that took up part of the main deck. Others were lowering barrels down a hatch; others were mending a sail. Passengers milled about—most of them men no older than Ronald, and a couple of women— helping themselves freely to a cask of small beer.

"Very well," Captain Stokes said. "I see no obvious defects."

Montgomery handed him the signed indentures, received three half crowns per person, and was gone. The captain left a deckhand in charge of Blair's group and went back to the quarterdeck.

"During the day ye'll come on deck, in groups, every four hours with the watch," the deckhand said. "The seats of ease are on the beakhead. The one on the port side is the men's; the one on the starboard, inside the roundhouse, is the women's. When the waters are choppy, hold on tight or ye'll find yerself shittin' midair. There's a line tied tae the railing behind each seat of ease. Pull on it until ye get tae the frayed end. Use that tae wipe yerselves, and drop it back into the ocean tae rinse it clean."

Blair's stomach turned just listening to the instructions.

The deckhand gestured to a man pissing into a metal half funnel on the port-side bulkhead. "There's a pissdale on each side o' the ship. Organize yerselves into messes of five and pick a different person every morning tae be in charge o' receiving the food rations."

There was a loud splash. "Cap'n!" yelled a deckhand. "One's tryin' tae escape!"

Blair rushed with the others to the handrail. The man who had just been at the pissdale was swimming toward the shore. Some pilots in longboats cheered; some didn't seem to care one way or another. Silently, Blair cheered him on; he felt elated when the man reached land and ran.

"Damned shitten elf!" screamed Captain Stokes. "All passengers, down to the hold!"

The deckhand in charge of Blair's group waved them to an open hatch. "Remember, one berth per two adults or family." Blair stepped through the hatch onto a staircase and was assaulted by the rancid smell of bodies and human waste. At the bottom left of the stairs, a male passenger was opening the door on what looked like a narrow closet. As the man stepped inside, Blair could see it was a privy. He walked toward the bow, flanked on each side by two levels of berths. Short curtains attached to the ends of each berth provided a semblance of privacy. Twin lanterns hung from the berths' framing every six feet. A table ran down the middle of the hold, a third of its length, and a lamp hung on the lower foremast above it. Two families with one baby and four children between them—the oldest a couple of years younger than Blair—occupied the table. Blair looked quizzically at a bucket with a lid that was secured with rope at the foot of the foremast. "That for emptying yer stomach if ye get seasick," he heard someone say. At the end of the hold, Blair finally found four empty berths. Samuel and Christy quickly claimed a bottom one.

"We'll take this one," Ronald said reassuringly to Aileen, pointing to the berth above it. "Ye wilna struggle climbing up and down."

Blair pulled his blanket out of his bag and stuffed the rest of his belongings—along with Ronald's, Samuel's, and Christy's—in the space under Samuel's berth.

"Lie down if ye want," Ronald said. "I'll stand for now."

Blair pulled himself up, groaning at the sight of the four-by-six-foot space. He swung his legs over a plank lining the outer edge of the berth and scraped his shin on it. He muttered a curse.

"That'll keep us from falling when the ship is rocking," Samuel explained.

Just then, Blair hit the crown of his head against the overhead with a loud whack.

"For why are ye being so clumsy?" Ronald asked.

"Just wait till ye climb up here!" Blair fought a feeling of claustrophobia as he plopped on his back and stared at the overhead, mere inches from his face. The entire hold went strangely quiet. He rolled on his side and peered down.

A family of three was making its way toward the bow. When the little girl started to whimper, the mother said, "*Bi samhach!*" in a tone that betrayed more fear than anger. Blair recognized the dialect well enough—*Irish*. The parents stopped when they reached Samuel and Ronald, who stepped aside but stared with hostility at the father. The man tried to keep an impassive face, but his eyes were anxious. The Irish girl who had been waiting at the bridge—Jean—glowed with relief at the sight of the family. She waited only long enough for them to set their belongings in their berth before she approached and introduced herself. As the parents and Jean chatted in muted voices, Blair lay down again and closed his eyes to shut out the planks above his head, which resembled too much the lid of a coffin. Having been surrounded by wide horizons his entire life, the mere thought of spending most of the next eight weeks like this was suffocating.

That night, jammed between the berth's outer plank and his brother, Blair lay awake, his limbs numb, Ronald's stockinged feet next to his face. The entire crew was holding a dance before they set sail; the music from violins and an oboe sounded to Blair as if they were right next to him, and the footfalls of crewmembers and prostitutes dancing on the deck above echoed loudly. The hold was filled with the cries of babies and toddlers, and the ship creaked and groaned. How his brother could sleep was beyond Blair. Suddenly Ronald kicked him in the nose, making his eyes water. The thought *I want to go home* repeated of its own accord in his head, over and over until he drifted off to sleep. He woke up some time later, feeling utterly disoriented, and found he was alone in his bunk. Everything was silent, except for the ship's creaking.

"Ronald?" he whispered urgently, terrified that his brother had changed his mind and had abandoned him. He looked down: sitting on the sole—the floor of the ship—was a very cross Jean. In her berth, Ronald and Aileen snuggled under a blanket, kissing. Moans and rustlings were coming from Samuel and Christy's berth and other berths besides. Blair pressed his palms hard against his ears. He was not willing to go without Janet another day, certainly not for four years. Tomorrow he would get off the ship.

A seagull, perched on the gunwale, stared stupidly at Blair as he sat on the seat of ease. He shivered in the cold, damp dawn, his breeches at his ankles, feeling more mortified than he had ever felt. Men were lined up waiting their turn. Most looked away with modesty, but some stared with impatience at him and Ronald at his side on the second seat of ease.

"We've chosen ye tae get our rations today," Ronald said. Blair shut his eyes and wondered how his brother was capable of such nonchalance at a moment like this.

"Why me? Ye get them."

"Ye're the one we trust the most," Ronald said.

"I'll do it tomorrow."

"It's decided."

It was impossible for Blair to relieve himself under these circumstances; exasperated, he gave up and stood, pulled up his breeches, then walked to the main deck. He leaned on the port handrail and scanned the water. Only one thing kept him from jumping: he could not swim. He stared at the longboats coming and going, remembering how some pilots had cheered the man who had escaped the day before. If he could make it as far as one empathetic pilot, maybe the man would row him to shore. He spotted a longboat gliding so close to the *King George*, he was sure he could splash down right next to it, if he timed it properly.

"What are ye staring at?" Ronald asked. Blair cursed under his breath when the longboat pulled away from the ship. *That's all right*, he told himself. *There's still time before we set sail.* He retrieved the rations and went with Christy to the camhoose, the covered area on deck where the food was cooked, and she boiled the beef and peas. Back in the hold, sitting at the table, he ate his breakfast distractedly.

"Why the sour face?" Ronald asked through a mouthful of bread and butter, almost indignantly.

The ship's bell rang once, announcing the start of the forenoon watch at eight thirty. The rhythmic cadence of a shanty filtered down into the hold.

"They're raising the anchor!" Samuel exclaimed. Blair jumped to his feet and headed to the hatch.

"Where are ye going?" Ronald called after him.

"Tae the seats of ease."

"But they said—"

Blair kept walking.

"What are ye doing out here?" a deckhand asked when he saw Blair on deck.

"I'm going tae the seats of ease."

"No, ye're not. Get back tae the hold. Hey!"

Blair slipped around the deckhand and headed toward the port side. Every longboat in sight was too far away. He tried to cross to the starboard side, but the deckhand intercepted him. "I said get back tae the hold!"

Blair slipped away again. He leaned on the handrail, hyperventilating. *Maybe I can reach that longboat right there.* He swung a leg over the handrail, but two pairs of hands yanked him back. "Let me go!" he screamed as he was dragged to the hatch. Ronald was standing at the top of the stairs, looking absolutely confused.

"Both o' ye, get down!" one of the deckhands said.

"What happened?" Ronald asked when Blair came back into the hold. Without answering, Blair walked past him, climbed into his berth, and covered his face with his hands. Now he was trapped.

Two hours later the *King George* was sailing northeast to the lough's mouth and then northbound. Tentacles of seasickness strangled Blair; every inch of his skin crawled. Men and women groaned, children and babies wailed. Blair barely managed to climb down the berth in time to empty his stomach in the pail at the foot of the foremast, and he didn't have the wherewithal to climb back up. The smell of vomit grew worse with each passenger who succumbed to nausea. Ronald looked down at him with pity. "Do ye need help?" he asked.

Blair groaned and shook his head.

Eight bells signaled noon; soon after, the wind died entirely. By nightfall the ship was still becalmed, granting the passengers a welcome respite. At sunrise the wind picked up, and the ship resumed its northbound course. Blair's seasickness returned. Although he was not in pain, he had never experienced anything as torturous. He was snarled in a whirlpool; it was as if maggots had sprouted inside his bones and were eating their way through, gnawing at his muscles and coiling under his skin.

"They say ye'll feel better outside," Ronald said when it was their turn to go on deck. Samuel and Christy moaned and did not budge. Blair forced himself to move. With painful slowness he climbed down the berth and groped his way to the stairs. Once on the main deck, he took wide and halting steps as the ship shifted treacherously under his feet, until he managed to lurch to the gunwale on the starboard side and take hold of it. He and Ronald contemplated a stretch of land rising on the horizon.

"What's that?" Blair asked.

"Scotland," answered a deckhand.

Blair could hardly believe how close it was. Until now he'd left Lisburn only a handful of times and never gone farther than Belfast. The home of his ancestors had always seemed so far off and otherworldly to him as to be almost mythical. He turned to his left and saw Ireland's coastline beyond the port handrail; then he turned back toward Scotland. A deep sense of loneliness and isolation washed over him. He was floating between the land his ancestors had abandoned and the land that didn't have a place for him anymore, on his way to another country where he would be an outsider.

July 11, 1729

Mallie stood next to Edina's bunk. The girl groaned, curled up tight, her palm pressing on her forehead. "I'm so cold," she muttered. "And my 'ead 'urts worse."

Mallie touched Edina's cheek; she was burning. When Mallie told a guard, he said he would inform the gatekeeper, but no physician showed up. For the next few days Edina left her bunk only once, with Mallie's help, to use the corner bucket. She refused food, grimacing with nausea at the very mention of it, but Mallie persuaded her to drink a bit of water. Soon other women began to fall ill too. Finally, a week after Edina had first gotten the headache, two prison nurses appeared. Mallie stood to the side as one nurse rolled up Edina's gown and shift, and the other held a lamp over her chest and abdomen. Edina squeezed her eyes shut against the light. At the sight of the rash covering the skin, the nurses looked at each other with knowing and fearful eyes.

"Wot's wrong with 'er?" Mallie asked.

"Gaol fever," said a nurse.

"Oh," Mallie replied, though it meant nothing to her. "Are yer giving her medicine?" But the nurses were already hurrying out, and although it was still daytime, Mallie heard the door lock behind them. A few hours later a nurse carrying a basketful of aromatic herbs entered the hold.

"Is that medicine?" Mallie asked hopefully.

"It's so the fever don't spread," the nurse said, scattering the herbs on the floor, and the door was again locked. That evening, the door opened just enough for a nurse to shove food and water inside. She stuck her head in, holding a candle that couldn't have aided her in seeing much, and then she was gone. The following morning, as soon as the metallic sound of the key rang through the hold, all those who were not ill—except for Mallie—ran to the door, begging to be moved, but the guard ordered them to step away and stay away. The empty basket and bucket were hastily replaced, but no one came inside.

Mallie lost track of the days. One afternoon, she approached the door and tilted her head back, directing her voice toward the grated window on the door.

"Our waste bucket is ready ter spill!" she said.

"Hold on," replied the guard. Several minutes later Mallie heard his voice again. "Place the bucket next to the door and step away."

Mallie did as told, with the help of another woman. When the door opened and the guard switched the full bucket for an empty one, she begged him to ask the nurses to check up on Edina. He said he would, but no one came. Soon, out of the fifteen women in the hold, only Mallie and four others showed no symptoms, and there was no rest from the sounds of dry coughing and moaning.

"It 'urts!" Edina cried out one morning, her eyes glazed and unfocused.

Mallie rushed to her side. "Is it yor 'ead?"

"Stop whipping me!" Edina wheezed. "I've changed me mind!"

Mallie stared, confused and scared at Edina's nonsensical words.

"Stop, please transport me!" Edina begged, her face contorting with the vigor her limp body did not have.

Mallie pounded on the door. "Is anyone there?" No one answered. She did it again.

"Stop that!" growled the gaoler on the other side.

One by one, every sick woman began to hallucinate. Mallie tore a thin strip of linen from her skirts and plugged her ears. Six days after Edina first became delusional, she fell quiet. Mallie inched her way to the girl's bunk, the sudden stillness now somehow more terrible than the fevered mumblings that had plagued her for days. Edina was the color of whipped egg whites. Her eyes fluttered open and Mallie let out a huge breath.

"Wot 'appened?" Edina asked feebly.

"You were feverish." Mallie touched Edina's cheek and smiled. "Yer cooler now."

When a nurse cracked the door open to shove in the day's food and water, Mallie excitedly told her of Edina's change.

"It's not over yet, lamb," the nurse said, and shut the door behind her.

Two days later Edina's fever returned, and Mallie watched in horror as her fingers, nose, and ears turned black with gangrene. She and the others who had not fallen ill moved under the window in an effort to escape the cadaverous stench emanating from the deteriorating prisoners. Mallie felt terrible, but she couldn't bring herself to approach Edina's bunk, which was covered in bloody diarrhea. Her only consolation was that Edina didn't seem to notice anything anymore. The following morning a terrified nurse walked in.

"Hurry up," urged a second nurse waiting by the door, her voice muffled under a handkerchief wrapped around her mouth and nose. The first nurse approached Mallie and the two other inmates, who were all three curled up like kittens against the wall. "Alive, alive, alive," the nurse chanted. She approached the wall where Edina's bunk was. "One, two, three, four dead."

As the nurse hurried to the door, an inmate called after her, "For the love of Christ, don't leave the bodies here!"

The door shut, and the nurse looked through the window. "Bring the bodies by the door, and we'll remove them."

Mallie covered her face with her hands as the women who were not incapacitated carried out the grisly task. The bodies being carted to Christchurch the day of her trial had been the first she had ever seen. Now she was surrounded by corpses. She clutched her doll, pretending the toy pulsed with the warmth and breath of the living, and remained awake until dawn, when male inmates appeared to wrap the bodies in linen and carry them away.

CHAPTER FOUR

August 5, 1729

Blair fumed as he carried the rations. In the hold, Ronald, Christy, Samuel, and Aileen stared in disbelief at the one and a half biscuits, three small potatoes, two ounces of salt beef, and three pints of water each had received for the entire day.

"Every Tuesday and Friday, instead o' the potatoes and beef, we'll get six spoonfuls o' pea soup," Blair said sullenly.

"I had a bad feeling when the cask o' beer that was on deck disappeared as soon as Ireland was out o' sight," Christy grumbled.

"What did ye tell them?" Ronald's accusing tone made Blair even angrier.

"I told them this wasna enough!"

"Ye should've demanded our proper rations."

"Ach! I did!" How did Ronald dare suggest Blair was at fault in any way? Maybe if Ronald had been the one facing five surly deckhands, he would understand.

"Jean!" A boy deckhand that looked all of ten years old stuck his head through the hatch. "Who's Jean?" Jean stepped forward, shy and uncertain. "Cap'n Stokes sends this." Baffled, she took a little bundle wrapped in paper. Inside was a piece of yellowman candy.

"Thank ye," she said, puzzled.

"The cap'n says if ye want more, ask."

Jean broke off a piece and offered it to the little Irish girl, who accepted it with delight. Ronald and Samuel glanced at each other, scowling, and headed to the hatch. "Ye stay here," Ronald said when Blair tried to follow.

"I'm too hungry tae stay here," Blair retorted. He'd be damned if he'd give Ronald occasion to blame him later for standing by. On the quarterdeck, Captain Stokes and his chief mate were with the boy who had delivered the candy. As the captain listened to the boy's report, he brought a fist to his mouth, popped something in, and chewed. When Blair, Ronald, and Samuel reached the stairs leading up to the quarterdeck, the chief mate stepped down to meet them.

"Ye're no supposed tae be out o' yer hold," the chief mate said.

"What do these roundheads want?" Captain Stokes asked, approaching. Upon hearing the derisive word mocking their haircuts, Blair felt his face warm up.

"We havena received the food we were promised," Samuel said.

"Is that so?" The captain smirked and turned to his chief mate. "Make sure that from now on these gentlemen get as much sausage, soda bread, and beer as they desire."

"We only demand our proper rations," Ronald said.

"You *demand*?" said the captain. He stepped down onto the main deck. "Go back to your hold, you fucking Irish."

Every indignity suffered in the past few days had been quietly gnawing at Blair. Like spoiled meat, it had fermented inside a thin layer of self-preservation. The word *Irish* pierced that layer. Blair threw a punch at the captain, who nimbly dodged the blow. Blair's fist missed its mark and instead hit the captain's closed hand, making his fingers open up and sending a handful of raisins scattering on deck. The chief mate grabbed him by the shoulder and effortlessly pinned Blair's arms behind his back.

"Dinna touch my brother!" Ronald yelled, lunging for the chief mate, but he was immediately restrained by two deckhands. When the captain struck Blair in the stomach, a third deckhand was needed to subdue Ronald. Several passengers and crewmembers had gathered around; Samuel stood by, impotent.

"Bring the cane and cat," the captain ordered. The bosun brought a rattan cane and a leather bag from which the captain pulled a whip. His fingers wrapped expertly around a grip from which hung nine cotton-cord knotted thongs, two and a half feet long. Ronald's jacket and shirt were pulled off him. "Tie his wrists to that belaying pin rail," the captain said, pointing to a sort of wooden rack that encircled the bottom of the mainmast, waist high. Wooden pins similar to cudgels were inserted all around the rack through holes; around each pin, lines were wound. Ronald's wrists were bound together, hooked over one pin, and secured with more rope.

"Bite this," the bosun said, holding a piece of leather to Ronald's mouth. Ronald glared at him and kept his mouth shut. He finally took the hide when the bosun said, "Ye'll crack yer teeth without it."

The captain raised his arm up and back and brought the whip down. Ronald grunted and his muscles rippled. Blair wanted to howl.

"One," the captain said calmly, pausing to untangle the bloody thongs. Blair shut his eyes, wishing the chief mate would release his arms so he could cover his ears. The way the captain calmly counted each blow—*two, three, four*—contrasted grotesquely with the sharp sound of the whip slicing flesh. Blair couldn't help but feel proud of his brother for not crying out; the only sounds coming from him were deep grunts and heavy breathing. Blair finally heard *twelve*, and Ronald stopped grunting. Blair opened his eyes; Ronald was on his knees.

"Oh God..." Blair groaned. Ronald's back was crisscrossed with gashes from which blood flowed freely. Two deckhands dragged his limp body next to Blair, and he collapsed facedown, drenched in sweat. When a pail of saltwater was poured on him, he finally cried out.

"Your turn," the captain said. The chief mate released Blair, who fumbled with the buttons on his jacket; he would not give anyone the satisfaction of undressing him.

"Not those," the chief mate said. "These." He pointed to the buttons on Blair's breeches. "Yer not old enough for the cat." When the captain grabbed the rattan cane, Blair understood.

"It'll be like when Da birched us," Ronald said, trying to sound reassuring, although his eyes blazed with fury. Desperately mortified and hoping the female passengers would avert their eyes, Blair allowed the bosun to drape him over a gun, tie his hands, and pull down his breeches. He took the hide between his teeth and pressed his legs together to shield his testicles. With the first blow he realized a cane was *nothing* like a birching rod. The stinging pain spread like hot embers through his entire body, and he moaned loudly with every blow. By the time the twelfth blow fell on him, tears and snot were streaming down his face. The ship's surgeon cursorily examined him and Ronald. Samuel and another passenger flanked Ronald, draped his arms around their shoulders, and helped him limp toward the hatch. Someone else offered a shoulder for Blair to lean on, but he refused. He grit his teeth as he limped behind Ronald, his glutes and hamstrings rigid. Once down in the hold, he looked straight ahead as he walked but could feel everyone staring in shock as they made their way to their berth.

"Lads," Samuel said, looking ashamed, "I'm sorry I didna step in. I have Christy tae think of."

"There was nothing ye could do," said Ronald in a hoarse voice. "Ye would've been whipped too."

With Samuel's help, Ronald painstakingly climbed to his berth and lay on his stomach. Blair climbed up behind him.

"Please forgive me," Blair said, glad to be facing his brother's feet and not his eyes.

"It wisna yer fault."

Blair breathed raggedly through his mouth, keeping as quiet as he could so no one would notice he was crying. A warm hand draped itself gently on his back. He turned his head and saw Christy standing next to the berth, handing him a handkerchief. He took it without a word, and without a word she went back to her berth. When the time for their next meal came, she and Samuel shared their rations with the two brothers.

August 15, 1729

"To Sir Richard Baylis, Lord Mayor of the City of London. The humble petition of Malvina Ambrose. That your petitioner was guilty of committing a crime which she never before did and hopes by the grace of God never to do the like again. Most humbly prays on account of her tender age not yet eleven years and only cast to the value of single ten pence that Your Honor out of your extensive goodness will be pleased to let her receive corporal punishment for the heinousness of her crime and not to transport her out of her native isle."

Mallie sat at the table in the men's Middle Ward and listened to the schoolmaster read her appeal letter. As soon as the gaol fever outbreak had subsided, she had gone looking for him, praying he had survived. He handed her a tattered quill and indicated where she should sign. She slowly scratched out a shaky *M.*

"Poor Edina," the schoolmaster mused. "She was so grateful to have survived the previous fever outbreak."

Mallie looked up. "When?"

"Oh, three months ago."

"When did yer write 'er appeal letter?"

"Maybe eight months ago."

Mallie's mouth went dry; her mind worked. Edina might still be alive if she'd been transported. What if there was another fever outbreak while Mallie waited for an answer to her appeal? What if next time it killed her? She put the quill down and ripped the letter in half.

August 23, 1729

A slender young man flanked by two gaolers exited through the prison gate, his pristine wig and the sparkling buttons on his black coat making him seem out of place. He and his escorts walked past the convicts standing outside Newgate, waiting to be taken to the ship that would transport them. The young man turned his warm brandy-colored eyes toward London's flotsam and jetsam, the impurities that needed to be constantly strained from polite society: criminals, beggars, abandoned wives, prostitutes, even a small girl holding a doll. A line of javelin men stood between the convicts and their weeping friends and relatives. He had firmly forbidden his own friends, sister, and niece from coming to bid him farewell; his sister's sobbing would have exposed him as just another convict, and he felt ashamed enough as it was. His gaze lingered on the girl with the doll, and his eyes stung with tears. The way she anxiously tucked her lower lip under her upper teeth reminded him of his beloved niece Penelope, whom he had not seen since his arrest. At the head of this group of convicts waited a cart with three men and a pregnant woman. As the young man and the gaolers walked past it, he felt the hint of a gag reflex. The men were not wearing stockings or shoes; their breeches strained over their swollen thighs, and their lower legs and feet were black. The woman's swollen, black feet peeked out from under her skirts. *Scurvy.* When the young man reached a luxurious carriage pulled by two glossy black horses at the very front of the procession, a footman opened the door, and the young man leaned inside.

"Mr. Forward," he said, extending his hand toward a gentleman with a double chin and no cheekbones to speak of. "I'm Esquire Wornell Bray. I'm much obliged to you."

"It's my pleasure, Esquire Bray," Forward replied, shaking hands. "I wouldn't dream of allowing you to embark unaccompanied."

Only when Bray climbed into the cart did his escorts return to the prison. A moment later a cry came from the front of the caravan: "Make way for His Majesty's seven-year passengers!"

The carriage lurched forward. With every block traveled, the mob that followed the convicts swelled, like flies drawn to the carts that carried night soil out of the city. *You're very fortunate*, Bray told himself as the mob flung curses and mud at the convicts. *Money is a wonderful buffer against the worst humiliations of transportation.* He had paid for the best accommodations inside Newgate, and Jonathan Forward, who controlled the transportation monopoly, was personally escorting him to the ship. Bray would share the captain's quarters—also for a price—and be allowed to spend as much time on deck as he wished. When the procession reached Blackfriars by the Thames, Bray and Forward stepped onto the wharf.

"Mr. Wasey!" called Forward. A chubby man wearing impeccably tailored clothes responded to the summons. "Esquire Bray, allow me to introduce my agent, Mr. Wasey. Mr. Wasey, Esquire Bray is taking his lawyering talents to America, much to our loss."

Bray gave a small smile; it was considerate of Forward to introduce him in such a way, although surely the agent had the ship's manifest and knew better. The agent shook Bray's hand amicably and then turned to a couple of the gaolers accompanying the convicts. "You can start loading the first group into this lighter," he said, indicating one of the flat-bottomed boats waiting at the dock.

"Let us oversee the loading of your belongings onto another," Forward said to Bray while a group of male convicts climbed into a lighter. The two lightermen plunged their long oars into the water and pushed off into the swarm of lighters and ships. Suddenly the oarsmen yelled out in alarm and waved their arms frantically. A jolly boat manned by four rowers was headed straight toward them. Bray gasped, and Forward cursed as the boats collided, sending his prisoners and rowers splashing into the gray waters. The two lightermen quickly rose to the surface, spitting and coughing, and swam to the overturned vessel; the convicts, still wearing their irons, did not.

Forward turned to his agent. "How many convicts were in that lighter?"

"Ten, sir."

Forward sighed. "That damn river just swallowed thirty pounds the Crown owed me, not to mention the expensive irons."

Bray pressed his lips together. This was yet another thing to be grateful for: he would not be sold once they reached their destination. He had used the last of his savings to buy his freedom once he reached the colonies. Maybe the name of the ship would prove to be a good omen: *Hopewell*.

"If it's any comfort, sir," the agent said, "those were young boys and old men. I'll have replacements before the ship sails."

"Please make sure of it." Forward motioned toward another lighter. "Esquire Bray, if you please."

Mallie felt a cold rush of fear when she and several women were ordered to step inside a lighter. Seeing those convicts sink to the bottom of the river had been excruciating; she could barely breathe the whole nine miles to the port of Blackwall. The journey took them past hundreds of ships moored along both sides of the river on countless quays and jetties before their oarsman pulled the boat up to a floating dock and wound a line around a bollard. As she and the other female convicts carefully stepped on the dock and made their way up the wobbling gangway, deckhands lining the handrail whooped and whistled. As soon as the women were on deck, the deckhands searched them for contraband, fondling their breasts and raising their skirts. A sob pushed up Mallie's throat: she had never been felt up by a man. She stared at the feet of the deckhand standing before her, anticipating with terror the moment when he would make a grab for her.

"Peter!" the deckhand yelled.

A boy—barely older than she—scrambled down the leeward shrouds like a spry monkey.

"These 'ere wenches are wily, Peter," the deckhand lectured. As he pointed a filthy index finger in Mallie's face, she noticed he was missing the little and ring fingers. "Ye should learn 'ow ter find things they try ter smuggle. Search 'er doll."

A squeal scuffed Mallie's throat as the boy snatched her doll away and pawed it with his tar-covered hands. When the three-fingered deckhand was satisfied there was nothing to find in the doll, he ordered Mallie to spread her arms out to the sides. She obeyed out of sheer terror, her heart palpitating like a cornered rabbit, while Three Fingers guided the boy on how to feel her arms, back, chest, and buttocks. Every inch of her skin crawled with revulsion as sticky hands ran up one leg and then the other, all the way to her groin. Her eyes glistened with tears.

"The more ye cry, the less ye'll piss," the deckhand said, chuckling. "Search 'er."

The boy slipped his hand inside Mallie's skirt pocket and found nothing. He stood there, thinking hard. "Take off yer shoes."

Mallie blinked and didn't immediately obey. The boy repeated the order. As soon as she removed her shoes, a row of coins under her threadbare stockings, arranged from little to big toe, was easy to see.

The boy grinned, revealing teeth yellowed from chewing tobacco. He made her sit on the deck, take off her stockings, and hand over the last of the coins she had gotten for her hair.

"Cap'n Jenkins!" the deckhand cried out.

"No." Mallie's voice was a pitiful whisper. A man wearing a beautiful light-blue velvet three-piece suit and black beaver felt cocked hat strode up.

"An auspicious beginning!" the captain exclaimed, his weathered face scrunching like an accordion when he smiled.

He took the coins, jingled them in his hand, and looked down at Mallie. "Thank you, my dear. We'll see whether it's the men or women who contribute the most to my purse today."

Mallie breathed again when her doll was back in her hands, but her limbs were flaccid and numb. She was made to step aside while the rest of the convicts were searched. A penny knife was pulled out of a woman's stocking, and a file was discovered inside a man's gingerbread loaf. Both convicts were made to sit against the starboard railing on the main deck to be whipped later. When everyone had been searched, the men were led down a hatch, the women down another. Mallie, at the head of her group, followed a deckhand with a lantern. They reached another deck filled with casks, boxes, and chickens in cages, and kept going down the narrow staircase. A thick smell of mold and decay stopped her like a solid wall. The woman behind Mallie bumped into her, and from the rear of the group, another deckhand yelled a curse at whoever was holding things up. Mallie moved again.

"All the way in," urged the lead deckhand, crouching at the foot of the stairs. "Make way for the ones behind." Mallie was short enough to stand, but the rest of the women had to crouch. She moved forward in the near dark until she bumped up against wooden planks, and body after body piled up behind and around her, like dominoes in a box. The deckhand hung his lantern on the lower foremast. "Make yerselves at home." Mallie looked around. The lantern revealed planks nailed along the length of the bulwark, covering the portholes. There was nothing in the hold but a pail secured with rope to the bottom portion of a mast and canvas spread at their feet. The women had begun to stake out spots on the canvas—damp from water seeping through the rotting hull—when the sound of shrieks from the deck above made everyone freeze: the whippings had begun. Mallie and the woman she was shackled to dug into the canvas as best they could. Mallie covered her ears, but the cries trickled through her small hands. Soon, the woman who had been caught with the penny knife shuffled down into the hold, sobbing, blood seeping through the back of her gown, and she did not quiet down for hours.

That night, after the lantern had been extinguished, Mallie cowered in the most absolute darkness that had ever engulfed her. All around, women cried and talked about how heart-wrenching it had been to say farewell to friends and family. Mallie only listened. No one had come to see her leave.

After an almost inedible breakfast of gruel, the *Hopewell* set sail. The decrepit ship creaked loudly, and Mallie feared it would crack open like an egg. Hours later the ship stopped, and Mallie and five women were ordered on deck to receive new canvas gowns. She was standing in line, squinting, the high noon sun stinging her eyes, when six figures climbed out of the men's hold, wearing irons and padlocks around their necks. Her pupils dilated as she spotted among the convicts the boy who had been blacking shoes the day of her arrest. She was thrilled to see a familiar and friendly face. As soon as Mallie received her gown, she and the woman she was chained to walked to the handrail where the shoeblack—himself shackled to another convict—was standing.

"Derby?" she called. He pivoted with his torso, the neck iron preventing him from moving his head freely. Mallie gasped at the deep purple bruise blooming around one of his blue eyes.

"Mallie! I 'eard yer were in Newgate."

"I was."

"Is Lizzie 'ere too?"

"No. She's being sent ter Tyburn."

"Oh. I'm sorry."

"Me too," she said in a somber voice. "Yer were arrested for blacking?" She was well aware that shoeblacking was tantamount to vagrancy.

"I was never in prison. I was spirited away last night in an alley. Me mum don't know where I am."

Mallie felt a deep sadness for Derby's mother, who had often fed her. She imagined the woman very well might suspect "spirits"—kidnappers—had taken her son, as it happened all too often, but she would never know for sure.

"Oh, Mallie, me neck 'urts so!" Derby brought a shackled hand to his neck. He looked at Mallie and frowned. "Ye're a pile of bones." A gust of sea breeze pushed her straw hat off her head; around the edges of her linen cap, black stubble was visible. "Wot 'appened ter yor 'air?"

She put the hat back on and rearranged the chinstrap. "Sold it," she said dryly.

Derby pointed to her doll. "She's being transported for fencing the 'andkerchiefs yer stole, ain't she?"

Mallie had to suppress a smile. She hugged her doll tighter and shook her head. Suddenly a man settled himself next to Derby; she recognized him as the gentleman she had seen ride in the fancy carriage the day before. He turned his head in her direction, pretending to look into the distance, but she could tell he was watching her. After several minutes she whispered to Derby, "Do yer know where we're going?" Derby shrugged.

"Maryland," said the gentleman, pointing to the coast. "That's Gravesend, Kent."

Mallie cringed, regretting having asked.

"Maryland?" Derby said, frowning. "Where is that?"

As the gentleman replied, Mallie turned her head in the opposite direction, not wanting to acknowledge his presence, and for as long as he remained in that spot, she avoided uttering another word or even glancing in his direction. She was glad when he finally walked away, and she stayed with Derby until it was time for another six female and six male convicts to go on deck.

Two days later the ship reached the North Sea. The ship swayed harder now, and Mallie's shackle rubbed her wrist raw. The women moaned and retched. The acrid stench of vomit made Mallie's stomach turn, but hour after hour passed, and still she was not seasick. They sailed south, dropping anchor at midnight at the port of Dover. In the morning they joined a flotilla of convict ships leaving from Ireland, Bristol, and Liverpool, headed for the American colonies. The women's shackles were removed for the rest of the voyage. Mallie looked out over the water, overcome with wonder. Having spent her entire life in London, she had no idea the world had so much space. A cold wave rushed over her feet. She jumped in surprise and looked down; seawater washed in and out through the scuppers. She took off her shoes and allowed the water to wash over her.

August 25, 1729

A strong southwest wind had steadily pushed the *King George* off course for three weeks; a near constant stream of rain kept the passengers confined to the hold. Water leaked through the overhead and the bulkhead alike, and Blair was damp through and through. Gales blew day and night, and the weather grew progressively colder. When the winds died down long enough for Blair's mess to go on deck, they all headed straight for the camhoose to dry in front of the stove. Blair closed his eyes, relishing the heat and trying to shut out the sight of two deckhands sitting to his right, gnawing on cheese. Hunger clawed at his stomach. Lice had infested the hold, and his head, armpits, stomach, and groin itched relentlessly. He scratched his scalp, stirring up shivers that spread down his back but did little to soothe his burning skin. Captain Stokes's voice boomed from the quarterdeck.

"All hands on deck!"

The deckhands in the camhoose cursed and ran out. A moment later one of them returned.

"To yer hold, now!" he ordered.

As soon as he stepped out of the camhoose, Blair saw a low cloud about half a mile away. It was shaped like a giant log, and it was rolling toward them. The captain yelled out orders; men rushed from one end to the other, striking sails. A deckhand followed the passengers to their hold, made sure the lamps were snuffed out, and battened down the hatch. Ronald climbed unto the berth first, and Blair took the outside. For fifteen minutes they lay in total darkness. The ship did not seem to be rocking any more than usual.

"What's happening, Ronald?" he whispered.

"I dinna ken."

Then the squall hit. The ship heaved and shuddered like a baited bear pulling on its chain, cornered by bulldogs. Screams, prayers, and curses pierced the dark. Water began to trickle, then cascade down the stairs, and Blair feared they all would drown in the hold like rats. The ship rolled and threw him against Ronald, crushing him against the bulwark. Blair clamped an arm over the berth's outer plank. Ronald, however, lacked anything to grip on to, and when the ship rolled back again, he flew into Blair, smashing him into the plank.

"Do ye want tae switch places?" Ronald asked.

"Aye!"

"When the ship rolls in my direction, let go and allow yerself tae roll over me. I'll push myself tae yer spot. Wait—now!"

Blair released his hold, but instead of rolling, the ship pitched, and he went flying. He landed hard on the sole at the same time that he heard other passengers being thrown from their berths.

"Are ye hurt?" Ronald asked.

"Some," Blair moaned, trying to catch his wind. His hands found the edge of the bottom berth on his right, and as he gripped it, his fingers briefly closed around a small hand. Its owner was praying ardently, and when he listened closely to the tremulous voice, he recognized that it was Jean's. Something banged against his side: the pail's lid had come loose, and the pail's contents were spilling everywhere. The pail under the seat of the privy was probably not faring much better. He clung to the edge of the berth as the hours dragged by. The muscles in his hands, arms, and shoulders burned. He could feel Jean's hand grazing his as every so often she readjusted her grip. From the depths of his weary mind a thought crept up: this ship *was* his coffin. Would it hurt much when his lungs filled up with water? Would it be quick? What would life with Janet have been like? He remained motionless long after the storm had died down, still feeling as if he were caught in a whirlpool. The sound of the hatch opening was one of the most beautiful sounds he had ever heard.

"Ye people stink," grumbled a deckhand as he came down with rags and a pail full of vinegar for the passengers to clean up the mess with. "I remember when our cargo was sweet-smelling wine," he said as he relit the lanterns.

Jean grabbed a rag, dipped it in the pail, and worked in silence. Blair had never seen a more desolate expression than hers at that moment, and he could not help but feel pity for her.

Shortly after the passengers had finished cleaning up, a deckhand stuck his head down the hatch. "Jean Ó Súilleabháin!"!" he called. Blair looked down from his berth. The curtains on Jean's berth parted. Her cheekbones pushed against her skin in a way they had not when they had found her by the bridge, and the hollows under her eyes seemed deeper. Blair reflected on the past weeks and realized he had rarely seen her take her fair share of food; an Irish surrounded by Ulster Scots, she had no choice but to resign herself.

"Over here," she called back, puzzled.

"The cap'n invites ye tae have breakfast with him."

The hold fell completely silent. Jean's eyes met Blair's for a moment. He saw she did not want to go, but at the same time recognized the same hunger that drilled his core.

"Make up yer mind," the deckhand said impatiently. Her eyes bleak, Jean got up and exited the hold.

At long last allowed to go on deck, Blair grabbed his Sunday clothes.

"I dinna feel well," Christy said. "You go, Samuel."

Outside, Blair took deep breaths, relishing the crisp, clean air. Ronald and Samuel stretched their arms. A few deckhands hung from the lee channels, relieving themselves; several crewmembers were rinsing their clothes in pails of seawater. As soon as a pail became available, Blair, Ronald, and Samuel washed their own clothes.

Later, when Blair was hanging his damp clothes over the side of his berth, Jean returned, wearing clean and dry clothes, certainly not the ones she had boarded with. She was gathering her belongings when the Irish mother—her wide-eyed little girl at her skirts—approached. Although Blair could not understand the words, it was clear the mother was trying to persuade Jean not to go. Jean said something back, never meeting the woman's gaze. She hugged her, kissed her cheek, crouched down to hug the girl, took her things, and headed for the hatch.

"Catholic whore," a woman muttered with disdain. In her nervousness, Jean stepped on her skirts halfway up the ladder and dropped her bag. No one moved as she scrambled to gather her scattered belongings. Maybe it was the image of Jean kneeling on the sole; maybe Blair simply needed to make a dent in the misery around him. Whatever the reason, he hurried over and helped her collect her things. She looked at him almost apologetically and, without thanking him, hurried out.

"Why did ye help her?" Ronald asked. Blair wasn't quite sure himself, but he gave Ronald the answer he knew would appease him.

"Her name reminds me o' Janet." He shrugged, as if the incident were inconsequential. However, even though he told himself that helping this Irish girl was of no more note than watering a cow, the tiny act of kindness had filled him with an unexpected warmth. Suddenly, the familiar sound of an instrument being tuned made him turn his head; a passenger had taken out his fiddle. The man began to play, and three other men quickly reached under berths and pulled out fiddles. Soon, the soothing and leisurely notes of four fiddles melded in perfect harmony, like yarns of different colors knitted into one pattern. Blair smiled. *Music.* In the midst of despair, music never failed to fill him with joy, or at least comfort. He joined in the singing:

> *Over the mountains and over the waves,*
> *Over the fountains and under the graves,*
> *Over the floods that are deepest, which do Neptune obey,*
> *Over rocks that are steepest,*
> *Love will find out the way.*
> *You may train the eagle*
> *To stoop to your fist;*
> *Or you may inveigle*
> *The Phoenix of the east;*
> *The lioness, you may move her*
> *To give over her prey;*
> *But you'll ne'er stop a lover—*
> *He will find out the way.*

August 28, 1729

For a second day, the *Hopewell* was becalmed. Mallie leaned on the port handrail, Derby whistling next to her, following the lead of several crewmembers in an attempt to summon the wind. The captain, as usual, occupied his commanding spot on the quarterdeck. Bray stood with him, conversing.

"Mallie, is it?" someone said, shoving Derby aside. "Peter wants tae spend time with ye."

Her stomach tightened when she saw Three Fingers and the boy who had searched her. The boy slunk next to her, switching his quid from one cheek to the other.

"Trying tae make a man out o' Peter, are ye?" joked the bosun on his way to the foremast.

"Since I failed with ye," Three Fingers shot back, "I have high hopes with him."

The bosun cackled and held up a needle. "I'm going tae pin this in the sails, and if that fails tae bring us wind, I'll pin it tae the lawyer's arse. It's him that's bringing us bad luck." He stuck the needle in his sleeve and climbed up the foremast shrouds. Three Fingers turned his attention back to Mallie.

"Ye could play cards with Peter in my cabin, have food and small beer."

"Leave her alone," Derby said, but his voice lacked any hint of confidence or bravado. Three Fingers's hand shot forth and clamped around Derby's neck.

"Talk again and ye won't make it tae Maryland," he growled.

Derby stared into the distance, looking pained. Three Fingers grabbed Mallie by the arm and dragged her away, stopping beside the foremast. Peter followed.

"Finney! Finney!"

Three Fingers looked up, annoyed. "What?"

Mallie followed Three Fingers's gaze. The bosun was on the shrouds right beneath the topgallant sail, making exaggerated jabbing motions with his needle at something on deck. Mallie turned her eyes to see what the bosun was jabbing at and saw that Bray was walking toward her. Three Fingers and Peter laughed. The bosun then reached for his marlinespike, which hung from his waist by a macramé lanyard. He detached the lanyard from his belt and pretended to throw the marlinespike toward Bray, like a javelin. Three Fingers and Peter stopped laughing.

"Don't do that, ye idiot—" Three Fingers muttered.

"What's going on here?" Bray asked, stopping next to Mallie. Three Fingers and Peter turned their attention to him, but she kept her gaze on the bosun a moment longer and saw him fumble the marlinespike, which flashed as the sunlight hit it on the way down. She gasped and thrust both hands against Bray's middle, pushing as hard as she could. Startled, Bray took a long step backward as the marlinespike came whizzing down between them and embedded itself on the deck, the lanyard hanging limp from its eye. Derby, Three Fingers, and Peter came close, their eyes wide. Bray reached down and freed the marlinespike, which was quite longer than Mallie's forearm.

"Esquire Bray," Captain Jenkins said, approaching, "are you unhurt?"

"Yes, thank you." Bray then turned to Mallie. "Thank you," he said earnestly. Mallie said nothing.

"Is everyone unhurt?" the bosun called out, scrambling down the shrouds onto the deck.

Captain Jenkins took the marlinespike from Bray's hand and whirled on the bosun, pointing the object at his chest as if it were a dagger.

"Please forgive me, Cap'n," the bosun stammered.

Captain Jenkins turned the marlinespike in his hand and shoved it lengthwise right under the man's rib cage. The bosun bent over, wheezing.

"Don't ever let that happen again," warned the captain.

"No, sir," the bosun squeaked, and he hobbled off.

The ship's bell rang, announcing another half hour gone by and the end of Mallie's time on deck.

"Come, Peter," Three Fingers said, and he grabbed Mallie by the arm. She had opened her mouth to beg to be left alone when Bray grabbed her other arm.

"Captain, I'd like this girl's company."

Mallie's *No!* might as well have been the squawk of a common seagull, for all anyone noticed.

"Release her!" the deckhand exclaimed, pulling on her. A sharp pain bit her shoulder and she yelped.

"Now, Esquire Bray," the captain said unctuously. "You've enjoyed a privileged situation. Why provoke my crew? Surely you can pick someone else."

Bray held the captain's eyes, smiled, and shrugged. "It's this girl I want."

Captain Jenkins harrumphed, reached into his vest pocket, and pulled out a coin.

"Cross," the deckhand said.

"Pile, then," said Bray.

Mallie, literally caught between the two men, watched the coin flip in the air. This was her worst nightmare: although she had never been with a man, she had seen stray dogs mating, and plenty at the brothel and Newgate to get a sense of what it was that men and women did. And it was abundantly clear that it was a revolting thing, to be avoided at all costs. The captain caught the coin and opened his palm.

"Esquire Bray, the girl is yours. Make good use of the time."

"Sit down," Bray said, scooting and patting the captain's bunk. Mallie pressed her back against the door, as far away as possible from him. He noticed her nose twitching, probably detecting tobacco and men's musk. "Sit down," he repeated. He chuckled when she sat on the sole. He opened a chest and pulled out an orange and a flask. "What's your name?"

"Malvina," she said, rushing the syllables.

"I'm Esquire Wornell Bray. What's your doll's name?"

Mallie shrugged.

"Do you want an orange, Malvina?" He stretched an arm toward Mallie so she wouldn't have to move. She hesitated for a moment, but he knew her hunger would defeat her fears. He smiled when she peeled the fruit and a tangy, fresh scent filled the cabin. Oranges were his niece's favorite fruit. Mallie's eyes sparkled when the juicy wedges burst in her mouth. Bray took a swig of whiskey from the flask and ran his fingers over its leather covering, remembering the beloved who had given him this gift. He had never felt such adoration for anyone, and it broke his heart to know someone else was bound to take his place. He returned the flask to the chest and thoughtfully ran a finger over the spine of one of his law books.

Weeks ago, he had left the library at Lincoln's Inn—the barristers' association to which he belonged, one of four Inns of Court—and headed toward a tavern, a poetry book secreted away in his bag. He wasn't supposed to remove the reference book from the library, but he planned to return it the following day, and no one would ever even notice. He fervently wished to read from this book to his lover, but it was unthinkable to allow any of the other barristers to see them together, no matter how innocuous the setting. He had just stepped inside the room he had rented for the afternoon, the day's usual vexations swept away at the sight of Howard, when the Inn's librarian and a constable had burst in. The librarian had seen Bray put the book in his bag and had followed him all the way to the tavern. Confessing the truth would have meant hanging in Tyburn for sodomy. Therefore, Bray had fabricated a story about trying to sell the book to an unsuspecting collector—Howard. Howard had thus escaped the incident unscathed, but Bray had been convicted of theft and sentenced to transportation. At least, as a member of the Inns of Court, he would easily resume his law practice in the colonies.

He looked at Mallie, who was eyeing him with distrust. She darted her eyes away, but when he produced more food and water, she accepted it eagerly. While she ate, he covered the entire bunk with a clean sheet to keep lice from getting into the bedding and mattress.

He reached under the bunk, pulled out a folding chair, and sat down. "Do you want to lie down?"

She shook her head.

"I promise I'm not going to touch you. Lie down." His voice was kind but firm. She could not hide the pleasure on her face when she lay down on the horsehair-stuffed mattress. He could see her fighting to keep her eyes open, but her tired muscles melted like ice in a kettle. She curled up in a fetal position with the doll, brought her citrus-scented hands to her nose, and inhaled. Moments later she had sunk into a deep, peaceful sleep.

CHAPTER FIVE

September 5, 1729

A blast sounded through the hold of the *King George*, jolting Blair awake. Ronald propped himself up on an elbow, eyes wide.

"Was that one of our cannons?" someone asked.

"I think it was," another voice answered.

About three minutes went by before another shot rang out, followed by three more at equal intervals.

"Blair," Ronald said, "get up. It's our turn tae go on deck."

Blair and the rest whose turn it was to go outside waited by their berths while the previous group came back down.

"Why are they firing?" someone asked the passengers who were returning.

"They espied a sail and are giving chase," a woman replied.

"Why?"

"We dinna ken."

When Blair climbed on deck, the ship was still tacking. He spotted another vessel on the *King George*'s starboard side, a quarter mile away.

"Ronald, isna that ship moving east?" Blair asked.

"It is," Ronald replied.

"Why are we chasing it? For why would we even if it were westbound?"

Ronald simply shook his head, his eyes flashing. For the next few days, Captain Stokes gave chase to almost every ship he spotted, and strayed farther and farther north. And the weather grew colder and colder.

September 22, 1729

The rations aboard the *King George* had been cut to three and a half pounds of bread per passenger a week, and one pint of black, stinking, worm-laden water per person per day. Christy developed a fever and body aches, but it wasn't until she was struck with diarrhea that the surgeon finally deigned to pay a call.

"Dysentery," he muttered bleakly.

Before the day was over, most passengers were showing symptoms, including Blair. That night he had just reached his berth—after having used the privy for the third time in the span of a couple of hours—when he heard the Irish mother's anguished voice. The father, who had been sleeping at the table, his head resting on his arms, ran to the berth and opened the curtains. Blair saw the couple's daughter convulsing. The mother held the girl down by the shoulders while the father held her legs and prayed out loud. Ronald stuck his head out, saw what was happening, and lay back down with the blanket over his head. Blair didn't dare move. He stayed put until the girl's tiny body went limp, and felt a lump in his throat as the parents wept. He finally climbed back up to his berth, afraid to fall asleep lest he never wake up again.

In the morning, Blair, Ronald, and Samuel stood with other passengers and crewmembers around a gun port on the starboard side. The Irish girl's body had been wrapped in canvas with a cannonball at her feet, and the canvas had been sewn shut. The small bundle now lay on a board. Jean stood next to the girl's mother, holding her hand. The girl's father stepped toward Captain Stokes and held out the family's Catholic Bible. Stokes waved it away and instead read from his well-worn King James Version. Two deckhands tilted the board, and the body slid through the gun port and splashed into the water below. The mother keened. All his life Blair had been told that Irish keening was a horrible thing, and he had believed it—though he had never heard it. Now, he found the sound melodious, haunting, beautiful.

The Irish girl was just the first domino to fall. Not a day went by without another passenger following her into the sea. The rations had dwindled to a pound and a half of bread a week, along with a single biscuit, a tiny amount of salt beef, and a quarter pint of barley, which the passengers were forced to eat uncooked, because there was no water to boil it in. Blair tried to eat the leathery beef, but the salt singed his dehydrated mouth, and he spat it out. He was more tired than he had ever felt. Chewing required all of his will. He simply didn't want to move anymore. He heard the ship's bell ring.

"Time tae go on deck, Blair." Ronald sounded winded. Blair felt him climbing down the berth.

"I'm not going," Blair replied.

"Samuel, are ye coming?"

Samuel's voice had a hollow ring. "She's dead."

It was as if a bolt of lightning had cut through Blair. He looked down. Christy's head was resting on Samuel's shoulder; Blair would have sworn she was asleep. Ronald crouched down and touched her cheek but immediately yanked his hand away. For the first time since leaving home, Blair saw fear in his brother's eyes. Ronald and Samuel conferred in low tones while Samuel gently stroked Christy's hair. Ronald picked her up gingerly and carried her out of the hold, but Samuel remained on the sole. Blair climbed down his berth and crouched next to Samuel.

"Need help?" he asked.

"Aye."

Blair stood up, took Samuel's hands in his, and pulled him up. By the time they had made it to the deck, Christy was already being wrapped in canvas. The weather had become frigid, and the passengers wrapped themselves in their blankets whenever they went outside. Blair stood next to Ronald and wondered if his brother was shaking so violently due only to the cold. Samuel's eyes seemed strangely vacant. Almost as soon as Christy's body had sunk beneath the waves, the captain approached Samuel, looking uncharacteristically troubled.

"You should know that when we reach Philadelphia, you'll have to be sold for your time plus your wife's," the captain said.

Samuel looked up with a curious expression that didn't match the gravity of the statement. "Why?"

"Your wife died past the halfway point of the voyage."

"Oh." It was as if Samuel had been told it was Friday instead of Saturday. Blair seethed as the captain walked away.

Couldn't the man have waited one day before breaking the news?

"Dinna worrit," Ronald said. "We'll find the way tae pay for Christy's term."

"It's awricht," Samuel replied, looking past Ronald and Blair. "It disna matter."

A deckhand hurried past them and scrambled over the leeward handrail. For a moment Blair thought the man would jump overboard, but he perched himself on one of two narrow planks bound to the ship's leeward side, dropped his slops to his ankles, held on to the shrouds, crouched with his bottom suspended over the channel's outer edge, and relieved himself. *Well*, thought Blair, *at least he waited until the burial was over.* Out of the corner of his eyes, he saw another figure climb over the handrail and disappear.

The deckhand yelled, "Man overboard!"

Blair ran to the handrail and saw Samuel's head sink beneath the waves and chunks of ice and then resurface, his lips blue, gasping for breath. "Samuel!"

"Captain!" Ronald yelled as he reached Blair's side. "We need tae retrieve Samuel!"

"If I turned the ship every time someone jumped overboard, we would never get to the colonies," the captain yelled back from the quarterdeck. The handrail was now crammed with people staring in horror at the water.

Blair grabbed a pail tethered to the handrail by a line and threw it over the side with all his might. The pail drew a small arch in the air, dropped uselessly next to the ship's hull, and was dragged alongside like a dog on a leash before a deckhand pulled it back up. Blair scanned the water and was shocked at how easy it was to lose sight of Samuel's location.

There! *He was still there.* He turned to Ronald, desperate for guidance from his big brother, but all Ronald could do was stare at the ocean with a look of anguish Blair had never seen before. Just then someone squeezed in between them.

"Take this," Jean whispered to Blair. She held a small bundle in her hands. "Take it," she insisted. He squirreled the bundle under his blanket; then she turned and was gone in a flash. When he returned his gaze toward the water, Samuel was out of sight once more. This time Blair couldn't spot him in the waves.

Two weeks later nearly all of the ship's passengers were short of breath, with aching bodies and spotted skin. Their gums bled and their teeth had become loose. Blair and Ronald exhibited none of their symptoms; the bundle Jean had given Blair contained about two pounds of raisins, which had protected them from scurvy. However, they had eaten the last of them. Curled up in his berth, Blair imagined death as a scythe that steadily and implacably swung to and fro, from bow to stern and back. He heard Ronald cry out from the berth that had been left vacant by Christy and Samuel. Blair looked down in time to see his brother wake up, wild eyed, his forehead beaded with sweat. Ever since Christy's death, Ronald had been plagued by nightmares. Blair wondered what it would do to his brother if he were forced to carry his corpse.

He waited impatiently until it was his time to go above deck, then climbed up to the channel where he had seen the deckhand. His fingers gripped the shrouds; the ship's swaying motion was more pronounced here than on deck, the stiff breeze even colder. His teeth chattered. He thought of the painful, drawn-out deaths he had witnessed. He thought of Samuel; it had been over quickly. Not a bad way to go, considering.

"I never saw anyone think so hard afore takin' a shit," a deckhand muttered as he walked past. Blair leaned back as far as his arms would allow. Tears trickled down his cheeks, leaving cold tracks on his face. It would be so easy to just let go. Surely Janet and his family would forgive him, wouldn't they? He glanced toward the quarterdeck; Captain Stokes stared back at him. An overwhelming, hot fury pulsed through Blair's limbs and dulled all cold and hunger and thirst and weariness. He swung a leg back over the handrail. *Not today. Not today, not tomorrow.*

September 27, 1729

Sheets of rain drummed deafeningly against the *Hopewell*'s hull all night long, seeping through seams and old nail holes, drenching Mallie and the other women. It wasn't until the forenoon watch the following day that she had a chance to go outside. She was struggling to wring the water from her clothes when Bray found her, took her to the camhoose, and parked her in front of the stove. Once she was dry, he took her to the captain's cabin, fed her, and put her to sleep. He sat down with a book, and read until it was time to return Mallie to her hold. The next day, gales again forced all convicts to remain in their holds. She was surprised to discover herself pining not only for Bray's food and bed, but also for his easy warmth and demeanor, which cloaked her with a heretofore unknown sense of safety.

"Are yer all right?" Derby had asked the first time they met after Bray had won the coin toss. She felt embarrassed, guessing what was on Derby's mind, but her flustered "yes" had also been confident. Derby had smiled and said, "Good."

Squalls continued to besiege the *Hopewell* for days, during which convicts were allowed on deck only a couple of times. Mallie's torpor was punctuated only by terror and pain when tossed about. At last the winds died down; the hatch opened with a screech, and she sat up immediately. Once outside, she was disappointed not to see Bray. Derby was leaning on their usual spot on the handrail, his eyes overflowing with anguish.

"That looks worse," she said worriedly.

"What?" he asked, as if he had just noticed her. She pointed to a red ring around his neck.

"We're always shackled in the hold," he replied. "Yer lucky yer not a man."

She did not reply but could think of numerous ways in which men were far luckier than women.

"I want ter go home, Mallie. Oh, I want ter go home."

The despair in his voice made her shudder; she didn't know what to say. Suddenly, a hand appeared from behind and snatched the doll she had been cradling. She whirled to see Peter skipping across the deck, holding the doll by the head.

"Give it back!" she cried, going after him as fast as the ship's swaying allowed her landlubber legs. "I'll tell Mr. Bray."

Peter gestured toward Derby. "Stop talking to 'im, or I throw 'er overboard."

"Please, give 'er back!" She looked around desperately for Bray.

"Do as I say."

Peter dangled the doll in Mallie's face. "Mallie! Save me! Ye may 'old her for a spell," he said cunningly, handing it to her. "But I'll take it again unless ye do as I say."

Mallie had felt sad and jealous whenever she saw wealthy children and their parents emerging from stores with a new toy: a hoop, a puppet. But the prospect of *losing* her doll—as opposed to never having had one in the first place—brought about a new, raw grief. How could an object cause her so much pain? She glanced at Derby, who was now sitting on the deck, his face in his hands.

"I'm too old ter play with dolls," she said, and threw the doll overboard. She walked back to Derby, sat down next to him, and quietly rested her head on his shoulder.

October 15, 1729

Mallie took a minute sip of water, then passed the two-quart can her mess of six was forced to share in the afternoon, the same amount that had been allotted in the morning. It had been that way for days. She fell asleep, back-to-back with another convict, their bodies craving any warmth they could find. Sometime during the night she woke up and felt something cold pressing up against her back. *Planks,* she thought. *I must have rolled.* When the hatch opened in the morning and a deckhand came in to light the lantern, Mallie sat up. In the second she realized she *had* slept all night leaning against the convict, the woman—now with nothing to buttress her—rolled onto her back. Mallie screamed and crawled backward, like a crab running away from a torch. The woman's expressionless eyes were fixed on an indefinite point, her mouth slack, a dribble of saliva running down her cheek.

"Ye scared me tae death!" the deckhand chided Mallie, almost as if his feelings were hurt. "There's no need tae scream like that!" He stood catching his breath, hand over his heart, and then he left. When the body was finally removed and she went on deck, she found Derby every bit as shaken as she was; two male convicts had died.

That night, in spite of the cold, Mallie slept alone. In the morning it was discovered that another woman was dead. From that day forward, she felt only half alive herself until she confirmed Derby was all right.

Deckhands carried five of the surviving female convicts up the stairs. Every single one, except for Mallie, was too weak to walk. As soon as she stepped on deck, she gasped; she could see land. Everyone, both convict and crewmember, looked toward the west, entranced. She scanned the crowd until she found Derby; then she approached Bray.

"That," Bray told her, "is Maryland's coast."

Twenty-six hours later she was sweeping her gaze over the clear waters of the Chesapeake Bay. A flock of snowy egrets flew overhead, an elastic white quilt that stretched and contracted as it glided. Two deckhands offered all convicts fresh water from pails. Everyone drank frantically.

"I thought the captain said we'd run out of water," Bray said brusquely when a deckhand walked up to him. "I bet he'll increase the rations too. It's a little late to fatten up his cargo."

Mallie touched a hand to her hip and felt bone. She knew very well she might have died had it not been for Bray, and had no words to truly convey her gratitude. Two days later the *Hopewell* sailed past the Potomac River and then Rickard's Cliffs, which rose majestically on the bay's western shore, its tree-topped sheer sides glowing warm orange in the sun. After another two days, the ship reached the port city of Annapolis, at the mouth of the Severn River, and on October 24 it moored in the harbor proper, eight weeks after leaving London. Out of fifty men, eight had died, and seventeen out of twenty-one women were still alive. Of the four young boys on board, only Derby remained.

October 14, 1729

So many passengers had died that Blair had taken a bottom berth. The sound of thunder reached his ears, and he moaned, anticipating another violent storm. He again heard thunder, and then joyful shouting. He propped his cheek on the berth's outer plank. A couple of passengers stood by the stairs, heads tilted back, mouths open. He crawled out of his berth and approached Ronald's. His brother was facedown, motionless.

"Ronald," Blair called in a breathless voice. His tongue felt so swollen, he couldn't properly close his mouth. He shook

Ronald by the shoulder. Nothing. In a panic, Blair yanked his hair. Ronald groaned and mumbled into the bedding.

"It's raining! Ronald, it's raining." Ronald didn't budge. Blair wrapped his blanket around his shoulders and made his way to the hatch, under which more passengers were now standing, their mouths open like chicks waiting to be fed by their mother. He pushed his way through and crawled up the stairs on all fours, every step chewing into his last ounce of strength. Several deckhands were busy securing empty pails and casks on the deck. Blair stood under the main staysails, tilted his head back, and opened his mouth to receive the rain streaming down the canvas. At once he spat out the tar-laced water and stepped away from the main staysails to allow the rainwater to fall directly onto his cracked tongue; it was manna. He filled a pail with rainwater and another passenger helped him bring it down to the hold. Blair helped Ronald to sit, then brought the ladle to his brother's parched lips. Once the fresh liquid touched Ronald's mouth, he sprang to life and began to drink eagerly. He put his hand behind Blair's head, pulling him close until their foreheads touched. For the first time Blair could remember, Ronald wept.

The view unfurling before Blair was dreamlike: at the mouth of Delaware Bay, to the west, the trees and white beaches of Cape Henlopen seemed like a vision. Never had his heart swelled with such adoration for land. The sky had never seemed such a dazzling shade of blue, nor the air so pristine. As the ship slowly worked its way along the western coast of the bay, his glee turned to impatience. Seeing land so close at hand, without being able to disembark, was like another maddening itch he could not scratch. That night they dropped anchor at Bombay Hook; the next day they reached New Castle in Delaware, where William Penn had landed forty-seven years before, and took on provisions and fresh water. Blair chomped off a huge chunk of an apple, the juice dripping down his chin. Nothing would ever taste as good.

"Eat slowly," Ronald warned. "Ye'll make yerself sick."

At long last, on October 24, almost fifteen weeks after leaving Belfast and having lost three crewmembers and sixty-four passengers, eleven of them children, the *King George* arrived in Philadelphia.

PART TWO

CHAPTER SIX

October 25, 1729
Philadelphia

Naked and shivering on the main deck in the early morning chill, Blair poured a pail of Delaware River water over his head, scooped a handful of soft soap from an open cask, and vigorously scrubbed himself. Not since leaving Lisburn for Belfast had he washed as thoroughly, and he felt reborn. Raw spots on his scalp burned, but feeling clean again was wonderful. He sluiced himself. The lather that pooled at his feet was teeming with crab lice. He scraped the water off his body with his hands and, still damp, dressed in his Belfast clothes. When all the men had finished, they headed back to the hold to allow the women to wash their hair and feet. Then the men were summoned again on deck to have a barber from the city shave them. Blair surveyed his surroundings. Back home, clouds had always seemed to hang so low, he felt he could almost touch them. Here, the clouds soared high in the sky. To the west, the outline of a range of mountains cut the sky; wooden wharfs lining the shore jutted out in every direction. He was eager to see the city, but the high riverbank concealed it. He could see nothing but crowded, wooden storehouses west of the river.

After every man had been shaved, a city surgeon came on board to determine if anyone carried any contagious diseases. Only after everyone had been given a clean bill of health—meaning they didn't show signs of smallpox or gaol or yellow fever—was the ship allowed to dock. Blair watched with a pang of envy as several crewmembers disembarked, whooping and laughing, followed by the handful of passengers who had paid for their passage, the Irish couple among them. Jean was also allowed to disembark; she did not look back once.

"Captain Stokes," Ronald ventured, "may we go on land for a couple o' hours?"

"I allowed that once, and everyone escaped. You'll remain here while your names are registered in City Hall."

Shortly after noon, all passengers were summoned on deck and lined up, facing two men.

"These are Edward Horne and William Rawle," Captain Stokes said. Blair recognized the names; these were the men who held his indenture. They were dressed exactly as linen-drapers in Lisburn were: their shirts had no ruffles, their black knee-length coats were plain, they wore broad-brimmed hats, and the captain had not addressed them as *Mr.* Horne or *Mr.* Rawle. *Quakers.* The Lowland Scottish Presbyterian pride that had kept Blair from weeping in public the day his father had been buried now made him bitterly glad his father was not there to witness Quakers selling his sons.

October 25, 1729
Maryland

"I'll never grow accustomed to the peculiar smell they have upon arrival," the American agent for the British government said as he held a scented handkerchief to his mouth and nose. Jonathan Forward's agent in Maryland, standing next to him, nodded in agreement. Mallie shrank in shame. Earlier that day, for the first time in her life, she had washed herself with soap. She surmised, from the man's disgusted voice, that she had done a subpar job. Like the other women around her, she kept her eyes down while the British government's agent reviewed the list of convicts and recorded the deaths. After the captain swore no Catholics were among his cargo, the agent handed him an arrival certificate.

Mallie tensed when she saw Bray's belongings brought on deck. He crouched down and looked at her with sad eyes. "I wish I had the money to buy you your freedom. Please take care of yourself."

She felt like a stray puppy that had tried to follow a stranger, only to be left behind. The following morning, after weeks of being allowed to remain in the hold without restraints, the women were once again shackled. Mallie heard the faint peal of a bell calling for Sunday service; to her it sounded like an omen. Regret washed over her. If she hadn't discarded her appeal letter, she might have been, even now, back in the streets of London. She wished she could stow away and sail back home. Terrible as it was, the ship had become a familiar place, preferable to all the unknowns out there. She had gone from her tenement to Newgate to the *Hopewell*, each place worse than the last, and now she cowered in the dark, terrified of whatever was lurking in Maryland, waiting for her.

———

The wooden planks of Annapolis's dock reverberated under the footfalls of customers heading to the convict ships. A tall, striking man in his midtwenties, wearing an impeccable black coat over green breeches and waistcoat, was the first to nimbly step onto the *Hopewell*'s deck. He turned and held out his arm.

"Step carefully, Cassie," he said with tenderness. A teenage girl wrapped her left hand on his steadying forearm as her right lifted her yellow skirts. Another man, evidently a servant, followed them both.

"Is this Mrs. Bradnox?" Captain Jenkins asked with surprise, approaching the couple and smiling openly.

The young man smiled and turned to the girl. *Not yet, but soon.* She blushed and returned the smile, her teal eyes shimmering against her porcelain skin. "Captain Jenkins, this is my cousin, Miss Cassie White. She recently moved in with me and my sister."

"A pleasure to meet you," said the captain politely.

"A pleasure to meet you," replied the girl.

"Please, help yourselves." The captain gestured toward a table with a bowl and tumblers. Bradnox served himself some punch but refrained from serving his cousin. She was fifteen, and her mother—his aunt—counted on him to keep her safe. They mingled with Forward's agent, several other planters, the wife of a judge of the Provincial Court, a storekeeper, a magistrate, a butcher, a wigmaker, a woman who made quilted petticoats, and another who was a tavern keeper. As Bradnox introduced his cousin, her sweet demeanor made him beam with pride. He loved seeing how everyone, whether Quaker, Episcopalian, or Catholic, succumbed to her unaffected charm. After a while everyone gathered around the captain, and he updated them with the latest news from England. He then ordered the convicts brought on deck, separated by sex, and displayed in separate lines.

A flurry of handkerchiefs flew to the customers' noses. Bradnox offered one to his cousin, whose eyes couldn't hide her pity and disgust. He sighed with resignation; someday he would be able to afford black slaves, but for now he'd have to settle for *this*. Prosperity, the 250 acres he had inherited from his father, had come cheap; labor would not. He would have preferred indentured servants, but convicts were cheaper, their terms were longer, and they were not entitled to freedom dues.

"I read your advertisement in the *Gazette*," the captain said to Bradnox. "Are you looking to replace your runaways?"

Bradnox's eyes glinted with irritation. One of his runaways was a common convict, but the other was a black slave he had splurged on. He had bought him together with a black girl in the hopes they would have children, but the girl had succumbed to the agues. Titus, the man who had boarded with him and Cassie, was his only indentured servant. "I've never failed to recover a runaway. But I do need a field hand and a carpenter."

"I have just what you need."

"Cassie, this way." His cousin seemed enthralled by a small girl, a tiny clump of skin and bones. "Cassie."

"Yes, Andrew," Cassie said. Captain Jenkins took them to a young boy. He was the surliest creature Bradnox had ever seen, but had survived the trip in remarkably good condition.

"What's your name?" Bradnox asked.

"Sir, I was spirited away. I should be returned ter England."

Captain Jenkins slapped the back of the boy's head so hard, the boy lost his balance for a moment. Cassie gasped. "Answer the gentleman's question," the captain growled.

"Derby Grange."

"Given that the boy has no papers," the captain said, "the Worshipful Commissioner will have to adjudge his age. The younger the commissioner determines him to be, the longer he'll serve."

Bradnox nodded thoughtfully, then turned to the man the captain claimed was a carpenter.

"What's your name?" the planter asked.

"Ellery Baylor, m'lord," the man answered respectfully. "I'm capable and 'ardworking. I won't disappoint yer."

Forward's agent was summoned to handle the transaction, and Bradnox noticed the flintlock pistol in the man's waistband. Envy needled him. Catholics, such as himself, were not allowed to own or carry firearms, although even the lowest sort of Episcopalian was.

"Thirteen pounds," the agent said.

"Ten," countered Bradnox.

"Sir," the agent reasoned, "he was not convicted for arson or horse-stealing. Will you pay twelve pounds?"

"Eleven, and I'll take the boy."

"Ah, Mr. Bradnox!" The agent laughed. "You'll drive me to ruin."

Bradnox felt a gentle tug on his sleeve. "Andrew," Cassie said, "can we take her?" She pointed to the small girl she had been eyeing before.

"Just a moment ago the soul driver took possession of her," the agent said, pointing toward a man who was inspecting the male convicts.

"What's a soul driver?" Cassie asked, blinking.

"He resells convicts around the countryside, far from the tidewaters. Are you sure you want the girl, Miss Cassie? I had to pay him to take her."

"You paid him?" Cassie asked incredulously.

"It's not the first time, and it won't be the last. Sometimes it's the only way to move cargo in such condition."

"Cassie, no," Bradnox said.

"But I like her." She gently pulled him to the girl. The girl's eyes were firmly cast down. Bradnox sighed. If his cousin were picking a puppy, of course she would want the runt of the litter.

"What's your name?" Cassie asked sweetly. The girl muttered something.

"Speak up," the agent ordered. The girl stiffened.

"Mallie Ambrose."

"*Malvina* Ambrose," corrected the agent.

"Look up."

"Oh dear Lord, look at her odd eyes!" Bradnox exclaimed with aversion. He made Mallie remove her tattered straw hat; her hair had grown barely a quarter of an inch since leaving London. "What happened to your hair?" he asked with disgust.

"I sold it."

"Do you know how to cook?"

"No, m'lord."

"Do you know how to sew?"

"No."

He turned to Cassie, eyebrows raised in exasperation. *Please*, Cassie mouthed.

"I see the lady is interested in the girl," the soul driver said, approaching.

"The lady will see what other ships have," Bradnox replied.

Smiling, the soul driver handed the planter some paperwork. "All she needs is discipline. At this age they're clay; your firm hand will mold her easily."

Bradnox took Mallie's conviction papers, and glanced at the charges that had been leveled against her and the court's sentence. He knelt down, motioned for her to open her mouth and looked inside it, then ran his hands over her arms and legs, and looked at her hands.

"Four pounds," the soul driver offered. Cassie pouted and brought a hand to Bradnox's arm. He felt her warm, delicate fingers close firmly around the solid muscle under his sleeve, the result of hauling corn, plowing and ditching the ground, and performing other chores middling planters couldn't avoid. A warmth spread in his belly.

"Three pounds," Bradnox said.

The soul driver laid a hand on Mallie's head. "She's yours."

October 27, 1729
Philadelphia

When the passengers were called up to the deck to be displayed, Blair's entire being refused. He reminded himself that Janet was counting on him, and his legs finally responded. Customers strode along the line of passengers, looking them up and down. Blair felt like one of the linen webs he had held up for inspection back home.

A muscular man with a tanned face and an unkempt red beard pointed at Ronald and demanded, "What's yer name?" His Ulster Scot accent clashed with his appearance. He wore a fringed jacket and leggings, both fashioned out of the same beige leather. A brimless fur hat sporting the ringed tail of some animal Blair couldn't recognize was pulled low over his matted hair, and his belt and shoes—also beige leather—were adorned with colored beads.

"Ronald Eakins." Ronald's voice was flat, but his expression was defiant.

"Let's see yer teeth."

Ronald opened his mouth. The muscles in his jaw rippled while the man patted his body. Then he was told to walk to the mainmast and back.

"What skills do ye have?" the man asked.

"I can weave the best linen."

"So can I."

"I can learn tae do anything."

"Friend," the man said, calling one of the Quakers selling the passengers. "How much?"

"Sixteen pounds."

The man pondered for a moment. "I'll take him."

Blair's alarmed eyes turned to Ronald. What about *him*?

Ronald wrapped his hand around Blair's arm. "Sir, what's yer name?"

"Thomas Burt."

"Mr. Burt, my brother, Blair, is a verra good…" Ronald hesitated, thinking hard. *A very good weaver*, Blair thought dejectedly.

"I only need ye," Burt cut in. *No*, Blair thought, *this cannot be*. He had never considered the possibility that he and Ronald would be separated.

"We can still see each other," Ronald said in a reassuring tone. "It disna matter if we're no living under the same roof."

"We'll have no roof but the sky," Burt said. "We're going west."

"West? Where?" Ronald asked.

"Four hundred miles west."

"Scurse the bit o' me!" Blair exclaimed.

Burt laughed at Blair's shock. "We'll be back in a few weeks. Ask anyone tae point ye tae the Penny Pot Tavern; that's where we'll be lodging. Go fetch yer belongings."

Blair stared after Ronald as he went down to the hold. What if he somehow ended elsewhere too?

"Ronald," he said when his brother returned, "if we lose each other, come back tae Philadelphia four years from now. Promise me ye'll be here."

"Ye heard the man. I'll see ye in a few weeks."

"Promise me."

Ronald hugged his brother. "I promise."

CHAPTER SEVEN

For a second day, standing on the *King George*'s deck, Blair watched the sun disappear behind the riverbank. He sighed. Empty berths were being dismantled, and their space was being taken up by iron bars and bags marked "Wheat." His disgust at being considered a commodity had given way to shame at not having sparked anyone's interest. Only two customers remained on the ship, and he tried to project strength and stand tall and steady. He licked his lips and swallowed. He was dying to set foot on land. He was also dying to lie down.

"What's thy name?" one of the customers—a Quaker—asked. It took every scrap of will for Blair not to scratch his burning scalp; as soon as he had returned to his berth the previous night, lice had crawled back on him.

"Blair Eakins."

"How old are thee?"

"I'll be sixteen soon." And then, the dreaded question: What skills did he have? Blair never imagined that the pride he felt at being an excellent weaver could turn into a feeling of utter unimportance.

"I'm a linen weaver."

The man nodded, as if he had known the answer. "Let us see thy hands." Blair ground his teeth at the feel of the man's fingers prodding his fingers and limbs. When he was told to open his mouth, Blair's eyes filled with tears, remembering the time he had accompanied his father to buy a horse. Finally, he was asked to walk to the quarterdeck and back. The man stood mulling, hands on hips, then went off to examine someone else. Blair leaned on a cask; the sky was darkening. The only other customer had left. Blair might as well call it a day. He had reached the hatch when he heard his name. Rawle, one of the two men who held his indenture, caught up to him, accompanied by the customer who had just examined him.

"Jeffrey Craig has bought thee," Rawle announced.

A thrill ran up Blair's spine; he would finally sleep on land. "Thank ye, Jeffrey Craig." He knew—after a lifetime of selling linen to Quakers in Lisburn—that both men and women were to be addressed simply by their names.

"The courthouse will be closed for the day," Rawle continued. "Thy master will retrieve thee early in the morning."

Blair stepped off the gangway onto the dock, delighted to be stepping onto firm land. Strangely, the dock felt anything but firm. He looked down, puzzled, and took a couple of tentative steps. His sea legs sent him stumbling headlong into two men.

"I'm verra sorry!" he exclaimed as Rawle helped steady him.

"Another Scotch-Irish, William Rawle?" one of the men said with distaste.

Another what? Blair thought as Rawle led him away. Blair turned to see the men glaring at him with a resentment he couldn't understand.

"Must our city be the refuge of the very scum of mankind?" the second man yelled after them.

Blair, Rawle, and Craig climbed into a cart and went up King Street. On their right they passed a seemingly endless row of wharves flanking the river. The other side of the street was lined with houses and boardinghouses, workshops and warehouses. There were throngs of people both on foot and on horseback, and doing all manner of work, but Blair's attention was captured by the numerous men, women, and children with skin as dark as coal. Horse manure lay everywhere, and the stench of garbage filled the air. Blair spotted, at intervals, staircases leading from the top of the bank down to the wharves. The cart turned onto a street cut into the bank and running perpendicular to the river. He looked up in amazement at the earthen walls, buttressed by wooden planks. They climbed the slope to flat ground, turned a corner, and in a few minutes were facing the courthouse, which occupied the middle of High Street, so that pedestrians, carts, and horses were allowed to move on either side.

White and black men, women, and children, and buyers and agents lined one side of the building. People snaked up an exterior staircase leading to a balcony where the main entrance was. Those who had just been registered as servants or slaves streamed down another staircase on the opposite side. Blair looked up with dread. Without thinking, he scratched his scalp; shivers rippled through him. He glanced at Jeffrey Craig; the man was scrutinizing him. He leaned on the wall, pinning his hands behind his hips to keep them from flying to his head. They slowly circled the building, inching their way up the stairs, until at long last, they were led into a courtroom. Six men sat at a raised bench, their distinguished demeanor intimidating. Greetings were exchanged all around, and Blair was introduced by Rawle. Learning that he was in the presence of the governor of Pennsylvania and the mayor of Philadelphia, both Quakers, added to his timidity.

At a table below the bench, a clerk turned over a page in the Philadelphia mayor's court indenture book. He scribbled and then read out loud, "William Rawle and Edward Horne assigned Blair Eakins, a servant from Ireland, in the brig *King George*, Captain Nathaniel Stokes, to Jeffrey Craig, from Philadelphia, cordwainer, to serve four years. Consideration fourteen pounds, with customary dues."

A cordwainer? Blair thought with some alarm. He did not know the first thing about making shoes.

Craig paid the twenty shillings tax due for every Irish imported, was given a declaration signed by Rawle stating that Blair was not a convict, and took possession of the indenture. Out on the balcony Blair struggled to breathe. The staircase swam before his eyes. By the time he reached the bottom, he was suffocating and his palms were clammy. He took a couple of steps and passed out.

CHAPTER EIGHT

October 28, 1729
Annapolis, Maryland

Mallie, Derby, and Ellery spent the night in the basement of an inn. The following morning, just as they and Bradnox and Cassie were stepping into the street, a man came running up to the planter.

"Mr. Bradnox," the man said, "we're holding your runaways in the gaol. Choptank Indians captured them on the eastern shore."

Bradnox seemed delighted. "You bring me good luck," he told Cassie, kissing her hand. "If my runaways had been caught by white men, I'd be out four hundred pounds of tobacco. As it is, the reward will be two matchcoats. I shall have to get you a gift." He escorted Cassie back to the comfort of the inn and left Titus to load the rest onto a cart. Mallie wrapped herself tightly in the blanket, wishing she could lean against Derby for warmth, but the boy's scowl repelled her.

It wasn't long before Bradnox and the messenger returned, leading two men—one white and one black—both in leg shackles and iron collars. Mallie was struck with a realization: it had been weeks since she had gone so much as a day without seeing someone in fetters. Bradnox and Cassie climbed up next to the cart driver, and they were off. Before leaving Annapolis, they stopped to buy shoes for the new servants and cloth to make them clothes. Mallie's eyes sparkled at the sight of the Irish linen, calamanco, and wool flannel meant for her, thrilled at the idea of having new clothes and shoes for the first time in her life. Maybe there wasn't anything to fear, she thought. Maybe, if she worked hard, her master would ask her to stay after her time was up.

The wagoner took the cart west, on a road lined by hickories, dogwoods, and beeches, until they reached a landing on the Patuxent River. Everyone climbed aboard a bateau, and Bradnox and Titus each grabbed a setting pole and pushed, skillfully avoiding dead tree trunks that jutted straight out of the water close to the shore. Trees lined both riverbanks, making a dense wall that at times seemed to close in on them. Mallie spied with delight great blue herons and snowy egrets perched on branches that hung far over the river. A deafening honking sound made her look up; a massive flock of geese flew overhead. They stopped in the early afternoon at a spot where the riverbank was bare and about six feet wide. Bradnox took Cassie in his arms, gently set her down on the bank, and spread out a blanket for them. Mallie hiked up her skirts, and Titus helped her step into the cold, crystal-clear water. She sat on the bank, and while Titus handed the convicts salted fish and a yellow-colored bread, she ogled the feast of apples, cured ham, pickled cauliflower, and pound cake that Cassie produced from a basket. Mallie sniffed the unfamiliar yellow bread and took a bite. Her eyes lit up; it was unlike anything she had ever tasted before, and it was good.

"Corn pone," Titus said, grinning.

She watched hungrily as Cassie cut an apple in three, the fruit's clear nectar dripping down the girl's palm, and was surprised when Cassie handed her one wedge and the other two to Derby and Ellery. Mallie ate her wedge in two bites and could not help but eye the pound cake. Incredibly, Cassie offered her a slice. Mallie reached for the cake and looked at Bradnox with a wide smile of gratefulness. His glacial eyes made her hand freeze midair.

"They're here to pay for their crimes, Cassie, not to be pampered," he said. Mallie immediately pulled back her hand, mortified.

"Andrew," Cassie said softly, "she's just a child." The planter didn't reply. Cassie extended her hand, offering the cake as if Mallie were a shy chipmunk. Mallie shook her head, feeling Bradnox's glare on her. Her throat tightened. He had been generous enough by buying her shoes and cloth; he had been generous by buying *her*. And she had pushed things too far by thinking she deserved anything more than that. Cassie's intentions were good, but Bradnox was right: Mallie was here to pay for her crimes, and she would. She would redeem herself.

The bateau reached Prosperity late in the afternoon. Titus stepped off onto a small dock and walked up a sloping hill, accompanying Cassie, then returned with a horse and another man, his face weathered by the sun, his bleached hair tied in a queue.

"This is Jason, my overseer," Bradnox said.

"Robert and Scipio!" Jason exclaimed, smirking, his hand on a flintlock pistol in his waistband. "I was heartbroken, thinking I would never see you again. You'll have to tell me how far you got this time."

Titus carried Mallie in his arms, Derby and Ellery mounted the horse, and they went up a sloping path cut through a meadow thick with tall grasses and wildflowers. The sun had disappeared over the horizon. Mallie breathed in the clean herbal scents. There were wide horizons and green, open spaces; an owl hooted and insects hummed, and from the north the wind carried the sound of a horn, signaling the end of the working day for the field hands. The sky and clouds glowed orange and lilac. Mallie had never felt lonelier. At the top of the path, occupying an elevated hill, she saw a two-story house. The group rounded the house and headed for another, smaller two-floor building. A covered walkway connected the two structures. When Bradnox opened the door, two women sitting in front of the hearth stood hastily. Titus stepped inside with Mallie, and she realized they were in a kitchen. Bradnox introduced the new servants to Polly, the cook, and Margaret, the housekeeper.

"Margaret," Bradnox said before walking out, "bring us milk and biscuits."

"Sit," Polly said to Derby and Ellery, gesturing to two chairs around the table. "You sit here, doll," she said to Mallie, patting the seat of the chair she'd been using. When Mallie sat, she glanced up at Polly; she seemed about Lizzie's age, with kind, nickel-colored eyes. "Dear me!" Polly exclaimed when her eyes met Mallie's. "Margaret, come see!"

"Well, I never!" Margaret murmured, leaning down to take a close look. An old scar above her left eye had practically replaced her eyebrow, but her expression and voice were warm.

"I think they're quite lovely," Polly chirped. Mallie frowned, unsure if Polly was teasing her, and wishing she could disappear. When Margaret left with the supper Bradnox had ordered, Polly produced a loaf of corn bread and a pitcher of apple cider. As she handed Mallie a mug, Mallie recognized a *T* branded on her thumb. After eating, Mallie, Derby, and Ellery followed the cook to the kitchen yard, a courtyard ringed by a garden, a milk house, a washhouse for the laundry, a henhouse, a carpenter's workshop, and a smokehouse. They walked to the south side of the yard to the privies, and Mallie took a couple of steps back to confirm that she had seen what she thought she had: on the other side of a fence, a few feet away, was a whipping post. She thought of Bradnox's refined presence and demeanor and was confused; a whipping post seemed out of place.

Back in the kitchen, Polly took two pine knots—resin-saturated sticks of pinewood—lit them in the hearth, and inserted each one into a clay holder. Sooty black smoke curled up from their bright flames. Using iron tongs she took four stones from the hearth and wrapped them individually in linen rags. "That'll keep yer warm while yer fall asleep." She handed them out, took one for herself, and grabbed a pine knot. "Ellery and Mallie, come upstairs. Derby, wait here."

In the women's quarters, a layer of straw and four woven pallets were laid out in front of a small and rather inefficient fireplace. Margaret, snoring softly, was cocooned in a blanket on a fifth pallet. A pine knot atop a stand on a table under a shuttered window illuminated three rickety chairs—the only furniture in the room. Rags were stuffed into spots on the walls where the clay between the logs had crumbled. A few tattered items of clothing hung from nails on the walls, and in a corner sat a chipped chamber pot. Polly rummaged through one of two baskets and pulled out used but clean clothes, gave Mallie a shift to sleep in, and sent Ellery to the kitchen with two pallets, linen sheets, and patched-up wool blankets. Polly chuckled at the sight of Mallie, the shift's sleeves hanging several inches over her hands, the hem dragging on the floor. This shift, unlike any Mallie had ever seen or worn, had an opening from the back of the collar to the waist, which Polly closed with laces. The cook spread sheets and blankets on a pallet, and Mallie curled up and watched sleepily as Polly changed into another shift. Her eyes popped wide open: Polly's bare back was covered in a crisscrossed pattern of thick, raised scars.

Blair strained to open his leaden eyelids. A fireplace burned to his left, illuminating a girl about his own age, sitting on a stool to his right, looking down at him with soft brown eyes.

"Hello, Blair. Do you know where you are?"

A blanket covered him, and under his hands he felt the weave of a mat. The room smelled of leather and burning wood.

"Philadelphia?"

"Yes, Jeffrey Craig's shop. I'm Betty."

"What time is it?"

"Almost ten o'clock. Jeffrey Craig is upstairs in his room. You'll see him in the morning."

Betty helped Blair sit up and rest his back against the wall. He was in a rectangular workshop, bigger than his loom room. Men's shoes in different stages of completion hung from hooks in the ceiling, and from cords strung across a window to the left of the front door. Large, rectangular pieces of tanned leather hung on a wall. To the right of the fireplace there was a rack with lasts. Opposite all this a counter ran from the east wall almost to the middle of the room. Tools, jars, boxes, and rags were everywhere: on two shoemakers' benches, on a narrow shelf that ran along two walls, and on additional shelving. Blair gasped; his hands jumped from his lap to the floor, as if to steady himself.

"The room is moving!" he exclaimed.

Betty chuckled. "It's because you were at sea for weeks. It'll pass."

He swept his gaze around the shop, fascinated albeit disturbed by the effect, and recognized his clothes, blankets, and bags draped on two chairs arranged around the fireplace. He looked down at the shirt he wore and looked under the blanket covering his legs. Neither the shirt nor the breeches he wore were his own.

"I washed everything with lye soap to kill the lice," Betty said, throwing more wood into the fire. "The physician who came to examine you used an ointment of stavesacre to remove the vermin from your hair, chest, and limbs." She set a jar next to Blair. "He left this for you to do the rest."

Blair blushed, embarrassed at having to be nursed like a baby, and astounded that he'd been oblivious to all that had happened. Betty set a mug and a wooden bowl with a wooden spoon next to him. He picked up the mug, his hands shaking like an old man's, and spilled warm cider down his chin and onto his shirt.

"Oh no! I've soiled someone's clothes."

"Don't worry, they were the Craigs' former servant's."

"Did he fulfill his indenture? Is that why Jeffrey Craig needed someone new?"

"He died."

Blair shivered. The dead man's clothes felt like worms squirming on his skin. "I think I'll change into my own."

"They're not dry yet." She brought one of his shirts for him to feel; it was very damp. He sighed and turned his attention to the bowl, eyeing with suspicion one of several doughy balls bobbing in milk. He tried to bring one to his mouth, but his hand shook too much.

"Let me help," Betty said, taking the bowl and spoon from him. Reluctantly, he let her feed him. The food was very good. In short order he had wolfed down the entire bowl and some porridge.

"May I have more?"

"You ate all the leftovers. You'll have to wait for breakfast. And don't ever think about taking any food from the cellar." She pointed to a closed door next to the staircase. "They'll miss it immediately."

He pushed himself off the floor and sat on a chair, winded by even this small exertion. "What are those for?" he asked, pointing at two leather buckets with the name "CRAIG" painted on them, hanging from pegs on a wall.

"Fire buckets. When you hear someone ringing a bell and screaming, 'Fire,' grab them and run toward the smoke."

He stood gingerly and took slow, uncertain steps to the window by the front door, shocked at how cold the room felt as soon as he stepped away from the fire, even though Betty seemed to be constantly feeding it. "Are we far from the river?"

"We're very close."

He pushed aside the curtains. Glowing pinpoints on first-, second-, and third-story windows pierced the inky blackness. "At home we couldna afford this," he noted, tapping gently on the glass window. "We had oiled paper."

"I should go to sleep," Betty said. "You should too."

"Where do ye sleep?"

"On the third story, on the floor at the foot of the children's bed. That's for you," she said, pointing at a chamber pot next to the fireplace. She lit a candle, banked the fire, said good night, and went upstairs, the stairs squeaking under her feet.

Blair realized that for the first time ever, he would sleep all alone. An entirely unfamiliar feeling overwhelmed him: homesickness. He took deep breaths and still felt as if he were suffocating. The house creaked and groaned. A group of men stumbled through the alley, their voices and laughter strident with the obliviousness of alcohol. He applied the ointment of stavesacre to his private parts, and then fatigue overcame him.

At midnight, the sounds of Betty and the Craigs stirring from their first sleep woke him up. A dog barked and howled, and dozens of others joined in. Blair moaned. After about an hour, things quieted down again. Then, a baby began to cry.

October 29, 1729

Water dripped on Mallie's nose, startling her awake. The stone had grown cold against her belly. Moonlight seeping through cracks on the walls showed Margaret placing a bucket under a leaky spot next to the door. Three additional buckets were scattered about the room; drops hit the bottom of the buckets with a monotonous sound.

"Scoot, child," Margaret said, taking another bucket and placing it where Mallie's head had been. Mallie listened to the drip-drip-drip until a rooster crowed and Polly told her to get up and dress.

"Do yer think yer could empty this in the privies?" Polly asked, handing her the chamber pot.

"Yes, ma'am."

"Call me Polly, luv."

Mallie could see her breath when she stepped outside. It had stopped raining, but the sky was overcast and gray. Her shoes sank into the damp earth and made sucking sounds as she walked. She could feel mud and water seeping in through the soles, and she shivered. A flock of chestnut-colored chickens pecking at the ground parted as she passed. She reached the privies—averting her eyes from the whipping post—emptied the chamber pot, and hurried back. Derby, Ellery, and Margaret were sitting at the kitchen table.

"Sit, luv," Polly said, indicating a chair next to Derby, who looked as miserable as ever. A woman—a younger version of Margaret—walked in.

Margaret rushed to her, gave her a long hug, and whispered something in her ear. She released her embrace and turned to the new servants. "This is my daughter, Rhoda."

She held the woman's hand, and her chin quivered. "Her indenture ends today, and she can leave the plantation."

Rhoda smiled, but there was sadness in her eyes.

"Happy birthday," Polly said, hugging the woman.

"Thank you, Polly."

Ellery looked at Margaret and Rhoda, puzzled. "When was she bought?" he finally asked.

"She was born here," Margaret said. "I was serving my term for Mr. Bradnox's father when I had her. Because of it I was given two additional years, and she had to remain a servant until she turned thirty-one. When my term expired, I couldn't go. Watching her grow was no punishment—it was a blessing."

"So ye're both leaving!" Ellery exclaimed with a smile. Rhoda's eyes welled up.

"Men bring nothing but trouble, don't you know, Mr. Baylor?" Margaret sighed. "I fell in love, had a son, and just like that I was a servant again, for seven years. He's eleven, and won't be free until he turns thirty-one. So, here we are."

Ellery's lips moved silently, the thumb on his right hand touching the other four fingers one by one, as if performing calculations. "But yor two additional years had expired when yor son was born; yer were no longer serving a term. Why did yer get another seven years?"

"His father is a slave."

"Oh," Ellery said, his eyes wide in surprise.

Mallie gaped at Margaret, in awe of her motherly devotion.

"When are yer leaving, Rhoda?" Polly asked while she served a breakfast of corn mush and boiled eggs.

"Next month, when Mr. Bradnox goes to Annapolis."

"Where will yer go?"

Rhoda shrugged. "I don't know. Everywhere."

"Polly, when does your term end?" Ellery asked.

"In a bit less than eight years. It would end sooner, but I ran away once." The faint sound of a horn came in from the north. "That's the field hands' call ter work, and mine ter prepare the Bradnoxes' breakfast."

An hour later, Mallie, Derby, and Ellery followed Margaret to the main house, their shoes splish-sploshing in the puddles on the brick walkway, rainwater dripping down the edges of the roof above. They wiped their feet on a folded length of linen before going in through the back door into a passage, at the end of which Mallie could see the front door. "Mr. Bradnox sleeps in the parlor," Margaret said, pointing to a closed door on their left, past a set of stairs leading to the upper floor. She stopped at an open door on the right. "This is the hall."

"Come in, Margaret." Bradnox stood in front of a fireplace. Cassie sat to his left, smiling. The optimism that warmed Mallie when she saw her was tamped down at the sight of another, slightly older, displeased-looking girl sitting to the planter's right. He introduced her as Miss Abigail, his sister.

"You have two days to recover from your journey," Bradnox began. "Derby, you'll then move to the field workers' quarters. Ellery, you'll sleep in the stable to be close to the workshop, and you'll eat with the women, unless you're working in the fields. Mallie, you'll help Polly and Margaret. When Rhoda leaves, you'll take her place and will alternate nights between Miss Cassie and Miss Abigail's room, except for Sunday nights, when you'll sleep in the women's quarters."

Mallie tried to catch Abigail's eyes, hoping she would smile like Cassie, but the girl slumped in her chair. "Margaret, have Polly wash that awful smell off of her."

"Yes, Miss Abigail."

"Your terms of servitude began the day I bought you," Bradnox continued. "You cannot travel more than ten miles from here without a pass written by me."

The image of Polly's scarred back flashed in Mallie's mind.

"If you run away, time will be added to your term, ten days for each day of absence. If you're foolish enough to run, I will find you, just like I found Robert and Scipio. Margaret, how many people have successfully escaped since my father bought you?"

"None, sir."

Bradnox sat at a table and waved a hand in Mallie's direction. "Bring her closer." Margaret placed a hand on Mallie's back and gently pushed her forward. Bradnox opened up a commonplace book to a blank page, took a sander, sprinkled pounce on the page, and dipped a quill in the inkwell. Margaret set a measuring rod behind Mallie's heels.

"Four feet one inch," she announced, and Bradnox scribbled. He studied Mallie from head to toe, looking for identifying characteristics, and wrote some more. Then he repeated the procedure with Derby and Ellery.

"You can take them back to the kitchen, Margaret," Bradnox said. "At the end of the workday bring them to the whipping post for Robert and Scipio's punishment."

In the washhouse, Polly stripped Mallie down and had her step into the large copper laundry pot. She could not stop thinking of the upcoming whipping. Maybe she could pretend to be ill when the time came, she thought as Polly poured warm water over her and began to scrub.

Blair woke up to Betty coming down the stairs carrying two chamber pots, feeling every bit as tired as he had the previous day.

"Good morning," she said brightly. "How do you feel?"

"Good morning. I feel better," he replied, not wanting to come across as a sourpuss.

While she stoked the fire, he walked to the front window and pulled aside the curtains. Outside, an alley stretched to his left and right. It was as if the cottages in Lisburn had been tipped on their ends: the houses were three stories high, with narrow facades. Signs hung above some doors. Several lots remained empty. He took his own chamber pot and followed Betty through a rear door to a courtyard. He watched in amazement as she approached a strange metal device and filled a bucket halfway with water.

"What's that?" he asked.

"You never saw a water pump?"

"No. Where's the water coming from?"

Betty thought for a moment and chuckled. "I never wondered about that. There must be wells under the city, because there are pumps everywhere."

They stood in line with other servants and slaves behind a privy, and Betty introduced him. They emptied their chamber pots in the privy, rinsed them, and washed their hands at the pump before going back inside.

"How old are the Craigs' bairns?" Blair asked after swallowing a mouthful of porridge. His hand was still too shaky to hold a spoon, so he had resorted to drinking straight from the bowl.

"Grace is three, Nancy is five, and Prudence is fifteen," Betty replied, stirring her porridge. "Baby Ewan is one."

"Where are ye from? Ye sound neither Irish nor English."

"I was born here."

"Where are yer parents?"

"My mother died. My father…" She shrugged.

"Oh. Yer not indentured, then?"

"I am. I was born a servant because my mother was indentured when she had me, but in two years I'll be eighteen and free, and I'll marry Johannes." Her eyes glimmered. "He works in a shipyard, and he'll also be free then."

They finished breakfast without saying much else. When Betty went outside to sweep the front steps, Blair followed her, eager to be outdoors, although he had to lean on the building for support.

"What's that?" he asked, pointing to a strange contraption attached to the Craigs' second-floor window. A metal rod jutted out from the bottom of the window frame, at the end of which were three small rectangular mirrors.

"A busybody," Betty said. "You use them to see who's at your door, for safety, or—if you tilt them—who's at your neighbor's, for gossip." Blair smirked, amused. When Betty finished sweeping, he sat on the steps until three journeymen arrived.

"Are you the new servant?" asked one.

"Aye," Blair said, standing up. "I'm Blair Eakins."

"Bartholomew, Derrick, Virgil," the journeyman said, pointing at his companions and himself.

"You look freshly arrived, which is to say, you look nearly dead," said Bartholomew.

"Pay no mind, lad," said Derrick. "Nothing that good eating won't fix."

"Don't expect that in this house," Virgil whispered.

"Are you all coming in to work?" asked Craig, opening the door. Blair followed the journeymen back into the shop. Two of the men sat under a window on one side of the room, the third under a window on the opposite side, rolling up their sleeves. The cordwainer's dress was different from the day before: he wore slippers and a leather apron, his sleeves were rolled, and the bottoms of his breeches legs were un-buttoned. Next to him was a plump woman, who seemed somewhat older than he.

"This is my wife, Tacey Craig," Craig said.

"Pleased tae meet ye, Tacey Craig," Blair said.

"Pleased to meet thee, Blair Eakins," she said, looking warily at him as he firmly grasped the back of a chair with both hands.

"I assume this is the first time thee has been indentured?" Craig asked.

"Aye." *There won't be a second time*, Blair wanted to say.

"There are some simple but important rules thee must follow. Thee shall live and sleep in this workshop and never go upstairs. Thee can't fornicate, nor marry without my consent, purchase liquor, visit taverns, or trade with others." Blair noticed all three journeymen smirk. "And thee must work a full day. After the workday is finished, thee may go out but must return by nine, before the doors are bolted.

First Day is thy day off. If thee runs away, five days for every day of absence will be added to thy indenture, as will the costs of capturing thee. Never stoke the fireplace; only Betty and I do that. Don't light any candles without my permission, and don't touch any tools or materials, anything at all on my shelves, ever, unless I tell thee to. Thee will run errands, such as going to the tanner. My wife will accompany thee to market once, and after that thee will go by thyself twice a week. Obey me and be industrious, and all will be well."

After the lecture, Craig's wife returned upstairs. Craig took down a wooden box from a shelf. "I'm going to teach thee to make wax. Roll your sleeves and sit down." Blair plunked down on a chair facing Craig, in front of the hearth. The cordwainer took a chunk of pine rosin and some pine pitch and dropped both in a small pot over the fire. The sharp smell of pine made Blair sneeze. When the rosin and pitch melted, Craig put tallow in the pot and mixed the ingredients together with a long wooden spoon. He poured the hot mixture into a larger pot full of cold water, dipped his hand in, and spun the wax until it had cooled down enough to be handled. He scooped it out and pulled and kneaded until it turned amber. Then he rolled it into a ball. "Now make one," he said.

Blair opened the wooden box, recalling the amounts of rosin and pitch used. With shaky hands, he repeated the steps Craig had demonstrated. He could feel the cordwainer's eyes drilling into him. He was swishing the wax in the water when a loud stampede of feet clattered down the staircase. He looked up and saw what he deduced were Craig's two eldest daughters, each with a hornbook in hand. The girls stared at him, intrigued.

"Don't linger," scolded their father. "You'll be late for school."

Blair returned his focus on the task at hand. When he finally cradled a ball of wax in his palm, the sense of accomplishment surprised him. Craig took the ball and unceremoniously put it in a small basket. Nervous but eager to tackle the next lesson, Blair waited. Craig handed him a book.

"Read out loud while we work," the cordwainer ordered. Blair saw the title and bit his tongue: *An Apology for the True Christian Divinity.* After showing Blair where to begin, Craig took a leather stirrup—a sort of belt with a buckle— and, sitting in his chair, looped one end of the stirrup under his left foot and the other end over his knee and the shoe he was working on. Resigned, Blair set to his task. However, thoroughly bored and having hardly slept the previous night, he was constantly yawning in the middle of sentences.

"Stop!" Craig finally said, rolling his eyes. "Lie down if thee wishes to."

Blair positioned his mat against a wall, out of everyone's way. He had just closed his eyes when a banging noise made him jump. Virgil, hammer in hand, a large, flat stone across his lap, was pounding away on a piece of leather. The noise made it impossible to sleep, and by the time the journeyman had finished beating the leather, Blair had a headache.

———

The Craigs' daughters returned at noon, and while the family had dinner on the second floor, Betty and Blair and the journeymen ate in the shop. Then the girls left for school again. A new customer walked in to order a pair of shoes.

While Craig measured the customer's feet, the man whistled absentmindedly. Blair seized an idea, something he was sure would entertain the cordwainer and the journeymen both, and, more importantly, something that would keep him from suffering through any more theological dissertations.

"Jeffrey Craig," Blair said when the customer was gone, "I can sing while ye work. *I once loved a lass and I loved her sae weel, that I hated all others that spoke o' her ill—*" The journeymen's heads snapped up, eyes wide.

"Stop!" Craig commanded. Stunned, Blair went quiet, his mouth still open. "God frowns upon singing, music, and dancing. I may forgive a new customer for whistling, but I shall not have thee singing." Blair sulked and his face burned. He was listless with boredom when the journeymen finally left and Craig went upstairs. It wasn't long before the cordwainer came back down.

"Don't touch anything," he warned before going out. Almost as soon as the front door shut, Betty came down the stairs.

"Would you like to take a walk?" she asked.

"Please!"

They stepped outside just in time to see other masters, servants, and slaves exiting their respective shops, some of them carrying unlit lanterns.

"Where are they going?" Blair asked.

"Taverns, coffeehouses."

"All o' them?"

"Yes."

"But servants and slaves are no allowed."

Betty shrugged.

"Has Jeffrey Craig also gone tae a tavern?"

"Yes."

"Quakers in Lisburn dinna drink."

"Wet Quakers in Philadelphia do."

They walked down the alley slowly, in the direction of the Delaware, Blair's legs getting reacquainted with solid land, Betty listing off the names of every tenant—shipwrights, river pilots, mariners, carpenters, and potters—as they passed their houses, and the names of their servants or slaves. At Front Street, at the alley's east end, they turned right. At the corner they went right again until they reached Second Street, and walked until they reached the alley's opposite end. A door beneath a sign with a blue ball signaling a chandler's shop opened, and a short, red-haired girl emerged.

"Betty!" she called out happily. Blair immediately recognized her Ulster brogue. "This is yer master's new servant?"

"Yes, this is Blair Eakins. Blair, Alice McLean works for the chandler."

"Pleased tae meet ye, Alice," Blair said.

"Pleased tae meet ye." Alice handed Betty three black candles. "I left the tallow cooking for too long but made candles anyway. Katherine Moore will no sell them. Blair, do ye wish tae come with me tae the tavern? Poor Betty canna get away on account o' the bairn."

"Now?" Blair asked, surprised at the invitation.

"Aye. We'll be back afore Betty bolts the doors."

"But we're no allowed," Blair whispered, glancing up nervously at the busybody.

"We wouldna tell anyone." Alice winked. Both girls looked at him, waiting for his decision. He chewed on his lower lip. He didn't want to get into any trouble, but if every day in the shop was to be as mind numbing as it had been today, he would go insane unless he found some diversion.

"I'm in no condition tae go tippling," he finally said. "I'm out o' breath after a wee walk. Maybe in a few more weeks."

"The Penny Pot isna far," Alice said. "But ye're right, I felt half dead when I first arrived."

The Penny Pot. The tavern frequented by the man who had bought Ronald! "I'm sure I'll feel better soon."

Betty watched longingly as Alice walked away. "She sees her sweetheart every day. I see Johannes only on Sundays." She looked toward the cordwainer's shop, and her shoulders slumped. "I should go back to the children and get supper ready."

"I'll stay outside for a spell. I'm no made for the indoors." From the shop's steps Blair watched children play until the twilight faded and their parents called them in. He remained outside until people started pouring back into the alley, their lanterns glowing orange. He and Betty were having supper when Craig returned. The cordwainer rested his back against the door and glared at Blair with bloodshot eyes.

"I should've bought a Palatine," he said, slurring the words as he walked to the stairs. His foot missed the first tread a couple of times before he clumsily made his way up.

"Pay him no mind," Betty said softly. "You're better than any German."

When Blair had bedded down for the night, he pictured himself in the cottage back in Ireland, trying to imagine every object with as much detail as possible, but the scent of leather kept shattering the image. He missed Ronald with a wretchedness he had never imagined. *This may be a good poor man's country*, he thought, *but it will never be home.*

The horn signaling the end of the workday spurred Mallie to hide under her blanket, hoping to be left alone, but Margaret roused her. She trailed behind the housekeeper, Polly, Rhoda, Derby, and Ellery, dragging her feet. The black runaway was already tied to the whipping post. The white runaway, Titus, Jason, another black man, and a boy with green eyes that seemed to glow against his mahogany skin—clearly Margaret's son—stood in a circle around the post. Mallie noticed Margaret glance from the black runaway to the boy, her eyes radiating fear. The silence seemed to grow heavier when Bradnox appeared. He rolled up his sleeves, and Jason handed him a three-foot-long plaited leather whip, tapered from the end of the handle and knotted at the tip.

"These men were gone for thirty-six days," Bradnox said, directly addressing Mallie, Derby, and Ellery; she felt every single word was its own warning. "Robert will serve an additional three hundred and sixty days, ten for each day gone. Additionally, he will pay the fees for the days he spent in jail, the reward paid for his capture, and the pot hook." He tapped the butt of the whip on the iron collar riveted around the white man's neck. "But he has no money. Therefore, I'll petition the commissioner to determine how many lashes he deserves."

Bradnox then walked to the black man. "I'll request that Scipio receive thirty-six lashes, the maximum allowed by law. And if he tries to run away again, I'll have him castrated." Everyone listened in stunned silence. Scipio shook.

"However," Bradnox continued, "I don't need a court's permission to give them ten stripes each." He adjusted his grasp on the whip as Jason placed a piece of leather between Scipio's teeth. Mallie hid halfway behind Polly, covered her ears, and looked down. Still, the muffled cracks of the whip and grunts made her shiver. When she looked up, Scipio's back was a mess of red slashes and rivulets. Derby and Ellery seemed ready to faint. Scipio was untied, and Robert was secured to the post. Mallie hid again behind Polly. Once the whipping was over, Titus stepped forward to loosen the rope around the man's wrists, but Bradnox stopped him.

"Leave him there until midnight."

"C'mon, luv," Polly said with a strained voice, taking Mallie's hand. "We can go now."

I'll never *run away,* Mallie promised herself later as she struggled to swallow her supper. *Never.*

CHAPTER NINE

October 30, 1729

Mallie staggered into the kitchen, her arms under a load of firewood, her apron wrapped around it. She released her cargo beside the fireplace, where Polly was busy with the Bradnoxes' breakfast. After she brought in another load, Polly took her to the well and filled two buckets halfway. She then positioned a yoke on Mallie's shoulders, trying to balance the buckets hanging from the ends. Mallie grunted, the buckets swaying capriciously this way and that, like a pair of drunks arguing about which way to go, the yoke digging painfully into her flesh. It was soon evident she would not be able to manage the fifty feet to the kitchen, so Polly hauled the water the rest of the way, then sent Mallie back to the well by herself, instructing her to fill each bucket only a third.

"It'll take yer more trips," Polly said, shrugging. "Just don't fall into the well, doll."

After the Bradnoxes had eaten, Mallie washed pots, pans, and dishes. Then, in the barn, under Polly's direction, she unsuccessfully tried her hand at milking the cow. Back in the kitchen, Polly demonstrated how to peel a potato. Mallie's hands were quite raw, and she wielded the knife so gingerly that it barely nicked the skin. The cook's patient expression kindled in Mallie such a desire to please her that she dug the knife in too deep, and it caught. She pulled it loose with such force that she accidentally drove it into the fleshy part of her left thumb. She yelped and dropped the knife, then did her best to fight back tears as a trickle of blood began to run down her palm.

"Oh, darling," Polly cooed, "yor first war wound. I'll fix yer up." Polly toasted a slice of cheese on a skillet over the fire, covered Mallie's cut with it, and wrapped it with a strip of linen. "Back ter battle," Polly said, squashing any glimmer of hope Mallie had that she'd be allowed to retire for the rest of the day. Working more deliberately now, she slowly made her way through two dozen potatoes. The fire was kept roaring as the oven spat out what seemed like an endless supply of corn bread, and the kitchen sweltered in spite of the wide-open door. A blue-and-buff-plaid handkerchief wrapped around Polly's forehead was dark with sweat, and her neck gleamed. The potato Mallie was peeling swam before her eyes. She blinked, nodded off, and almost fell off her stool. She moved to the floor, leaned her back against the wall, and kept working.

"I'll be right back, doll," Polly said. Mallie rested the knife and potato on her lap and fell asleep. A cracking sound and a stinging pain on her hands jolted her awake. Abigail, the planter's sister, was standing over her, a crop in her hand.

"Stand up."

Mallie obeyed, her lips quivering, looking around for Polly, chiding herself.

"Don't cry. There's no reason to cry."

"Miss Abigail, is everything all right?" Polly was standing at the door.

"She was sleeping. We don't need another lazy servant."

"Yes, Miss Abigail, I'm sorry."

The planter's sister stood guard while Polly transferred the noon meal to pewter dishes. Mallie stood by, rubbing her hands, taking staccato breaths. When Margaret arrived to fetch the food, Abigail left with her.

Mallie fetched more water, washed the morning's pots and dishes, pulled garlic from the garden, and then helped knead dough for bread.

"Check ter see if the crust is golden yet," Polly said half an hour after placing the bread in the oven, built into one of the walls of the hearth. Mallie grasped the oven door and immediately released it with a howl.

"What are yer doing, child?" Polly grabbed a pot holder, pulled the bread out, and turned her attention to Mallie, who had dissolved into tears. Her palm was crimson and blistering. "There, there," Polly said, sitting Mallie on her lap and wrapping her in her arms. "I spent my first two weeks here crying day and night."

Mallie couldn't remember a time when she had ever been cradled. Polly's warmth swaddled her and seeped into her belly. She leaned her head on the cook's chest. For the very first time in her life she felt soothed and, in the midst of her loneliness, sheltered.

October 30, 1729

"We heard that on Monday last, a cart and five horses, together with their driver, fell from the top of a stone bridge at Darby, which is near fourteen foot high, and came out all unhurt," Blair read out loud. He paused to listen to the booming sounds coming from the Delaware; ships had been firing cannons since dawn to celebrate King George's birthday. His heart sank when he reached the end of the half sheet that made up the Pennsylvania Gazette. Craig took the paper and with great care placed it on a shelf, on a stack of past issues. Blair held his tongue when his master handed him An Apology.

After supper the entire household walked to the Delaware to watch fireworks. The wharves and streets teemed with people. Blair watched in awe as the crackling, sparkling white lights bloomed like fantastic dandelions and spumed like a million fireflies against the black velvet sky. He oohed and aahed with the crowd but went quiet as they shouted their huzzahs for the king.

"Blair, did thee see where Betty went?" Tacey Craig asked when the last of the fireworks had faded away. She cradled baby Ewan as she searched the crowd. Blair looked around, puzzled as well. He had been so entranced, he had not noticed Betty's absence.

"No."

Back in the shop, Tacey Craig stood at the door for a moment before going upstairs, her face tensed in displeasure. Blair sat in front of the fire, elbows on his knees, chin in his hands, staring into the flames. His eyes drifted to the shelves. The floors creaked with such ease under the lightest pressure that he felt sure he could tell the moment anyone stepped on the staircase. He snatched a couple of *Gazette* issues from the stack and sat down. He scanned something about a message sent by Governor Burnett to the House of Representatives in Boston, but his eyes lit up when he found an advertisement by the publishers of the *Gazette* offering "Bibles, bills of lading bound and unbound, servants' indentures" and numerous other paper items. *Paper.* Surely quills and ink too, to write letters home! If only he had money. He sighed and turned to the second sheet, where a very different advertisement caught his attention.

Run away on the 25th of September past, from Rice Prich-ard of Whiteland in Chester County, a Servant Man named John Cresswel, of a middle Stature and ruddy Countenance, his Hair inclining to Red. He had on when he went away, a little white short Whig, an old Hat, Drugget Wastcoat, the Body lined with Linnen, coarse Linnen Breeches, gray wool-en Stockings, and round toe'd Shoes. Whoever shall secure the said Servant so that his Master may have him again, shall have Three Pounds Reward, and reasonable Charges paid by Rice Prichard.

A second advertisement was also an ad for a runaway servant, this one from Germantown Township. He stared at the newspapers in his lap, deep in thought.

"Blair."

"Dear God!" He nearly jumped out of his skin and slid the sheets under his bottom.

"What are you hiding?" Betty whispered, appearing from the rear of the shop. Blair looked at her, unblinking, doing a deplorable job of appearing innocent.

"I was only reading," he said, pulling the sheets from under him. They both gasped; in his hastiness to hide them he had creased them.

"Man dear!" he exclaimed, smoothing them out.

"Betty! Where were thee?" Tacey Craig was coming down the stairs. Blair sat again on the papers.

"I'm sorry," Betty replied softly. "I was with friends."

Tacey Craig brought her open hand across Betty's face. "Don't go off frolicking again."

Betty lowered her teary eyes and brought her hand to her reddened cheek.

"Don't linger locking up."

"Are ye awricht?" Blair asked when Tacey Craig was gone. Betty nodded but went about her nighttime chores in complete silence. Blair returned the *Gazette*s to their spot, feeling terribly sad for her, and wondering if Tacey Craig would have dared slap him if she had caught him reading the newspapers.

November 1, 1729

"Thank ye for another year o' life," Blair prayed upon waking up, though this was not a birthday he was looking forward to. Later that morning, carrying an empty basket, he followed Tacey Craig south on Second Street as bells rang to announce market day. In less than five minutes, they came upon the courthouse, which sat at the intersection of Market and Second. Blair followed Tacey Craig as she turned right on Market, toward the roofed building that was the butchers' stalls, and went inside. Signs advertising "raccoon" and "bear's foot" intrigued him, but the beef hanging on hooks made his mouth water. After buying a cut of beef, they went out into the street the way they had come.

They walked past the courthouse, past a whipping post, stocks, and a pillory, all empty. Past these, stalls had been set up down the middle of Market. Tacey Craig bought apples, cider, butter, sugar, flour, Indian corn, pumpkins, and onions. Blair's stomach growled at the amazing cornucopia displayed before his eyes. The journeyman was right: the meals he was getting were not enough.

The Presbyterian meeting house was south of the stalls, where Alice had said it would be. Five Indian couples had staked out different spots to display brooms and woven baskets and mats, and Blair couldn't help but stare openly. Their skin and long black hair glistened with bear oil, their posture was straight, and their expressions were so serene as to nearly be inexpressive. Four of the women sat on mats, but one was standing, as tall as any white woman out shopping, even taller than some of them. Blue and red ribbons decorated her knee-length stroud dress, and an animal pelt shawl was draped over her shoulders. Next to her, on the ground, securely tied to a flat cradleboard resting against a stall, a baby slept. The Indian man was as tall as Ronald, his oval face was hairless, and he wore a shirt and matchcoat. Both he and the woman wore deerskin leggings and moccasins decorated with shell beads. They seemed to take no notice of Blair's gawking.

"We're going back to the courthouse," Tacey Craig said after buying some poultry. She had the look of someone who was about to undertake an unpleasant and unavoidable chore. As they retraced their steps, Blair heard jeering sounds coming from beyond the stalls. His stomach clenched. A man was now in the stocks, another in the pillory, their faces and hair dripping with rotten egg and mud. A black man and two white women in shackles cowered in a cart. Blair glanced at Tacey Craig, who seemed to be gauging his reaction. He gaped as one of the women was made to descend the cart. She was then tied to the whipping post, with her back exposed.

"That's the sheriff." Tacey Craig nodded toward a man holding up a notice.

"Jane Linch," the sheriff read, "having been found guilty of stealing the goods of Benjamin Gibbs and having been sentenced to twenty-one lashes, the judgment will now be complied with."

"That's enough," Tacey Craig said, walking away before the whipping began. Blair was confused. It was evident the sordid scene had disturbed her deeply, so why had she stopped to watch? "That girl about to be whipped is a servant," the cordwainer's wife said.

Suddenly, Blair understood: although he had done absolutely nothing wrong, the Craigs believed him capable of stealing and deemed this warning necessary. It was humiliating. An old woman dressed in rags stepped in front of them. Her mouth was almost toothless, her eyes bloodshot. Blair saw recognition creep very slowly into Tacey Craig's eyes.

"Frances?"

"Yes, Tacey Craig. As you see, I'm reduced to begging." The corners of the old woman's mouth quivered with shame. "I fell off a wagon and injured myself. Would you be so kind as to help me?"

"Thee should remove thyself before a constable arrests thee," Tacey Craig scolded, hurriedly giving the old woman a couple of pennies. "And wear thy letters." She pointed to the old woman's right sleeve.

"I would've loved to see her!" Betty exclaimed when she came down for the noon meal and Blair told her about the encounter. Her smile faded as Blair described the woman's sad condition.

"What are 'letters'?" he asked.

"All paupers must wear a blue or red *P* and the initials of the city. Oh, why isn't she wearing them? She'll be whipped and sentenced to twenty-one days' hard labor." Then, almost to herself, she said, "She was a good, hardworking woman."

Dear Lord, Blair thought, I've done nothing but work hard since my head reached my father's hips. I understand why Frances would not wear those "letters." I swear I'll wear a shroud before I ever wear a P.

Mallie, Margaret, and Rhoda hauled almost one hundred pounds of wood to the washhouse, then thirty gallons of water to fill the copper pot to boil the first load of clothing, table linens, and bedding. While Margaret started the fire, Mallie and Rhoda hauled another ten gallons for the scrub and rinse water.

"The clothes must be stirred," Margaret said, dipping a flat-sided wooden paddle into the copper pot and demonstrating. "Here, Mallie, try it."

Mallie took the washing bat, expecting the task to be just like stirring a huge pot of soup, but the clothes were like molasses. Her arms and shoulders burned with exertion, and she was breathing hard. The washhouse was thick with steam; sweat trickled into her eyes. After only a couple of minutes, she couldn't stir anymore.

"Go get our clothes and anything Polly wants washed," Margaret said, taking the bat. Mallie stepped outside just in time to see Bradnox walk into the kitchen and shut the door behind him. She stood there for a moment, unsure what to do; Polly always kept the door open to let the heat escape. She peeked through a window. The planter had Polly against a wall, hands under her skirts. He whispered in her ear, and she turned her head away, looking frightened. Then he took her hand, and they disappeared up the stairs. Mallie ran back to the washhouse.

"Where's the linen?" asked Margaret.

"I couldn't get it. Mr. Bradnox was there. He went up with Polly."

"Oh no..." Margaret sighed and shook her head.

"I'm glad I'll be gone soon," Rhoda said sullenly.

Margaret stirred the clothes in silence, then with Rhoda's help lifted them out and dropped them into another pot with warm water, grabbed a washing board and lye soap, and showed Mallie how to remove stains. After rinsing the clothes in cold water, they wrung out everything by hand and hung it to dry in front of the washhouse's fireplace. They filled the copper pot with clean water and started the process over again with a second load. Once they were finished, Margaret said, "Go back to the kitchen, Mallie. Mr. Bradnox should be gone by now."

The kitchen door was open. Polly was alone.

"Polly," Mallie said softly, entering. Polly stood over the table, lost in thought, her hands sunk in dough. "Margaret wants the dirty linen."

"It's in a basket," Polly replied without looking up.

Mallie climbed the stairs, haunted by Polly's distressed look. It was a look she was familiar with. She had seen it back in London, when unwilling girls at the brothel had been forced to service a client.

"Are you all right?" Margaret asked Polly during supper.

"I wish he would marry Miss Cassie already."

"When has marriage ever stopped a man?"

Mallie wrapped her red, raw, throbbing hands around her bowl and tried to keep her tired arms steady as she brought it to her lips.

"At least Rhoda will finally be out of his reach," Margaret said.

"She'll be old enough to catch his attention before her time is over," Polly whispered.

Mallie looked over the rim of the bowl and caught the women staring ruefully at her. Rhoda yanked her eyes to the fire, Polly pretended to busy herself with her sleeve, and Margaret took a big gulp of cider. Mallie had understood Polly's meaning, but she was not worried. Mr. Bradnox was a handsome man. Handsome men didn't care for ugly women, and ugly girls like herself surely grew up to be ugly. With that comforting thought, she went back to her porridge.

CHAPTER TEN

November 2, 1729
Morning

When the rooster crowed, Mallie slowly got to her feet, every muscle in her body sore and stiff.

"It's Sunday, luv," Polly said in a groggy voice. "Lie back down."

Mallie fell asleep again as soon as she lay her head on her mat. When she woke up, she was alone. She got up and went down to the kitchen, where Polly and Margaret were seated at the table with Ellery. Mallie joined them for a leisurely breakfast. When they finished eating, Polly asked Ellery if he would be so kind as to fix their leaky roof. He gladly agreed, and Polly gave him directions so he could join them at the field hands' quarters once he was finished.

"Is Rhoda's father a field 'and?" Mallie whispered to Polly as they strolled behind Margaret and Rhoda, who walked hand in hand, completely engrossed in each other's presence.

"He was," Polly whispered back. "Now he's there. As is Rhoda's babe." She pointed to a small clearing bordered by a low, slanting fence, where six wooden grave markers jutted crookedly from the ground. Mallie shivered. Lowering her voice ever further, Polly said, "Rhoda's leaving tomorrow."

When they passed an apple orchard, music and singing reached Mallie's ears. They arrived at a one-room log cabin built next to a half-plowed field. The pungent steam of boiled crabs rose from a pot hung over a blazing bonfire. Bradnox's field hands and a black man Mallie had not seen before sat on logs encircling the fire. Titus played a fiddle while the black man and the green-eyed black boy pounded a rhythmic beat on a hollowed-out log. The runaways still wore their iron collars. Mallie was delighted to see Derby again, although his head was turned to the side and he seemed lost in thought. The unfamiliar black man swept Margaret up in his arms and spun her round and round; she shrieked and laughed.

"This is Mallie, the new girl," Margaret said when she was back on firm ground. "Mallie, this is Isaac. He lives at Mr. Hearne's plantation. That's Charles, our son, and Cumby." She gestured toward the boy and the black man. The boy waved and smiled shyly, and Cumby raised a hand. Mallie smiled back. Derby turned his head toward her, and she gasped. A red line ran across his face, from the left side of his brow, over his left eye and all the way down to his chin and part of his neck. Their eyes met, but before she could say anything, he turned away.

"He refused to work," Titus said. "He's lucky to have his eye."

Mallie sat next to Derby, who stared into the fire. Polly took a crab from the pot, placed it on a wooden plate, handed it to Mallie, and sat down next to her. When the crab was cool enough, Polly removed the legs and claws and cracked it open.

"Derby, do yer want some?" Mallie asked, trying to get him to talk. He only shook his head. She ate in silence, then leaned her head placidly on Polly's shoulder and closed her eyes.

"Ellery!" Polly chirped, then jumped to her feet, toppling Mallie over. Polly introduced Ellery and then went to the pot to get him a crab. He sat next to Mallie, and she looked at him out of the corner of her eye, irked at the attention he was commanding from Polly. But when Polly brought his food, she asked him to scoot so she could sit between him and Mallie. She reached out and patted Mallie's hand.

"Yor like a chunk of ice, doll!" she exclaimed, taking Mallie's hands in hers.

"It seems you found yourself a pet," Ellery observed, smiling at Mallie. Mallie smiled back.

For the rest of the day Mallie alternated between sitting around the fire, listening to the singing and music, eating, and taking short walks with Polly, Isaac, Charles, and Ellery. Margaret and Rhoda seemed not to notice anyone else, and everyone let them spend their final hours alone together.

"Take care of Mama," Rhoda told Charles when it was time to go back to the women's quarters. "And take care of yourself." She hugged him and kissed his cheek.

"I'm sorry I can't see you off tomorrow," Charles said, his voice catching.

"I know you would if you were allowed."

"Bye, Derby," Mallie said timidly. "See yer next Sunday." He did not reply.

That night, Mallie was awakened by Margaret and Polly whispering to each other, and she strained to hear them. "Seeing Rhoda leave this plantation is the one thing I most wanted in the world," Margaret said. "But that day seemed so far away, and now...I'll never see her again, Polly, you know I won't."

Mallie could hear muffled sobs coming from Margaret's pallet.

"Maggie," Polly said, "calm yerself down. Ye'll wake 'er, and then the three of us will cry all night."

November 2, 1729
Morning

Blair took a seat on one of the red-painted pine pews. He had hoped to warm up in the Presbyterian meeting house, but it was every bit as cold as the shop, if not more so. From his perch on the gallery he looked down at the preacher, who stood on the elevated pulpit, his voice projected through the church by a pyramidal sounding board suspended above him. Blair had hoped that surrounding himself with his countrymen would ease his homesickness, but the sermon could not be any more boring. His eyelids grew heavier and heavier. A man gently shook him awake.

"Lad, it's allowed tae stand up." Blair looked around and noticed several people were on their feet. "Standing will keep ye awake when Reverend Andrews wilna."

At long last the morning session came to an end, and he eagerly burst out into the street and headed for the shop, hoping the Craigs were back from the Quaker meeting house. Otherwise, he had no idea what he would do with himself during the noon break before the afternoon sermon. He was hungry, and the cold was making him dizzy. He knocked and waited, shivering. The door opened. "Betty, thank God…" He stopped midsentence. It was Prudence who had opened. "Thank you, Prudence," he said as she stepped aside.

"Betty left some food for thee."

"Thank ye."

Prudence skipped up the stairs. After eating, Blair decided he simply could not drag himself back to another boring sermon. He stared at the banked fire, wishing he were allowed to stoke it, and wrapped himself in his blankets. He woke up an hour later, went out to the privy, and returned to lie down and stare at the ceiling, bored and restless. He sat up and glanced at Craig's shelves. He looked toward the stairs and listened. He went to the shelves, pulled down one issue of the *Gazette*, quickly read it where he stood, and placed it back. He waited a moment, then took another issue and made his way through it. He turned to grab a third sheet and gasped. Prudence was at the foot of the stairs, staring at him.

"Prudence," he stammered in a low voice, "I was only reading them." He returned the sheet to its place. He waited anxiously for her to say something, but she only studied him with a serious expression and then made her way out the back door. He sat twiddling his thumbs until she returned.

"Prudence," he said, standing up, "please dinna tell yer father."

"I should."

"I promise I will no touch them again."

She stared into his eyes, her cheeks flushed. *I've angered her*, Blair thought.

"Prudence! What are thee doing?" Tacey Craig called.

The girl hurried up the stairs, and Blair plopped down in a chair and buried his face in his hands. Although he could not make out the words, he could hear Tacey Craig asking something, and Prudence replying.

Monday morning Mallie walked with Polly, Margaret, and Rhoda to the dock. Derby was already sitting in the middle of the bateau, sulking, Scipio in front of him and Robert behind, all three of them shackled. Titus stood at the bow, Bradnox at the helm, both leaning on their setting poles.

Rhoda gave her mother a coiled basket. "Something to remember me by, Mama. It's not as fine as the ones Mr. Hearne's slave girls make, but…"

Margaret took the basket lovingly. Its bottom was no wider than the palm of her hand, and its delicate body tapered to a narrow, round opening at the top. She didn't utter a word, her expression stoic. She kissed Rhoda's cheek one last time.

"Goodbye, Mallie," Rhoda said.

"Goodbye."

Rhoda climbed into the bateau, and Bradnox and Titus pushed off. As soon as the bateau glided around a bend and disappeared from sight, Margaret's stolid mask crumbled, and she sobbed uncontrollably. While Polly consoled Margaret, Mallie tried to understand why Rhoda would leave. If she had a mother who loved her half as much as Margaret loved her daughter, she would be willing to spend her life in hell to be with her.

November 8, 1729
Saturday

Blair held his cap against the cold wind as he followed Alice to the two-story brick building that rose right in the center of the wide street. A sign reading "Penny Pot Free-Landing" hung above the entrance. She turned right, led him toward a landing on the Delaware, and pointed to a half-built ship on a slipway on the banks of the river, just a few yards away. The ship was so close to the buildings on the street that its bowsprit practically reached their eaves.

"Johannes and my sweetheart, Raimond, are working on that ship," Alice said. She pointed south. "Stay away from the stretch that starts here and goes all the way tae Market Street. That's Hell Town, and ye want nothing tae do with those people."

The Penny Pot was crowded and thick with pipe smoke, humming with conversations in English, Dutch, Swedish, and German. A fiddler was playing, his dubious talent making Blair wince. The patrons were a mix of artisans and laborers, white and black, and even the odd gentlemen. What few women there were all belonged to "the lower sort." Blair followed Alice to a long, oblong table. A tall, blond man stood up and kissed her once on each cheek.

"I'm Raimond Tiel," the man said with a thick German accent, "and this is Johannes Fretzel."

"Betty has told me about you," Johannes said, also with a German accent. He turned to two men sitting to his right. "Blair Eakins is Scotch-Irish, like you. He just arrived."

"Welcome tae Philadelphia," one of the men said, scooting one chair over. "I'm Edward Cole. This is William Gardner."

Blair sat down and turned to his countrymen. "Why do so many insist on calling us Scotch-Irish? We're nothing o' the sort."

"We are now, lad," Edward replied, slapping Blair's back good-naturedly. "What will ye drink?"

"I dinna have money."

"That's never a good excuse. William and I will pay for yer first drink. Susannah!" A girl who was walking by with a tankard in each hand flashed Blair a smile. "It's Blair's first time in a Philadelphia tavern. Bring him a flip, will ye?" He turned back to Blair. "Did ye come by yerself?"

"With my brother. He was indentured tae a fur trader called Thomas Burt."

"Ah…Thomas Burt," Edward said, cocking his head, and he and William exchanged intent glances.

"Ye ken the man? He said he was taking my brother four hundred miles west."

Edward pondered a moment before replying. "Thomas should keep his mouth shut. That'll be west o' the Alleghenies, and that's against the law. Easy tae get swallowed up there too. If the bears or mountain lions dinna kill ye, the Indians might."

"Dinna scare the lad," William chided, seeing Blair's dismayed look. "They'll be back soon, Blair. Tell the tavern keeper where tae find ye, and when Thomas returns with yer brother, he'll tell him."

"Here's your drink, handsome," Susannah said, approaching the table. Her sparkling blue eyes held Blair's gaze with a brazenness he had never seen in any girl.

"To the queen's health!" Edward said, and he raised his tankard. Blair, William, Alice, Johannes, and Raimond raised theirs and echoed the toast.

"Prost!" Johannes and Raimond added.

"And tae Blair," Alice said. "Betty told me he turned sixteen a week ago."

"To Blair!" everyone repeated. Blair took a swig of his flip. The warm, creamy, bittersweet fluid swished in his mouth like liquid candy. He smacked his lips. "That's perfect for a birthday."

"It's beer with molasses, rum, eggs, and nutmeg, and we dip a red-hot iron in it," Susannah said. She winked. "You should have *anything* you want for your birthday."

"Leave him alone," William said. "He disna have money. But I'll dip my hot iron in ye."

Blair cringed, embarrassed at William's vulgarity and expecting Susannah to slap his head right off. To his surprise, she was unfazed. "I'm not working tonight, but I can fetch Emma."

"Ye can always count on Susannah and Emma," Edward said when Susannah walked off. "Detta over there decides two or three times a year she's done whoring, but she has a son tae feed."

Blair was, all at the same time, disappointed to realize Susannah saw him as a client and titillated. William studied his expression for a moment and said, "Ye've never been down a cock alley, have ye?"

Blair's face flushed hot. No stranger in Lisburn would dare ask such a question. Indeed, no acquaintance would either. "Of course I have."

William laughed. "If ye say so."

"Are ye two also indentured?" Blair asked, eager to change the subject.

"Oh, of the bunch Raimond's the only freeman."

"How then do ye have money for drinks?"

Edward and William looked at each other. Almost imperceptibly, William shook his head.

"We find odd jobs here and there," Edward said.

"Do ye no get into trouble for it?" Blair asked.

"Not yet."

"In the mood for rogering, William?"

Blair almost choked on his drink, scandalized by the filthy mouth and nonchalance of the petite girl with black, sleepy eyes who had appeared behind William's chair. William got up, and he and the girl went up a staircase at the far end of the room. Blair finished his drink, and Edward insisted on buying him a beer. Susannah had just set it down in front of him when Alice said, "Raimond is walking me home, do ye want tae come? Betty will be bolting the windows and doors soon."

Blair looked with disappointment at his beer. He hated leaving it untouched. "Aye, I'll come with ye."

"Gentlemen—and ladies!" boomed a voice behind Blair. "May I have your attention?"

"That's the tavern keeper," Edward said. "Before ye go, talk tae him."

"For your entertainment," the tavern keeper announced, "a number of cock matches are about to begin, two guineas a battle."

"Blair, stay for one match," William cajoled. Blair glanced with longing at the crowd heading out the back door of the tavern, to the patio. The cordwainer hadn't scolded him for taking the *Gazettes*, so he surmised Prudence had taken pity on him—at least for the time being. He shouldn't push his luck. Then again, one cock match would last one minute at most.

"Go, Alice. I'll catch up."

"If ye're having only one more drink, make it a real one. I'll take yer beer," Edward said, calling Susannah over. "Bring Blair a rattle-skull."

They joined the crowd heading to the courtyard. Blair winced at the volley of curses coming from laborers and gentlemen alike. It was "bloody this," "bloody that," "damn this," "damn me," and even a "rascal" and a "fuck." When he tasted the rattle-skull Susannah had brought him, the mix of porter, rum, and brandy singed the inside of his mouth. He vigorously shook his head.

"Do you like it?" she asked.

"Aye." He cocked his head. "Yer English sounds... English."

"You have something against the English?"

"Ye're a verra bonny lass, ye may be forgiven."

Their eyes locked. He felt dizzy but could not tell whether it was because of the alcohol or her proximity. She motioned for him to lean in. "I like you very much," she whispered, her warm breath tickling his ear. She strutted back inside, leaving him simmering with desire. Dazed, he turned too fast and bumped into a man, spilling half his mug on the man's jacket.

"See what you've done!" the man cried. Before Blair could apologize, Edward had dragged him away.

"I like ye, lad! I'll talk tae William, and we'll include ye next time there's a job." Edward started to sing. "*I went tae the alehouse like an honest woman should, and a knave followed after as ye know knaves would...*"

I'll be able to buy paper and write home, Blair thought happily. He joined in the song, his voice drowning out Edward's: "Knaves will be knaves in every degree. I'll tell ye by and by how this knave served me!"

Mallie stood at the foot of the staircase in the main house, holding a candlestick, her face contorted with dread. This was her first night sleeping in the house.

"Go on," Margaret coaxed. "Remember, it's the door on the right."

Mallie reached the top of the staircase, took a few steps down the hallway, and knocked gingerly. Abigail opened the door and looked down at her with aloofness. Mallie timidly stepped into the clean but simple room. There was a small table with a washbowl and pitcher; a delftware pitcher and mug on another table; a dresser, a vanity, and a chair; and a pewter crucifix above the door. Against a nightstand on which a candle flickered, she spotted the crop Abigail had hit her with a few days before.

Abigail pointed to a mat and blanket on the floor, at the foot of the bed. "You sleep there." As soon as Abigail blew out the candle, Mallie was asleep. She woke up some time later to a foot being shoved against her forehead. "Wake up. I'm thirsty, and the pitcher is empty."

Mallie shook off her grogginess and stood, then took the delftware pitcher in one hand, the candlestick in the other, and stepped out while Abigail held the door open. She stood for a long moment staring into the dark hallway, her breathing shallow and fast, before she gathered the courage to take the first step. The floorboards seemed to retreat under her feet, and by the time she made it down the stairs and reached the back door, she was dizzy with fear. She set the pitcher down on the floor to free her right hand, and as she reached for the knob, her foot accidentally bumped into the pitcher. With her heart in her throat she watched it wobble, then right itself, and let out a deep sigh of relief. She picked it up, stepped outside, set it down, closed the door, and picked it up again. She turned, her heart pounding in her ears, terrified of what sprites or trolls could be lurking in the dark edges of the walkway. She was halfway to the kitchen when a gust of wind blew out her candle. She whimpered and blinked, trying to pierce the dark. She took two steps and bumped into a solid figure. She screamed and dropped the candlestick and the pitcher, which shattered on the ground.

"Don't scream!" Derby hissed.

"Wot are yer doing 'ere?" Mallie asked, her voice panicky.

"I'm running away."

"Why?"

"I told the Worshipful Commissioner I was spirited out o' England without me consent. He said the law allows for kidnapping and transportation o' vagrants. I said I ain't a vagrant, but 'e wouldn't listen, and 'e insisted I'm thirteen, no matter 'ow many times I said I'm sixteen, and 'e sentenced me ter nine years, and Robert told me it shoulda been seven."

"If Mr. Bradnox catches yer, ye'll be whipped!"

"He won't."

"Mallie?" Mallie gasped at the sound of Polly's voice coming from the kitchen door.

Derby vanished. Polly and Margaret, their white faces trembling in the light of a pine knot, found Mallie looking as guilty as if she'd been running away herself.

"What happened?" Polly asked.

"I dropped a pitcher."

Polly crouched down, the pine knot in her hand. She and Margaret looked as if they had stumbled upon a corpse. Margaret groaned.

"Was it very dear ter her?" Mallie asked with dread.

"If the house caught fire, the first things Mr. Bradnox and his sister would save would be their looking glass and their three—their *two*—delftware items."

"Well," Polly said, "they never use the other pitcher, which is exactly like this one. We can replace it."

Margaret shook her head, looking frightened.

"Maggie," Polly said, glancing at Mallie, "she's only ten. We can't let them find out."

Margaret looked at Mallie's huge, scared eyes and sighed. After finding the candlestick and relighting it, she made her way to the house. Polly and Mallie retreated to the kitchen and waited. Thoughts tumbled through Mallie's head, like dry leaves swirling in the night wind. If she didn't give Derby away, might he make it? How could he? Bradnox's runaways were grown men who knew the area, and yet they had been caught. When Margaret returned, Polly filled the replacement pitcher with cider and accompanied Mallie to the back door.

"Take deep breaths," Polly said as Mallie wrapped her shaky fingers around the handle. "We'll clean up. Go." Another gust blew, and something cold peppered Mallie's cheek. Snow. It was coming down hard now.

"Polly, I dropped the pitcher because Derby startled me. He's running away."

———

The following morning, Mallie, Margaret, Polly, and Ellery walked through seven inches of snow on their way to the field hands' quarters. Mallie's breath condensed in the bracing cold; she was haunted by images of a frozen Derby. She clapped her hands delightedly when she saw him with the rest of the workers around the bonfire. She skipped to him.

"Yer 'ave tongue enough for two sets o' teeth," he snarled. Mallie halted, flustered. She turned to Polly, who was glaring at Derby. Ellery grabbed Derby by the arm and yanked him to his feet.

"Yer should thank Mallie for telling Polly, and Polly for alerting us!" he scolded. "Yer think yer would've made it far? Titus and I won't come fetch yer next time, will we?"

"Nah," Titus said. "Too much trouble."

Derby's chin trembled. He sat down, crossed his arms on top of his bent knees, and buried his face in them. Mallie sat next to him as she had done so many times on the ship, but her eyes filled with tears when, without raising his head, he said, "I'll never talk ter yer again."

Blair's head throbbed. The previous night, after the rattle-skull, he had had another flip. Upon arriving at the shop, he had found the doors bolted and had simply crumpled on the steps, where Betty found him in the morning, snoring and very hung over. Now, Craig stood before him, his leather stirrup dangling in one hand.

"Pull down thy breeches and kneel in front of the chair," Craig ordered.

"Jeffrey Craig, I ken I did wrong. But I'm begging ye, please forgive me this once."

Blair's remorse was sincere, but it was not the pain he wished to avoid. His pride rankled at the thought of any man, other than his father, physically disciplining him. The caning he had received on the ship had been the first time that had ever happened, and he had sworn to himself it would be the last.

"It's my right and obligation to discipline thee. I can wait until tomorrow and ask one of my journeymen to hold thee down."

There was absolutely no way Blair would put himself in that spot. He knelt, pulled his breeches down, and rested his forearms on the seat of the chair. His fingers clenched around the stiles with the first blow. Needles of pain coursed through him, each smack of the leather stirrup on his backside burning more and more. Drops of sweat trickled down his forehead. The second Craig delivered the seventh and final blow, Blair jumped up. He pulled up his breeches, his hands shaky. He had never been hit with a strip of tanned leather, and the pain had a blistering bite of its own.

"Thee can come in," Craig said, opening the front door. Betty walked in, broom and dustpan in hand, avoiding Blair's eyes. While she went out the back, Craig went upstairs and Blair quickly changed into his Sunday clothes.

"I'm sorry," she said when she returned. "I waited as long as I could."

"Oh, lass, I dinna blame ye." He brought the mug of cider to his lips, the only thing he could stomach for now. When Craig came down with his wife and children, Tacey Craig gave Blair a cold, hard look.

"Don't get into any trouble," Craig said as they all headed out. "And be back at a prudent hour."

Almost as soon as the Craigs were gone, the door swung open. Edward and William, accompanied by a third man, let themselves in and bolted the door.

"What do you think you're doing?" Betty asked, alarmed.

"We need privacy, and someone with good handwriting," Edward said, grasping Blair's shoulder tightly and winking at him. He unfolded a piece of paper and placed it on the counter. Blair and Betty gathered around. The paper read, *Please to let Samuel Donaldson pass to Mr. Watson's in the Province of New Jersey and return on Saturday next to Philadelphia, for Mrs. Lock. November 9, 1729.* The seal of Philadelphia was stamped next to the date. Edward pulled out a penknife and carefully scraped off the *S* in *Samuel* and moved on to the *a*. "Mr. Donaldson has unfortunately passed away, and wastefulness is a sin. So we're making a new pass for Mr. Olof Sandel here."

"You can't do that here!" Betty protested.

"It'll only take a minute."

"Edward," Blair pleaded, "go somewhere else!"

"Ye'll get a penny if ye write Olof Sandel's name on the pass. Betty, ye'll get a penny just for being bonny."

"What we'll get is oil of stirrup," Betty said, wringing her hands.

"May I see that for a moment?" Blair reached for the pass, and before Edward could object, he snatched it away.

"No!" cried Olof Sandel. Blair stood next to the hearth, holding the paper just out of reach from the flames. Edward looked more surprised than upset.

"Will ye leave now?" Blair asked.

"I told ye—Blair's no the kind," William said. He seemed strangely pleased.

Edward sighed. "Aye, ye were right. We're leaving, lad."

Blair returned the pass to Edward, who pointed a finger in his face. "Ye cost me a bet."

Before the men walked out, he patted Blair on the cheek. "Mayhap 'tis best."

CHAPTER ELEVEN

November 15, 1729

M allie knocked nervously on Cassie's bedroom door. "Come in," came a happy voice from inside. Mallie walked in. Cassie was sitting at a small desk and motioned for Mallie to sit down in the chair next to hers. Mallie obeyed and sat quietly, staring down at her hands in her lap. "Do you know how to read and write?"

Mallie looked up in surprise. "I can write an *M* and an *A*."

"I wish to teach you to read and write properly."

Mallie thought for a moment. "Why?"

Cassie smiled sadly. "I know my father—God rest his soul—would be pleased." She looked at Mallie with tenderness, then pulled from a chest a book: *A Little Book for Little Children: Wherein Are Set Down, in a Plain and Pleasant Way, Directions for Spelling and Other Remarkable Matters.* She handed it to Mallie, who looked at the cover in fascination.

"This is also for you." Cassie gave Mallie a commonplace book.

"Wot is it?" Mallie leafed through the book's blank pages.

"It's to practice your writing in. You may write your initials on the first page. And I can also teach you embroidery." Cassie took from a basket a rectangular piece of linen, and

Mallie ran her index finger over the embroidered pattern of blue and pink flowers and green leaves.

"I can learn 'ow ter do this?" she asked, smiling.

"Of course. Now"—Cassie took Mallie's hands and looked earnestly into her eyes—"Mr. Bradnox must not know about your lessons. He's very busy, and we must not distract him with trivialities."

"With wot?"

"*Trivialities.* Things that are not important. Can you keep this secret?"

"Yes, Miss Cassie, I promise."

"Wonderful! Do you want to start now?"

"Yes!"

After the first lesson ended, Cassie had Mallie kneel next to the bed, bow her head, and clasp her hands under her chin. "Jesus Christ my God," began Cassie, "I adore you and thank you for all the graces you have given me this day. I offer you my sleep and all the moments of this night, and I ask you to keep me from sin. I put myself within your sacred side and under the mantle of our Lady. Let your holy angels stand about me and keep me in peace. And let your blessing be upon me." Cassie took Mallie's hand and guided it over her face in the sign of the cross. "In the name of the Father, the Son, and the Holy Ghost."

Mallie went to sleep at the foot of the bed that night, feeling happier than she had in years. Before she fell asleep, she promised herself that she would not write her initials on the book, but would wait until she could write her entire name.

November 15, 1729
Saturday

Blair thirstily eyed the drinks that Susannah had brought, and the aroma of the bread and food on the table caused his stomach to growl audibly. He had been hesitant to return to the Penny Pot, but Betty had assured him that as long as he returned before she bolted the doors, everything would be all right. In truth, he hadn't been hard to convince. The cold, short days allowed only for the briefest of walks after the workday was over, and he was desperate for a change in routine. However, he still had no money and no way to get any, and he had resolved not to allow anyone to pay for his drinks. The same fiddler from the previous week walked into the tavern, took out his instrument, and began to play. The music did anything but help Blair's mood.

"Oh, tae show him how it's done!" Blair muttered to himself.

Alice turned to him with surprise. "Ye play the fiddle?"

"A little," he replied dismissively.

"I want tae hear ye play," William said enthusiastically.

"William, no!" Blair called out, but William was already walking over to the musician, and, after a brief talk, returned with the fiddle in his hand. Blair took it with a scowl. He pulled the bow over the strings and winced at the instrument's horrid tuning, then corrected the inadequacy and began to play.

"'The Lads o' Wamphray'!" exclaimed Edward.

Blair's apathy quickly melted away; the music filled him with joy.

"Can ye play 'The Lochmaben Harper'?" a man yelled out as soon as Blair had finished the first tune.

"What are ye doing?" Blair asked when Edward jumped to his feet and snatched his cap.

"Trust me." After going around the tavern, Edward returned Blair's cap with a triumphant flourish. Inside were several coins.

"But the law…" Blair said.

"Just take it."

"I'll have my fiddle back now, if you please."

Blair turned to see the none-too-pleased fiddler and grudgingly returned the instrument and gave the man five pennies. He counted his remaining coins. He could buy a beer and still have enough to buy paper, ink, and quills. He summoned Detta and ordered a tankard, but it was Susannah who brought it.

"That was beautiful," Susannah cooed. She sat on his lap and stroked his fingers. He broke out in goose bumps. "You should play me sometime." She kissed his fingertips and walked off.

"She will no rest now, not until ye let her hold yer fiddle-stick in her hand," William said.

Blair drank, trying to hide his blushing face behind the tankard.

"Excuse me, lad, what's your name?"

Blair stood up, mystified by the well-dressed gentleman who had just addressed him.

"Blair Eakins, sir."

"My name is Lucius Groom. I heard you sing last week out in the yard. You have a rare voice, in addition to being one of the best fiddlers I've ever heard."

"Thank ye, sir."

"I'm entertaining some guests in my house next Saturday, early afternoon. I will pay for you to play for us."

Blair was speechless for several long seconds. "I...I dinna have a fiddle," he finally stuttered.

"I have one."

"But I'm no allowed..."

"A shilling for an hour of your time." The man offered his hand. Blair hesitated for a moment. Shaking hands was an Englishman's custom. *A shilling for an hour.*

"Aye, sir, I'll play for ye," he said, taking the man's hand.

A pair of warm, soft lips touched Blair's, and his skin tingled when silky hair brushed against his face and neck. Somewhere in the back of his mind he knew he was dreaming of Janet, and he prayed it was still hours before Betty came downstairs so this wonderful moment could last. The light weight of a body settled on top of him and he wrapped his arms around it, his hands feeling childish curves under thin linen. He slid his hand between two coltish legs. He heard a gasp, and sharp teeth closed on his lower lip. The pain woke him up in an instant.

"I'm sorry, I didn't mean to bite thee like that," someone whispered.

This cannot be, he thought, certain he was still dreaming. He ran his tongue over his lip and felt a bump that stung.

This could only be Betty, overcome by a moment of inexplicable, terrible judgment, but for the *thee...*

"Prudence?"

"Yes."

"Go back tae yer room."

"My parents won't wake up for hours."

"Ye'll get me in trouble!" he whispered urgently. There was silence, and then he heard sniffles. "Oh no, dinna cry!"

"I didn't tell my father. I thought thee would be pleased with me."

"I am, ye dinna ken how grateful I am, but ye really canna be here."

"Sit with me for a while. I promise I'll leave soon."

"Soon," he muttered. He sat up and threw his blanket over himself, and she leaned her head on his shoulder contentedly. He clenched his teeth when her hand slid down the inside of his thigh, but he tried to ignore it. In spite of how worried he was, the sweet scent of her hair was intoxicating, and her hand running from his knee to just below his groin was too. He felt her breath quicken, and when she placed her hand over his groin, he let her. He closed his eyes, and his breath quickened. *Please don't do that,* he feebly thought as his will slipped away. Then baby Ewan started to cry. Blair's heart jumped to his throat. They remained perfectly still, ears perked, hearts pounding. They heard footsteps, then Tacey Craig's soothing voice. They remained frozen for what seemed like ages, and the house was silent again.

"I think ye can go now," Blair whispered. This time the girl did not object. She stood up and gave Blair one last smitten smile. He watched her go up the stairs, her progress agonizingly slow as she tried to keep the treads from creaking. He lay down and stared at the ceiling, troubled by how easily things had escalated, by the fact that Janet had so easily slipped from his mind, and grateful that he had been snapped back from the brink.

Two days later, whenever Craig's daughters passed through the shop on their way to school and back, Blair kept his eyes glued to his work, but it was simply impossible to keep Prudence out of his mind. On one occasion he was forced to wait several minutes before going to the privy, lest it became evident to everyone that his head had been swimming with unchaste thoughts.

Later that night, a tickling sensation on his head woke him up. He batted at it and realized fingers were twirling locks of his hair. He groaned. Prudence scooted closer. Fuming, he went to the fireplace, lit a spill with an ember, and lit a candle.

"Are thee going out *now?*" she asked when he put on his shoes. He grabbed his blanket and headed to the rear of the shop, Prudence at his heels. A frigid blast of air hit him when he opened the door; the candle was immediately snuffed out. Snowflakes sprayed his face. Mouthing a curse, he stepped outside, with Prudence right behind.

"Dinna follow me." He walked all the way to the middle of the courtyard. Prudence's bare feet and lack of a coat, if not his request, prevented her from going any farther. His teeth clacked in his ears. Soon, the cold impelled Prudence back indoors. Blair waited a few more minutes and then cracked the door open, trying to detect the slightest sound.

Convinced the girl had returned to her room, he made his way back in, angry to have lost what precious little warmth his body had. When he opened his eyes the following morning, Betty was stoking the fire.

"Why did you go out last night?" she whispered.

"I didna."

"You did."

"How would ye ken?"

"The rear door was not bolted, and I never forget to do it. And there's that." She pointed to muddy tracks on the floor.

"I must've walked in my sleep."

Betty crossed her arms and tilted her head at the sorry excuse. The suspicious looks she gave him all throughout dinner and again during supper persuaded him to confess. "I swear, Betty, I did nothing tae encourage her."

She nodded. "I believe you."

"I'll sleep in the cellar tonight."

"It's cold down there."

"Where else can I go?"

That night, he waited until the house grew still and then grabbed his two bags, mat, and blankets. He groped his way to the cellar door in the dark, then realized that the cellar would be even darker. He found the same candle he had used the night before and lit it and began to descend the stairs. *Betty was right*, he thought as he stepped down into the frigid cellar; it was so cold, he might as well sleep outside. The candlelight revealed shelves with pots, jars, and containers, baskets with soap, eggs, butter, and bags of flour. His mouth watered at the sight of apples, blocks of cheese, and chunks of bacon. He dug inside a bag, pulled out a slice of dried peach, and popped it in his mouth, savoring the tart fruit. He took another and was about to bite into it when he stopped himself, remembering what Betty had said about the Craigs keeping close scrutiny of their food, then returned the slice. He searched among an old broom, brushes, old lasts, and a broken clock until he found a long piece of twine. He tied one end around the door's knob and the other around a hook on the wall to the right of the door, keeping the length of twine taut. He tried to open the door, testing the makeshift contrivance, and was satisfied. He put on both his pairs of stockings, then forced his second pair of breeches over the ones he was already wearing. He stuffed himself inside two shirts and one jacket and still spent the next few hours shivering, barely able to sleep, trying not to think of the jars of preserved strawberries and peaches within reach. He was wondering if this was all for nothing and he should go back to the shop when the doorknob turned. He listened with apprehension; the twine squeaked gently, and the floorboards outside creaked. After one last attempt, whoever it was gave up.

"How was your night?" Betty asked the following morning, noticing the dark circles under Blair's eyes.

"Someone tried tae open the door. I'm sure it was her."

He spent all morning fighting to keep his eyelids open, and his voice was hoarse as he read for the cordwainer and the journeymen.

"Are thee all right?" Craig asked.

Blair sneezed. "I might have caught a wee cold."

"If thee can't read properly, don't read at all." Craig took the newspapers from Blair and returned them to their shelf. He turned on his heels, looking indignant. In his hand was the candle Blair had lit two nights in a row. "I told thee not to use my candles!"

Blair searched desperately for an explanation. "I needed to use the chamber pot."

Craig gave Blair a wholly incredulous look. "Don't do it again."

At noon, Blair ate as quickly as possible and took a nap until Craig woke him up. As soon as the workday was over, he fell asleep, woke up only long enough to have supper, and went down to the cellar before Betty closed up for the night. He was angry with and resentful of Prudence, mostly for being so warm and soft and making him so irritatingly restless.

November 22, 1729

Mallie hummed joyfully as she worked in the kitchen next to Polly; they had been instructed to prepare a special dinner. Margaret, her eyes and ears alert to everything that went on in the main house, had learned a few days before that Bradnox was summoning Cassie's mother from Annapolis so he could ask for Cassie's hand. Even better news was that Ryan Hearne, the man who owned Isaac, the father of Margaret's son, intended to marry Abigail. The weight of Mallie's years of servitude seemed to shrink in an instant, now that she could count on Cassie's continued presence and Abigail's permanent absence.

The kitchen door swung wide open, and Abigail stuck her head in, looking furious. "To the main house. Both of you."

When Mallie and Polly walked into the hall, Margaret was already there. Bradnox was holding a riding crop in his left hand. "Who took Miss Abigail's delftware pitcher?" he asked Margaret. A cold wave rushed from Mallie's belly to her head and down her arms.

"I don't know, sir," Margaret replied. Bradnox slapped her. He then faced Mallie. She was caught; tears pooled in her eyes.

"Mr. Bradnox," Polly said, "I broke it."

Mallie snapped her head toward Polly. She opened her mouth to protest, but Polly spoke again. "It was an accident. I'm very sorry."

Mallie looked at Margaret, who brought her finger to her lips, just for a second. Bradnox took a sideways step to face Polly. She looked him straight in the eye, half defiant, half beseeching him to be forgiving. He slapped her, twice.

"Finish cooking, and come back when we've finished eating."

A thick lump in Mallie's throat made it impossible to swallow any of her supper. *Maybe*, she thought desperately, *Bradnox will be so happy about his engagement that he will forgive Polly.* But when Margaret returned to the kitchen, the look on her face made any hope Mallie might have harbored shrivel up.

"He's in a foul mood. Mrs. White didn't object to the match, but she won't let Miss Cassie marry for four years. She wanted to take her back to Annapolis, and the only way she agreed to let her stay was if Miss Abigail stayed too. Miss Abigail is furious, because her brother won't grant his permission for her to marry Mr. Hearne now."

"Keep Mallie company," Polly told Margaret when Bradnox called for her.

"Is 'e going to beat 'er with the crop?" Mallie asked Margaret when Polly left.

"Yes."

"Where?"

"On her back."

"I shoulda told the truth." Mallie's voice quaked.

"It would've just made matters worse," Margaret said, stroking Mallie's cheek. "He would've been angry at Polly for lying and punished her anyway."

"Mr. Bradnox 'as beaten yer?"

Margaret chuckled mirthlessly. "He's beaten everyone." She hung a pot of water over the fire and threw a handful of mustard seeds in.

It was not long before Polly returned, her faced flushed and her eyes teary, her stay in her hands. When she sat down and Margaret untied the laces in the back of her shift, Mallie understood why this article of clothing was different from the ones she had seen and worn in London: it was for the planter's convenience. Margaret soaked a square of linen in the mustard seed water, wrung it, and let it cool before applying it to Polly's back. Polly sucked in air through her teeth.

"I need to go to the privy," Margaret said. "I'll be back soon."

The last thing Mallie wanted was to be left alone with Polly. Surely, she would forever hate her after this. But Polly turned to her and, in spite of the sadness in her eyes, smiled. It was a sincere smile.

"Why did yer do that?" Mallie asked.

"I don't know. I kept thinking of the fright I felt when me mother beat me."

"Did it 'urt?"

"Oh yes. It's not the first time, mind yer, and it always 'urts. But I feel 'appy." Polly shrugged.

"Thank yer," Mallie said. "No one 'as ever been this kind ter me."

Wornell Bray had been kind, but Mallie understood that being a man of his station was much easier than being a woman like Polly.

November 22, 1729

The feel of the lathered brush on his face and neck lulled Blair, and he promptly fell asleep in the barber's chair.

"Wake up, lad," the barber said. "I can't work unless you hold your head up."

Blair nodded off repeatedly while the barber worked on him, worried about what sort of performance Lucius Groom was going to be treated to if he could not shake off his lethargy. Thirty minutes later he had changed into his Sunday best and was running his hand over his smooth chin. Following Groom's directions, he easily found the house. A young black woman opened the door and showed him to the drawing room, where a group of young gentlemen were conversing, smoking, and drinking wine and punch. Groom got up from a table where he had been playing cards.

"This is Blair Eakins," Groom said, turning to his friends. "You'll find he's every bit as talented as I've promised."

Blair's stomach clenched when, among the guests, he recognized the man who, only days before, had been to the shop to have his feet measured. *Please, please, please don't remember me*, he thought, avoiding the man's eyes.

"You're Jeffrey Craig's servant, aren't you?" the man asked.

Groom raised his eyebrows. "The cordwainer?"

"Aye, sir," Blair replied in a defeated voice. "Mr. Groom, ye ken I'm no allowed tae work for anyone other than my master. Mayhap 'tis best if I leave. I'm sorry tae have wasted yer time."

"Nonsense." Groom grabbed his arm and walked toward a table where a violin sat in its open case. "Is anyone going to tell Jeffrey Craig that Blair played and sang for us?"

"Of course not!" everyone chorused.

The man who had recognized Blair scoffed. "Just because the Society of Friends wish to deprive themselves of the joy of music and would deprive us as well, that doesn't mean we'll let them."

Blair picked up the violin, thrilled at the feel of the smooth wood. He turned it over and read a label on the back: *Joseph Guarnerius fecit Cremone anno 1729 IHS*. It meant nothing to him, but it was evident this instrument was much different from any he had ever seen. "This is the most handsome fiddle I've ever held."

"That's because it's not a fiddle; it's a violin," Groom said. "Please, start with whatever you want."

At that moment, Blair yawned like a bear. He clamped a hand to his mouth, embarrassed. Groom laughed. "Flora!" he called, and the black girl appeared. "Make a pot of coffee and bring Blair a cup."

An hour and a half later, Blair was outside Groom's house, exhilarated. Never had he heard such beautiful sounds as those that had taken wing from Groom's violin. He had his shilling and then some, thanks to the generosity of Groom's guests. He would be heading straight to the shop but for the fact that the coffee—this being the first time he had tried it—had put wind in his sails, so it was off to the Penny Pot. He had taken but a few steps when he heard a deep voice behind him, calling his name. He turned and saw a black man.

"Blair Eakins," the man said when he caught up, "my name is Abraham Fry."

"What do ye want?" Blair asked warily; this was the first time he had ever spoken to a black person.

"I was in the kitchen and heard you play. Mr. Groom's servant girl and me, we getting married. We want you to play at our wedding."

"Have both yer masters given their permission for you to marry?"

Abraham smiled, a radiantly white smile against his dark skin. "I have no master; Mr. Groom ain't Flora's master neither."

Oh, thought Blair, *they're the* free *kind.* He was unimpressed: Reverend Andrews's sermons clearly pointed out that blacks were inferior to whites and slavery was biblically justified. No blacks, no matter how free, would ever be allowed to marry in the Presbyterian meeting house.

"Where are ye getting married?"

"Gloria Dei."

"Where?"

"The Swedes' church."

Knowing this man had the means and freedom to marry made Blair very bitter.

"I work as a blacksmith; I can pay you fair," Abraham said.

"I'll think about it," Blair replied, but his tone made it abundantly clear he had no intention of doing so. Abraham's smile disappeared, and a wounded look flitted over his eyes. He straightened his shoulders, nodded, and returned Blair's hard look with steady but conciliatory eyes.

"There's time. I hope you say yes," Abraham said even as Blair turned his back on him and walked away.

November 26, 1729

A sharp and pleasant scent of lampblack, linseed oil, and resin filled Blair's nostrils when he stepped inside the print shop of the *Pennsylvania Gazette*. Being sent alone to market had its advantages; he could buy what he needed to write letters without the Craigs figuring out he had money to spend.

"Good morning," Blair said. "I'm looking for Mr. Franklin."

A man fumbling with the drawers of a letterpress cabinet looked up with bloodshot eyes. Another young man working a press at the far end of the shop wiped his ink-stained hands on a rag.

"Good morning," the man at the press said, walking toward Blair. "What can I do for you?"

"I need three sheets o' paper for letters, please. Do ye have ink and quills?"

"One packet of powdered ink for seven pence, twelve quills for three, and each sheet of paper is one penny."

Blair noticed the printer give him a strange look as he wrapped everything up.

"You don't remember me." The printer's demeanor was rather chilly as he handed Blair the bundle.

"Forgive me, Mr. Franklin, have we met?" Blair scrutinized the man's unfamiliar face.

"You spilled your drink on me about two weeks ago."

Blair gasped. "Oh no! Please forgive my clumsiness!"

"You sound Irish," Franklin said with distaste.

"I came from Ireland, from"—Blair lowered his voice, horrified at the dreadful impression he had made—"Ulster."

"Let me guess—you're indentured."

"Aye," Blair replied reluctantly.

Franklin gave an exasperated grunt. "We're verily being swarmed as Ireland seems determined to send us every one of her impenitent citizens."

Blair blinked, not understanding what he had done to deserve such animosity. Surely an accidental spill did not justify it, especially when he had just offered a heartfelt apology. A slurred voice came from the letterpress.

"Din' you run 'way from your 'ndenture, Benjamin?"

Franklin glared at the man, who was evidently in his cups. "I ran away from my brother's beatings, Meredith. And I never stole horses or burglarized houses like all these Irish are wont to do." He gave Blair a look as if he'd caught him in the act of stealing. "Maybe you can explain to me why you've come to a land whose inhabitants hold such disrespect and aversion toward your nation."

"I…I came because…" Blair stuttered, taken aback by the hostility.

"We keep advertisin' 'em." The drunken man held up a copy of the *Gazette*. "And we keep buyin' 'em."

Blair turned back to Franklin. "I'm verra sorry I've offended ye."

As he left the money on the counter and scrambled out, his face flushed, he could hear Franklin still complaining: "They bring the smallpox…"

"I wish I had family to write to," Betty whispered as she ate her supper and watched Blair write his letters. He first wrote to Joseph Shipboy, telling him about his brother and sister-in-law's deaths, and addressed the letter to Donegal, the Ulster-Scot town west of Philadelphia, hoping it would somehow find him. He wrote another to his mother, uncle, and grandfather, telling them about the inadequate rations and how long the voyage had taken, but not the whipping and caning. He told them about Christy's and Samuel's deaths, but wrote in optimistic tones about Ronald's placement with one of their countrymen and said he himself was happily situated with a cordwainer. Finally, he wrote to Janet. He promised he would do nothing but work toward their future, and said he was eager for the day when they could be together again. He carefully folded the letters and sealed them shut with wax. He would drop off Joseph's letter at the postmaster's on Second Street, and at the Penny Pot he would find a ship's captain to carry the other two to Ireland. He hoped his family and Janet could cobble together the necessary money for postage.

He should have been overjoyed, but the printer's words had made him homesick all over again. He stared sadly at the letters, wishing it were him on the ship headed back home.

November 26, 1729

On her chair next to Cassie, Mallie swung her feet back and forth as the young girl reviewed a page full of *A, E, I, O, U.*

"Mallie, this is lovely! You deserve a good night's sleep."

"Please, I want ter do another page." It didn't matter how tired she was at the end of the day; Mallie lived for these lessons. "Wot do I do now?"

"Not *wot*," Cassie corrected patiently. "*What.*"

"*What*," Mallie repeated. She had just begun another page, the tip of her tongue pressed between her teeth in concentration, when someone knocked, just once, and the door opened.

"Cassie, forgive my intrusion. I'd meant to…" Bradnox stopped midsentence, a small box tied with yellow ribbon in his hand. Mallie jumped to her feet. Cassie also stood up, flustered. "What are you doing?" the planter asked, walking to the table and studying Mallie's work. From his expression, Mallie now understood why Cassie had wanted to keep these lessons a secret.

"I thought I would teach her a few basic things," Cassie said, trying to hide her nervousness.

"Why didn't you tell me?"

"It's not really a serious endeavor. It's more like…a game."

"She's not here to play. Why do you wish to do this?"

"Because my father took to heart his obligation to teach his apprentices to read the Bible, write, and cipher the Rule of Three. I want to follow his example."

Mallie furtively looked from one to the other, hating being the cause of a lovers' quarrel.

"Your intentions are noble," Bradnox lectured. "But she's not an apprentice—she's a convict. Convicts don't get the benefit of lessons."

Now Mallie glanced at the door. Maybe she could inch toward it...

Bradnox's tone would have made anyone think that his cousin was much younger than she really was. "I told you when I bought her: she's not a kitten or a puppy. She's not your pet."

"I know she's not a pet," Cassie said, frowning. "She's a girl."

"She's a pickpocket."

It was all Mallie could do not to crawl under the bed. She knew what she was, but hearing it made her feel painfully insignificant.

"Why didn't you tell me?" Bradnox insisted. Cassie wrung her hands.

"I'm sorry, Andrew, you're right," she blurted with sincere regret. "I should've told you. This is your house, and she's your servant."

Mallie glanced sadly at her commonplace book. There would be nothing at the end of the day to look forward to. Bradnox took Cassie's hand in both of his; there was genuine adoration in his eyes. "You may continue giving her lessons, if she receives ten blows with the crop."

Mallie clenched her skirts in her hands.

"She's done nothing wrong!" Cassie cried. "If anything, she was being obedient!"

"I agree. This isn't her punishment. It's yours. From now on, Mallie is your whipping girl. If a whipping boy is good enough for *Sa Majesté* Louis the Fifteenth, surely it's good enough for my Cassie."

Mallie's mouth had gone dry as cornmeal. Cassie shook her head slowly, thinking, torn.

"If you don't agree, you can't continue with her lessons," Bradnox said.

"I can't bear the thought of her being whipped."

"This is why a sincere bond and fondness between whipping boys and princes is encouraged. The entire exercise would be futile otherwise."

Cassie looked at Bradnox, brokenhearted. "No."

"Yes," Mallie said. "Please."

In Bradnox's hall, a distressed-looking Polly faced Mallie. The top of Mallie's shift hung loose around her waist, her back and chest covered in gooseflesh. Their fingers were wrapped around each other's forearms, but Mallie was shaking so much, she could barely maintain a grip. Bradnox loomed behind her. Before closing her eyes she glanced one last time at Cassie, sitting rigid by the fireplace, pale and aghast. She heard the sharp crack of leather against flesh at the same time as the searing pain bloomed on her skin. She yelped and her fingers clamped down; her eyelids squeezed shut with each blow, and tears poured down her cheeks and dripped down her jawline. When it was finally over, Polly helped her slip her arms back into the sleeves of her shift, and they walked in silence to the kitchen.

"It stings!" Mallie blubbered when Margaret applied the prescribed cloth dampened in mustard-seed water.

"I know, but it'll make it better. Why did he hit you?"

When Mallie explained, both Polly and Margaret looked bewildered.

"But yer don't need ter read or write ter be a good cook," Polly observed.

"I know."

"Why then does this matter so much to you?" Margaret asked.

"I don't know. In London it was a terrible feeling when I looked through the window of a shop selling sweets, and I couldn't eat them. That's 'ow I feel when I can't read something."

"Well," Polly said, "when yer learn, read me a sweet story."

November 29, 1729

After one single beer, Blair folded his arms on the tavern table, laid down his head, and fell asleep. Not until the cockfights were announced did he wake up. *It was a mistake to come*, he thought. The following Saturday he would stay at the shop.

"Are ye awricht?" Edward asked when they walked to the courtyard. "Ye've terrible dark circles under yer eyes."

"Betty told me their master's oldest daughter has taken a liking tae him," Alice said, tittering. "Two nights in a row she tried tae seduce him, so he's been locking himself up in the cellar since." Edward, William, Johannes, and Raimond burst out laughing.

"It's no laughing matter," Blair said, annoyed. "I canna sleep in that freezing dungeon, and I'm surrounded by food I canna touch. Even if she left me alone, the baby cries at all hours o' the night."

"When did this start?" William asked.

"I've spent nine nights in the cellar."

The men groaned. Outside, Blair confided in Edward. "I canna go down tae the cellar anymore. I really need tae sleep. But I'm afeared I'll give in tae the temptation if she keeps trying."

"Her father may be a pacifist Quaker, but it won't mean anything where his daughter is concerned. He'll kill ye."

"How much does one have tae pay a whore?"

"Two guineas is the going rate."

"Two guineas?"

"If ye're desperate, ye can go tae Hell Town for a three-penny upright."

"I am desperate." Blair looked around. As always, the women were greatly outnumbered by the men, and the only two that he found attractive, other than Alice, already had company.

"Blair! Am I glad to see you!" Groom was striding toward him. "Can you play for me next Saturday?"

Some good news, at least. "I'll be verra happy tae, sir."

"And would you be willing to play for us twice a month? Not the same day every time, but every two weeks without a doubt."

"Yes, sir!"

Blair called Emma over and ordered beers for everyone, thrilled to be treating his friends. Edward stared after her when she left the table, then whispered something to William, who snickered. William then called Johannes and Raimond, their heads came together, and all three grinned. Blair felt a pang in the pit of his stomach; his "friends" were clearly leaving him out of the joke, and it appeared the joke was him.

December 6, 1729

Blair's plans to go straight back to the shop after playing at Groom's changed after he was again given a cup of coffee. Emma practically bounded to him as soon as he stepped into the Penny Pot. "Blair! Are you hungry?"

"Hullo," he said, flustered at the effusiveness. "What's there tae eat?"

"Tongue pie."

"I'll have that. And a beer."

Emma skipped away, giggling at something that was clearly lost on him. When he found Johannes, Alice, Raimond, William, and Edward, the strange way they smiled at him made him self-conscious.

"Now *that* looks tasty and juicy," Edward said when Emma returned with the pie. Feeling all eyes on him, Blair focused his attention on his food. Not only had Johannes, Raimond, William, and Edward left him out of their joke the previous Saturday, but apparently Alice was now also in on it. Maybe after eating he would leave. First he needed to ask Alice something.

"Alice," he said, "would ye be willing tae cook supper for me, Monday through Saturday? I'll give ye money for market and for yer work. If I ask Betty, Jeffrey Craig will wonder why I have money."

"I'll be happy tae."

Suddenly, Susannah was whispering in his ear. "Come with me. I want to show you something."

"Hey! Where're ye taking him?" Edward demanded, strangely upset, but Susannah had already pulled Blair away.

"Come to my room," she said.

Blair sighed with exasperation. "I dinna have the money yet."

"I'll give you time to pay."

He turned; everyone at the table was staring at them expectantly. He turned back to Susannah. "What are ye all scheming?"

"Just come with me."

"Not until I ken what ye're scheming."

Susannah pouted. "Your friends paid Emma to take you to bed."

"Oh, did they?" This time he did not dare glance at the table. "And ye wish tae deprive Emma of her guineas?"

Susannah seemed flustered. "They told her that...she would be your first woman—*in Philadelphia. I* want to be your first."

Blair knew his face had to be as red as an English soldier's uniform. "*No one* is paying on my behalf."

"I won't take their money." When he hesitated, Susannah rested one hand on his chest. "Let me know if you change your mind." She turned to walk away and then smiled when Blair reached out and grabbed her arm.

The thrill coursing in his veins like cold whiskey, however, seemed to paralyze his limbs as soon as he crossed her threshold. He stood with his back against the door, like a block of ice. Susannah lit two candles on a nightstand and faced him, her eyes mischievous. He swallowed, doing his best to hold a steady gaze but failing spectacularly. She took his hands and placed them on her hips, threw his cap on a chair, and ran her fingers through his hair. He stopped her, self-conscious about the bald spots that had yet to fill in, so she lowered her hands to his face and kissed him. She tasted of small beer and rosemary. When she cupped his groin, he gasped and closed his eyes. He was a brand-new frame drum in Susannah's able hands: she applied pressure, again and again, and every single cell in his body reverberated in time with her rhythm. He felt her fingers opening buttons, and then his breeches were around his ankles. He braced, expecting her hand to close around him—nothing. He opened his eyes. She was staring at his erect member.

"What's wrong?" he asked, alarmed, afraid he was about to be failed in a test he was unaware of.

"Nothing," she said resolutely. With no small amount of awkwardness, she helped him discard his shoes and stockings.

"Ye're still wearing all yer clothes," he observed as he removed his jacket.

"Close your eyes."

He complied, rustlings and swishing of linen and hemp caressing his ears and promising new vistas. The bed squeaked.

"Open them."

For a moment he could not breathe. She had lain on the bed without any attempt at exotic or provoking poses—her head rested on her pillow, arms at her sides, legs straight. The light from the candles varnished her skin and twinkled on her hair; her nipples were the color of clay marbles. She patted the bed. He sat next to her and—almost reverently—placed both hands over her breasts. He squeezed gently, soaking in their plumpness. His mouth closed with such hunger on a nipple that she shivered.

"Lie down," she said. He discarded his shirt and lay on his side, resting his head on his left hand while she guided his right hand past her belly. Her thighs parted. He caressed her, and she melted like sweet butter left to soften in the sun. "Oh, Blair!" Her words made his cock jolt. He drew circles, and as she moaned, he remembered a man he had once seen in Belfast who made a crystal cup with water sing by running his finger around the rim. Her hips rose and fell, matching the undulation of his fingers, and her cheeks flushed. He studied her with fascination: her eyes were closed, her lips parted, and her fingers were tangled in the sheets. She cried out, and her hips froze in their upward thrust, her legs shuddering. Her hand flew to his and gently held his fingers. She lowered her hips, panting, then opened her eyes and smiled at him.

"Are ye awricht?" he asked. She nodded. "What did ye feel?" he asked, as if he were inquiring about the secret to immortality.

"I'll show you. Lie on me."

If she had been warm butter on his fingers, she felt like hot flip on the tip of his cock. He thrust and she stiffened. He paused, unsure how to proceed.

"Go slowly," she whispered.

When he fully slid into her, it was as if a blanket—left for hours by the fireplace—had opened up and then wrapped around him. Completely unprepared for the overwhelming sensation, he immediately climaxed, every muscle fiber straining like sails catching a gale.

"How can that be a sin, when it feels like heaven?" he panted once he had rolled onto his back and caught his breath. *If only I had the money to have her again*, he thought. He wondered how much time had passed since he'd walked into her room; it seemed time had stopped. Betty would bolt the doors soon. He forced himself to sit up, picked his breeches off the floor, took every coin he could find in the pockets, and placed them on the bedside table.

"Don't go," Susannah said.

He chuckled. "Are ye trying tae get me indebted for life?"

"You only have to pay me for the first time."

"Are ye feeling charitable?"

"I assure you, that's not what I'm feeling."

CHAPTER TWELVE

December 8, 1729

Blair's temples throbbed as he stood, seething, and pulled his breeches up. Craig hung his stirrup on the wall. When he had finally arrived at the shop that Monday morning, Blair had argued in vain that, although he had not returned Saturday night or at all on Sunday, he hadn't missed any work, but Craig was furious and unforgiving. At least the journeymen had not arrived yet and so had not witnessed the beating. Craig, however, made sure to share the story with them as soon as they walked in the door, much to Blair's chagrin.

"Where were you?" Betty asked later, during dinner.

"At the Penny Pot."

"Was it worth it?" She bluntly looked at the blanket Blair was using as a cushion on his chair.

"I assure you, Betty, it was," replied Bartholomew, and the other two journeymen laughed.

In the afternoon, the cordwainer showed Blair how to untwist a length of hemp thread by rolling it on his knee to separate the strands. Then he demonstrated how to wax the strands and how to twist any number of them together to achieve the thickness desired. He instructed Blair to try it himself. When Blair was finished, Derrick waved him over.

"You'd never done this before?" Derrick asked, studying Blair's handiwork. "You did a great job."

"It can be better," Craig said, taking the thread from Derrick's hand. When the cordwainer turned his back, Derrick rolled his eyes at Blair.

Later, as soon as the journeymen had gone, Blair approached Craig. "Sir, if I promise tae be here in the mornings before breakfast, do I have yer permission tae lie out?"

"Are thee displeased with thy lodgings?" Craig asked in a sarcastic tone.

"I'm no used tae babies crying. I promise I'll work harder than any servant ye've ever had."

Craig thought for a moment and almost imperceptibly glanced at the basket where he had put the thread Blair had waxed. "Yes. But if thee is ever late, I *will* discipline thee."

"I have Mr. Craig's permission to lie out," Blair happily announced when Craig retreated to the second floor and Betty came down.

"Are you going to the tavern tonight?" she asked.

"Aye."

"You won't get much more sleep there than in the basement," she said, unable to contain a mischievous smile.

"At least I'll be warm."

"How odd to see you on a Monday!" the tavern keeper exclaimed when Blair walked into the Penny Pot. "Susannah, bring what I bought."

Susannah's eyes shone at the sight of Blair. A moment later she was back with a used fiddle.

"You can play it whenever you're here," the tavern keeper said, "and keep every penny you get."

Blair tuned the fiddle, played a few notes, and smiled. "It's a good fiddle," he said. "Thank ye."

As a customer called him over, he crossed paths with Susannah, who flashed him a blissful smile.

"Will you play 'Tam Lin'?" the customer asked Blair. Blair was silent for a moment.

"Would ye prefer something livelier?" he offered.

"You don't know it," the customer said with disappointment.

"I do, I do," Blair replied, adjusting the fiddle under his chin. As the melody flowed, the words played in his head.

O I forbid you, maidens a',
That wear gowd on your hair,
To come or gae by Carterhaugh,
For young Tam Lin is there.
There's nane that gaes by Carterhaugh
But they leave him a wad,
Either their rings, or green mantles,
Or else their maidenhead.
Janet has kilted her green kirtle
A little aboon her knee,
And she has brooded her yellow hair
A little aboon her bree,
And she's awa to Carterhaugh
As fast as she can hie.

The song went on with Janet—the leading lady in the story—appearing in verse after verse. Was he betraying his own Janet? Blair asked himself. No, this meant nothing. If she were here, things would be different. This was just so he would not lose his mind while they were apart. He caught Susannah glancing at him. The thrill she had evidenced upon his arrival had subsided. He realized that although he had simply assumed he could spend the night, maybe he was just being presumptuous, and Betty would have bolted the doors by now. All he could do was wait. When the tavern keeper was saying good night to the last customer, Blair was relieved that Susannah invited him upstairs, although she still seemed uneasy. She shut the door, turned, and leaned back on it. He waited. She said nothing, so he came closer. Still nothing. He pinned her against the door and kissed her. Maybe he had imagined things. If she had something on her mind, it was evaporating quickly.

"Wait, stop!" She pushed him away and slithered out. He rested his forehead on the door, groaning.

"What's wrong?" He turned and saw her pulling some strange-looking thing from a box. She held it up for him to see.

"You need to wear this. It's a cundum."

A what? He listened while she explained that he was to put his member *inside* that thing—that *thing* made of linen, like an empty sausage casing closed at one end. Then he was to fasten it with a ribbon running through the casing around the open end. By the time she had finished talking, his arms were tightly crossed over his chest. He looked down at himself, imagining a ridiculous little bow, and scoffed.

She sighed. "Why is it always a struggle with men? We're not doing anything unless you wear it."

"For why?"

"It keeps me from getting pregnant and from catching the pox."

"I dinna have the pox."

"Not yet."

"How would I catch it?"

She rolled her eyes. "From another woman."

"I dinna desire another woman."

The unexpected words left her speechless for a moment. "It's a matter of time before you very much desire another woman."

He seemed very skeptical at this declaration. "For why didna we use it afore?"

"I don't know; I just didn't want to use it the first time. But I must be cautious. Trust me, it's for your own good too."

He took the "cundum" from Susannah, pinching it between his thumb and forefinger like a venomous insect. "I dinna want tae imagine any linen I ever made was used tae make these." He held it up and scrutinized it. Susannah squealed when he accidentally dropped it.

"Be careful!" she cried, picking it up. "Ship captains bring them from London, and they're not cheap."

Blair thought for a moment. He approached her and nuzzled her neck. "If ye want my prick tae wear a dust bonnet, I'll do it." She burst out laughing. "But I dinna need it just yet, do I?" He moved his mouth to her bosom and squeezed her bottom with his hands.

"Oh no, you're not going to trick me," she said.

Hours later the nightstand candle was halfway spent and the linen accessory lay untouched in its box.

January 5, 1730

All the servants gathered in front of the main house on the twelfth day of Christmas to receive gingerbread—baked by Cassie and Abigail themselves—and rum. Some servants and slaves from Ryan Hearne's plantation had been invited too and were mingling with Bradnox's servants. Taking advantage of the gathering, a slave wedding was being held. Cumby and a black girl from Hearne's plantation sat in chairs while everyone formed a ring around them. Facing them, a black woman offered prayers in a tongue only the slaves understood, then smashed a ceramic pot on the ground. The slaves cheered and whooped as the woman gathered up the shards of the broken pot and placed them in the black girl's outstretched palms. "Four pieces—four children!" the woman exclaimed. Bradnox looked at Cassie and smiled; she smiled back.

Polly and Ellery followed the field hands to their quarters, to fight off the bitter cold with rum and music and dancing. Mallie sighed when Derby walked past her as if she were invisible. She had tried to talk to him every Sunday since his attempted escape, but to no avail.

"Will Cumby move ter Mr. Hearne's plantation now that he's married, or will 'is wife move 'ere?" Mallie asked Margaret back in the women's quarters.

"They'll stay where they are. They're not really married, because they're slaves."

"Oh."

"Here, child, eat your gingerbread."

"If Polly ain't back soon, I'm going ter eat 'er portion," Mallie said through a mouthful.

"I suspect we won't see her till morning, but save her share."

"Maggie, wot—*what's* this?" Mallie showed Margaret her wrists and the back of her hands, which were covered with flat, red spots. Margaret raised her eyebrows.

"Well, my dear, you have the cowpox."

"*I do?* Is that bad?" Mallie studied the spots with great alarm.

"No. These spots will bleed, then fill up with pus"—Mallie's eyes grew wider and wider—"you'll get scabs, and they'll fall off. It hurts, but you'll be over it in a few weeks, and you'll have these." Margaret showed Mallie her own hands and wrists, which were covered with a smattering of scars. "Polly has them too."

Mallie looked from Margaret's scars to her own lesions, not entirely convinced there was nothing to worry about. But because there was nothing to do but trust Margaret, she returned to her gingerbread.

Polly spat into the chamber pot, heaved, and threw up again. She wiped her mouth with a rag. The rooster's crow pierced the morning air.

"Yer don't look like yor with child," Mallie noted. When Polly and Margaret stared at her in surprise, she said, "I saw whores who were childing."

"Is it Ellery's?" Margaret asked.

"I hope so," Polly said feebly.

"Well, Mallie's right. Hopefully no one will notice until the baby's born."

"No one has ter notice ever."

Margaret frowned. "I don't want to hear you say that."

Polly chewed on her nails. "Ellery will notice soon."

"Does he know about Mr. Bradnox?"

"Of course not!"

Margaret turned to Mallie with a solemn look. "Mallie, this is very important. We need to take care of each other as much as we can. Do you understand?"

"Yes."

"You understand you should never mention to anyone that you have seen Mr. Bradnox in the kitchen with Polly, or that she's with child?"

"I do, I promise."

Polly's eyes brimmed with tears. "Sometimes," she said sadly, "yer seem so much like a grown-up, and so little like a small girl."

January 5, 1730

Susannah maneuvered around Rosina, the new girl at the Penny Pot, carrying a tray with food. As usual, stirred by novelty, the patrons were, to a man, enchanted by Rosina's sandy-brown eyes. Susannah set her order on a table, then went to the taproom and picked up a round of drinks. She was on her way to deliver them when she saw Blair and Rosina together and stopped dead in her tracks. Rosina had one hand resting on the back of Blair's chair and was giggling as if she had just downed a rattle-skull. He looked at her like an eager puppy, straining against its leash, eager to go play. Rosina licked her lips sensually before sauntering off, and Blair stared after her. Susanna walked to his table.

"Blair." He turned, startled. "Do you want a drink?"

"No. Aye...the new girl is bringing it. Thank ye."

"All right."

Susannah walked out to the courtyard, went into the privy, and allowed the tears to come, her arms hugging her aching stomach. She had known this would happen; Blair had done nothing wrong. She, on the other hand, had allowed them to fall into a kind of...domesticity. She had refused him when he had offered money but had happily accepted the little gifts he had brought her: ribbons, a ball of soap, candles. She'd learned a long time ago that she could depend only on herself, yet Blair had almost made her forget the lesson. She had seen other girls destroyed by their sentimental fantasies, and she resolved that now, for her own sake, she had better set the world right again. As she was walking back inside, she bumped into Edward.

"Susannah," he said, "how much longer are ye going tae refuse me? Ye'll end up injuring poor Blair."

Susannah was coming down the stairs with Edward when she spotted Blair glaring at her from his table. He emptied his tankard and slammed it down, startling the men around him. She and Edward made their way to him.

"Blair," Edward said with a sincere smile, "have a beer with me."

"I'm leaving." If he left now, he could still sleep in the shop.

"Are you abandoning me tonight?" Susannah asked nonchalantly.

"Go," Edward chimed. "I need tae wait for William."

Blair followed Susannah up the stairs, his feet hitting the treads as if he would pulverize them. Once inside her bedroom, she could see his lower jaw sliding side to side as he glanced at the bed, which she had been careful to make again with fresh sheets.

"Are you angry with me?" she asked.

"No."

"You are."

"I have no reason tae be. I owe ye money, and ye've requested no more payment for yer services."

She cringed. No matter how kind men might seem, jealousy always turned them cruel. Her eyes blazed but were steady. "Would you marry a whore or someone who's been one?"

"I'm going tae bring back a lass who's waiting for me in Ireland and marry her."

He might as well have punched her in the stomach. It was small comfort to confirm that she had done the right thing in correcting the path she and Blair had stumbled on.

"In a few years," she said with as much composure as she could muster, "you'll be gone to some other city, married or not, just like most of the men who pass through here. I've been avoiding customers because...well...I like you." She made sure her words came out sounding lighthearted. *Because I needed this brief, beautiful respite.* "But I need the money. I'll be dead before I wear paupers' letters. You'll see paupers being whipped, but you'll never see a woman whipped for being a whore in Philadelphia. I know very well what my station in life is, but I don't have a master, no one has beaten me in years, and I'm free to go where and when I please."

Blair blinked. She could see his anger ebbing. "I understand," he said, although his voice was strained. "I truly do."

"Will you spend the night with me?"

He glanced at the bed and shook his head. "I should first pay what I owe ye and what I would've paid for lodgings."

Susannah kept her hands at her back, fighting back tears and the desire to hug him as he walked out the door.

Blair stood outside the tavern, holding the lantern the tavern keeper had lent him, thinking. He couldn't quite understand why he had been so upset with Susannah; he knew she wasn't *his*. He realized now that although he had always treated her kindly, he had considered himself above her. He had been wrong. Just what had he been thinking? That they would live together until Janet arrived? He peered down the dark street and wondered if it had been a mistake not to spend one last night at the tavern. He couldn't risk the cordwainer catching his daughter if she went back to her mischief, and he definitely would not sleep in the basement. He remembered something Alice had said about her mistress having boarders, and headed for the alley. He knocked on the chandler's door. A moment later Alice answered.

"Blair! What can I do for ye?"

"May I speak tae yer mistress?" Blair stepped inside while Alice fetched Katherine Moore. The chandler studied Blair with curiosity as he asked if he could lodge in the shop.

"Does Jeffrey Craig know about this?"

"I have his permission tae lie out, as long as I'm back by morning."

"Would thee be willing to do small chores for me, in addition to the rent?"

"I would."

"If Jeffrey Craig asks, I'll say thee does chores for me, then."

Ten minutes later Blair was lying on a woven mat, in the third-story room, beside two other boarders who were sleeping, thinking of Susannah. He had not been blind to the fact that she was brokenhearted, and he was in no way indifferent to it. In a way, he was brokenhearted too.

"Janet," he whispered, just to hear the name.

January 7, 1730

Mallie observed Polly with curiosity. For the fourth time in about a minute the cook had checked the pot hanging over the fire. Then she rearranged some jars that were in perfect order, glanced at Margaret, who was finishing her breakfast, and suppressed a sigh.

"At last," Polly muttered when Margaret left. She hurriedly pulled some seeds from her pocket and swallowed them, chasing them down with cider.

"Was that a remedy?" Mallie asked.

"Yes."

"Wot's wrong?"

Polly moved her chair and faced Mallie. "This is ter restore my menses, but I didn't want Margaret to see, because she would disapprove and be upset."

Mallie nodded slowly and knowingly, her intelligent eyes fixed on Polly. Some things were, by necessity, learned in a brothel.

"I don't want a child keeping me 'ere after I've finished my time."

A couple of hours later Polly was curled up on her mat, having practically crawled up the stairs. Margaret looked down at her, livid. "I thought the cramps would begin tonight," Polly groaned.

"If you were going to do it, it shouldn't have been in the middle of the week, when Mr. Hearne is coming to dine," Margaret said. "Who's going to cook?"

"I can cook," Mallie said. "No one will know."

Polly gave Mallie an unconvinced look.

"We don't have many options," Margaret observed. "I have my hands full."

"I can do it," Mallie insisted.

"Mallie, if it doesn't come out right, we'll get a beating," Polly warned.

"It *will* come out right."

The two women looked at each other, rather more reassured. Margaret helped Polly to the kitchen and left her at the table, squirming in pain. Polly watched as Mallie filled a pot with water and hung it over the fire, then stuffed a chicken with dry oysters and skillfully sewed it shut with twine. When the water was boiling, Mallie dropped the chicken in and stirred in salt and thyme. When she took parsley and began working on a sauce, Polly, unable to sit any longer but satisfied things would not end in disaster, limped back upstairs.

———

Two figures sneaked away into the inky night, a safe distance from the main house. Mallie held a bundle of bloodied linen while Margaret lit a fire. Once it was roaring, Margaret took the linen and threw it into the flames.

———

March 22, 1730

Inside the Presbyterian meeting house, the pews and galleries were quickly filling up. Tables dressed with white tablecloths had been arranged in the aisle. A pewter flagon, cups, and a paten heaped with strips of thin, unleavened bread were arranged on a small head table. Blair was sitting in a pew, lost in thought, absentmindedly tapping his Communion token on a front tooth. He stilled his hand when the church elder in charge of collecting the tokens shot him a disapproving look.

"I want a token!"

All heads turned toward the angry, strident voice coming from the main entrance to the church. Reverend Andrews was arguing with an agitated man. As the elders and the sexton rushed over, Blair jumped to his feet; it was the man who had bought Ronald.

"Please leave. Yer condition is an affront tae the Lord's house," Reverend Andrews said.

"I want a token!"

"Reverend," Blair said, approaching, "if ye've run out o' tokens, he can have mine."

"That's very generous, but misguided. Thomas was examined and questioned beforehand, like everyone else, and he failed tae show that he's prepared in mind and spirit. He's welcome tae return in six months tae take Communion, in a sober state."

"Have I seen ye before?" Burt asked Blair. His mouth exuded rum.

"Ye bought my brother five months ago."

"Ronald Eakins!"

"Aye, sir. Ye said ye'd return soon, but never did. Where is he?"

"Yer brother was much too much trouble. I sold him."

"Thomas," Reverend Andrews interrupted, "ye need tae leave. Blair, ye can talk tae him outside—not in front of the meeting house, please—or ye can go back inside."

Blair saw Burt's eyes sweep over Reverend Andrews and the scowling male congregants who gathered around him. If the man had any sense at all, he knew better than to defy his own countrymen, who were every bit as keen to fight as they were to pray. He tried to slam the door on his way out, but Blair caught it and followed him to the street.

"Please," Blair pleaded. "Where may I find my brother?"

Burt stopped and said, "I sold him tae an Indian." Then he took two lunging steps toward Blair and shoved him. Blair steadied himself and kept a prudent distance away. "Come and fight, you weasel!" Burt hollered.

"I dinna wish tae fight ye, sir."

Burt swung wildly, but Blair easily avoided the blow. Although it was useless to try to reason with the man in his current condition, Blair resolved not to let him out of his sight. He would follow him to wherever he was lodging, wait for him to sleep it off, and get the truth out of him, one way or the other. This drunken blather about selling Ronald to an Indian made no sense. Blair followed Burt as the man stumbled down the street.

"Stop following me!" Burt cried out, looking over his shoulder. Blair slowed down, but kept walking.

"Blair!" A man came jogging up to him. "Reverend Andrews sent me tae retrieve the token ye took, and I find ye provoking Thomas!"

"I just wish tae ken where my brother is."

"I'll fight both o' ye," slurred Burt, turning toward Blair and the man.

"Blair, go back tae the meeting house!" the man ordered.

"But…"

"Go, or ye both will be my first arrests as new constable!"

"Mr. Burt," Blair begged, "I'll pay for the information. When ye feel better, ye can leave word for me at the Penny Pot or at the chandler's shop in Preston's Alley." He marched back to the meeting house, feeling as desolate as he had the day he saw Ronald step off the *King George*.

April 24, 1730

Lying on his pallet in the third-floor room at the chandler's, Blair listened to the other two boarders snoring. The previous day, after his encounter with Burt, he had run to the Penny Pot during the noon break and again at the end of the workday, but the trader had not been seen. He had waited in the tavern as long as he could before he knew Alice would lock up the chandler's shop. In the morning, Susannah had come to the alley bearing a message: the trader would be waiting for Blair at the Bear's Inn the next day, Saturday, at the crack of dawn, before leaving the city. He slid his hand through an opening in one of his pillow's seams and grasped a bag of coins. He had found work playing at several taverns and had stopped spending money on tobacco and cock-fights, which he missed quite a bit, and sex, which he missed terribly. He needed to transfer the coins to his secret hiding place. Although he carried the bag with him all day, carrying it at night was an invitation to be robbed, and it was time to empty it.

He sat bolt upright when a bell clanged out in the alley; he had quickly learned to recognize the alarm and in the past few months had joined in efforts to fight several fires. He moved to the window. It was ten o'clock and most windows were dark, but a full moon illuminated the alley. He waited for the location of the fire to be yelled out while the other boarders, now awake, put on their shoes.

"Fire in the wharves south of Chestnut!"

They ran down the stairs, and the two other men grabbed the chandler's fire buckets from their hooks by the door on their way out. In the alley, men were pouring out of houses, all of them carrying buckets. Blair ran to Craig's shop; Betty was already in the doorway.

"Did Jeffrey Craig take his pails?" he asked.

"He's not home."

Blair ran inside, pulled the buckets from their pegs, and, along with dozens of other men, raced toward the smoke and orange glow. He flew down Carpenter's Stairs to the wharves just in time to see a group of men carefully rolling the fire engine down the last few treads. The five-foot-long, three-foot-wide, five-foot-high wooden device set on four wheels was rolled to within a safe distance of the burning building. The night resounded with shouts and cries for help. He heard someone call out his name and turned to see Johannes and Raimond running toward him. Men were already filling buckets in the river and rushing to the burning warehouse.

Blair, Johannes, and Raimond stood in a line of fifteen men stretching between the Delaware River and the fire engine. Being at the river's edge, Blair filled his bucket, handed it off to Raimond on his right, took an empty bucket from the man standing in front of him in a parallel line, and filled it while Raimond passed the first bucket to Johannes. The bucket was passed down the line until it was dumped into the engine's trough, which fed a cistern. Fifteen buckets full of water were constantly zipping toward the engine, and fifteen empty ones were making their way back to Blair. On top of the cistern, at the aft end, was a pyramidal case from which protruded a brass pipe. Over the middle of the cistern was an iron shaft, attached to two levers on each side, which were attached to long wooden bars. Six men, three on each side of the engine, ran up and wrapped their hands around these bars while another man jumped on the pyramidal case and directed the brass pipe toward the fire.

"Ready?" cried out one of the men on the left side of the engine.

"Ready!" replied the two men next to him.

The three men cried out, "One!" in unison as they lowered the left bar, thus raising the bar on the right; then, the men holding that bar lowered it, and cried out, "Two!" In this manner, the men vigorously cranked the bars up and down, working the pumps, to the rhythmic cries of *one, two, one, two.* A wide arch of water spewed from the pipe's spout. After a few minutes, however, Blair could see they were not making any progress. Even though he was the farthest from the fire, hot air buffeted him, and he was drenched in sweat.

"The warehouse is lost!" someone yelled out. "Let's not waste the water here!"

The engine was repositioned, and the men's efforts were directed toward the building to the left of the warehouse, to prevent the fire from spreading.

"Fire priggers!" someone shouted. Blair saw several dark figures slink out of the burning building, their arms loaded with bolts of cloth, then flee into the dark. A group of men assembled to keep away opportunistic thieves, although it was impossible to protect every single window and door. Blair kept working the bucket brigade, watching with dismay as the adjacent buildings and two cooper shops caught fire, until the searing heat finally forced them to give up and roll the fire engine away.

"The fire has spread to Mr. Fishbourn's new tenements!" someone shouted.

Blair, Raimond, and Johannes ran toward the new conflagration. The fire had jumped to the two-story tenement building, and faces of men, women, and children peered down from the upper-floor windows, screaming for help. Volunteers ran inside and emerged with furniture, chests, and other goods and heaved them into the street. Blair looked up to see a man standing atop a ladder propped against the building, wielding a metal pole with a hook on its end. The man started pulling shingles off the roof, and Blair and several others steered clear of the rectangular cedar cuts plummeting down. He saw two men carrying what seemed to be empty fire buckets and darting around the side of the building—William and Edward. Blair followed them and came around the corner just in time to see them break a bottom-floor window and disappear inside. He stuck his head through the broken window.

"Edward and William! What the hell are ye doing?"

The pair, who were in the process of filling their buckets with anything of value they could get their hands on, paused only long enough to see it was Blair who had discovered them.

"I'm sorry, lad," Edward said. "Not all of us sing like ye."

Blair pulled his head out of the window, furious. He rounded the corner back to the front of the house, lost in thought. He heard a voice from above yell, "Watch out below!" and then the butt of the metal pole that the man had been using to remove shingles crashed on his head and everything went black.

CHAPTER THIRTEEN

May 4, 1730

Weeding time had arrived; extra hands were needed in the fields, and Mallie and Ellery had been recruited. As Mallie was led to the field, she saw five long wooden planks set across the width of five tobacco beds. Two short legs at the end of each plank made them slant. Sitting on the planks, the field hands reached down and pulled weeds. To her dismay, Jason ordered her to climb on a plank already occupied by Derby. For eleven hours his hostility radiated like heat from an oven, competing with the sizzling sun. Mallie groaned and stretched her back. She had by turns lain on one side and then the other, sat with legs stretched in front of her, then with knees bent, and still her legs felt numb.

She kept track of the sun's path, willing it to disappear beyond the horizon. The horn finally blew, and the workers trudged to the edges of the field. She turned in the direction of the kitchen and accidentally stepped into Derby's path. Before she could sidestep him, without hesitation or warning, he slapped her. She gasped, bringing her hands protectively to her face. She cringed when he reached out and peeled one of her hands away. He plucked something off her cheek and showed her: a mosquito. She brushed her cheek with her sleeve and began to thank Derby, but he had already turned and walked away.

———

May 8, 1730

All except one of Groom's guests were gone. Flora, his black servant girl, had started picking up empty glasses and dirty ashtrays. Blair kept his back to her, waiting to get paid, while she worked in complete silence.

"Flora," Groom said after giving Blair his money, "please give Blair the bread that's in the kitchen. I'm walking Mr. Lynn to the stables. Blair, I'll see you in two weeks."

"Aye, sir. Thank ye for the bread." Blair paced around the room, waiting for Flora, and sighed dejectedly. After being knocked unconscious during the fire the previous month, he had missed his meeting with Thomas Burt, and Blair had been unable to ascertain where he might be. A flash of something red under a chair caught Blair's attention. He crouched down to look and found it was a snuffbox. He picked it up just as Flora returned.

"That belong to Mr. Lynn," she said.

"I'll take it tae him," Blair said, running out the door. When he reached the end of the block, the stable boy was standing on a bale of hay, looking in through one of the stable windows.

"What are ye doing?" Blair asked.

"Shush!" the boy whispered, smiling wickedly. "Take a look." He jumped to the ground, and Blair, intrigued, climbed up the bale. Groom and Lynn were standing close—much too close—to each other. Lynn held Groom's arm firmly, saying something that was inaudible. Groom looked nervously toward the door.

"Did ye hear them arguing?" Blair asked.

"Just wait!"

Lynn tightened his grip. His words, whatever they were, seemed to become more fervent. Blair tensed, alert to the moment when Lynn might strike at Groom or otherwise attempt to harm him. But then, Groom kissed Lynn, and Lynn returned the kiss. Blair stared in disbelief, unable to look away, while the men kissed with as much passion and tenderness as if they were man and woman. Groom opened his eyes and met Blair's stare. He pushed Lynn away, Blair jumped to the ground.

"Well?" the stable boy asked. "What did ye see?"

"Nothing," Blair stammered. "I didna see anything."

"Ye did! They're mollies!"

"Here," he told the stable boy, handing him the snuffbox. "Give this to Mr. Groom." He would simply run back to the chandler's. He had just stepped onto the street when the stable door opened.

"Blair," Groom said, looking grave, "what are you doing here?"

"Mr. Lynn forgot that." He pointed at the stable boy.

"Magnus, you left your snuffbox at my house," Groom said, his voice empty of all expression. Lynn stepped out of the stable, also looking grave.

"Thank you, Blair," Lynn said, offering Blair some coins. "For your troubles."

"That's no necessary."

"I insist."

The stable boy elbowed Blair but received a glare such as made him step away.

"Why don't you add that money to Blair's gratuities next time he plays for us?" Groom said to Lynn.

"That's a good idea," Lynn replied.

"Good night," Blair said, eager to leave. As he walked away, he knew he would never return to that house.

——————

Betty interrupted her breakfast to answer the knock on the door.

"Is Blair here?" Blair heard Flora ask.

He jumped to his feet and pushed past both girls, muttering, "Follow me, Flora." He hurried to the end of the alley and one block down, with Flora struggling to keep up. He finally stopped and whirled on her.

"What are ye thinking? The Craigs will ask who ye are and why ye're looking for me!"

"You forgot your bread." In her hands was a bundle wrapped in linen.

"*The bread?* I forgot the—Ye came looking for me on account o' the *bread?*" he asked, exasperated.

"You saw Mr. Groom and Mr. Lynn."

Blair was taken aback by her bluntness.

"Aye, when I returned the snuffbox."

"You saw them like man and woman."

Blair was at the same time annoyed and mortified. Who did this girl think she was, to bring this subject up? How dare she? Did she suspect him of being a mollie too? What did she even want?

"I dinna ken what ye mean."

"My ancestors consider people like Mr. Groom spirits of the gods."

Her statement confused him even more. "Well, this is America. Do they know what ye think about this at the Swedes' church?"

A pained look clouded Flora's face. "In church they say, 'Ye shall know them by their fruits.' God make everything, so God make Mr. Groom. He a good man, a generous man. I know what it's like to be treated like nothing. Judge not—"

"I get my sermons from Reverend Andrews."

Flora offered Blair the bread. He snatched it from her hand, turned, and walked back to the shop. For the rest of the day he debated with himself. He thought of the day he disembarked, when two complete strangers called him *dishonest*, and *scum*, and of the time when Franklin had insinuated he had inclinations toward criminal activities. The Craigs had also harbored suspicions. Flora was right about one thing: Groom was nothing if not kind and generous. True—men weren't supposed to kiss men, but Blair wasn't supposed to fornicate, and he was no model of restraint. And there was another quite weighty, less enlightened consideration: money. If he wanted to bring Janet to America at the end of his indenture, he needed the money. In the end, although unsure whether his decision sprang from following the maxim "Judge not lest you be judged" or from pure self-interest, he resolved to mind his own business.

———

May 14, 1730

Mallie woke up in the middle of the night, freezing cold in spite of the late spring weather, and lay awake until dawn. She spent the entire day shivering and coughing. By suppertime, when she complained of a headache, Margaret touched her face and gloomily announced, "I'll tell Mr. Bradnox she's got the fever and agues."

Polly bundled her in sheets and blankets and sat down to watch over her, fidgeting with a strip of leather in her hands. A short while later Bradnox came in and put his hand to her face. "It might simply be catarrh," he mused without much conviction.

Mallie pushed away his hand forcefully. "Don't touch me, Lizzie!" she yelled. She made a choking sound, her eyes rolled back in her head, and her body began to shake violently, her limbs jerking uncontrollably. Polly held her head while Bradnox forced a strip of leather between her clenched teeth.

"So it is the agues," he said dolefully when Mallie's seizure had passed and she was lying in a stupor. "I'll get my medicine chest."

"Polly?" Mallie's eyes fluttered open.

"Yes, luv, I'm here."

"Wot 'appened?"

"Ye're sick. Mr. Bradnox is going ter treat yer."

The planter returned with a chest from which he took a brass lancet and a bowl. Mallie sat in a chair, and Polly held her arm while Bradnox picked a vein. Mallie closed her eyes as the planter placed the lancet on the crook of her arm, cocked the steel blade, and pressed the trigger with his thumb, firing the blade. A warm, deep-crimson jet gushed out. When the bowl was filled to his satisfaction, Bradnox took a long strip of linen and wrapped it tightly around Mallie's arm, then wiped the lancet with a handkerchief and placed it back in the chest. Through her stupor, Mallie watched warily as Bradnox took a bottle full of a syrupy brown substance labeled "Ipecacuanha," poured a bit into a cup of water and stirred it, then handed the concoction to her. She grimaced as she downed the drink, then drank a large mug of water to wash the taste from her mouth.

The planter handed Polly a four-ounce tumbler and a corked decanter. "Do you remember when to administer this liquor?"

Polly nodded. "One tumbler when this fit ends, then another every three hours, except when she's sleeping, and stop when the next fit begins."

"Good. I'll come back tomorrow." Bradnox set an empty pail next to Mallie. She looked at it, then up at the ceiling, puzzled; it wasn't raining.

"I'll be back soon, luv," Polly said. She returned about twenty minutes later, sat next to Mallie, and waited. Mallie's stomach churned like two feral cats in a sack.

"Polly!" she cried out. Polly helped her sit up and placed the pail under her chin while she threw up violently.

"I don't want it!" Mallie complained when Polly handed her another mug of water.

"Yer have ter drink it, luv."

Mallie drank, fighting every gulp, and immediately vomited again. She crumpled on her mat, moaning. Never had she felt so wretchedly sick. Shortly after the evening horn had sounded, Margaret came up the stairs with someone in tow. "You have a visitor."

For a moment, the sight of Derby made Mallie's discomfort disappear. He himself looked sick with worry. He sat next to Mallie and told her a few simple stories about his day: a grasshopper he had caught and a new song he had learned from the field hands. Afterward, she could not have repeated anything he said, but his presence was a wonderful balm.

"Please take good care of 'er," she heard him whisper when Polly ushered him out. "Two of Mr. Hearne's workers 'ave already died."

"Am I going ter die, Polly?" Mallie asked hours later while Polly changed her sheets and blanket, which were soaking wet.

"No," Polly replied. "I got the agues before, and 'ere I am."

Margaret changed Mallie's bedding again before dawn. Her temperature had finally dropped, and she wasn't sweating as badly now. Polly fetched the decanter Bradnox left, poured a tumbler, and gave it to Mallie. She eyed it with mistrust.

"Wot's in it?"

"Claret wine, lemon juice, Jesuit's powder and other things."

Mallie took a sip and grimaced. "That's bitter!"

"Well, medicine is bitter. Drink the rest."

"'Ow much are yer going ter make me drink?" Mallie asked after she had managed to gag down the revolting concoction.

"Morning and evening for six days."

"Six days?"

"Six days this first infusion; then eight days a second infusion; then a third infusion two fortnights."

"No, no, no..." Mallie grumbled, nauseated at the mere thought.

"Yer will get better," Polly said, stroking her hair. "I promise."

Feeling as if her body were melting through her mat and into the cracks in the floorboards, Mallie whimpered and waited for the next fit to come.

May 27, 1730

Bradnox, with Margaret's assistance, bled Polly. Her body shuddered so violently that the jet of blood streaming from her arm missed the bowl and splashed on the floor. Mallie gasped and looked away. As he had done with Mallie, Bradnox gave Polly a purgative and left the decanter of medicine. When Polly started to vomit, Mallie gently stroked her back while Margaret held the pail.

"Is that wot I sounded like?" Mallie asked with concern some time later. Polly's breath was coming in wheezing exertions.

"No," Margaret replied, "and she didn't sound like that either the first time she came down with the agues. I have chores in the main house now; I'll tell Mr. Bradnox about it. Before I go, you should drink your tumbler."

For the first time since her treatment had begun, Mallie drank the potion without complaint. Two hours later Margaret still hadn't returned. Polly stood up and walked toward the table by the window.

"Polly, wot do yer want?"

"I have ter chop those onions," Polly slurred, pointing at the empty table. Her legs buckled, and she stumbled forward and caught herself on a chair.

"Polly!" Mallie tried to coax the cook back to her pallet. When Polly refused, Mallie stuck her head out the window and screamed for Margaret, again and again.

"Oh heavens!" Margaret rushed in, took Polly by the arms, and gently steered her toward her pallet.

"Please don't leave again, Maggie," Mallie begged.

"Don't worry, I'll be here for the rest of the day."

Mallie lay back down, reassured even as she felt a fresh fit coming on. She shivered and watched helplessly as Polly's hallucinations grew worse. At some point, completely drained, she fell asleep.

Mallie woke before sunup. Bradnox and Margaret sat next to Polly's pallet. The planter was holding the mouth of a small bottle under Polly's nostrils; she did not move. He corked the bottle, put it inside his medicine chest, and slammed the lid shut.

"I'll send Titus and Cumby," he said coldly, then stood up and walked out.

Margaret began to weep. Mallie crawled toward Polly on all fours, her heart splintering. The twilight coming in through the open window gave the scene an unreal tinge.

"Polly!" she cried. "Wake up! Yer need ter take yor medicine!" She gently shook Polly. Even through her linen shift, the cook's shoulder was unnaturally cold. Not even when she had learned her mother had died had Mallie felt as much an orphan as when she gazed into Polly's clouded, lifeless eyes.

June 5, 1730

A ghastly scream made Blair look up from the leather he was polishing. The cordwainer and the journeymen had heard it too. It seemed to have come from an upper floor.

A moment later the cordwainer's wife was in the shop, her face ashen. "Betty is having a baby."

The men looked at each other in disbelief. *When was she even with child?* Blair wondered.

"Blair, go find the midwife," Tacey Craig ordered. "She's at Arch and Third."

Blair ran the whole way. He was soon in the midwife's hall watching her hurriedly throw the disassembled parts of a birthing chair and other implements into a bag.

"I see the girl has been screaming," the midwife commented shrewdly when she and Blair arrived at the alley. A gaggle of neighbors had gathered in front of Craig's shop. At the sight of the midwife, the neighbors' chatter intensified. Blair opened the door to find Craig peeking through the window, looking annoyed. As soon as the midwife had been taken to Betty, Tacey Craig left with baby Ewan and returned with Alice, who looked utterly surprised.

"Katherine Moore will pick up the girls at school and take them to her shop," Tacey Craig said. "And she has lent us Alice for a few days."

Blair tried to focus on his work, but every so often he could hear Betty's cries and moans, and he was dying to go find Johannes.

"I ken who the father is," he finally told Craig. "Should I go get him?"

"No," Craig answered sharply. "Keep working." A couple of neighbors opened the door in the course of the morning, asking if they could help, but Craig curtly refused them.

At noon Alice came down briefly to serve Blair and the journeymen and to get a quick bite herself.

"We need tae send word tae Johannes," Blair told her.

"Aye, but I canna go now."

Betty seemed to quiet down for a while, but in the early afternoon it was evident she was again in agony. The cordwainer put down his tools in frustration.

"It's impossible to work like this," he grumbled, and stomped upstairs. As soon as his footsteps had ebbed, Blair burst out the door, broke into a run, and didn't stop until he reached the shipyard next to the Penny Pot.

"Johannes! Johannes!" he yelled, trying to be heard above the noise of the men working on the ship. A couple of men noticed him and alerted Johannes.

"Blair, what are you doing here?" he said, looking down from the quarterdeck.

"Betty's having a baby!"

Johannes climbed down and took off running, his long strides making it impossible for Blair to keep up. He reached the alley in time to see Johannes at the shop's doorstep; Craig was holding the door open, looking furious. As Blair approached, several upstairs windows began to open. Craig glanced at the neighbors peering out and reluctantly ushered

Johannes inside. As Blair followed at Johannes's heels, the bleating cries of a baby could be heard coming from the third floor.

"Jeffrey Craig, my name is Johannes Fretzel. I'm the father of Betty's baby," Johannes said as soon as Craig shut the door.

"And what is thy trade, Johannes Fretzel?"

"I work at West's shipyard."

"Thee is a freeman?"

Johannes voice dropped slightly. "No." He glanced at the stairs with impatience. "Friend, I take full responsibility for this. May I please see them?"

"No."

"Please, I'm begging you."

"I don't see why thee would want to see the baby; he'll be indentured until he turns twenty-one."

Johannes's face glowed at the news that he had a son, and then his expression turned forlorn. He fell to his knees, his usually gruff voice deflated. "I'm *begging* you."

"Blair, go get a constable," Craig ordered. "Thee should find one at the Crooked Billet."

Blair took Johannes by the elbow and gave a firm tug. Johannes didn't budge. "Johannes, please go."

"Not until I see my boy."

"I'm warning thee, I will have thee put in the stocks!" Craig threatened.

"Johannes, please!" Blair begged.

"No."

"I said go find a constable!" Craig barked.

Blair ran out the door, but as soon as he was out of the alley, he slowed down to a leisurely walk, hopeful that if he could buy some extra time, Johannes would be gone and Craig would have calmed down before he returned. But when thirty minutes later he and the constable turned the corner at Second Street, his heart sank; Johannes was sitting on the steps of the shop.

———

June 13, 1730

Standing next to the whipping post, waiting for Johannes to be untied, Blair felt as if he would empty his stomach. Johannes had been tried and found guilty of fornication. Once he was freed from his bindings, Blair and Raimond flanked him, draped his arms around their shoulders, and helped him to a cart that would take them to the shipyard. Johannes howled in pain when they hit a pothole and his back bounced against the side of the cart.

"You won't be playing at our wedding next year after all," Johannes said, and Blair nodded sadly. Betty's indenture had been extended two years and, given that Johannes didn't have money to deposit a security with the court for the maintenance of his son, his term had been extended a year. "You'll have time to learn something new. I know all of your songs by now, anyway."

Blair tried to smile. "I'll learn some German songs."

"Tell Betty I'll come by tomorrow after the Craigs have gone to meeting."

Blair discreetly studied Johannes: he was lithe and strong, and yet he seemed shriveled after the whipping. It was inconceivable that Betty would soon be subjected to the same twenty-one lashings Johannes had just received.

Blair scowled when a knock came at the door. "That had better not be Johannes," he told Alice, getting to his feet. "He's supposed to wait until the Craigs are gone." He opened the door to find a nervous-looking woman.

"Let her in quick and shut the door," Tacey Craig said, running down the stairs. "Are thee David Fisher's girl?"

"Yes."

"Come upstairs."

Blair and Alice looked at each other questioningly. They heard Betty, her tone pleading and distressed, Tacey Craig's impatient voice, and the cordwainer, commanding and unyielding. Betty's sobs intensified and then Tacey Craig and the woman, with the baby in her arms, came down again.

"Give this to thy master," Tacey Craig said, handing the woman a letter. Blair and Alice watched in shock as the woman and her delicate bundle were all but shoved out into the alley. Tacey Craig shut the door, leaned on it, and sighed with relief. Then she turned guilty eyes to Blair and Alice, who were staring at her, stone faced. "Hurry up with breakfast, Alice."

As soon as Tacey Craig was gone, Blair ran outside. The woman and the baby were getting into a cart on Second Street. He looked up and saw Betty's face pressed against the second-floor window, her face streaked with tears. Then Craig's hands clutched her shoulders and yanked her back.

Blair stood next to one of the windows on the front of the shop, once in a while pulling the curtain aside just enough to steal a nervous glance out into the alley. Johannes was sitting in one of Craig's chairs, Betty on his lap, her head on his shoulder, her hands grasping at the back of his jacket like claws. She cried as if she would never stop. Johannes rocked her and whispered soothing words in her ear. Alice sat in another chair. Both she and Blair looked dejected. It had taken several minutes to piece together Betty's frantic and disjointed account: the baby had been taken to Clearfield, the summerhouse of one of Jeffrey Craig's customers. They wouldn't even let Betty name the baby.

"I...I'm so-sor-ry..." Betty hiccupped. "I...couldn't stop..."

Johannes stroked Betty's hair. "Don't blame yourself."

I will follow Susannah's advice and be careful, Blair promised himself. For if I have a child, bastard or not, son or daughter of a whore or not, I'll kill anyone who tries to take it away. His resolve only strengthened two months later, when word came that the baby had died.

CHAPTER FOURTEEN

October 1730
One year after Mallie's and Blair's arrivals

Mallie sat at the kitchen table and pretended to work on a cross-stitching project, but her attention was really on Bradnox's newly arrived convict, who sat across from her. The man had been bought to replace Robert, who had died of the bloody flux. There was something about him Mallie did not like one bit. She glanced at Margaret, sitting to her right, and saw she did not like him either.

"I hope you like this, Ephraim." Biddy, the new cook, set a plate of boiled eggs and corn pone in the middle of the table and took a seat.

"Mr. Bradnox knows how to choose stout wenches," Ephraim said, taking an egg and studying Biddy. Under his disturbing gaze, her friendliness quickly cooled.

"The only thing on your mind should be whether you'll catch the fever and agues or the bloody flux," Margaret said as she began to peel an egg for herself.

"No disease can kill me. I survived the pox," Ephraim said, cocksure, before smacking his own pocked cheeks. He turned his attention to Mallie. "You're a runt now," he said, flashing her a smile that made her recoil. "But that'll change in a few years."

"You watch yourself," Margaret warned. Mallie stood up, placed three stones in the hearth, and went back to the table and ate her supper. When she finished eating, she used a pair of tongs to transfer the stones to a widemouthed pot, and set it on the table. Biddy held out a folded length of linen, and Mallie fished out a stone and placed it in the cloth. She handed Margaret her stone, and then walked around the table to Ephraim and reached inside the pot. As soon as she approached him, he grabbed her by the waist and pulled her close.

"Let me see those eyes," he said.

"Let her go!" Margaret cried, but the man had already wrenched his arm away from Mallie, the color drained from his face. He screamed and jerked his bare foot to one side. The hot stone that had been intended for him rolled once and settled on the earthen floor. He propped the heel of his foot on the chair and groaned; the tops of his toes were red and blistering where the rock had landed. He looked up and glared at Mallie.

"You did that on purpose, you bitch!"

"Don't touch me again," Mallie replied coolly. She set the pot by the fire, her back to Ephraim so he could not see her hands shaking.

"Well," the man was saying, "is someone going to get me an ointment or something?"

Mallie calmly headed for the door. Once she was outside, she ran all the way to Cassie's room.

Under Cassie's watchful eye, Mallie dipped her quill into the inkpot and filled the last page of her book.

"Oh dear," Cassie said, "I'll have to get you a new one."

Mallie sat back while Cassie assessed her work. Cassie placed a hand on Mallie's dust bonnet and looked at her with tenderness. "You've made wonderful strides."

Mallie smiled sadly; Polly would have been proud. She held the book in her hands, remembering how its blank pages had seemed so intimidating, its lines impossible to fill. Now, her very own handwriting filled it, cover to cover. *This is how I'll get to the end of my sentence*, she thought, *one page at a time.* She flipped to the first page and wrote: *Commonplace Book for the year 1729–1730. Malvina Ambrose.*

October 1730

Blair watched as Alice poured tallow into a pillar candle mold. "Can you pour me a wee bit o' tallow?" he asked, offering his empty pewter cup.

"Whyfore?" Alice asked.

"To amuse myself. I dinna need tae be in the shop for another half hour."

She rinsed out the cup with a small amount of water and poured about half an inch of tallow into it. When the tallow had cooled down a little, Blair scooped out a small amount with his fingers and played with it, rolling it into a ball and flattening it. He molded a cylinder, like a tiny pillar candle, and looked at it thoughtfully. He scooped out some more, took a coin from his breeches pocket, and rolled it in the tallow.

"Ye're like a bairn of ten," Alice said, chuckling.

"From now on will ye save me the tallow when ye cook my meat, and burn it tae make it black, like the ones you gave Betty when we met?" he asked.

"I can. For why do ye want it burned?"

"Tae make my own candles and use them at the shop. Jeffrey Craig will no be able tae say I'm using his."

There was a timid rap on the door, and Blair got up. When he saw who it was, he almost slammed the door shut.

"Hello, lad." Edward was smiling sheepishly. "These were left in the Penny Pot for ye. I had tae beg Susannah tae let me bring them myself."

Blair had kept his distance from Edward and William since the wharf fire and had kept quiet about what he had seen. Now, he crackled with excitement when he saw what his former friend had in hand.

"From Ireland," Edward said, handing him two letters.

"Thank ye," Blair said, taking the letters and reaching into his breeches pocket. "How much was postage?"

"It's paid."

Blair insisted but was firmly rebuffed. "I'm happy for ye, lad. I truly am," Edward said after an awkward silence. "I hope it's good news."

Blair waited for Edward to leave and then opened up his mother's letter, quivering with anticipation.

Anne McKay, Lisburn, County Antrim, Ireland
To Blair Eakins, Philadelphia, Pennsylvania
July 20, 1730

My dearest Blair,

I am the happiest mother in the world, knowing my two sons have landed safely in a land where justice and fairness will allow them to prosper as their efforts dictate. Your grandfather was blessed to read your letter before he left this world, and he and your father will now look upon you and Ronald and guard your steps.

Blair put the letter down. His sight blurred, but he suppressed the tears and continued reading.

We still await news from Ronald, but we trust you both are sitting together, reading my words. By the time you receive this letter, a year will have gone by since you left home, and only three will remain before you earn your freedom. You are daily in my prayers.

I am your loving mother,
ANNE MCKAY

He sighed. He would have to tell her the truth about Ronald. He would not, however, tell her what he sometimes feared: that the West had indeed swallowed his brother. As he stared down at the letter, a sense of unease swept over him; his mother had not mentioned Janet. He took the second letter and ran his fingers over it, chewing his lower lip. He slipped a finger under the wax seal, broke it, and unfolded the paper.

Janet Ferry, Lisburn, County Antrim, Ireland
To Blair Eakins, Philadelphia, Pennsylvania
July 21, 1730

Dear Blair,

I can barely keep my hand steady as I write this. Since the day you left, I have prayed night and day for your safe arrival, and my heart bursts with joy and gratitude knowing my prayers have been answered. Time crawls without you by my side, but scarce a handful of years is naught when I think of a lifetime as your wife. I long for the day when we never part again.

I am your faithful lass,
JANET FERRY

He pressed his knuckles over his eyes, reminding himself of the promise he had made himself aboard the *King George*: he would not cry.

PART THREE

CHAPTER FIFTEEN

September 1733

The afternoon sun glinted off the apples that Mallie had just washed in the river. She held the basket out to Margaret, Derby, Biddy, and Ellery, and then sat down next to them in the shade of a tree. Derby studied her and smiled. Under her curled, dark lashes, both her eyes glinted with gold in the autumn light. She bit into a crisp apple and smiled back. Life had settled into a predictable rhythm: Mallie now slept in the passage outside the parlor—which was now Bradnox and Cassie's room—except on Sunday nights, when she slept with Margaret and Biddy. Abigail had married Ryan Hearne and had moved to his plantation.

Derby playfully bumped his bare toes against Mallie's, and she recognized the invitation to take a walk. They followed the glimmering river until they were out of sight of the others. Mallie hiked up her skirts and waded into the river until the water reached her calves. Derby removed his shirt and dove in. "Come all the way in," he beckoned.

"I'll drown."

"I'll teach yer 'ow ter swim."

"I would need to undress, and my shift would get wet."

"I would need *to* undress, and *my* shift would get wet, *m'lord,*" he said, playfully mocking how proper her speech had become. She gave him a flustered look, and he splashed her while she screeched with laughter.

"Stop that!" She stepped out of the water, sat on the bank, and watched Derby dive and surface, again and again. He finally got out and sat next to her. She glanced at his back, which was scarred from a whipping at the hands of Jason. His neck would forever bear the marks from the irons he had worn on the ship. She lowered her gaze and noticed the outline of his member, straining against his wet breeches, and immediately jerked her head back toward the river. He leaned in and kissed her ear, his lips cool and wet. Mallie's skin tingled, but she did not budge. He took her chin in his hand, turned her face, and looked directly into her startled eyes. She placed one hand on his chest as though to push him away. He gently pressed his mouth to hers and waited. Mallie felt time stand still. At last she parted her lips and kissed him back. He slid off her cap, his fingers undid her bun, and her long hair cascaded down her shoulders, black and glossy like licorice Pontefract cakes. His fingertips grazed her scalp; blood rushed to her head, and she moaned. He laid her down, hiked up her skirts, spread her legs, and pulled down his breeches.

"No!" She pushed him away, this time forcefully.

"Mallie, please…"

"No!"

"Why?"

"I don't want to be trapped like Margaret."

"I promise I won't get yer with child."

"No."

He relented and rolled on his back, arms folded over his face. "I should go back ter me quarters," he said curtly.

"Please don't be angry with me."

She watched him walk away, her body roiling with unfamiliar sensations. Wishing to be alone, she started walking back to the kitchen, stuffing her cap in her skirt pocket. When she reached the orchard, she walked along its edge, picking up stray apples that had fallen to the ground. Suddenly, someone jumped out of the bushes from behind, seized her by the hair, and dragged her into the brush. She screamed, but the man pinned her on the ground and covered her mouth with a dirt-covered hand, pressing down so hard that her lips and gums hurt. She saw Ephraim's pocked face hovering an inch away from hers, and from her throat came a muffled cry. She jerked her head furiously left and right until her teeth found his fingers. She bit down as hard as she could and heard a rabid howl. His grip loosened and she screamed again. He punched her, sending a flash of pain through her head. Then his weight was being lifted off her, and through blurred vision she saw Derby wrestle him to the ground. Derby flipped the man onto his stomach, hooked an arm around his throat, and choked him until he went completely limp. He released him, and Ephraim's head hit the ground with a dull thud. Derby rushed to Mallie's side and knelt down at her side.

"Are yer all right?"

She buried her face in his chest, sobbing. A hacking sound made them both turn. Ephraim had come to.

"If yer ever touch 'er again, I will kill yer," Derby snarled, standing over the cowering man. He helped Mallie to her feet and joined arms with her for support. As they walked away, she turned and looked back nervously. Ephraim was still on the ground, rubbing his neck and wheezing. They had almost reached the kitchen yard when they ran into the last person she wanted to see.

"Mallie! What happened?" Bradnox stared in shock at Mallie's swollen blue and purple eye. He whirled on Derby. "Did you do this?"

"No, sir!" Derby protested.

"No, sir, it wasn't him." The irony of the planter's indignation was not lost on her.

"Who was it?" Bradnox asked, his eyes smoldering with subdued fury.

⸻

Mallie, Margaret, and Biddy stood over Ephraim's freshly covered grave in the workers' burying grounds. The planter had beaten him—with his bare hands—so badly that the man had died the next day.

"He deserved it, you hear me?" Margaret asked. Mallie nodded, but her face was tight. "He would've raped you."

"I know."

Mallie stared at the mound. In London, even as a child, she had been aware of the fact that murders were as much a part of the city as its fog. But—as far as she knew—she had never before lived in such proximity to anyone who had killed another human being. Worse—killed them with impunity. Now she knew that no matter how elegant and handsome, no matter how well spoken, compared with many of the stinking, toothless, crass men who frequented the Covent Garden brothel, Bradnox was far more dangerous.

September 24, 1733

Blair woke up bursting with joy. He would soon, at long last, be sailing to Ireland to marry Janet. He had not heard from Ronald in all these years, but he was confident his brother would keep his promise and return to Philadelphia. He combed back his hair, which now reached his shoulders, tied it with a black ribbon, put on his cap, and went downstairs to the chandler's shop.

"Good morning, Alice," he said.

"Look who's in a bright mood today!" she replied. Having finished her indenture, she was now working for the chandler for wages.

In the cordwainer's shop, Chastity, the slave girl whom Craig had bought when Betty's indenture had ended, was stoking the fire. Craig wasn't there. Blair and the journeymen, used to their boss's absence, began to work alone. It was not until after dinner that Craig came down, his face puffy and his belly like a pregnant goat's.

"I do believe there'll be days when I'll miss yer shop, Jeffrey Craig," Blair said, looking all around.

Craig looked up from the shoe he was working on. "What?"

"My indenture expires next month."

"No, it doesn't."

I must have misheard, Blair thought. "I'm sorry, what did ye say?"

"Thee is mistaken. Thy indenture doesn't expire yet."

"It does." Blair felt a pinch at the base of his neck. "It's hard tae believe four years have passed."

"Thee signed an indenture for seven."

Blair went mute for a moment. The journeymen had stopped working and were looking from Blair to Craig.

"I most certainly didna."

"I'll show thee."

Craig went upstairs and returned with the indenture. Blair's blood drained to his feet when he saw that, where it should have said *Willing to serve William Rawle or Edward Horne or his Assigns 4 Years in Philadelphia,* the number *4* had been replaced by a *7.*

"That's no what I signed," Blair said, completely bewildered.

"It's in writing."

"Ye altered it."

"That's a scandalous accusation."

"I'll go tae the mayor."

Craig cleared his throat and took back the indenture. "Thee may certainly do so."

"It was written in that book, the day ye bought me," Blair said confidently. All that was needed was to go to the courthouse and ask to see the records. And he wasn't about to wait. "I'm going now," he announced, and walked out the door.

Standing on the courthouse balcony, Blair gnawed on his thumbnail. Craig had of course followed him, indenture in hand, straight past the line of immigrants and agents waiting their turn, and up the stairs. Blair had knocked on the courtroom's door with determination and had stated his predicament with such conviction that Mayor Griffitts had sent the clerk to find the indenture book for the year 1729 right away. In the meantime, Blair and Craig had been asked to wait outside, and the mayor, Governor Gordon, and four aldermen were left to scrutinize the original indenture. Blair gazed down at a gaggle of Palatines waiting to come up and take the Oath of Allegiance to Pennsylvania.

"Blair Eakins, come inside."

Blair's insides bunched up when he turned and saw the clerk standing at the balcony door, empty-handed. Inside the courtroom, he and Craig stood side by side—Blair now a full head taller—facing the mayor, the governor, the aldermen, and a German interpreter.

"We don't see any indication that there was a *four* where there's now a *seven*," the mayor declared, returning the indenture to Craig. "Does thee have the book?" he asked the clerk.

"It was lost in a fire two years ago," the clerk replied.

Blair had not felt the ground drop under him like this since the time Janet had been raped. "Are ye sure ye looked everywhere?"

"Yes."

"I can help ye look again." Blair's eyes were wild.

Governor Gordon looked at Blair with impatience. "Our clerk has done his best, and we have work to do."

"The man who was clerk at the time might be able tae find it," Blair insisted.

"He was taken by the smallpox last year."

"What about the agent who sold me?"

"Young man, that's quite enough," Governor Gordon said, raising his voice. "It's inconceivable that William Rawle would remember, and I'm not going to inconvenience him."

"Jeffrey Craig's wife must remember!"

"Blair!" The governor slammed his hand on the desk. "We're not going to bother Tacey Craig either."

Blair's chest heaved, his breathing audible through his nose. "Am I tae remain indentured an additional three years?"

"No," the governor said, "you're not serving any *additional* time at all. This document shows you signed up for seven years, and that's what you'll serve. My clerk will make a new entry this very moment, so that three years from now there's no question about it."

"Thank thee very much for thy assistance in settling this misunderstanding," Craig said, taking Blair by the arm. "We'll leave you all to your busy day."

Blair pulled free, his face red. "I can buy that time from Jeffrey Craig."

Mayor Griffitts raised his eyebrows. "Thee has money?"

"Aye."

"How much?"

"Nine pounds." That would buy about ninety gallons of rum, or 560 pounds of muscovado sugar, which Craig's wife liked so much.

"How did thee come by this money?"

"I earned it."

"How?"

"Playing the fiddle."

"Where?"

Blair realized he had just confessed to breaking the law. The truth was, however, that everyone knew servants went to taverns, and no one could do much about it. Maybe Craig would accept the money.

"In taverns."

Mayor Griffitts turned to the cordwainer. "Jeffrey Craig, did thee know this?"

"I did not. For the past four years he's had my permission to lodge with Katherine Moore. I assumed she gave him boarding in exchange for small chores. He had assured me he was not involved in any illegal activities."

Blair's voice seethed with indignation. "I've *never* missed a day o' work."

The mayor was unmoved. "Blair Eakins, thee will not lie out anymore. All the fruits of thy labor during the time of thy indenture belong to thy master. Therefore I order thee to deliver all thy money to Jeffrey Craig."

At the chandler's shop Blair crossed his arms and ground his teeth as a constable grabbed his bag and poured its contents onto his pallet. The chandler looked on, indignation gleaming in her eyes. Craig picked up a wooden box and opened it; there was nothing inside but a few farthings and pennies, two black pillar candles whose shape left much to be desired, a comb, and writing implements. The few coins in Blair's pockets, plus the coins in the box, added up to nowhere near the money he had claimed to have.

"Mought it be he doesn't have that money?" the constable suggested.

"It could be a ruse he conjured up in his desperation," Craig conceded. He turned to the chandler. "Katherine, I thank thee for lodging him all these years. I apologize for any inconvenience."

"It's been no inconvenience at all. I wish all my boarders were as trustworthy as he."

Blair gathered his things and followed Craig, all the while suppressing an overwhelming desire to either take off running, or jump on him and vent his anger until the cordwainer was unrecognizable.

September 30, 1733

Mallie returned from the privies to the kitchen to find an angry Bradnox standing at the door.

"Come with me," he grumbled. Ever since Ephraim had attacked her, she had been spending Sundays in her quarters, mostly to avoid Derby, but now she wished she had gone to the field workers' quarters with Margaret and Biddy after all. She followed Bradnox to the hall in the main house, where Cassie waited. It was clear she had been crying, but there was something else that made her look odd. It took Mallie a moment to figure out what was different: it was her eyebrows.

"I told my wife she wasn't allowed to pluck her eyebrows," Bradnox said in a stern voice. "But she disobeyed me."

"Can't you wait until tomorrow?" Cassie asked. "It's *Sunday.*"

It took one single piercing look from Bradnox to keep Cassie from uttering anything else. Mallie groaned inwardly.

She knew what was coming. Over the years Bradnox had embraced her role as "whipping girl" with enthusiasm: whenever Cassie upset him, he would take out his anger on Mallie. Five minutes later Mallie was walking back to her quarters, her back burning with fresh marks from Bradnox's crop. She had managed not to cry, as an act of defiance.

"What's wrong, Mallie?"

She turned and saw Derby approaching. She tried to say nothing was wrong, but as soon as she tried to utter one word, she began to sob. He put an arm around her, and she hugged him tightly. He held her until she had spent all her tears. They walked to the kitchen, where he listened in livid silence, as she told him about being Cassie's whipping girl.

"Do Margaret and Biddy know?"

Mallie nodded. "I tried to hide it, but…they're not stupid, and Mr. Bradnox is not discreet."

"Yer poor, sweet girl." Derby reached out and tucked a strand of hair behind her ear. "Do yer want ter be alone?"

"No, don't go." She sat on the edge of her chair and nestled her head on Derby's shoulder while he determinedly kept his hands on his thighs. She brought her cheek to his and nuzzled against it, feeling the unfamiliar roughness. In one quick motion Derby sat her on his lap. As he looked into her eyes, she could feel her heart pumping. He kissed her, and she kissed him back. The warmth she had felt that day by the river spread through her, like water spilling over fertile soil. She ran her fingers through his hair. He picked her up and carried her upstairs.

"Which is your spot?" he panted.

He should go, she thought. "That one."

He laid her down gently and lay next to her. He slid his hand under her skirts, brushing the inside of her thigh. Her mind made a feeble attempt at being judicious and then capitulated. She was ensnared in a vortex in which she and Derby spun and tumbled. She felt so light-headed, she was certain she would pass out, but instead her senses were heightened. Derby's eyes seemed to radiate light; when his hands caressed her, she jerked as if embers grazed her skin. She felt him sliding into her, then a bite of pain that could not be pain because she craved more of it, and she wanted to cry with joy. Pain and pleasure fused and rushed through her veins and converged in one focused burst of ecstasy, catching her completely unawares.

"Are you all right?" Derby asked afterward when they were lying side by side, holding hands and catching their breath. She stared at the ceiling, deep in thought. He propped himself up on an elbow and looked into her eyes, forcing her to return his gaze.

"I think you can teach me to swim now."

His laughter echoed in her ears as her limp body succumbed to sleep. When she awoke, she found him staring at her. Startled, she tried to sit up, but he gently stopped her.

"It's all right; I've been keeping watch."

"What time is it?" she asked, alarmed.

"It's early." His hands immediately went about removing her skirts.

"Stop! What if Margaret or Biddy walk in?"

"Mallie!" he replied, playfully mimicking her tone. "Yer know that as long as 'tis light out, they'll stay out."

She could not argue. The sun was starting to set when he finally left. Perched on the window, she watched him go, her heart swelling. He looked back, a drunken and satisfied smile on his lips, and she shooed him away with a wave of her hand.

———

December 1, 1733

Blair walked into the Three Mariners Inn and approached the tavern keeper. "Has anyone collected the letter I left with ye?" he asked.

The tavern keeper reached into a basket on a counter and pulled out a folded and sealed letter; *Ronald Eakins* in Blair's handwriting was written on it. "I'm sorry, lad, no one has claimed it."

Ronald's indenture had ended more than a month earlier, and still Blair had found no word or sign from him at any of the city's taverns. He had inquired and left letters at every one of them—except the ones in Hell Town—and there were close to a hundred. He squelched a feeling of abandonment. Ronald would not disregard his promise, would he? Maybe, for some reason, he had tried to run away and had gotten more time. "Do you want to take the letter?" the tavern keeper asked.

"No. I'll leave it here."

Blair headed to the Penny Pot, trying not to entertain the thought that Ronald might have fallen victim to any one of the wilderness's many dangers. He knew, from his mother's letters, that she had not heard from Ronald either. Although Blair endeavored to sound positive when writing to her and encouraged her to keep hope, he could tell that after all these years, she had none left.

Blair sat at a table at the Penny Pot, staring impatiently at the door. At long last Johannes arrived. With him was a stocky man, a man who would show Blair how to get to Donegal. Johannes perfunctorily introduced them, and they sat down. The man pulled out a map and splayed it on the table. Blair leaned forward, eagerly scanning the paper.

"This is Philadelphia," the man said, pointing to a black dot on the lower right-hand corner of the page, with the letters *PH* next to it. Blair followed the man's index finger as he traced the paper and described the path to take: northwest about four miles to a fording spot on the Schuylkill. Just the thought of fording the river made Blair anxious, but he would have no choice: no bridges crossed the river, and although he could easily pay the ferriage fee, ferrymen were required to ask for passes in an effort to catch runaway slaves and servants. Blair paid close attention to the rest of the man's directions, then gave him some money, folded the map, and put it inside his jacket.

"If you're traveling by yourself, this isn't the season," the man warned as the tavern door opened and snowflakes blew in. "Walking over the frozen river will be easier than fording it, but you might freeze to death before you make it to Donegal."

"I understand," Blair replied. If Ronald was not back by the first sign of spring, he would go looking for him.

March 1, 1734

Over the rhythmic sound of streams of milk hitting the bottom of the pail, Mallie heard the barn door open. Her heart fluttered, and she turned, Derby's name on her lips. Disappointment stung her when she saw Bradnox. She stood and wiped her hands on her apron. "Do you need something, sir?"

"I didn't mean to kill the man. I want you to know that."

"Yes, sir," she stammered, confused. If Bradnox had a heavy conscience, wouldn't it be enough to confess to his priest? He strutted straight to Mallie and grabbed her by the waist. Her mind buzzed with alarm; he had never done such a thing.

"You're not a child anymore." His speech was slurred, and he reeked of tobacco and rum.

"Sir, please let me go!"

She tried to peel his arm off, but it was like trying to bend an iron bar. He dragged her to the rear of the barn, muffling her protests with a hand over her mouth. He pushed her down on loose piles of straw behind some bales, pinning her down under his weight. "I'm not going to hit you, and I'm not going to hurt you. Just stop fighting me. I promise I'll be kind."

She banged her fists against his solid back and shoulders until her hands hurt, then grabbed at his hair. He wrapped his fingers around her wrists; it took one single squeeze for her to release her hold. He clamped one hand around both wrists and brought them behind her head, while with the other hand he pushed her skirts out of the way. She screamed.

"Scream again, and I'll sell Derby."

She stopped fighting. She turned her head, eyes tightly shut, Bradnox's grunts and hot breath in her ear.

CHAPTER SIXTEEN

April 3, 1734

As Blair played the fiddle in the Penny Pot, he noticed a man wearing an eye patch, sitting at a table and looking at him in a strange way. When Blair decided to rest for a while and walked past him on his way to the tavern's privy, the man bluntly stared, squinting his one good eye. Blair tried to remember if he knew the man, but he was sure he did not. When he came out of the privy and was halfway to the tavern's rear door, a hand grabbed him by the shoulder, from behind, and spun him around hard. It was the man with the eye patch.

"Did you buy new clothes with my money?" the man asked, in quite an unfriendly tone.

"What?"

"Give me my money."

Blair was more perplexed by the minute. "What are ye talking about?"

"Take off your cap."

"Ye're confusing me with someone else."

"That's why I said take off your cap, to see if that's the case."

"I'm not taking off anything. I'm not who ye're looking for." *Damn it*, Blair thought, *I can't afford trouble now*. His plan was to run away in three days, and if this escalated into a full-blown fight, he might end up in jail.

The man was carefully studying Blair's face. When he reached for Blair's cap, Blair quickly grabbed the man's wrist, pulled him close, and punched him in the stomach. The man crumpled to the ground at the same time that the tavern door opened and the tavern keeper walked out.

"What's this?" the tavern keeper asked.

"This man tried to rob me!" Blair exclaimed.

"I played cards with him last night at the Bear's Inn, and he lost," the man with the eye patch said. "He owes me my winnings."

"He was here all night," the tavern keeper said.

The man stared at Blair; he didn't seem so sure anymore. "Maybe, maybe not."

"Let's say you made an honest mistake," the tavern keeper said, "and I'll let you back inside."

Blair glanced at the tavern keeper, none too happy with this arrangement.

Eye Patch smirked. "My mistake."

The tavern keeper let the man walk ahead of him and Blair, and patted Blair's back. "It'll be all right, lad."

Blair made sure to keep a constant eye on the man, and noticed the man did the same to him. After a while he realized the man was gone. When it was time to leave, he walked faster than usual and kept looking over his shoulder. At the shop he quickly bolted the door. He replayed the incident in his mind, failing to make sense of it. He had to acknowledge that as angry as the man had been, he seemed sincerely confused. Whatever the case, he hoped he did not run into him again before Saturday came.

––––––––

April 4, 1734

"That isna a fiddle; that's a cat in heat!"

Blair's right arm stopped midstroke over the fiddle's strings. *The man is back*, he thought with dismay as he turned. But what he saw was so incredibly wonderful that he was sure he was about to wake up in Craig's shop, alone in the dark. The man who had mocked him wore deerskin, moccasins, and an otter-skin hat with flaps to cover his ears, and was looking him up and down, a broad smile on his tanned face.

"Well, here dear! Where did my little brother go?" Ronald exclaimed as he took Blair by the upper arms. Blair was shocked to see he was now a good three inches taller than his older brother.

"I thought I might never see ye again," Blair stammered as the brothers hugged. Under Ronald's clothes Blair felt rock-hard muscle.

"Ye dinna look like my little brother, and ye dinna sound like him either," Ronald said.

"My brother wasna built like a bull."

"That's what wielding axes and tomahawks do tae ye." The brothers released their embrace, and Ronald looked at Blair and smiled. "Ye let yer hair grow."

"So did ye."

"Ma would disapprove."

"She would."

They found an empty table. "Ye never wrote tae Ma," Blair said, trying not to sound too accusatory.

"I did! Twice! I wrote tae ye! For all I ken, the ships sank with the letters I sent her."

Blair did not know where to begin, but once he started, he hardly took a breath. When Ronald heard their grandfather had died, he gruffly rubbed his eyes with his knuckles. When Blair told him about his encounter with Thomas Burt, Ronald's face darkened.

"The bastard sold me tae a damned Shawnee," he said, removing his hat. Blair gasped. On the right side of his brother's head, where the ear should have been, there was nothing but a thick, crooked scar. Ronald ran his fingers over the scar. "Ye should see what he did tae my body with red-hot embers." A surge of fury rushed through Blair.

"But"—Ronald took a tomahawk from his belt and placed it on the table—"I earned my freedom with one single blow." Blair stared at the tomahawk, not sure he understood. Ronald winked and smiled.

"Ye killed him?" Blair whispered.

"Aye."

The answer shocked Blair. Sure, Ronald was never going to be a model of decorum and pacifism, and Blair would not expect him to meekly take such physical abuse. But the cold, matter-of-fact attitude revealed a side of Ronald that was very disquieting. Blair was grasping for words when Susannah approached their table. She stared at Ronald, then at Blair, then back at Ronald.

"You're Blair's brother," she said confidently.

"Aye," Ronald replied, straightening his shoulders. "I'm Ronald Eakins. And who are ye, bonny lass?"

"My name is Susannah." She smiled. "Finding you is a dream come true for Blair."

It was Ronald's turn to look from Blair to Susannah. "Ye're the lass who made a man o' my brother."

"Ronald!" Blair groaned as Ronald smiled wickedly. "I'm sorry," he muttered apologetically.

"I didn't *make* him into anything," she said, looking at Ronald with such poise, he actually seemed a bit flustered. "I only discovered what he was."

"Bring us two flips, please," Blair said, eager to put an end to the topic. Once Susannah had gone, he lowered his voice. "Were ye playing cards at the Bear's Inn the night before last?"

"How do ye ken?"

"A very angry man was here last night. He thought I was ye, and he wanted his money."

"He cheated."

"I had tae punch him."

"Good!" Ronald laughed.

Blair sighed, but he laughed too. Then he became serious again. "For why weren't ye arrested for—the Shawnee?"

"I've told no one. People die and disappear on the frontier all the time, and the authorities dinna care about going after white men over dead Indians. But I dinna like tempting fate either, so I went tae Donegal looking for Joseph Shipboy; he had moved tae Pextang. Ye should see the frontier, Blair! It's full of our countrymen."

"What have ye been doing since ye've been without a master?"

"I work with men who trade with the cursed Delawares, Shawnee, and other Indians."

"The *cursed* Delawares? Ye dislike the Delawares? Why? They're peaceful."

Ronald leaned in. "Damn the peaceful Delawares. I had built a log cabin, cleared a good patch of idle land not far from Donegal, and last year Governor Gordon and James Logan—that lackey of the Penn family—evicted me and burned down my cabin and those of many others, all because the Delawares claimed those were their lands! Weel, if I canna take 'their' lands, I'll take their furs. The minister at the Donegal church reminds his congregation of Joshua's command: *utterly exterminate the inhabitants of the land.* Havena ye heard the same here?"

Blair nodded, frowning.

"What do ye think they mean?" Ronald asked.

"I thought Reverend Andrews was just teaching us history."

"I imagine I'm making history, then." Ronald shook his head and smiled. "I canna believe we're reunited."

Blair smiled too; it was wonderful. "Two days from now ye wouldna have found me. I was running away tae look for ye."

"Ye were *running away*? Ye havena finished yer time?"

The word sat on Blair's tongue like a chunk of iron. "No."

"Why? How long after we arrived were ye bought?"

As Blair explained what happened, Ronald's face turned redder and redder under his tan. "Damned Quakers!" he exclaimed. Blair could see his mind was racing. "This morning I traded furs and skins for merchandise and rum. I need tae leave tomorrow tae meet a trader called Peter Cheaver, not far from Nutimus's town, the Indian village. There we'll meet a band o' Delawares and trade with them. Ye're coming with me."

"See ye tomorrow evening at Pegg's Run, at the York Road," Ronald whispered, standing on the steps of Craig's shop. It was growing dark, and one by one the alley's windows were beginning to glow with candlelight. Blair hugged his brother, walked into the shop, and looked out the window just in time to see Ronald spit purposefully on the steps before walking away.

April 5, 1734

Mallie dashed through the kitchen yard, her hand clasped to her mouth. Unable to contain herself, she threw up a few feet before reaching the privies. She spat, wiped her mouth, and slowly straightened herself. So far she had been able to hide her morning sickness from Margaret and Biddy, but they were bound to notice, and she would eventually show. She slipped her hand into her pocket and felt the same type of seeds Polly had taken years before. After burying the vomit with a spade, she headed back to the kitchen.

"You're very quiet, Mallie," Margaret observed during supper. "Are you all right?"

"Yes. I was remembering Polly."

As soon as Margaret and Biddy went out to the privies, Mallie took out the seeds. She was studying them—wondering how many to take—when the door opened.

"Wot are yer doing?" Derby asked, smiling. Mallie closed her fist and let it fall to her side.

"What are you doing here at this time?" she asked, feigning worry. "You'll be punished if they find you here."

"No, I won't. The bell 'as been rung. Wot's in yor 'and?"

"Nothing."

"Mallie, I was watching yer through the window."

"Margaret and Biddy will be back soon."

Derby cocked his head at Mallie's odd behavior. She retched.

"Mallie!" Derby exclaimed, closing his fingers around her elbow. "Are yer sick?"

She retched again, more violently, and the seeds fell from her hand. Derby picked them up and stared at them. "Ye're childing," he finally said.

She held out her palm. "Give them back."

"I know what this is. Where did yer get them?"

"Give them back."

"*No.* 'Tis our baby."

Oh, Derby, Derby, she wanted to say, *it might not be your baby at all.* Not content with raping her once, Bradnox had sought her out regularly, and she had no choice but to submit. But she would die before Derby found out. "If I have a baby," she tried to reason, "I won't have the heart to leave when my time ends, and I don't want a child of mine to be Mr. Bradnox's property."

With his free hand Derby took Mallie's and looked intently into her eyes. "I'll talk ter 'im. I'll offer ter stay two more years in exchange for our baby's freedom. When ye finish yor time, ye'll take the babe; when I finish mine, I'll join yer."

"You'll be whipped."

"I don't care."

Mallie groaned at his stubbornness. If only she could be assured his plan would work as he envisioned it, she might acquiesce. "I'll be whipped," she said, certain Derby would prefer anything over that.

"I'll ask ter take yor punishment."

She choked up, moved by his love. *Well*, she told herself, desperately grasping at any sliver of hope, *the baby will look like either Derby, or me, or Mr. Bradnox*. She and Derby made two, two was more than one, and she somehow knew this was good.

"Please," Derby begged. Mallie finally nodded. He threw the seeds into the fire as another bout of nausea struck her.

April 5, 1734

"Who were thee talking to last night?" Craig asked Blair the following morning before the journeymen arrived. Blair winced. The cordwainer must have been looking at him and Ronald through the busybody.

"That's my brother," he replied. "I hadna seen him in four years."

"It's good to reunite with family. Does he live in the city?"

"No," Blair said, growing nervous. "But he'll visit often from now on."

Craig approached a wall on which hung a couple of tanned hides. He looked at them for a moment and said, "I need thee to go to the tanner's."

When Blair returned with the new hides, the journeymen were busy working, but Craig was gone. Two hours later, when he returned, he sent Blair to the blacksmith's. As Blair walked down the street, an uneasy feeling crept over him, but he told himself he was fretting too much.

"Jeffrey Craig sent me for two of his knives," he said upon arriving at the blacksmith's shop. When the blacksmith's apprentice approached him and stood much too close, Blair frowned and stepped away.

"I'm sorry about this," the blacksmith said, "but you're having an iron collar fitted."

"What?"

"Your master believes you're running away, so he got a court order, which I have to follow."

Blair tried to push past the apprentice, but the black-smith's iron-hard hands clenched his shoulders. "Don't resist. If I have to tie you up like a hog, I will."

An hour later, an enraged and humiliated Blair was being escorted back to the alley. In the end, it *had* been necessary to tie him down and even gag him, as he had almost bitten off one of the apprentice's fingers. The blacksmith had fashioned two semicircles of three-quarter-inch round forged iron, each with a bladelike projection made according to the length of Blair's shoulders. The semicircles enclosed his neck and were riveted, and the blades rested on his collarbones.

"Is that Blair?" he heard someone say as the blacksmith escorted him back to the shop. He lowered his head as much as the collar would allow, keeping his eyes down, and walked faster.

"Let's be jovial, fill our glasses, madness 'tis for us to think, how the world is ruled by asses and the wise are swayed by chink! Fa-la-ra, fa-la-ra!" A group of young men announced their presence in the street by singing at the top of their lungs. Blair pressed his back against a brick wall, his bag clutched in one hand. He had waited until everyone at the shop had fallen asleep and then had sneaked out. He was not headed for Pegg's Run, however. He did not want to travel for miles on busy paths wearing an iron collar, not knowing when he'd find someone who would remove it. He had also discovered that the bladelike projections on the collar made it extremely uncomfortable to lie down.

He waited, listening as the singing faded away. He turned the corner and almost ran into one of the revelers who had fallen behind. The man stared at Blair.

"'Scuse me," the man muttered, and he sidestepped Blair, tottering in admirable defiance of the law of gravity. Blair ran and was soon standing at the door of a house. The inhabitants should be up after their first sleep. Blair knocked and waited. A muffled male voice came through the door.

"Who there?"

"Blair Eakins. I'm looking for Flora and Abraham."

After several tense seconds, the door opened a crack. Then an arm shot through, and Blair was pulled inside. Abraham bolted the door again and walked to the fireplace to stand next to Flora. Another black couple had also gotten up from their chairs around the fire. Everyone stared at Blair in disbelief. Now—facing Groom's servant and her husband, and the additional couple he had not expected—he almost wished he had gone directly to Ronald.

"Flora, I need yer help, please. Abraham…" The words choked him. "Can ye remove it?" Abraham looked at Flora, and she nodded. "I can pay ye," Blair said, setting his bag on the floor and taking out his wooden box.

"No," Abraham replied categorically. "I take no money."

"Please, ye should be paid." When Blair opened the box and looked inside, he froze. The map showing the way to Donegal wasn't there.

"No," Abraham said.

Blair shut the box and put it back in the bag. He couldn't worry about the map just now. He swallowed hard, ashamed. "Awricht."

Abraham turned to the other black man, who nodded knowingly and took a candlestick. Blair followed them out the rear into a small shop. Abraham pulled a stool next to a post vise, a couple of feet behind it, and took a hammer and chisel. "Sit," he said. Blair looked warily at the tools in Abraham's hands. "Don't worry," Abraham reassured him. "We do this many times."

Blair gulped and bent at the waist, and Abraham's friend repositioned the stool so that one of the collar's projections could slide between the vise's jaws. The man then tightened the jaws shut. Blair felt the man's hands firmly holding his head and the collar pressing on the nape of his neck as Abraham positioned the chisel on the rivet. He held his knees in his hands and tensed.

"One, two, three…"

Blair grunted and braced himself as the collar bore down painfully on his neck. Metal clanged against metal. Abraham struck a second time, then a third, and Blair heard the broken rivet clatter to the floor. Abraham opened the collar and removed it.

"Thank ye!" Blair exclaimed, jumping to his feet. Back in the house, he turned to Abraham. Never had he felt so humbled. "Please forgive me. It's been a long time since ye asked me tae play at yer wedding. I was petty and...envious. Flora, forgive me. Ye could have turned me away, and I dinna deserve yer generosity. Thank ye all."

Flora smiled sadly and understandingly. "All is forgiven."

"Go, before Craig know you missing," Abraham said, and he handed Blair the collar and broken rivet. "Throw this in a river."

Blair ran faster than he ever had. He should have reached the fording spot seven hours earlier, and he could only hope Ronald would still be waiting.

April 6, 1734

"By God, I was afeared ye wouldna come!" Ronald exclaimed. Behind him, a black saddle mare and six packhorses were grazing.

"I was delayed." Blair held up the disassembled iron collar.

Ronald's nostrils flared in anger. He grabbed the collar from Blair's hand and heaved it into the river. "This will go much better around yer neck." He pulled a leather necklace from which hung a sheathed knife over his head and pushed it into Blair's hand. "It's yers tae keep." The blade was roughly five inches long, attached to a horn handle, and its leather sheath was beautifully adorned with red, yellow, and blue quill-work, a thong attached to both upper corners.

"Never travel without at least a knife." Ronald nimbly mounted the saddle mare, and Blair mounted up behind him. He had not ridden a horse since their arrival in Philadelphia. "The horses are Peter Cheaver's, but I'll have my own soon; *we'll* have our own soon. This is mine, though," Ronald said proudly, patting a long gun in the mare's saddle sling. "And this is the powder." He pointed to a polished animal's horn that was slung over his shoulder. Blair felt elated when the pack string finally started moving. They crossed Pegg's Run, then Cohocksink Creek. They spoke very little; when they did, they whispered.

"Isna giving rum tae Indians illegal?" Blair ventured.

"Aye, but Governor Gordon will never enforce *those* laws," Ronald scoffed. "He will no allow something like the law tae get in the way of his profits."

Every hour or so they would stop and let the horses graze. They passed Germantown and rode through densely wooded areas, crossing stream after stream. They reached Sandy Run when the sun came out, and began to encounter other travel-ers. Blair hid his face behind Ronald's back and pretended to sleep, sure that anyone looking into his eyes would recognize him. The sun was directly above them when they set up camp a distance from the main path. Blair slid off the horse with a groan and crumpled on the ground, his legs cramped and sore. Ronald laughed and practically jumped off his mount.

"I'll stand guard while ye sleep," Ronald said, spreading a blanket on the ground.

While his brother hobbled the horses, Blair carefully searched his bag. The map was nowhere to be found. He replayed the day, starting when Craig had asked him about Ronald. The more he thought about it, the more certain he felt that Craig had rummaged through his belongings while he had gone to the tanner's and had found the map. Maybe he had not only seen him talking to Ronald; if his window was open, he might have heard what Ronald said. Well, it didn't matter. Blair had managed to get away. With his brother standing guard a few feet away, he sank into an easy, smooth sleep. When the last of the sunlight had drained away, they took to the path again. They stopped at midnight, and Blair took the first watch. Ronald was snoring when a branch snapped somewhere to Blair's right. His hand flew to his neck knife and unsheathed it.

"Ronald!" he yelled.

A dark shape lunged at him, and he lost his grip on the knife. The attacker sat on his chest, his considerable weight crushing his lungs. Gasping, he wrapped his hands around the man's neck and extended his arms as far as they would go. Blair's face was now out of the man's reach, so the man resorted to pounding his fists against Blair's arms. Blair squeezed with all his might and resisted the pummeling.

"Let him go, Blair!" Ronald yelled. The man had stopped throwing punches; his hands feebly plucked at Blair's fingers. "That's Peter Cheaver!"

Blair released his grip and the man fell onto his side, wheezing.

"I wasna expecting tae find ye for another fifteen miles," Ronald said, helping the man sit up.

"I recognized my horses," Cheaver said with a strangled voice, "but your head was under the blanket, and I didn't recognize the watchman."

"This is my little brother I told ye about. Ye almost killed him," Ronald said, turning to Blair, half in disbelief, half in admiration. Blair rubbed his aching arms, ignoring the compliment.

It was noon the following day when Blair and Ronald reached a clearing where a group of eight Delaware men sat around a campfire, a delicious scent of roasting meat wafting in the air. Cheaver had stayed behind, having downed quite a bit of rum the previous night, and there was no rousing him. "He'll catch up soon enough," Ronald had assured Blair. "*Hè! Kulamàlsihëmo hach?*" he called out, raising his hand.

"*Nulamàlsihëna,*" replied one of the Delawares. Ronald introduced Blair, and then they unloaded the wares and displayed them on the ground: blankets, metal cooking pots, beads, and a cask of rum. Ronald inspected the Indians' deerskins and fox and otter furs, and then he and Blair sat by the campfire. They partook of the meat while Ronald and the men chatted rather amicably, half in English, half in Lenape.

Suddenly, two Indians emerged from the woods, bows and quivers at their backs, one of them holding a tomahawk, their eyes hard and their jaws set. The one without the tomahawk angrily addressed the Indians sitting around the campfire. Ronald mouthed a curse and quickly stood up. Blair jumped to his feet, as did the Delawares.

"Cheaver!" the man with the tomahawk cried out, pointing at the horses and the cask of rum. "Break law, again. Eakins"—he pointed at Ronald—"no trade license." He marched resolutely toward the cask.

"Don't you dare stave it, Gray Wolf!" Cheaver emerged from the woods, pistol in hand. Gray Wolf stopped in his tracks. With the tomahawk still poised to strike, he glared at Cheaver, then Ronald, and finally Blair, who slid the neck knife from its sheath, his hand trembling.

"Step out of the way of this peaceful commerce, or you'll force me to act unpeaceful-like," Cheaver warned.

One of the Indians who had brought the furs addressed Gray Wolf urgently, in a clear attempt to defuse the situation. In turn, Gray Wolf beseeched the band. One of the Delawares from the first group, looking ashamed, broke off, picked up a number of furs—his share of the merchandise—and stood next to Gray Wolf. Gray Wolf waited for a moment; when it became clear no one else would join him, he disappeared into the thick woods, followed by his companion and the one convert. Blair slid the knife back into its sheath and wiped his sweaty hands on his breeches.

"We can celebrate now," Cheaver said, opening up the cask himself. He poured rum into tankards and passed them around while Ronald retrieved a jug of whiskey.

"Are ye all right?" Ronald asked when they were all seated around the fire. Blair snatched the jug and took two huge pulls, the jug shaking in his hand. "They wouldna have attacked us," Ronald said reassuringly. "Years ago, the Iroquois declared the Delawares to be 'as women,' and they're no allowed tae fight."

Copious amounts of meat and rum calmed Blair. Strangely, Ronald and Cheaver drank rather moderately while regaling the Delawares with a series of greatly embellished stories of their adventures, supplemented with pantomime. A Delaware approached Blair and, smiling, pointed at his neck knife. Blair removed it and handed it to the man, who studied the quillwork with approval before returning it. Soon, the Delawares' cheerful demeanor morphed and soured. When two of them got into a heated argument, Ronald and Cheaver stood up.

"Let's go," Ronald said. "Time tae keep our distance."

Blair looked back one last time. The two Delawares were now rolling on the ground, going at each other like rabid dogs.

Astride a horse, behind Ronald, Blair felt like a six-year-old who had disappointed his big brother. The previous night, after the Delaware had handed back his neck knife, Blair had set it at his feet and forgotten about it. Now, the brothers had to retrace five miles while Cheaver waited, and it was evident Ronald was annoyed. When they reached the Indian campsite, Blair could not believe the pathetic picture before his eyes: the men were sprawled on the ground, every single one bruised and bloodied, the acrid smell of vomit heavy in the air. He scanned the ground with urgency. "Oh, thank God, here it is," he said, picking up the knife.

"Dinna dare lose it again," Ronald scolded. He looked at the drunken men with a sneer. "Believe it or no, if we waited for them tae wake up, they'd exchange their clothes for more rum. But that wouldna be treating them fair, would it?"

Blair glanced at the blankets and cooking pots and empty cask. Nothing about this seemed fair to him.

"Once we trade our remaining goods, I'll return tae Philadelphia with the furs," Ronald said as they headed back. "Ye'll go with Cheaver tae Donegal, and we'll meet there. Then ye and I alone will head west o' the Alleghenies." He snatched Blair's cap from his head and ruffled his hair, the way he used to back home. Blair took his cap back glumly. He did not share his brother's excitement. *Going west of the Alleghenies is against the law*, he wanted to say, but he knew it would be useless, and he did not want to be thought a coward.

"Peter and I could lend ye the money for Janet's passage," Ronald said.

Blair was deeply touched. But it was precisely the thought of Janet that made him wonder now if running away had been such a good idea. Given that he could not set foot in Philadelphia, she would have to travel by herself, and Blair could not imagine her braving such a journey on her own. Maybe he could sneak out and back in through a different port. But he did not want to *sneak* at all; he wanted to travel as a *free man*. Assuming he could get her to Pennsylvania, what then? She certainly could not go trading, so she would have to stay in Donegal or Pextang. After having her wait patiently all these years, was he to dump her for weeks or months at a stretch? He would forever be a runaway. Forever looking over his shoulder. Craig, unlike Ronald's last master, was a

Quaker, not a dead Indian, and Blair's indenture increased with every passing day. Back at their campsite, over breakfast, Blair summoned the courage to talk to his brother.

"Ronald," he finally said, "I need tae talk tae ye, privately." They walked until they were out of Cheaver's sight. Blair had a hard time holding his brother's gaze. "I'm going back tae Philadelphia."

Ronald shook his head, as if trying to clear his ears of an obstruction. "Why would ye want tae go back?"

"What sort o' life can I offer Janet if I'm a runaway?"

"I wilna let ye go back."

"Ye *what?*"

"What kept me going all these years was the promise we made tae each other! *Nothing* was more important tae me than tae find ye. We were supposed tae stay together."

"I'm no free yet tae keep my promise."

"Ye did yer time; ye should be free!"

"God's curse, how the damned hell do ye think I feel? I'm rippin' mad at that bastard, lying chancer!"

Ronald was taken aback. "Ye never cursed like this."

"Ye said ye'll be back in Philadelphia when ye've traded yer goods. I'll see ye then," Blair said with a conciliatory tone. "And every time ye return with furs."

After a very long pause, Ronald said, "Will ye promise tae join me when ye've finished yer time?"

"Aye."

Ronald thought for a moment before speaking. "I'll let ye go. Ye'll have tae walk, though."

"Thank ye for finding me." Blair pulled Ronald to him. He could feel his brother resisting the embrace, his muscles twitching with frustration, but he knew the next time they met, Ronald would greet him with a big smile.

CHAPTER SEVENTEEN

April 12, 1734

Blair was seriously wondering if returning had been one big mistake. He had been fitted with a new collar, but this was much worse: attached perpendicularly to the collar, at the nape of the neck, was a fifteen-inch-long strip of iron, about an inch thick, with a curled tip from which hung a bell above Blair's head. Every time he moved, the bell clanged.

"Dinna beat me, Jeffrey Craig," he had warned upon his return when the cordwainer had threatened to use the stirrup. "I'll continue working in spite o' the fact that ye and I ken the truth. But if ye dare touch me, I swear I wilna work at all."

Whether it was to vent his anger or to assert his authority, Craig had gone ahead with the punishment. Two of his journeymen had reluctantly held Blair down; it had taken all their strength to keep him from bolting. The pain had been excruciating, as Craig had struck him with the stirrup's metal buckle. Afterward, frothing with fury, Blair had refused to work. Craig had threatened to put him again in an iron collar. Blair held firm, and Craig had fulfilled his threat. The collar was a miserable thing to wear in the daytime, and much worse at night, but still Blair would not yield. Craig had even threatened to go to Mayor Griffitts, to no avail. The cordwainer had finally given up and advertised Blair for sale. Several cordwainers had immediately offered to buy him, but Craig had refused; he would not hand him over to his competitors.

"He had them in a stretcher, Mr. Chisholm," Blair said when a customer came in to try on his new shoes. "Tomorrow morning they'll have shrunk."

"Ignore him—he's nothing but a rascal," Craig snapped. "The sooner I sell him, the better."

"It's only this master that I refuse tae work for." Blair shifted again. *Clang, clang, clang.*

"How much time does he have?" Chisholm asked.

"Considering the added time for running away, two years and eight months. You can have him for six pounds."

"Well, if I can break in these shoes, I'm certain I can break any pigheaded servant. I'll take him."

Blair heard the screams half a block before he and Chisholm reached the ropewalk. A worker came running toward them.

"Mr. Chisholm! Doyle fell into the kettle!"

Blair followed the men to a large wooden structure. Inside, surrounded by workers, a man lay on the floor, moaning, his head, neck, upper torso and arms thick with black tar. The crowd parted to let Chisholm through.

"How the bloody hell did this happen?" Chisholm asked.

"We were laying down a new bridge." The worker gestured toward an oak plank, half of it covered in tar and lying on the ground next to a huge kettle encased in brickwork.

"He was talking to me, and then he swooned and ended up draped over the rim."

The injured man was hoisted onto a piece of canvas, and four men carried him away.

"Have Blair tar with you," Chisholm ordered.

"Why not Tom? Blair doesn't know anything about tarring." Blair glanced nervously at the tar kettle.

"Teach him. Everyone back to work!"

"I've often heard ye play," the worker said when they were alone. "My name is Edan Campbell. Are ye running away again?"

"No."

"That's a shame. I was hoping we could run away together. I'll fetch another bridge. Leave yer things in that corner for now." Edan dragged the plank away and returned with a new one. "Grab that end and help me lay it over the mouth o' the kettle. That's the step," he said, pointing to another plank attached to a tackle and hanging vertically from the ceiling above the kettle. Blair paid close attention as Edan described how they would dip the 160-fathom haul of yarn in the tar and thread it through a "nipper" on the wall to be wound to a capstan outside. Through another wide opening in the structure, Blair saw four men leaning on the four poles of the capstan, waiting. Edan's explanation seemed to go on and on.

"Mind yer fingers and hands," Edan warned when he finished the lecture. "I'd hate it if ye could never play the fiddle again. Questions?"

Blair wiped his hands on his vest, the spicy scent of tar tickling the lining of his nose. "No."

A cacophony of snoring, coughing, and farting rose from about fifteen dark lumps surrounding Blair. He stared into the darkness of the workers' sleeping quarters, absentmindedly picking at the mat under him with thumb and forefinger, his belongings nestled between his left arm and flank. His clothes and hair reeked of tar. While he tried to push it away, one thought kept flashing through his mind: he had to write to his mother and Janet. *I hope Janet has enough patience and love left to wait for me*, he thought anxiously.

The following evening he went to Groom's house. "I would be verra grateful if I could leave my belongings with ye for safekeeping. I'm afeared something—or everything—is bound tae be stolen in the ropewalk quarters."

"I'll be happy to. Let's go to my desk; we'll make a list of everything, and you'll keep the list."

Groom sat at his desk, and Blair took out of his worn bag three large black pillar candles, a wooden box that contained a comb, his ink pot, sealing wax, two quills, a penknife, the neck knife, and his mother's and Janet's letters.

"The only thing of value is the neck knife," he said. "My brother gave it tae me. I'll keep the comb, and I need my writing implements tae write home tonight, but may I bring them back tomorrow?"

"You may use my desk before you leave, if you wish; it'll be more comfortable than your quarters."

Blair agreed once Groom accepted payment for his paper.

"Will you continue to play for me?" Groom asked when Blair was ready to go.

"I would like that verra much. But if ye asked me tae play today," Blair said, rolling his sore shoulders back and forth, "I dinna think I would even manage tae hold up the violin."

June 16, 1734

"Andrew, Mallie's with child," Cassie said.

Bradnox looked up from his desk, his chest tightening. Of course she was. It had been obvious for at least two weeks, but he wasn't about to be the first to point it out. "Is she?"

"You men! If I hadn't told you *I* had conceived, you would've found out the day I delivered." Cassie patted her abdomen, which at eight weeks was barely noticeable.

"Do you know who the father might be?" Bradnox asked.

"I have no idea. But we must find out and punish him."

"You realize she's to be punished too."

Cassie looked anguished. "I know."

"We'll question her, then. It could be someone from another plantation."

"Mr. Bradnox?" The planter and Cassie turned at the sound of Mallie's voice. She and Derby stood in the open door. "May we come in?"

"We have something ter tell," Derby said as he and Mallie entered. Mallie kept her gaze down, unable to even glimpse at Cassie. She knew how much this woman loved Bradnox, and she felt as much embarrassed and guilty as she felt angry and impotent.

"Go ahead," the planter said, intrigued.

"I'm the father of the baby Mallie's carrying. Don't waste yor time with the commissioner requesting permission for me whipping. I'll submit ter the thirty-six lashings."

"Very well," Bradnox said, unmoved.

"And I wish ter receive Mallie's lashings."

Mallie scowled at Derby, but he kept his eyes on the planter. Bradnox was speechless for a moment. "I'll think about it," he said at last.

"Sir," Mallie said, "if you please, I'll take my own punishment."

"Sir, please don't…"

"I said *I'll think about it*," Bradnox snapped.

"Yes, sir. I have only one small request," Derby continued. Bradnox raised an eyebrow, turning to Cassie as if to say, *The nerve of some convicts*. "I'd like ter offer two years beyond me term, in exchange for the baby's freedom."

Bradnox crossed his arms and leaned back in his chair, thoughtfully looking from Mallie to Derby. "Yes."

The answer was so unexpected that Mallie blurted out, "What?" She looked at Cassie, who was smiling, her eyes brimming with tears, moved by her husband's generosity.

"Thank yer, sir," Derby gushed. "God bless yer."

Bradnox looked out the window. "I'll give instructions to have the workers gather at the post tomorrow after work."

"I'll tell Jason meself, sir."

"See you tomorrow, then."

Derby walked out, but Mallie remained where she stood.

"Mallie, I think you should thank Mr. Bradnox," Cassie said.

Mallie glared at Bradnox. No two words had ever been harder for her to utter.

"Thank you." Her voice was flat, but her eyes smoldered. She turned and walked out.

December 4, 1734

Mallie lay on her back on the floor of the women's quarters, her knees bent and spread apart, her face flushed and glistening with sweat. A blanket was rolled up behind her head, and a sheet covered her naked body. Margaret knelt between her legs while Biddy sat behind her head.

"I can see its head!" Margaret exclaimed. Mallie felt like her insides were being ripped apart. "Keep pushing, luv."

After one last agonizing surge of pain, Mallie heard the staccato cries of a baby.

"It's a girl!" Margaret held up the tiny, blood-and-slime-covered body while Biddy wiped the sweat from Mallie's face, then washed the baby and placed it on Mallie's chest. Mallie looked down at her daughter, studying her features, but the baby still didn't look like anyone. Mallie was overwhelmed by the love she felt for this little creature.

"I want to name her Polly," she said. Margaret smiled and nodded.

The heart-wrenching sounds of a field hand being whipped blew in through the open window. Mallie turned her head and saw, on the table, the coiled basket Rhoda had given Margaret the day she left.

———

Two weeks later Margaret was trying to keep her trembling fingers steady as she untied the back laces on Mallie's shift. Not only had Bradnox decided not to allow Derby to take her punishment, but he would whip her himself. Jason had his flintlock pistol in hand and kept a watchful eye on Derby, whose veins bulged in his forehead, his nostrils flaring and his chest heaving. Bradnox had given Derby permission to remain in the men's quarters during the whipping, but he had chosen to stay.

Mallie wrapped her arms around the post, and Titus tied her hands. He placed a strip of leather between her teeth. "I'm sorry, pretty girl," he whispered. She leaned her forehead on the post and closed her eyes. In the past, Bradnox had hit her with a bucking paddle or crop for a myriad of imputed faults, both hers and Cassie's, but never once had he flogged her. She had been telling herself all day long that this would be over in one short minute, but now, the anticipation drowned any rational thoughts she had tried to comfort herself with. She heard the gravel crunching beneath Bradnox's leather soles as he approached; each passing second stretched terribly. She breathed in, out, in, out, her nerves hissing until she wanted to yell out, begging for mercy or for the punishment to begin already.

The first blow landed, carving deep into her skin, the pain scorching like a thick stream of boiling oil splashed across her back. Her head snapped back, her hands pulled against her restraints, and she heard a feral wailing pulsate from her throat. The sizzling agony had just reached its peak when Bradnox delivered the next blow. When it finally ended, she knew so only because Titus was untying her abraded wrists.

Margaret and Derby helped her to the women's quarters and gently laid her down on her stomach. Derby sat on the floor, caressing her hair, his face blanched but his eyes dry. Not until he was alone—in the farthest edges of a fallow field—would he allow himself to weep with rage.

"Give her to me," Mallie said to Biddy in a weak voice when the baby began to fuss. "She's hungry."

Derby helped her sit up and caressed the baby's downy brown hair as she suckled.

"She's beautiful," he said.

Mallie looked at the baby's placid face. *Please, Little Pol,* she secretly implored, *please look like me.*

December 28, 1734

"Thank ye, Mr. Bradford." Blair's heart kicked in his chest like a bucking colt as he paid the postmaster and took the letter. Out on the street he stared at his name in Janet's handwriting. He felt at once excited and afraid. He broke the seal and held the paper tight against a cold gust of wind.

Janet Ferry, Lisburn, County Antrim, Ireland
To Blair Eakins, Philadelphia, Pennsylvania
October 7, 1734

Dearest Blair,

We all feel wretched to hear of such an injustice done to you, and we pray that somehow this wrong might yet be righted. Still, nothing has made your mother happier than to know her two sons have finally found each other. Blair, I've missed you so. There was nothing in the world I wanted more than for us to be together. When you asked that I wait, the only answer I could give was yes. For four years I drew strength from the knowledge that the fulfillment of all my hopes was inexorably approaching. Now I must ask for your forgiveness, for I'm not as strong as you deserve. This loneliness and constant longing weakened me, and my heart cries out for a home of my own. Someone has remained steady in offering such a home and a hand to hold. It's only right that you know this from me: I've accepted to marry your cousin Gilroy. He's a good man, and he's kind to me. We're to be married 16 November. Please remember me with joy, and keep me in your prayers. I shall never forget you, and I desire nothing more than your happiness.

Blair clenched his jaw and crumpled the paper. *She's been married for six weeks.* During a past winter, the temperature had dropped so much in Philadelphia that trees along the Schuylkill had snapped like pencils, the exploding sound traveling through the cold air all the way to the city. That was how Blair's heart felt. But he could not blame Janet.

She had kept her promise, and he had not. He tossed the letter on the snow, pulled his jacket close about him, and headed back to the ropewalk.

CHAPTER EIGHTEEN

July 1, 1736

Mallie walked into the milk house with a bucket of fresh milk. Once she had shut the door, she poured the milk into a shallow lead pan. She was going to set it down on a shelf when she noticed a dish containing some cream cheese that Cassie had begun working on three days before, sitting too close to the edge of the shelf. She carefully moved it until it touched the brick wall, and then placed the lead pan with milk next to it.

She stepped out of the coolness of the milk house into the drenching heat of the Maryland summer. On a blanket, in a shady spot in the kitchen yard, Biddy watched over Little Polly and Cassie's daughter. The girls hugged each other, squealing with joy. At that moment, Cassie emerged from the main house, her belly quite large again. She walked toward the little girls, unsmiling, and avoided so much as glancing at Mallie. Both mothers knew what was evident to all but no one dared point out: the girls, born two months apart, were so similar, they could be twins. Both had Bradnox's coffee hair, olive eyes, and shapely mouth.

"Annie," Cassie called, "let's go inside."

"No, Mama!" The girl hugged Little Polly even tighter. Cassie unceremoniously separated the girls and picked up her daughter.

Mallie's daughter cried out, "Papa!"

Mallie felt a chill when she turned and saw Bradnox and Derby approaching, Derby pushing a wheelbarrow with a freshly butchered and dressed hog. The planter walked past Little Polly and gave his wife and daughter a quick kiss. Cassie received the kiss with a blank expression, her cheeks flushed. Little Polly had crawled to Derby and grabbed his breeches with her little hands.

"Not now, Pol," he said with a hard voice.

Mallie pulled her away. "Papa's busy, luv."

"Salt this hog," Bradnox ordered Mallie. "Next week my sister and her husband and Mrs. Bradnox's mother will visit us for a few days, and I want this to be ready by then."

Mallie followed the planter and Derby to the kitchen. Bradnox set the meat on the table and walked out.

"Can yer give me some salt?" Derby asked, pointing to the bags lined up on a wall. "We've run out, and Jason won't give us more."

"Will you spend some time with Pol tonight?" Mallie asked while she filled a linen pouch. Little Polly was again clinging to Derby's breeches, looking up at him, trying to get his attention with babbling sounds. "She keeps asking for you."

"Don't ask me ter do that."

"Please, the babe is innocent."

"Yer should've told me. I would've protected yer."

"How?"

"We would've run away."

Mallie shook her head in frustration. "Don't punish her for what happened to me."

"I can't punish a child that ain't mine."

Mallie cringed. She handed him the salt and rested her hands and forehead on his chest, her shoulders shaking while Derby's arms hung limp by his sides. "I'm sorry," she whispered, but even if he forgave her, she would never forgive herself for having allowed him to be whipped and for having cost him two years of his freedom. As soon as it had been abundantly clear to him that he was not the father, he had asked Bradnox to rescind their agreement. Bradnox had insisted with a straight face that the girl was undoubtedly Derby's.

Derby stepped back, and Little Polly protested when he plucked her hands from his breeches. "I'm going ter court," he said. "I'll ask the commissioner to see her. He'll know who's the father." Then he walked out as Little Polly began to cry. Mallie picked her up and peppered her face with kisses.

"I promise I'll never, ever leave you. You're the most important thing in the world to me."

After breakfast Bradnox appeared in the kitchen. "Jason told me you gave Derby salt," he told Mallie. "Come with me."

Resigned to the coming punishment, Mallie handed her daughter to Biddy and followed Bradnox. Instead of heading for the main house, however, he headed for the barn. He ordered Mallie up to the hayloft, and she glanced at him with suspicion. Since her pregnancy, he had stopped forcing himself on her, so this had to be a new penance. But masters were capricious, if nothing else, and being spared the pain of a beating was not a bad thing. She climbed up, and he removed the ladder.

"You'll stay here for the rest of the day."

By noon Mallie was wishing she had been hit with the crop; the barn was stifling and the air completely still despite the loft's single window. Most of all, she was desperate to see her daughter. She considered yelling out to Biddy, but was afraid to get her in trouble. At long last, she heard someone propping up the ladder. When she leaned over the edge, she saw Margaret, climbing up with a pail of water. Mallie drank desperately and splashed her face while Margaret climbed back down.

"What did Mr. Bradnox say? When will he allow me to come down?" Mallie asked as Margaret reappeared with a basket containing boiled potatoes and eggs.

"I don't know," Margaret answered, still standing on the ladder but not quite meeting Mallie's gaze.

"How's Pol? I hope she's not crying for me and carrying on."

"She's with Biddy."

"Can you ask her to bring her? Just for a few minutes."

"I should go. I have work to do." Before Mallie could say another word, Margaret had climbed down the ladder and was gone, leaving her perplexed. She sat in front of the window and chewed her food slowly, replaying in her mind the brief exchange with Margaret. The hours dragged on, and the heat only got worse. Mallie stripped down to her shift and fell into a groggy sleep, drenched in sweat, her heart pounding. When the sun went down, she dressed again, looked out the window, and saw Ellery on his way to the kitchen.

"Ellery!"

"Mallie? What are you doing up there?"

"Mr. Bradnox put me up here for the salt I gave Derby. Do you know what he did to him?"

Ellery shrugged. "Nothing. I worked all day on a fence where the field hands were. Mr. Bradnox never summoned him."

And then it hit her like a thunderbolt. How had she missed it? Bradnox's sister and brother-in-law and Cassie's mother were to be here in a week. They were sure to see the striking resemblance that had developed between Annie and Little Polly. And did Bradnox know Derby intended to present Little Polly in court to plead his case?

"Please ask Biddy to bring me Pol straightaway," Mallie begged, her voice becoming panicky. When Ellery returned with Margaret, one look at their faces confirmed Mallie's worst fears. "Where's my daughter?"

"Mallie, I'm so sorry, luv. He threatened to sell my son if I said anything. I'm so, so, so sorry..." Tears streamed down Margaret's face.

"Where is she?" Mallie bellowed.

"Mr. Bradnox took her and Biddy to Annapolis."

"Get me the ladder!"

"There's nothing to be done, dear. I'm sorry, I'm sorry..."

"Let me down!"

"He said to leave you there until he returns tomorrow."

Mallie turned away from the window, walked to the very edge of the hayloft, and looked down about eight feet, trying to determine where the hay was thickest. She lay flat on her stomach and swung her legs over the edge just as Margaret and Ellery were rushing through the door. She wriggled and pushed herself backward until her entire torso cleared the floor of the hayloft. She landed with legs bent and rolled onto her side, clutching her right knee, howling in pain and rage.

———

July 8, 1736

"She won't move, and she won't talk to us, sir," Margaret said, distraught.

Bradnox pulled off the blanket Mallie had cocooned herself in. She was curled up in a fetal position, her arms covering her face, her hair a mess of knots and straw. After discovering her daughter had been taken away, she had wailed for a day and night, sunk into a stupor for several days, and barely moved since. Before calling Bradnox, Margaret had summoned Derby, but Mallie had ignored him.

"That's quite enough." Bradnox pulled her to her feet. Her face was deathly white. "Biddy, clean her up and begin preparing dinner. If she refuses to work, let me know immediately."

"Where is she?" Mallie asked once the planter had gone and Biddy was picking straw from her hair.

"I told you, I swear I don't know," Biddy whispered sadly.

Mallie moved about the kitchen as if she were sleepwalking, her hands chopping and mixing and seasoning out of habit, answering curtly when Biddy attempted to make conversation.

"Dinner looks wonderful, Mallie," Margaret said when she retrieved the soup bowl, and she smiled hopefully when Mallie offered to help carry the food.

When Mallie walked into the hall, Bradnox and Cassie looked at her with apprehension from opposite ends of the table but said nothing. Mallie walked past Bradnox, Cassie's mother, and Abigail and Ryan Hearne, toward the end where Cassie sat, in her hands a delftware plate with the cream cheese she had seen in the milk house.

"That looks absolutely exquisite," Cassie's mother exclaimed.

"It is so laborious!" Cassie said, glowing with pride. "The worst part is turning the mixture of cream and rennet, salting and covering it with nettles every single hour for an entire day. The final seven days are not so bad…"

As Cassie kept talking, Mallie stopped at her side. She raised the plate over her head; the whole room gasped. Cassie, startled, stopped talking and turned toward Mallie.

"No!" Cassie cried.

Bradnox and Ryan Hearne both jumped out of their chairs, but the cheese and plate were already smashed on the floor, and Mallie was stamping on them with all her might.

———

Mallie supported her right hand with her left and mindlessly scribbled with a piece of coal on the wall of the inn's basement. The shackles around her wrists clanged. Dougal—Titus's replacement after his indenture had ended—glanced up at her from the game of cards he was playing with another four men, then went back to his hand. The morning after she had ruined the cream cheese, Bradnox had brought her to Annapolis. The following day they had appeared before the Worshipful Commissioner, and the judge had granted the planter's request to give her thirty-six lashings. At dawn they would head back to Prosperity.

"Mallie?"

Mallie blinked, not believing her eyes. Lizzie stood next to her, a beer mug in each hand.

"Lizzie!" one of the men playing cards with Dougal called out. "Bring me my beer and your arse."

"Shut up and don't rush me," she replied. She crouched next to Mallie.

"I thought you were dead," Mallie said, eyes wide.

"I did too." Lizzie stared at Mallie's neat, flowing handwriting. "I'll be damned...yer can write."

"How did you get here?"

"And yer sound like a lady! Me sentence was commuted ter a fourteen-year term. I was transported a few months after yer left." Lizzie stood up and delivered the drinks. She returned, crouched again, and ran a finger over Mallie's charcoal writing. "Can yer make me a pass?"

Mallie chuckled dryly; Lizzie had not changed. "I wouldn't know how."

"I can get a real one. Yer just have ter copy it. I can get paper for both of us, and yer can make a pass for yerself. I'll bring yer with me on the ship that'll take us back ter England."

"I don't think you can."

"I swear I can. I can bring a blacksmith right now."

Mallie frowned and swept her gaze around the basement.

"I guarantee no one will say anything," Lizzie reassured her.

Mallie's heart raced. Her daughter might still be somewhere in Maryland, but with each passing day the chances of finding her grew dimmer. If Mallie broke free, she could go looking. Sure, Bradnox would hunt her down, but she had to try.

"I don't want to go to London; I want my shackles opened, one shilling for your pass, and paper. You have to get rid of him." She pointed to Dougal. Lizzie jumped to her feet and walked out. Soon a girl appeared, approached Dougal, and whispered in his ear. He smiled, threw his cards down as the other servants laughed and whistled, then eagerly followed the girl out the door. Lizzie reappeared with a man carrying a bag of tools. They approached Mallie, and she offered up her wrists, exhilarated. At that moment the basement door opened, and Bradnox and a chastened-looking Dougal walked in. Without wavering, Lizzie threw her arms around the blacksmith and kissed him. Startled, the man dropped his bag of tools, which fell to the floor with a racket. Lizzie released the blacksmith, feigning embarrassment.

"Sir! We'll move ter different quarters," she said as the blacksmith gathered his tools. Bradnox snatched the bag, looked inside, and thrust it against the man's chest, knocking the wind out of him.

"Get out before I call a constable," the planter ordered. "You too, wench." When the pair slunk out, Bradnox turned on Mallie. "You're spending the night in my room."

She walked ahead of him, her eyes glowing with hatred, feeling the blacksmith's chisel inside her pocket softly bouncing against her thigh.

The air in Bradnox's room was thick with tobacco smoke. He and another man sat at a table, a cribbage board in front of them and cards in their hands. The man reached into a basket next to the board and popped a biscuit into his mouth. "These are delicious," he said, licking his fingers and wiping them on his breeches.

"You should try the ones my girl makes. She's a heavenly cook," Bradnox said, proudly pointing at Mallie, who was curled up in a corner, wrapped in a blanket, watching the men warily; both had drunk prodigious amounts of wine over several games.

"Is that so?"

"She needs to be disciplined every so often, though."

"What servant doesn't?"

Bradnox laughed. "Being a master comes with responsibilities." He took one of three cards in his hand and set it on the table, faceup: three of hearts. "Three," he said.

The man did the same: seven of clubs. "Ten."

Bradnox smiled when he set down his next card: five of hearts. "Fifteen for two." He took his peg from its spot on the cribbage board and moved it two holes to the very end of its track. The man groaned and shook a fist good-naturedly as the planter grabbed the coins next to the board.

"I've left my best bet for last," the man said. "I'll return shortly."

When the man exited the room, Bradnox turned to Mallie. She recognized the look, and it revolted her. She pressed a finger against the tip of the chisel inside her pocket.

The man returned with a wooden chest, set it on the table, and opened the lid. Bradnox's eyes lit up at the sight of about two pounds of Hyson tea. He placed eight crowns on the table.

"I don't want your money," the man said.

"My bet against your tea is fair!"

"It is, but I wish to play my tea against your servant girl."

Mallie's arms tingled.

"I see." Bradnox stared at her, seemingly running calculations in his mind. "My Mallie it is, then."

At that, Mallie jumped up and pulled a chair next to the table.

"What do you think you're doing?" Bradnox exclaimed. "Go back to your spot!"

The man laughed. "What a sprightly filly! Please, sir, let her watch. I don't mind."

"Are you sure you still want to play for her? I would understand if you changed your mind."

"I want her that much more."

Bradnox shrugged, moved the two pegs to the starting point of their respective tracks on the board, and shuffled the deck. Even if she did not know the game, Mallie reasoned, maybe she could read the men's faces to discern the outcome. She had already figured out that each round lasted roughly ten minutes. Bradnox offered the deck to the man to cut. Then each took a card and showed it to each other.

"Nine of diamonds," said the man.

Bradnox smiled as he showed his card. "Two of hearts." He shuffled the pack again, the man cut it once more, and then the planter dealt each five cards. Each discarded two into a pile, facedown. Bradnox turned up the top card in the deck, a jack of diamonds. "Two for his heels," he said, taking one of his pegs and advancing it two holes.

It's a race! Mallie thought. *The pegs are racing, and the one to make it to the end of its track first wins.* For the next few minutes she watched as the men laid down cards, calling out things that sometimes made sense to her and sometimes did not, things like "nine," "twenty," "thirty, and one for the go." The men took turns shuffling and dealing, all the while their pegs advancing, sometimes just a couple of holes, sometimes making large leaps forward. When Bradnox looked at his hand and then glanced at the tea as if it were already his, Mallie's heart stopped. But then she noticed that, as the cards were laid down one by one, the planter bit down harder and harder on the stem of his pipe.

When both hands were finally on the table, Bradnox's cockiness had shriveled like the tobacco in his pipe, even though he was only four holes from reaching the end of the board, while the other man had fourteen to go. The planter stared in disbelief at the man's two fives and one jack of spades and the turn-up card, a five of spades: a perfect cribbage hand, adding up to fifteen. When Bradnox turned his smoldering eyes on Mallie, she immediately knew.

He had lost her.

Mallie lay on the floor, at the foot of the bed occupied by her new master. His snores were so loud, she could feel the floorboards vibrating. She was glad Bradnox had lost her, and his dejection gave her immense satisfaction. She was relieved that her new master had fed her a decent supper and had refrained from touching her, but when he kept her in fetters and she realized they were leaving Maryland, her despondency was overwhelming. She turned the chisel round and round in her palm. Maybe, in her wrath, she really could have stabbed Bradnox, but she could not bring herself to kill this other man. She extended her arm as far as it would go under the bed and released the chisel. All hope of looking for Little Pol was gone. She felt as if she were being sucked down into a black hole. Then, just as she felt she would crash at the bottom of the pit, all emotion seemed to bleed out of her, and nothing but a painless vacuum remained.

PART FOUR

CHAPTER NINETEEN

July 13, 1736

The reddish dog bounded joyfully from its spot in front of the fireplace in the kitchen, sweeping Mallie aside.

"Good boy!" Chisholm exclaimed as the dog ran circles around him. "I brought you a treat." The man offered the dog a bone, and the animal closed its jaws around it with a soft clunk. Two women wearing aprons got to their feet, greeting Chisholm respectfully, studying Mallie with curiosity.

"I brought you a treat too," Chisholm said, placing a broad hand on Mallie's back and pushing her toward one of the women. "Her name is Mallie, and you'll be very pleased with her."

"Aye, sir. Thank you, sir," the woman said. Her pale-blue eyes stared into Mallie's with fascination.

"C'mon, boy, let's allow the girls to get on with breakfast."

Mallie remained where she stood, waiting for instructions. The blue-eyed woman smiled at her. "You must be tired from traveling. Sit down. My name is Clara, and this is Hedevi."

Above and to the right of the fireplace, Mallie saw something she had not seen since leaving London: a four-spoke wooden wheel about four feet in diameter was hanging from a ceiling beam. A rope ran from the wheel's hub to a pulley at the end of a spit, on which a big cut of meat had been skewered. Mallie watched as Clara took a black turnspit dog from inside the wheel and set it on the floor. The dog hurried to a water bowl and slurped noisily. Clara picked up a second dog—a gray turnspit with black spots—and placed it inside the wheel. The dog's short, crooked legs moved mechanically, turning the spit.

"Did Mr. Chisholm buy you in Annapolis?" Clara asked.

"He won me in a game."

"I wish he would lose me in a game," Hedevi said as the black turnspit sniffed at her heels. Mallie winced when she kicked it away. "What do you want, Edan?" A young man had poked his head inside the kitchen and was staring at Mallie. She returned the stare with such impassivity that he looked away.

"I was just...I was looking for..."

"Oh, get out!" Clara waved him away with a rag. "You're here to gawk at the new girl. Well, you've seen her, now scat and let us work."

"Before the workers have sat down to eat," Hedevi warned Mallie, "Edan's report will have spread. You'd best be ready for a lot of unwanted attention."

Mallie's eyes turned to a table. "Are you using this?" she asked, pointing at a rolling pin.

"I saw the new cook," Edan said as he and dozens of workers—black and white—filed into the building where they were served their meals. "She's a regular beauty. From far away ye wilna notice anything odd, but wait till ye see her up close. Do ye wish tae run tae the kitchen and steal a look at her, Blair?"

"No." Blair grabbed a wooden spoon and bowl from a stack on a table. He stood in line, steadily moving toward a boy doling out servings from a huge pot of porridge, then got his portion and sat down at a long table. A flurry of hands reached out for beer pitchers and into baskets containing slices of scrapple. Blair was chewing his pork and cornmeal loaf, deep in thought, when he sensed a girl standing next to him. He turned his eyes just enough to see a fresh pitcher in her hands. Absentmindedly, he leaned to the right to give her room, then looked up at her. A warm, tingling sensation coiled itself around his heart. Though he could see only her profile, her face seemed to glow, as if her skin gave off light of its own. The crown of black hair peeking out from under her cap contrasted strikingly against the white linen; her perfectly drawn lips seemed raspberry stained. His eyes were tracking a scar running across her right cheekbone when she turned her head slightly toward him, and he was struck by the mineral green of her eyes. She turned toward him and caught his gaze. A pressure settled on his chest. Her *eyes* were not green: her *left* eye was a burnished chestnut—and the effect was breathtaking.

Men at the table whistled, clucked their tongues, and called out.

"Leave her in peace," Hedevi said, but it did no good.

Mallie ignored them. As she set the pitcher on the table, the man on her left brazenly squeezed her bottom. She immediately reached for the rolling pin she had tucked in the pocket of her apron and brought it down on his forearm with as much force as she could muster. The man yelped and released her, and the table erupted in laughter while he cradled his arm, fingers bent like claws, a string of curses spilling from his mouth. As she calmly walked away, Blair stared. Edan had been wrong. She was not a *regular* beauty. She was the most heavenly creature Blair had ever seen.

"Give me two weeks," one of the workers said, "and I'll woo her. If she has any brains about her, she'll fancy someone who'll become a freeman before fall begins."

"Keep yer freedom, Silas, because I'll keep her," Edan said. Blair glanced at the two. Silas didn't stand a chance. Edan, on the other hand, was a pleasant, good-looking lad. And Blair could not let him have her.

Back in the kitchen, Hedevi and Clara were bent over with laughter, hands holding their bellies, while Mallie watched them in silence. Clara wiped tears from her eyes and glanced at Mallie, whose expression was blank. Clara and Hedevi looked at each other and shrugged. In the course of the morning they had tried to strike up a conversation with Mallie several times; her responses had been polite, yet terse, and they had dropped their efforts to include her in their chitchat. But she had proved her competency, immediately earning their approval.

Later, sharing her mat with the turnspits, Mallie closed her eyes and, as she did every single night, thought of her daughter. As she mentally reviewed every detail of Little Pol's face, she felt no sadness. Nothing. Her last thought before falling asleep was how not feeling much of anything was not a bad thing at all.

July 18, 1736

Blair tossed and turned on his mat, unable to shake Mallie from his thoughts. For the entire week, men had tried talking to Mallie whenever she approached the table—some lewdly, some politely—all striving to win her attention. But no one dared touch her. Blair never spoke to her; it was clear the men's advances made her recoil. She never uttered a single word. Blair had been eagerly waiting for Sunday to come. To-morrow he would have the chance to approach Mallie when she wasn't busy working, and when he wasn't just another face among dozens. He would get her to talk to him.

Try as she might, Mallie could not summon Little Pol's face. Each time it seemed to be coming into focus, another emerged, entirely of its own accord. The face was Blair's. She knew his name because Hedevi was infatuated with him. She brushed the image away, annoyed at this intrusion. At no time when she had brought beer or food to the table had he come up with an excuse to talk to her. Why was she even thinking of him? She forced her mind to go blank.

Blair pressed his back against the wall of the ropewalk warehouse, stepping out of the way of the workers heading out to enjoy the day. He ran his tongue over his teeth, tasting the mixture of cinnamon, dragon's blood—a red resin from an Arabian tree—and cream of tartar with which he had cleaned them, wishing he still had clothes he could call "Sunday best."

Edan broke off from the group. "Who are ye waiting for?" he asked, parking himself next to Blair.

"I was making up my mind as tae where tae go."

"I've made up my mind," Edan said.

Blair followed Edan's gaze; Mallie was coming out. Blair cursed under his breath. The two vying for her attention would guarantee failure for both. But then he saw Hedevi catch up with Mallie, and he smiled. His chances had just improved.

"Good morning," Edan said, launching forth, stepping right into Mallie's path. She tensed and took a small step back.

"Good morning," Blair said to Hedevi, flashing her a smile.

"Good morning," Hedevi replied, pleasantly surprised at this unexpected friendliness.

"Where're ye going?"

"To church."

"Church?" Blair asked, sincerely surprised. "I've never seen ye go tae church."

"Mallie wants to go, and then I'm showing her the city."

"May I walk with ye?"

"*Ja*, thank you!" Hedevi exclaimed, delighted. Blair purposefully fell behind Mallie and Edan, and Edan glanced back at him triumphantly. Blair returned a smile of acquiescent defeat. He asked Hedevi questions, let her talk to her heart's delight, and watched with satisfaction as Edan launched into a soliloquy and Mallie's shoulders rose and fell with a deep sigh.

"I thought ye were going tae the Swedes' church," Blair said when Hedevi turned right at a corner.

"Mallie wanted to come here," Hedevi said as they walked into an alley and stopped in front of a building. "Are you coming in?" she asked hopefully.

"I will," Edan said. Blair cleared his throat. He looked at Saint Joseph's church as if it were a spitting skunk with its tail up. Reverend McCracken had made it clear that kneeling and making the sign of the cross was the devil's yoke and the way to hell.

"I wilna," he said politely, "but thank ye for allowing me tae keep ye company."

"Maybe I'll see you later?" Hedevi chirped, batting her eyelashes.

Mallie said nothing, but as the girls and Edan went inside the church, she turned her head and her eyes met Blair's. Her flustered look made him smile, but he felt foolish. *Such a shame*, he told himself: *beautiful, feisty, and* Catholic. *And I never heard her voice.*

The late-morning sun strained through the leaves of sycamores and willows on the Schuylkill's eastern shore, mottling everything with light and shadow. Blair sat with his back resting against an oak tree, lazily watching the river's surface as it gently rippled in the breeze. Two squirrels chased each other up a willow. He might get a scolding from Reverend Andrews next week for skipping church yet again, but he could not waste such a golden day indoors. He inhaled the scent of grass and water and listened to the birds chirping. He was about to get up when he spotted Mallie, walking all by herself. He sat still, and his heart skipped a beat when she noticed him. She quickly turned away and gazed toward the water. He waited and held his breath as she started walking toward him.

"Hullo," he said with a smile when she stopped in front of him.

"Hello."

"Where's Hedevi?" Blair knew he did not need to ask about Edan. He had had his chance.

"She ran into a friend and went with him."

So, Blair thought, this is your voice. It's without a doubt the saddest I've ever heard.

"Do ye wish tae sit?" He moved over to leave the oak's trunk free for Mallie to lean on. She hesitated for a moment before sitting down. He reached for a couple of broken branches that lay between them and moved them behind him. "We wouldna want any weapons within yer reach," he muttered, and one corner of her mouth moved ever so slightly. How he wanted to make her smile.

"My name is Blair Eakins."

"My name is Malvina Ambrose."

"Please tae meet ye, Malvina Ambrose. Ye come from Maryland, aye?"

"Yes."

"What do ye think o' Philadelphia?"

She thought for a moment. "I don't know. It's smaller than London and bigger than Annapolis. I miss the quiet nights at the plantation where I lived."

"Were ye born in London?"

"I think so."

"Ye *think* so?"

Mallie shrugged matter-of-factly.

"How old are ye?" Blair asked.

"Sixteen, maybe seventeen."

Blair mulled that over. He had never met anyone who didn't know their date and place of birth. At any rate, she had a hint of a London street accent, though her speech was far more polished than one would expect from a servant.

"Are yer parents in London?" he asked.

"They're dead."

"Oh. I'm sorry."

When she caught his gaze lingering on her scar, she lowered her eyes. After a brief but awkward silence, he spoke again.

"If ye dinna ken when ye were born, ye can pick any day ye fancy, and that'll be yer birthday."

Mallie looked at him, startled. "I like the idea," she conceded. And smiled. It was a tiny smile, but it was something. He felt as if he had just planted his flag *in terra nullius*—no-man's-land.

"Do you know when your birthday is?" she asked.

"The first o' November. I'll be twenty-three."

"Were you born here?"

"In Ulster, Ireland. Do ye no hear it in my voice?"

"You sound different, but everyone sounds different in this city."

"That's true, they do."

"I never met anyone in Maryland who sounded like Hedevi," Mallie observed.

"She's from Sweden."

"Why didn't you come to church with us? She was disappointed."

Oh no, he thought. *It was going so well.* He might as well get it over with. "I'm Presbyterian." To his immense relief, her face showed neither surprise nor disapprobation. He realized she did not know they were supposed to hate each other. "Come," he said, standing and offering his hand. "Let's dip our feet in." When she didn't move, he asked, "Are ye afeard o' the water?"

Unbelievably, she smiled again, although Blair could have sworn this was more of a smirk. She accepted his hand, and he helped her to her feet. They left their shoes and stockings by the tree and stepped into the water. Under the hot sun Blair's thick ponytail flashed with streaks of copper and bronze.

"When did you arrive?" she asked.

"Almost seven years ago."

"Are you free?"

The huge smile that bloomed on his face made Mallie become aware of her own heartbeat. Underneath his gilded eyelashes his amber eyes glowed like warm copper reflecting a hearth's fire. It was as if she had taken that first drink of warm cider after coming inside from a snowstorm.

"I will be, the second o' December. When does yer term expire?"

"I have a little over two years." After a pause she asked, "What will you do when you're free?"

"Join my brother as a fur trader. He's somewhere out west now. He comes tae the city every few weeks."

Mallie turned to Blair, eyes glinting. "You have a brother, and you see him *regularly*? What I wouldn't give to have a sister!"

"Aye. I'm lucky tae have Ronald."

Mallie shielded her eyes with her hands and looked toward the western shore. "Have you taken the ferry to the other side of the river?"

"No, I dinna have a pass. But I've walked across in the winter when the river freezes, tae remind myself I'm no permanently shackled tae the city."

A child's giggling made them turn. On the bank a woman was holding a little girl by the hand. The girl laughed as a butterfly fluttered in front of her face. Mallie stared at her with longing. A strange movement on the sandy bank caught Blair's eye.

"Wait here," he said. A moment later he called, "Mallie, come see!"

When Mallie joined him, he was cradling a tiny turtle in his hands.

"May we see that?" the child's mother asked, approaching. The girl's mouth formed a tight little O, and she swiftly hid her hands behind her back.

"It's just a baby, like ye," Blair said. The girl gingerly touched a finger to the green and yellow carapace. "It flipped onto its back and couldna right itself. Look, its belly is red. Here," he told Mallie, "ye hold it."

As soon as he put the turtle onto her outstretched hand, its little legs churned, and it ran across her palm. She swiftly put her other hand in front of it to catch it, and it raced across that hand too, forcing her to repeat the gesture. She smiled at the turtle's determination and, for one fleeting moment, seemed ensconced in a bubble of pure glee. Blair was bewitched. Then, the bubble burst, and her eyes clouded over.

"I think it's eager to go home," she finally said, handing it back to Blair and snapping him out of his reverie. He waded back into the water and released the turtle, and then he and Mallie returned to the cool shade of the tree. A cool breeze rustled the leaves and grass; a wild turkey clucked and purred. Mallie's head dropped, and she startled awake.

"Ye should lie down and take a nap," Blair suggested.

"I don't want to."

"Ye've fallen asleep three times in as many minutes. I promise I'll watch over ye."

She rubbed her eyes with her knuckles, unsure and not altogether trusting.

"If I sing a lullaby, will ye at least rest yer eyes?"

She finally acquiesced and lay down, resting her head on his rolled-up jacket. He began to sing:

Matthew, Mark, Luke, and John,

Bless the bed that I lie on.

Four corners tae my bed,

Four angels round my head;

One tae watch and one tae pray

And two tae bear my soul away…

He watched her eyelids twitch, and finally her features softened as she gave in to slumber.

Mallie and Blair spent every evening of the following week together. They saw the slow progress made on the statehouse's construction and walked to the falls of the Delaware.

They strolled alongside the Schuylkill, played cards, read the Gazette and the American Weekly Mercury, and talked about anything and everything. On Saturday evening Blair took Mallie to the Penny Pot, where Susannah greeted her with sincere friendliness and brought her a mug of punch. Mallie loved the lemon, sugar, and rum drink, but after half a mug she could hardly keep her eyes open, so Blair finished it and ordered her a mug of small beer. That Sunday, the thought of going to service didn't even cross his mind. He took Mallie to watch horse races on Sassafras Street and Center Square.

"Are ye hungry?" he asked after a while.

"Yes."

"I'll take ye tae meet my good friends. They sell delicious oysters."

As they walked, Blair fought the urge to reach out and take Mallie in his arms. Every day he had found himself more and more eager for a kiss. But every time he believed he had detected just enough of an opening in Mallie's armor, she closed off, and all progress was lost.

They reached the courthouse. All around it, several black vendors sold oysters from carts, while black men and women danced and sang and banged rhythmically on milk pails. Blair and Mallie walked up to one cart in particular, and he introduced her to Abraham and Flora. Abraham held an oyster in a linen towel, shucked it open with a knife, placed it on a wooden plate, and handed it to Mallie. She slurped the delicious, creamy flesh, and sighed with pleasure.

"Keep shucking," Blair said, taking his coin purse from a pocket in his jacket and handing Flora some money. "We'll tell ye when tae stop."

"I have big news," Abraham said as he handed half a dozen oysters to Blair. "We moving to French Louisiana."

Blair's hand stopped halfway to his mouth. "What? When?"

"Next week."

"So suddenly? Why?"

Abraham glanced at Flora; she nodded. "She making me a daddy," he whispered.

"Abraham! Congrat—"

"Shh!" Abraham put a finger to his lips. Flora seemed nervous. "The baby can't be born here. Babies of free blacks are bound; twenty-four years for boys, twenty-one for girls."

"Oh!" Blair exclaimed. He nodded emphatically. "I'll miss you dearly, but I wish ye the best o' luck." He winced, returned his uneaten oyster to the plate, and pressed his palm to his forehead.

"Are you all right?" Mallie asked.

"My head hurts." In fact, it hurt quite a lot. For the rest of the afternoon he tried to keep a happy countenance, but his headache grew still worse, and he was uncharacteristically sleepy.

"I think I've caught a cold," he told Edan that night in their quarters.

"It's yer punishment for stealing Mallie away from me," Edan said jokingly.

In the morning Blair's body ached so badly, he could not get up. Several workers started to complain too.

Blair was on his side when he saw Chisholm—a stool in each hand—ushering a middle-aged man into the quarters. They headed straight for Blair, and Chisholm set the stools down.

"Good morning," said the man, his voice confident and kind. "Would you take a seat facing me?" Blair sat on one of the stools. "I'm Dr. Bond. I understand you're not feeling well."

"I feel like I was in a tavern brawl."

The doctor chuckled. "You probably were." He leaned forward, pulled on Blair's lower lip, and examined the inside. "Open wide and stick your tongue out. Tilt your head back. All right, I've seen enough."

When Blair brought his head forward again, the doctor's jovial demeanor had vanished.

"What is it?" Blair asked.

"I'm sorry, lad. It's smallpox." Dr. Bond sighed in despair. "If only we could go two years without a smallpox outbreak."

Dr. Bond and his two assistants, both of whom had pock-marked faces, made the rounds between rows of moaning patients lying on mats and sheets on the floor, handing out doses of Dr. Bateman's Pectoral Drops.

"Mallie?" Blair's voice was the thinnest of wisps.

"I'm here."

"Thirsty."

She left her chair and knelt next to him. Leaning on the heel of his pustule-covered palms, he struggled to sit up. Mallie brought a mug of small beer to his lips. When she had first showed up to watch over Blair, Dr. Bond had tried to keep her from coming inside the warehouse where the ailing were quarantined, but when he saw the cowpox scars on her hands, he let her in.

"Too hot," Blair complained, although he was completely naked, save for a folded sheet covering his groin.

"All the windows are open," Mallie said, wishing he would lie down again and close his eyes. But, as he had been doing for days, he carefully scanned his body, taking stock of the progress of the pustules on his arms, chest, abdomen, legs, and the soles of his feet. She did not say it, but Hedevi had died that morning.

A panicky voice called out, "Doctor! Silas is bleeding!"

Blair turned his head and stared at Silas, the worker who had declared he would win Mallie. His indenture had ended the previous week. His skin was hemorrhaging so profusely, he seemed to be a melting red wax statue. All Dr. Bond and his assistants could do was wrap him in sheets. Mercifully unconscious, Silas choked on the blood pouring from his mouth and nose. Mallie moved in front of Blair to shield him from the nightmarish scene.

"Blair, please don't look."

He lay back down. "Ye shouldna be here. How will I bear the guilt if ye fall ill?"

"I've been ill before, and I got better. So will you."

He licked his lips, wincing. "If my tongue and throat were no covered with pustules, I would sing so ye wouldna get bored."

"I'm not bored." She looked at the doctor's assistants, who were placing in a wheelbarrow the disintegrated body that had heretofore been Silas, and shut her eyes against the awful image. *Please, God*, she prayed, *please, don't take him from me too.* When she looked back at Blair, he was staring at the ceiling. His lips moved. She leaned closer.

"I couldn't hear you."

"I was *so close*…I was so verra close…"

CHAPTER TWENTY

August 28, 1736

The early evening air quivered with crickets and katydids. Mallie could feel the very last of the sun's rays on her back. She had not felt this happy in a very long time. Blair's last scab had finally fallen off, and he had been allowed to leave the quarantine warehouse. In spite of his lingering weakness, he had insisted on walking to the city's western outskirts at Fourth Street.

Blair himself felt reborn. For the first time, he and Mallie walked hand in hand, at least as soon as they were outside Philadelphia. However, something troubled him somewhat: Groom had fled to New York to avoid the outbreak, taking Blair's possessions and leaving a letter at the Penny Pot saying he might not return but would send Blair's belongings whenever he requested them. And there was something else in the way of his complete happiness. He stopped and faced Mallie.

"Is it difficult tae look at my scarred face?" His question and the sadness in his voice took Mallie completely by surprise.

"No," she said, looking up at him. "Why would you think that?"

"Ye shy yer eyes away too often."

You have no idea how happy you make me, she wanted to say. I felt like I would die when I thought you would, and sometimes I can't believe you're still here. But in a few weeks, I'll lose you anyway. You'll be gone with your brother. I look away because when I look in your eyes for too long, my heart feels like it will explode from both happiness and despair.

He misinterpreted her long silence and forced his mouth into a smile of resignation. "At least I didna go blind," he offered.

She cupped his cheeks with her hands, gently running her thumbs over them, taking in with her sense of touch and sight every indentation, every discoloration. His skin might be scarred, but his eyes were as expressive and bright as ever.

"My mother threw a mug at me when I was a child," she said. "That's how I got my scar. She left me in our tenement, crying and bleeding, and went in search of more gin. I never saw her again."

Her fingers slid down his jawline and caressed his chin, then drew a fingertip over his lips. He took her hand and kissed her palm. She placed her other hand on his chest, closed her eyes, and sighed serenely.

"What is it, Mallie?"

"You're warm, and your chest is filling up with breath and your heart is beating," she replied, her voice full of wonder. He guided her behind a thick grove of walnuts, placed a strong hand on the nape of her neck and the other on the small of her back, and pulled her close. He barely touched the tip of her nose with his.

"I canna wait tae kiss ye," he said. "But not yet. Not with such fresh scars on my face and mouth."

"Don't wait too long. You'll be gone soon," she whispered.

It seemed like a long time before he finally replied. "I dinna wish tae go."

Hope sparked inside her, like a lone firefly in a moonless meadow.

"What do ye think I should do?" he asked.

She pulled back, looked down at her feet, and kicked a pebble, wishing he hadn't asked. *I wouldn't hesitate to join my brother*, she thought. *I wouldn't wait another two years for...*me. And yet, although she felt selfish and unworthy, she spoke up.

"Don't go. Please stay."

The ground beneath him dropped at those words, the same words he had heard so very long ago in the loom room of his cottage. He looked into a pair of liquid, pleading eyes.

"Ye never left my side while I was ill," he said, his voice warm with emotion. "Listen tae me, Mallie Ambrose: I love ye. I promise, on my life, that I will never, ever leave ye, no matter what. Do ye believe me?" She nodded. "*Do ye believe me?*" he repeated.

"Yes." She did, but the only other man to say he loved her had been Derby. Derby had meant it too.

"Do ye love me?" Blair asked.

She felt the same as when Derby had been teaching her how to swim and had instructed her to jump into the deepest part of the river. "I won't let yer drown," he had assured her. She took a deep breath and jumped, hoping Blair would still be there when she came up for air.

"I do. I love you."

September 19, 1736
Sunday

"Does yer face hurt from smiling like a fool?" Edan playfully asked as he and Blair exited their quarters. Blair chuckled. He had caught himself smiling at all hours of the day, like a drunk trapped in a wine cellar. Today he would ask Mallie to marry him and if it was the last thing he ever did, he would kiss her.

"Where is she?" he asked Clara when she and Lydia—Hedevi's replacement—appeared by themselves.

"She's not feeling well. She said not to wait for her."

"What's wrong?" he asked, alarmed.

"Don't worry, all she needs is rest. She'll be better tomorrow."

Blair bit his thumbnail, thinking. Reluctantly, he walked out of the ropewalk grounds, but he soon turned around. He should at least ask if he could bring her something to eat. He ran up the stairs to the women's quarters and opened the door slowly, in case she was sleeping. His scalp prickled at the sight that slowly took shape in the low light. She was lying on her mat, completely naked, seemingly asleep, and Chisholm was sitting next to her, his fingers in her hair, which was spilled in a dark fan around her head.

"What are ye doing?" Blair snarled.

"Just walk away, lad."

Blair pushed the door wide open and stepped inside. "Take yer hands off her and get out, ye impudent cur."

Chisholm stood up and strutted toward Blair. He was shorter, but heavy with muscle after a lifetime at the rope-walk. "I said, *walk away.*"

Blair charged. He slammed his shoulder into Chisholm's chest with his full force, hurling him against the wall and knocking the wind out of him. Chisholm slid to the floor, gasping for air. Blair stood over him, his chest heaving, fighting the urge to kick the man's head to a pulp. Mallie moaned softly, and Blair turned his head. Chisholm took advantage of the moment, balled his hand into a fat fist, and hit Blair on the side of his right knee. As Blair's knee buckled and he fell forward, he saw a fist; his field of vision erupted in a shower of sparks. His cheeks felt as if they were being pricked by needles, and the pain inside and behind his nose made his eyes water. Something wet flowed down his nostrils and over his mouth and chin. Unable to see, he kicked wildly. His foot connected with Chisholm's body, and he heard a cry of pain. He tried to crawl away, but Chisholm's hand caught him by the ankle and clamped onto it like a vise. He dug his nails into the floor and kicked with both feet, hard and fast. The hand slipped, then grabbed hold of his shoe, pulling it off. Freed, he crawled on hands and knees, managing to crack a single eye open. With blurred vision, he found a pewter mug, slipped his fingers through its handle, and flipped onto his back just as Chisholm lunged for his neck. Blair slammed the mug on Chisholm's forehead as he fell onto him, the liquid splashing both men's faces. Blood poured from Chisholm's forehead, his eyes went white and limp, and he collapsed onto Blair.

It took all of Blair's strength to push Chisholm off him. He wiped his nose and realized he wasn't bleeding; it was only snot. He tried to stand up, but nausea brought him back to his knees. He crawled to Mallie, who was still unconscious. A sweet scent caught his attention. He ran a hand over his wet face again and sniffed his palm. He picked up the mug and brought it to his nose. A chill ran through his body. *Laudanum.* He examined Mallie and was relieved not to see any bruises or marks. He quickly dressed her and retrieved his shoe. He poked his head out the door, made sure no one was outside, covered Mallie with her shawl and blanket, and carried her out, his right knee throbbing.

There was no one to go to for help while he figured out what to do. Abraham and Flora were gone, Alice and Raimond had left for Lancaster three years before, and Johannes and Betty were in Germantown. So he headed to the only place where no one would ask questions: Hell Town.

———

Blair fanned Mallie's sweaty face with an old newspaper and wiped his brow with his sleeve. The early afternoon sun fell through the open window, and a rat scurried across the yellow rectangle of sunlight drawn on the dirty floor. Heavy footsteps echoed on a staircase. A door opened and slammed shut. On the street cacophonous noises jumbled together; the sound of a bottle being shattered punctuated the cackling and yelling and cursing. Mallie's eyelids fluttered open, and she smacked her lips.

"Where are we?"

"In a tavern."

The words percolated slowly in her sluggish brain. "Annapolis?"

Blair smoothed a lock of hair off her forehead. "Philadelphia. Hell Town."

"Why?"

"Do ye remember Chisholm coming into yer quarters?"

Mallie smacked her lips again. "I need something to drink."

Blair helped her sit up. Her bleary eyes widened when she saw his face; the hollows of his eyes were black and blue.

"What happened?" She brought a hand to Blair's cheek. "Is this blood?" she asked, pointing at spots on his jacket.

"Aye, but it's not mine." He poured cider from a chipped pitcher into a mug and handed it to her. Slowly, Mallie drained the mug. "What's the last thing ye remember before waking up here?"

"Mr. Chisholm gave me pain medicine. It worked, so he gave me some more."

As Blair described the scene he had come upon and what had happened next, what little color Mallie had drained from her face. "I don't want to go back," she said with a tremulous voice.

"I'm no letting ye go back."

"What am I going to do?"

"We could go tae the authorities, tell them what happened." There was no confidence in Blair's voice.

"No!" Mallie grabbed his wrist. "The judge in Maryland wouldn't believe this one boy when he said he'd been spirited away and what his age was and the judge said he should be glad he was taken from England and—"

Blair placed his own hand over Mallie's. "Dinna worrit. We will no go back."

"What then?"

"We'll run away."

"But your indenture has almost run out."

He sighed. "Eleven weeks."

"You can't run away."

"I will no leave ye."

Mallie wrapped her arms around him, her shoulders shaking. He worked his jaw, his guts clenching with anger and frustration. Mallie pulled away. "We can walk as far as possible for a day or two, find someplace where I can stay, and then you come back and finish your time. No, wait! Will they whip you for beating up Mr. Chisholm? I don't want you to be whipped!"

"Mallie, I will no leave ye. We'll leave tomorrow morning and go west," he said firmly. "If we find help in Donegal, we'll stay there. Otherwise we'll keep going until we reach Pextang. I need tae go find us supper, but I'll be back soon." He slipped his hand inside his jacket, and his face blanched. "My coin purse!" He searched himself frantically. There was nothing. "I must go back tae the ropewalk."

"Don't! What if someone sees you?"

"I ken someone who might help me."

———

Just as Blair thought, he found Edward and William playing cards and drinking in their favorite spot outside the city.

"Happy tae help, lad," Edward said after Blair laid out the favor he needed. "We're indebted tae ye for not turning us in; I quite like my forehead without a *T* branded on it. I dinna need tae ken what caper ye've gotten yerself into."

In an alley some distance away from the ropewalk, Blair impatiently waited for Edward to come back. It was late enough that some workers might have already returned to their quarters. When Edward finally arrived, he was empty-handed, and his perennially carefree and impish look had been replaced by an ashen tint.

"Let's go," Edward said, grabbing Blair by the arm and dragging him along.

"For why?"

"Just walk."

After only two blocks Blair couldn't wait any longer, and he stopped. "What happened?" he demanded.

Edward looked at him with a mix of shock and pity. "Yer master is dead."

CHAPTER TWENTY-ONE

September 20, 1736

They set out with the first light. Mallie pulled her shawl over her mouth and nose against the cold with one hand and clutched Blair's hand with the other. A bag the tavern keeper had given him was thrown over his shoulder. He had paid for it, the night's lodgings, and barely enough food with the money Edward had to give him. Once they had crossed Fourth Street, Blair breathed a little easier. They passed herds of cattle and swine, and pear and apple trees, from which they stuffed the bag with as much fruit as it could hold.

Blair grimaced at the bitter taste in his mouth. He had emptied his stomach when Edward had finished his account. Edward had found a group of workers crowded around the door of the women's quarters, talking excitedly.

"I'm telling you," one was saying, "I couldn't revive him. As they say, he's gone to the diet of worms."

Edward had tried to steal a look at Chisholm, but when he heard that the sheriff was on his way, he decided it was best not to linger.

Blair hadn't told Mallie the story, only that his coin purse was lost.

When they reached the Schuylkill, Blair focused his eyes and ears. Bears, wolves, and even mountain lions prowled the area at dusk, night, and dawn. They followed the river north, startling rabbits and woodchucks, crossing paths with a fox, and eventually passed the Upper Ferry, which was moored on the western shore. An hour later they reached the fording spot. The sun should have been just over the eastern horizon, but it was completely hidden behind dark clouds. Blair stripped one long sycamore branch and balanced his bag on his head with his left hand, holding the branch in his right as a staff. He silently prayed that Mallie would not panic in the water.

"Hold on tae my..." he said, but Mallie had already stepped into the river without a trace of hesitation, her rucked-up skirts in her hands. He stepped into the water and took the lead. While he plumbed the river, she held on to his jacket, bracing against the southwest pull of the current. When they had almost reached the midpoint, he noticed with alarm that the waterline was above his knees. He turned to check on Mallie; the water reached halfway up her thighs. If they kept going and the water became deeper, she might be swept away. But they could not stop. There was no other way.

His heart raced when the water reached midthigh, but soon the waterline began to drop steadily. They headed for Old Peter's Road, their feet squishing in their shoes, crossing creek after creek, farm after farm, one township after another. It was impossible to avoid crossing paths with other travelers, and every time someone going in their direction caught up to them, especially those on horseback, they glanced at each other with anxious eyes. Only a handful of times, when they needed to rest and eat, did they step off the narrow Indian path. Mallie looked nervously at the woods; they were so thick, she did not know if she could find her way back if she strayed more than a few feet.

"Oh, lassie!" exclaimed Blair when they stopped at noon and removed their shoes. Mallie's stockings showed a big, bloody spot on her left big toe, another on her right heel. Blair's feet were not faring any better, what with one of his soles having a sizable hole, and he had unbuttoned the bottom of the right leg of his breeches to relieve his swollen knee. "Do ye want tae stop for the day and continue tomorrow?"

"No," she said adamantly.

They reached Milltown and Brandywine Creek just before it grew dark. They gathered fallen leaves into a pile, then removed their wet shoes, wrung out their stockings and hung them on a shrub, and nestled in the leaves. The nights were not yet unbearably cold, and even if he'd had time to buy a tinderbox, Blair would not have lit a fire for fear of attracting someone's attention.

The river murmured gently. Here, the Brandywine was but a few feet across and a few inches deep, so fording it should be a lark. However, in their urgency they had pushed themselves thirty miles. Blair felt his throbbing feet and knee, thought of Mallie's bloodied feet, and wondered if they would be able to move at all come morning.

———

Blair kissed Mallie on the tip of her nose and hobbled off to find a private spot. He was buttoning up his breeches when he heard an awful scream. He turned and sprinted, then burst through the foliage to face the most horrifying, nightmarish sight he could have imagined.

On the riverbank, a bear had Mallie by the upper left arm and was flinging her in the air like a rag doll. Her shoes went flying. The bear released her; she twisted in the air and landed feetfirst in the shallow water, crashing onto her side with a sharp smack, water splashing around her. Blair yelled and frantically waved his arms to capture the bear's attention. When that failed, he hurled a rock, which splashed next to the bear's front paw. The animal turned its head in Blair's direction, opened its mouth to reveal a set of massive teeth, and sounded a deafening roar. Blair's hair stood on end. In a split second the bear had advanced an incredible distance. Blair bolted. Behind him, the bear's rhythmic grunts grew closer and closer, and he knew that in a couple of breaths it would be upon him.

Out of nowhere, a loud, sharp crack rang out. It was not until he had run several more yards that Blair realized he was no longer being pursued. A man's voice called out, but Blair could not make out the words. He leaned his hands on his knees, gasping for breath, muscles primed to sprint, his eyes trying to pierce the vegetation. He almost took off again when the foliage parted just in front of him. Instead of the pursuing beast, an Indian materialized, a quiver at his back, a bow in his hands—by all appearances a Delaware. The Indian was saying something in his language, waving a hand back toward the river. He took two steps in that direction, again talking to Blair. Finally, Blair nodded and moved toward the Indian, who began to jog. As soon as they cleared the woods, they came upon the body of the bear; an arrow protruded from its side, and blood poured from a gunshot wound to the neck. A long gun was propped against its shoulder.

A second Indian had already ripped open the left sleeve of Mallie's gown and shift, washed her wounds, and carried her to the riverbank. Blair skidded to a stop next to her, light-headed at the sight of the deep bite marks on her arm, which were bleeding profusely. She was deathly pale and coughing up water, the side of her face abraded, thin lines of blood trickling down her cheek and temple. He crouched next to her as the Indian who had saved him stood at his side. Blair watched with apprehension as the Indian who was tending to her examined her arm. He was not entirely sure he was willing to entrust her to the care of a man with a stylized beaver tattoo on his chest, but the Indian moved with ease and confidence, and the truth was that Blair would have had no idea what to do. The Indian tore off a strip from the hem of Mallie's skirt and tied it tightly around her arm, at the level of her armpit.

"My ankle!" she sobbed.

Blair pulled back her wet skirts, and she moaned when he removed her right stocking. Her ankle was not misshapen, but it was starting to swell.

"Does this one hurt?" Blair asked as he removed her left stocking. She shook her head no. The Indian examined her ankles and returned his attention to the bite. He took what appeared to be bark from his shoulder pouch, chewed it, then mixed it with tobacco taken from another pocket inside the pouch and applied it to her arm wounds. He carried her closer to the river's edge—Blair right behind them—and washed the paste off with water. He applied more of the same paste on the smaller gashes, stemming the bleeding.

He took a bone awl and a strand of horsehair, which he drew a few times through his water-moistened fingers until it was pliable. Blair felt woozy when he realized what the Indian intended to do, but Mallie nodded her compliance. Blair decided it was a good moment to look for her shoes, but the current, gentle as it was, had washed them away. When he returned to Mallie's side, he saw that the Indian had applied three stitches to each of the two deepest gashes.

"Thank ye," Blair said when the crisis was over. "Ye saved our lives."

"*Yuh*," replied the man who had chased after Blair. He was also covered in smallpox scars, and a snake tattoo wreathed his right arm from shoulder to elbow. When the Indian who had nursed Mallie stood up, Blair felt a rush of alarm at the thought that the men were leaving.

"Wait," he said. "We were going tae Donegal." He pointed at himself and Mallie, and with his index and middle finger mimicked two legs walking west. "*Donegal.*" He pointed at the men and to the four cardinal points. "Where are ye going?"

The Indian with the snake tattoo pointed northwest. "*Shahëmokink.*"

Blair's heart dropped. He had been hoping they were headed for the Indian town of Conoy; Donegal was on the way. He abruptly picked Mallie up. "We'll come with ye. Please."

"Blair! What are you doing?"

"Ye're hurt and have no shoes. We need their help."

The Indians talked briefly. Then, while the Indian with the snake tattoo—whom Blair thought of as "Snake"—disappeared in the direction of the slain bear, the one with the beaver tattoo—"Beaver"—stepped into the river and gestured for Blair to follow.

"Do you know where we're going?" Mallie asked.

"The Indian village o' Shamokin."

A few steps after crossing the Brandywine, Blair's knee was buckling under Mallie's weight. Beaver saw the pain in Blair's face and motioned for him to set Mallie down. Blair swallowed his pride and complied. The Indian handed him a sturdy branch to lean on and carried Mallie himself. They soon came upon a group of men, women, and children, about fifteen people in all. Beaver put Mallie down, and the men and women studied her and Blair with quiet curiosity. A handful of children swarmed them, fascinated by Blair's hair and Mallie's eyes. After speaking with an older man, Beaver mounted one of two horses grazing nearby and trotted off in the direction of the Brandywine.

A woman motioned for Mallie and Blair to sit on a blanket. She reached into a pouch and offered Mallie a piece of willow, gesticulating as if she were chewing. She pointed at Mallie's ankle and injured arm and spoke in a reassuring tone.

"Should I accept it?" Mallie asked, looking at the bark with reticence.

"Try it and see what happens," Blair said.

Mallie popped the bark into her mouth and grimaced at the taste while the woman got busy wrapping her injured arm and ankle in long strips of soft deerskin hide. When she was finished, she pointed at Blair's right knee, holding out another piece of bark.

"Uh…no, thank ye."

"Blair!" Mallie exclaimed.

"Awricht," he answered sheepishly, taking the bark. "Ye made it seem as if it tastes horrible, that's all."

In time, Beaver and Snake returned with the horse, loaded with the dressed bear. Beaver helped Mallie mount the second horse, which she shared with bundles and a baby secured to a cradleboard hanging from the saddle horn. The men picked up their bows and quivers, and the women hoisted packs of supplies and fur blankets onto their backs, securing them with straps on their upper chests or foreheads. Beaver and Snake loped to the front and rear, respectively, to resume their scouting posts, and the band started moving, two abreast. Blair walked next to Mallie's horse.

"Is this village that we're going to close to Donegal?" Mallie asked.

"No. But dinna worrit. All that matters is that ye heal." Blair mustered all his strength to sound confident, knowing she was relying on his good judgment. This was not the time to tell her that Shamokin was a full eighty miles from Donegal.

The next morning, after a breakfast of bear meat, Mallie sat on a blanket and watched as everyone prepared to break camp. Blair was engaged in a minor struggle with the woman who had wrapped her wounds. He had tried to take her pack, but the Delaware was having none of his attempts at chivalry, and in the tug-of-war that followed, her pelt shawl slipped off, revealing her bare torso. The rest of the band paused in their preparations to watch the spectacle with amusement, and they erupted in laughter when Blair gasped and covered his eyes with his hands. It dawned on Mallie that the women in this band wore shawls, but not blouses or dresses like the Delaware women she had seen in Philadelphia.

Defeated, Blair walked up to Mallie's horse. "I was trying tae help," he said humbly.

"It's better if you take up a knife."

Mallie and Blair turned at the strange accented voice. A white man, dressed like an Indian, his long, sun-bleached hair tied in two braids, was walking up the path in long, easy strides. After talking to the band's chief, the man approached Blair and handed him a neck knife. "The men need their hands free in case we're attacked by an enemy or animal. I'll be in the rear, scouting. When we rest, we talk."

It was almost noon when they stopped. Blair and Mallie settled under a tree, and she rested her head in his lap and stretched her stiff legs. The white man, Snake, Beaver, and a Delaware couple joined them.

"My name is Remi Boucher," the white man said. He pointed at the Delawares who had saved Blair and Mallie. "These are Beaver Heart and Night Cat." Then he introduced the couple. "Half Moon is Beaver Heart's sister, and Looks to the East is her husband. Their chief is Lone Bear. They call you *Maxkandep*, their word for a redheaded person, and *Chipshkingwet*, 'strange eyes,'" he said to Blair and Mallie respectively. "What are your names?"

Mallie was about to give a false name when Blair replied, "This is Mallie; my name is Blair." She bit the inside of her cheek; even offering their first names made her uneasy. She noticed that Boucher, Beaver Heart, and Night Cat were studying Blair with growing interest.

"The Indians say a bear attacked you," Boucher said to Mallie.

"Yes," she replied. "We were lucky they were by the Brandywine."

"Logan and the Penn brothers have threatened all *Loups* who refuse to leave the Forks of the Delaware. Many are still there, but chief Lone Bear doesn't want problems."

"*Loups?*" Blair asked.

"That's what we French call them: *Wolves.* 'Delaware' is the name the English gave them. Lenape is what they call themselves, their real name. Where are you from, Mallie?"

"London."

"And you, Blair?"

"Ireland."

"Ah! Scotch-Irish."

Blair shrugged. "That's what the English call us in America."

Boucher laughed. He pulled out from a bag several sheets of paper secured with twine. "The *Pennsylvania Gazette* and the *American Weekly Mercury*," he said, setting the packet down with care. "I stock up when I visit Philadelphia. People who know me will bring them to my village."

"Shamokin?" Blair asked.

"No. I'm headed there because my Shawnee wife is visiting relatives. We live elsewhere." From the same bag, Boucher produced dried meat and distributed it. While they ate, Mallie could see Boucher sneaking glances at Blair; it was clear he was itching to say something. Surely he suspected they were runaways. Was he after a reward?

"Is your brother Ronald Eakins?" Boucher finally asked.

Mallie breathed with relief.

Blair perked up and smiled. "Aye! We were on our way tae Donegal, hoping to find him there."

Boucher did not reciprocate the smile. As he translated for the Delawares, Mallie felt an uneasy tension in the air. Beaver Heart said something earnestly, and the other three Delawares nodded in agreement.

"He said it would be good if one brother would ask the other not to take the Indians' furs in exchange for rum, which causes so much trouble," Boucher said.

Mallie had always heard Blair speak of his brother with nothing but pride and affection; now, he looked ashamed.

"I'm sorry he does that. I swear I would entreat him tae stop if he were here. It's the least I could do tae show my gratitude."

Night Cat and Looks to the East spoke through Boucher. "They thank you for the offer and wish your brother's heart were as yours."

Mallie was glad when Boucher and the Delawares stood up, announcing it was time to move again.

"I'm going tae walk with Remi and ask him tae point out the names o' paths we take and creeks we cross," Blair said as he helped Mallie mount her horse. As she watched him follow Boucher, she wanted to hold him in her arms and comfort him. He had been so joyful to hear his brother's name, and his happiness had been snuffed, like a length of black muslin draped over a window.

———

From her position on the horse, Mallie could see Beaver Heart appear on the path at the front of the line. The Delaware loped straight to Lone Bear and said something, and the chief held up his hand and yelled out some words. The band came to a stop. Beaver Heart ran past Mallie while everyone cleared the path and the women put down their loads. A Delaware man helped Mallie dismount. She waited anxiously, leaning on the horse. It wasn't long before she saw Beaver Heart and Boucher approaching and Blair—leaning on his walking stick—struggling to keep up.

"What happened?" she asked Blair when he was by her side.

"Apparently the Iroquois chiefs were visiting Shamokin and are on their way tae a council fire in Philadelphia."

Mallie, Blair, and Boucher stood together and waited. The band's excited chattering subsided when an Iroquois scout appeared on the path. In a low voice, Boucher pointed out the Seneca, Onondaga, Cayuga, Oneida, and Tuscarora chiefs as they rode past on their horses, regal and dignified, their attendants following on foot. Mallie was awed; she glanced at Blair and saw the same admiration in his eyes. Lone Bear's people watched in quiet deference. One chief who sported a fitted deerskin head covering, with one feather pointing up and one down, swept his piercing black eyes on Lone Bear's band, studying them with particular interest.

"That's Shikellamy," Boucher whispered, "the Oneida chief in charge of watching over the Lenape and Shawnee in Shamokin."

"There must've been about a hundred men," Blair exclaimed when the last of the contingent had disappeared down the path. Mallie tugged at his sleeve.

"I need to ease myself," she whispered. While the Delawares prepared to resume their journey, Mallie and Blair stepped some distance away. They were walking back when they ran smack into an Iroquois rear scout. Mallie yelped and Blair pulled her close. The Iroquois stared into her eyes, enraptured.

"Blair! Mallie! We're moving!"

"We're coming, Remi!" Blair yelled back. As they hurried off, Mallie glanced back. The Iroquois stood still as a statue, his eyes fixed on her.

September 24, 1736

"These damned farms sprout like mushrooms!" Boucher growled. He spat on the ground while Lone Bear's people observed in silent resentment an area that had been cleared of trees to accommodate a log cabin, smokehouse, barn, and outhouse, along with three acres of crops. Night Cat stormed toward the cabin. Beaver Heart tried to follow but was emphatically called back by Lone Bear, who—along with Boucher—rushed to catch up with the angry young Delaware.

"Blair, please don't—" Mallie begged, but Blair was already following them. A cold wave rushed through his chest when a bearded man stormed out of the cabin, musket in hand, a big black-and-white snarling dog at his side.

"Stop!" The farmer raised his musket and aimed. Night Cat, Lone Bear, and Boucher froze, Blair right behind them. "What do you want?"

Night Cat spat out a string of angry words.

"You're squatting on Indian land and you know it!" Boucher yelled.

"I improved this land, so it's mine now."

That voice, thought Blair. I know that voice.

There was a sharp click as the farmer cocked the musket; in the blink of an eye Night Cat had his tomahawk in hand. As Blair stepped between the two, he heard Mallie's faraway cry: "*No!*"

"Raimond, it's me, Blair!"

The farmer's eyes shifted from Night Cat to Blair. Lone Bear had stepped in front of the young Delaware and was haranguing him.

"Blair Eakins!" Raimond exclaimed, still aiming, his index finger caressing the trigger.

"*Please* lower yer musket."

Raimond sidestepped Blair and put Night Cat in his sights again. Blair moved with him.

"Get out of the way, Blair!" Raimond warned.

"Put down your weapon!" Boucher exclaimed. "The Indian has put his tomahawk away."

Raimond finally uncocked his musket. "Weber, it's all right, boy." The dog relaxed his threatening stance. The front door opened and Alice came out, looking scared and very pregnant. Lone Bear spoke to Night Cat; the chief didn't yell, but his voice was sharp as flint. The young man, chastised, headed back to the band. Blair saw Beaver Heart—his expression both relieved and angry—meet him halfway and firmly grasp his arm. When Blair turned his attention back to Raimond, Alice was embracing him.

"Blair? What are you doing here?" she asked, releasing Raimond.

"What are you doing *with these Indians*?" Raimond asked.

"Me and my sweetheart were on our way tae Donegal, and then maybe Pextang, when we were attacked by a bear. They saved us. She's hurt, and we couldna continue on our own."

"Are you hurt too?" Raimond pointed at Blair's walking stick.

"Aye, but that was not the bear."

"Pextang is thirty-seven miles from here." Raimond gestured toward the setting sun. "Stay with us; I'll take you there myself."

Blair's eyes lit up. "Thank ye!"

Raimond turned to Boucher. "Tell the chief he should remind his men they are to be 'as women.'"

Remembering the time when Ronald had said the same thing about the Delawares, Blair looked back at Lone Bear's men, who were watching them closely, muscles rippling on their lean frames. *They don't seem "as women" to me at all,* he thought. *They seem as nocked arrows, and the moment they're let loose, I wouldn't want to be their target.*

Instead of translating Raimond's words, Boucher muttered some choice curse words in French. Lone Bear yelled out an order, and Beaver Heart helped Mallie dismount and carried her to Blair. As soon as she was on the ground, she hugged his waist and buried her face in his chest.

"Chief Lone Bear," Blair said, "we'll never be able tae thank ye and yer people enough."

The cabin's front door opened into the kitchen, which led into an adjoining room. Mallie and Alice took two chairs at a table, while Raimond and Blair sat on stools. Over supper, Blair told them about the extra time he was serving and why they had run away, omitting the fact that he had killed their master. Alice and Raimond listened empathetically.

Raimond examined Mallie's arm. "The swelling is normal, and it'll be tender, but it'll heal. Stay as long as you need. Alice and I sleep in an upper room, so you can sleep here; it's less smoky than the kitchen."

"Show Blair around the farm," Alice suggested. "Mallie and I will arrange sheets and blankets."

Blair followed Raimond, the dog happily panting at their side. The work put into the farm was admirable. Still, Blair had to ask, "Raimond, for why did ye settle on Indian land?"

Raimond smiled. "It won't be Indian land forever. It's only a matter of time before it's included in new treaties between Thomas Penn and Logan and the Iroquois. The Iroquois are going to Philadelphia for a council that's to take place in just a few days. You must've crossed paths with them."

"Aye, we did."

"The German who interprets in these meetings is my friend. I assure you that when that council is over, more Indian lands will have passed to white hands." Raimond pointed to the west. "Over that way is a beautiful spot where you could build a cabin. Just imagine: your own piece of land, clear streams, blue skies above, blissfully quiet nights. In a few years, you'd be able to claim title."

Blair took in Raimond's splendid three acres. The picture he described would be a dream come true, and there was nothing that Blair would have liked more than to give Mallie exactly that. But he could not stop thinking about the Irish rising up to recover their lands. Later, lying next to Mallie, his heart heavy and his head aching, sleep escaped him. He felt her soft breath caressing his ear.

"Thank you for keeping me safe," she said. Headache or not he suddenly wanted her very badly. More than anything, he needed to be as close to her as possible, to feel she was his and only his, to pretend for a moment that they were shielded from the world. He turned to her and cautiously brought his lips to hers. He felt her hand settle on the back of his head and he kissed her. She eagerly returned the kiss, and whimpered. He could sense her aching for him, and yet…

"No," she begged when he tried to slide his hand under her skirts. "Please don't."

He stopped, catching his breath. "I'm sorry. I didna think o' yer injuries."

"It's not that. It's…" She hesitated to form the words. "I'm still afraid I'm going to lose you."

"It's awricht," he said, pondering how the same fear that fanned his need for closeness made her push him away.

"Don't be angry."

"Oh, lassie…" He smoothed her hair. "There's nothing ye can do tae make me angry. Go tae sleep now."

Blair and Mallie were jolted awake by Raimond's dog barking furiously and a loud knocking on the door. Raimond flew past them, musket in hand, and Blair jumped up and followed him to the kitchen door.

"Who is it?" Raimond asked through the closed door.

"It's Remi Boucher."

Raimond opened the door, and Blair squinted against the dawn light. Boucher was with Beaver Heart, who seemed very pleased.

"What is it, Remi?" Blair asked.

"A couple of Delawares on their way to Philadelphia camped with us last night. They saw Ronald at John Scull's store, between Mahantango Creek and Mikquar town. Night Cat is on his way to find him."

"That's wonderful!" Blair exclaimed. In spite of what the Delawares had said about his brother, Blair could not help but feel relieved to find Ronald so soon.

"Extraordinary, *oui,*" Boucher said, and Blair was struck with the impression that the Frenchman was not pleased to bring such a message. "Chief Lone Bear asks that you come with us. We will meet Night Cat and Ronald ten miles south of Shamokin. Lone Bear will invite Ronald to smoke, and you can ask him not to sell rum to Indians. *D'accord?*"

Oh no. Blair had been sincere when he said he would gladly pose this request to his brother. However, it was one thing to talk to him in private; he never imagined he would have the chance to do so in front of the entire band of Delawares. But he had promised. He turned to Raimond.

"Can I leave Mallie here? I'll return soon with Ronald."

"I'm not staying!" Mallie had come into the kitchen with Alice.

"Mallie, please," Blair begged. "It'll be but a few days."

"You promised you would never, ever abandon me," Mallie said, biting each word.

"I'm no *abandoning* ye. Ye'll be much safer here."

"That's true," Raimond agreed.

"Blair," Boucher said with urgency in his voice, "Lone Bear is breaking camp."

Blair opened his mouth to argue his case further, but the look on Mallie's face stopped him. "Ye're right," he conceded. "I promised." His voice sounded sharper than he intended it to, not out of frustration with Mallie, but because he did not want to unnecessarily expose her to the perils of travel.

Alice quickly prepared a bag filled with bread, butter, smoked sausage, bacon, and dried fruit. She handed it to Mallie and gave her a hug. "Come back soon."

"At least take this," Raimond said, giving Mallie a well-carved and sturdy cane. Once outside the cabin, she refused Boucher's offer to carry her.

"I won't be a burden," she muttered, limping as fast as she could.

CHAPTER TWENTY-TWO

"I should've left ye at Raimond's," Blair grumbled. Huddled under a raccoon-fur cloak, Mallie leaned on him. All around them, under a canopy of trees, the Delawares and Boucher huddled too, under a steady rain that had forced them to stop two days after leaving Raimond's cabin.

"I don't mind a little wet," Mallie said lightly. She snuggled closer and smiled to herself. She was not comfortable, but being with Blair was enough. She was almost content. Almost, because it had been unnerving to see how willingly he would have left her behind. It wasn't his intentions she didn't trust; she simply knew better. If she let him out of her sight, even for a split second, she might never see him again. She looked up to find Night Cat and Boucher crouched in front of them.

"Night Cat left your brother on this side of Mahanoy Creek," Boucher said, raising his voice over the hissing rain. "He's very glad to know he'll soon see you. When the rain dies down, we'll keep going until we reach the creek."

"Is Peter Cheaver with him?"

"*Non.*"

Mallie felt Blair relax a little. "Good," he said, "good."

Boucher carried Mallie in his arms, one step ahead of Blair. As they passed several hobbled and grazing packhorses, she spotted the outline of a man crouched in front of a bonfire. The man turned his head, and Mallie saw his big smile morph into a grimace of chagrin at the sight of Blair's scarred face. Boucher set her on the ground as the brothers crushed each other in a bear hug. She had never seen Blair be this affectionate toward anyone other than herself, and it was a wonderful thing.

"This is Malvina Ambrose," Blair said. "Mallie."

"I'm very pleased tae meet ye, Mallie."

"Pleased to meet you. Blair has told me a lot about you."

"Come sit. Ye too, Remi."

Mallie saw Boucher nod, but his usually friendly disposition had vanished. After they settled around the fire, Ronald turned to Blair.

"Remi told me about the bear attack. What were ye doing by the Brandywine? I thought ye had weeks before yer indenture ended."

"We've run away."

Ronald frowned. "Why?"

"Our master tried tae hurt Mallie."

Mallie saw Ronald's eyes darken in exactly the same way Blair's did when something upset him.

"I'll wager he's sporting darker bruises," Ronald quipped. "Isna that right, Blair?" Blair's nostrils flared. Ronald stoked the fire thoughtfully. "I wish those bastards would allow ye tae finish yer time in peace."

"So do I," Blair said, his voice gravelly. A horse snorted. "Ye have three more horses, I see."

"Aye. Business is good." Ronald checked on the meat. "Are ye hungry, Mallie?"

"Yes."

They made small talk as they ate. When they had finished, Blair said, "Remi, will ye please take Mallie back, while I talk tae ma brother?"

"Bien sur."

Before Blair could help Mallie to her feet, Ronald had already done so. He leaned into her ear and whispered, "I can see my brother has lost his head over ye." She grinned, embarrassed and delighted at the same time.

"Remi," she asked when Boucher was carrying her back to Lone Bear's camp, "are you and Ronald not friends?"

"I would not say so."

She felt somewhat guilty talking about Ronald behind Blair's back, but she needed to know more about him. She liked him, but sensed he was the only other person with whom she shared a place in Blair's heart.

"Why not?" she asked.

"He does not treat Indians fairly."

"But Blair is going to talk to him."

Boucher scoffed. "*Oui*, he is."

"When did ye get smallpox?" Ronald asked.

"Last month."

Ronald looked about to cry. "I dinna ken what I would do if ye died."

Blair was overcome both with love for his brother and dread for the two things he had come to say. He rubbed his face with his hand, trying to alleviate a creeping dizziness. "I canna go back tae Philadelphia. Ever. Our master is dead. I killed him."

The stick with which Ronald had been stoking the fire fell from his hand. He stared at Blair.

"I didna mean tae kill him. And Mallie disna ken."

"What happened?" Ronald asked, distraught. As Blair spoke, Ronald listened with more care and sympathy for his younger brother than he had ever displayed before.

"Can ye take us tae Pextang or Donegal?" Blair said after recounting their entire ordeal.

"Of course. Mallie can stay with Joseph Shipboy and his family in Pextang. Ye can come trade with me."

Blair took a deep breath. "Ronald, I promised I wouldna leave Mallie, and I dinna want tae lose her like Janet. I'm sorry, but I canna go trading."

"But she would be surrounded by people who would care for her. Plenty o' traders have wives. Ye wouldna lose her." Ronald's excitement was a dagger in Blair's side.

"I'm sorry," he repeated. "I canna go trading."

"But three years ago ye said—"

"I did, but I canna."

Ronald's mouth snapped shut. He flung a pebble at the fire. "I let ye finish an unjust term, and now ye refuse tae join me?"

Blair felt a bitter taste in the back of his throat. He wanted to say, *You didn't let anything; there was nothing you could have done to keep me from going back to Philadelphia.* Regardless, they *had* an agreement. How could he bring up the other subject? He simply let the words tumble out. "Lone Bear wants tae smoke with ye."

Ronald blinked, confused at the odd change of subject. "What? Whyfore?"

"I promised the two Delawares who saved us that I would ask ye tae stop selling rum tae Indians. They requested we all meet so they can witness my request."

Ronald stared at him, perplexed. "Man dear! For why would ye promise such a thing?"

"Because they saved our lives, and they're good people and they dinna want rum coming into Indian land. *Ye* showed me what alcohol does tae them."

"I dinna *force* Indians tae take my rum. Have ye ever been forced tae drink at a tavern?"

"No, but…it disna affect us the same way."

"I'm teaching them how tae drink."

Ronald's flippant tone made Blair snap back, "Yer lessons will ruin them."

Ronald glared in astonishment. "Only a few days were enough for ye tae become an Indian lover?"

"But it's just one thing out o' so many ye can trade! One wee thing!"

"If I dinna trade rum with them, it wilna make a difference! What about all the other traders?"

"The other traders are no my brothers. Please, just sit there and smoke while I make this request."

Ronald was seething. "Ye won't trade with me, but ye would lecture me as a bairn in front o' those savages?"

Blair's shoulders slumped. Well, he had tried. He could honestly tell the Delawares he had tried. Unexpectedly,

Ronald jumped to his feet and said, "Let's go smoke with the Delawares."

———

Blair inhaled the smoke, relishing it after years of not even having held a pipe in his hands. He handed the pipe to Ronald, seated to his left, who took a pull and passed it to a Delaware next to him. Once everyone had smoked, Lone Bear sprinkled tobacco on the fire around which the men were seated. Behind this ring sat the women and children and Mallie. Boucher interpreted as Lone Bear offered some words welcoming Ronald, thanked the Creator for bringing them together, and prayed so that everyone's ears would be opened in order to hear the truth. Finally, it was time for Blair to speak. He glanced at Mallie and she smiled, nervous but proud.

"I have a request tae make o' my brother, something I believe will be good business for everyone. If Indians' furs were no longer traded for rum, the men would have clearer minds and stronger bodies, making them better hunters and trappers; everyone's profits would increase. I love my brother and want tae see him prosper. Therefore, I want tae humbly ask him tae stop trading rum with Indians, since he has so many other good and needful items tae offer."

While Boucher interpreted, Ronald looked straight ahead, his expression completely blank. Blair waited for a reply. And waited. Boucher leaned toward him. "It's the Indian custom to give speakers time to consider if they've said everything that's on their minds. You must tell us when you're finished."

Blair looked around. The Delawares were looking at him with perfect patience. It was a little disconcerting. "That's all."

Lone Bear spoke up, and again Boucher interpreted. "We're happy to be shown so much love and friendship by our brother Blair, and we desire that the road between us and Ronald be open and clear, free from all stops, while the earth endures. That's all I have to say." All eyes then turned to Ronald.

"I'm very grateful tae Lone Bear's people for having saved Blair's life. He's my only brother; in truth he's my only family. I'll be happy tae grant him this request…"

Gratefulness and relief surged through Blair.

"…if he agrees tae one thing."

Something in Ronald's tone made Blair stop breathing.

"As ye see, I'm on my own. I need someone I can trust tae come west with me. If Blair agrees tae accompany me, I'll forever stop trading rum with Indians. That's all I have tae say."

Blair's stomach dropped. He turned to Mallie and saw in her desolate expression that she was convinced he would agree. He stared at his brother in disbelief. "Nothing would make me happier than tae be free tae join my brother, but I promised Mallie that we would never be separated; I canna break that promise. That's all I have tae say." Blair hoped Ronald could hear in his voice how such a proposal felt like the lowest of betrayals.

"Our heart is on the ground," Lone Bear said, "because we see that Ronald's cause is bad. Blair requests a good thing, which Ronald has to give. He in exchange demands something that Blair doesn't have. How is this fair? That's all I have to say."

Ronald turned to Lone Bear. "Chief, my brother promised me years ago he would join me. That's all I have tae say."

"Is this true, Blair?" Boucher asked for himself.

"Aye, it's true. I see now I must break one of my promises." For the first time since the assembly began, Ronald looked at Blair. Blair glanced at Mallie. Not since he had fallen ill with smallpox had she looked as grief-stricken. When he spoke, he could hardly hear himself. "Ronald, please forgive me."

"Chief Lone Bear, thank ye for sharing yer pipe," Ronald said, standing up and walking away while the Delawares murmured among themselves. With a buzz like a swarm of bees in his ears, Blair sprang after Ronald. When the light from Lone Bear's bonfires was behind them, he grabbed Ronald by the arm and spun him around.

"How could ye do that?" Blair sputtered.

"How could ye break the promise ye made tae *me*? I told ye many traders have wives."

"I dinna care what other traders do! I care about my own brother setting me a trap!" Blair had never in his life yelled at anyone like this. No doubt he could be heard in Lone Bear's camp, but he did not care. It seemed Ronald did not care either.

"I only wish us tae be together! Wasna that what we said we would do, ever since we left Ireland? There's no better way tae elude Philadelphia's authorities than tae go west. Ye need my help!"

"I dinna need ye, Ronald," Blair spat. "I survived without ye for the past seven years."

Ronald's eyes were bloodshot, his expression both wounded and enraged. The tone of his voice completely belied his next words. "*A cheil maun dree his weird.*" *A person must just accept his fate.* He turned and walked away.

Livid, Blair watched the darkness swallow Ronald. He could not imagine ever talking to him again. At the same time, he knew he probably would never see his mother, uncle, or any other member of his family. He felt like a castaway. Thinking about what his mother would make of it all broke his heart. On his way to Lone Bear's campsite he walked past Beaver Heart standing guard; the Delaware gave him a troubled and sad look. At the camp, Mallie limped toward him. For a moment it seemed she would say something, but then she simply reached out for his hand.

"We'll remain with the Delawares," he said, mustering all of his will to hide his crushed spirit. One look into her eyes assured him he had done the right thing. He pulled her close. "No one is more important than ye. I'm no leaving ye behind."

She looked into his eyes, with a confidence that wasn't there before. "I know."

CHAPTER TWENTY-THREE

From the eastern bank of the main branch of the Susquehanna River, Blair and Mallie swept their gaze north. Blankets of smoke hanging in the air betrayed three palisades: one beyond the woods on the eastern bank, one on the western shore, and one on the island that lay between the junction of the main and west branches of the river.

"Lone Bear's people will be guests on the island until they raise their own wigwams," Boucher said. "You'll go with them."

A group of Shamokin Delawares came out to welcome the new arrivals and guided them to a landing spot for dugout canoes. Night Cat, Beaver Heart, and a Shamokin man talked to Boucher.

"You and Night Cat and Beaver Heart will stay with White Turkey and his wife, Red Leaf, and her parents," Boucher told Mallie and Blair as their host turned his friendly eyes on them. "When you're ready to leave, ask White Turkey to come find me and I'll give you directions to a trading post twenty miles from here. There, you'll find people from Pextang."

With everyone seated inside the dugout, White Turkey and Night Cat each grabbed an oar, faced the bow, and started rowing. Around them, other canoes carried the rest of the band. They beached on the east side of the island and walked a short distance until they reached a log palisade, Mallie in Night Cat's arms. An army of women with bare torsos and baskets worked among crops of squash, beans, and corn spread outside the palisade walls like a patchwork quilt. The newcomers crossed the open gate. Dogs followed at their heels, sniffing, and everyone inside the palisade turned to look at them. Children flanked the procession, talking to their new playmates and reaching out unblushingly to touch Blair and Mallie. They passed several round, windowless wigwams, the exterior surfaces covered in bark and mats made of grasses, columns of smoke rising from holes in the middle of their domed roofs. When they reached the middle of the palisade, they passed a longhouse.

When they reached White Turkey's wigwam, he pulled aside the animal-skin curtain covering the only entrance, and his guests followed him inside, ducking to avoid braided strings of Indian corn that hung from the roof. Mallie blinked as her eyes adjusted to the gloomy interior. Skin-covered wooden platforms abutted the entire inner perimeter of the single room, and served as sitting space and bedsteads. On shelves above the platforms were a variety of sacks, bundles, and bark boxes. In the middle of the earthen floor, which was covered with rush mats, a kettle with bubbling hominy hung over a fire surrounded by stones. White Turkey addressed an old man and woman sitting on the platform, and they uttered a few warm words of welcome, their eyes opening a little wider at the sight of Blair and Mallie. A woman came in carrying a basket with several juicy, red cuts of meat.

"That must be his wife," Mallie whispered.

White Turkey seemed to explain matters, and with a smile, Red Leaf invited everyone to sit. Mallie was startled when—without a trace of shyness—the woman removed her shawl, revealing her breasts. Mallie almost laughed when Blair's eyes determinedly fixed on the fire. When Red Leaf skewered several pieces of meat and approached the fire to set them on the hot stones, Blair immediately jerked his eyes away and glued them to his lap. Mallie chuckled. Blair raised an eyebrow.

"Just ye wait until one o' the lads removes his breechclout. Ye'll no be mocking me, Miss Ambrose."

Mallie stopped chuckling and glanced nervously at the men. White Turkey took tobacco from a pouch, sprinkled it on the fire, and said a prayer. While Red Leaf filled two bowls of hominy for her parents, White Turkey invited his guests to help themselves to skewers of fragrant, sizzling meat. Red Leaf took from the hot ashes a number of ears of corn on the cob, husks still on, and distributed them. Blair was handing a skewer to Mallie when he saw Night Cat offer one to Beaver Heart, and in that simple gesture he noticed for the first time—in both men—a tenderness directed at each other that belied their virility. When Beaver Heart took the meat, the look that passed between the Delawares was unmistakable. At that precise moment, White Turkey said something. Blair cringed, certain that their host had noticed and in short order they would all be kicked out in ignominy. Instead, the Delawares engaged in brisk conversation. Red Leaf's parents did not seem troubled either. While pretending to watch Mallie eat, he paid closer attention and concluded that he was not imagining things. He was not shocked; he had already been shocked by Groom and Lynn. He was perplexed. Perplexed by the fact that these young Delawares did not feel the need to hide anything. And given the others' reactions—or lack thereof—it was plain they did not have to.

When Mallie yawned, Red Leaf pulled back blankets made with fox skins that were draped on an empty stretch of the platform and motioned for her and Blair to lie down. They eagerly accepted the invitation. Blair took the outer edge and faced Mallie. "Mallie..." he whispered.

"Mmm?"

"This...*friendship* between Night Cat and Beaver Heart, it's verra strange."

"It's more than a friendship."

"How do ye ken?"

"I knew when Raimond almost shot you and Night Cat and I saw in Beaver Heart's face the same fright and relief I felt."

"Oh."

"This is the warmest place I've ever slept," Mallie murmured. For the first time since leaving Philadelphia, she felt safe enough that the eerie howling of wolves somewhere outside the palisade failed to pluck at her nerves. Her tired muscles relaxed, and she sank into an exhausted, exquisite sleep.

The respite from danger had a very different effect on Blair. His mind was free to focus on something that, until that moment, he had not had time to dwell on: he had killed a man.

White Turkey ladled water over a pile of hot stones. The water spat and hissed until the sweat lodge was full of steam. Sitting between Night Cat and Beaver Heart, Blair wiped sweat from his eyes as his heart thudded laboriously in his chest. Remi had brought news that Sassoonan, the principal Delaware chief in Shamokin, wished to meet Blair and Mallie, so both were making themselves presentable. After a while, the Delawares backed out of the lodge on all fours, and Blair followed.

"Oh, man dear!" he groaned when the men plunged into the river. Remi, leaning against a tree, doubled over with laughter; Red Leaf's father, sitting at the foot of the tree, chuckled. Blair forced himself to step into the cold river up to his ankles, his arms wrapped tightly around himself. To his chagrin, White Turkey came up behind him, put his hands on his shoulders, and gently but firmly coaxed him forward until the water was up to his chest.

"Oh God, I'll die o' cold if I dinna drown!" he stuttered.

Facing Blair, White Turkey took a big gulp of air and closed his lips, his cheeks puffed up. Blair watched, teeth chattering, and mimicked him. The Delaware pinched Blair's nose and with his other hand pushed his head under water, just for a second, then let him come back up. Blair gasped as if he'd been underwater for ten minutes. White Turkey laughed.

"Can we get out now?"

Understanding the tone, if not the words, White Turkey nodded, and they headed back to the riverbank, where Beaver Heart and Night Cat were wringing their hair. White Turkey handed Blair a deerskin thong and loincloth—a rectangular piece about four feet long and a foot wide. Blair—following the Delawares' example—tied the thong around his waist, then brought the loincloth between his legs and tucked the ends in the belt, leaving one end hanging in the front and one in the back. He slid his feet into a pair of moccasins, and they went back to the palisade, the sun warming their backs.

Red Leaf's mother, sitting on a log around an outdoor fire at the entrance to the wigwam, uttered enthusiastic words of approval at the sight of Mallie. Beside her, Red Leaf glowed with pride. After accompanying Mallie to the river so she could wash herself, the Delaware woman had dressed her in deerskin leggings, a knee-length skirt, and a fox pelt to use as a shawl. The clothes smelled wonderfully of the sassafras bark and leaves they had been stored with, but Mallie felt almost naked without her shift and no laces or buttons to keep the shawl closed. The fact that Red Leaf was uncovered did nothing to assuage the feeling. Mallie sat down and tried to pull a horn comb through her damp hair with her right hand while clutching the shawl closed with her left. Her hair was hopelessly tangled. Red Leaf fetched a bowl filled with bear grease, took a dollop, and spread it through her own hair to show Mallie. The grease smelled gamey and pungent, but the alternative was for Mallie to leave her hair looking like a rat's nest. She draped the shawl on the log, daubed the grease onto her hair, and combed it out as fast as she could. When she untangled a section, she was amazed at the results: her hair positively glowed. She finished and was handing the comb back to Red Leaf when she spotted Blair and the men returning. She snatched the shawl and quickly covered herself, deeply embarrassed: it must have been impossible for Blair—and the others—not to catch a glimpse of her chest.

"Ye look like an Indian angel," Blair exclaimed. Mallie could see he was forcing his eyes to focus on her face. She—on the other hand—could not avoid scanning him from head to toe in spite of his near-nakedness, and her breath unexpectedly faltered. For the first time since they met, Blair blushed. Mallie was glad when Boucher and the Delawares dragged him off to finish getting him ready.

Inside the wigwam, Blair accepted the bear grease that White Turkey offered and spread it on his hair, chest, and limbs like the rest of the men, then combed his hair. White Turkey had him step into a pair of deerskin leggings and draped a fox pelt over his shoulders. Blair's greased skin felt odd, and he tried not to fidget in the unfamiliar outfit. He was wholly unprepared for the reaction he elicited outside. Red Leaf and her parents laughed good-heartedly and smiled. Mallie's eyes twinkled.

"You're ready to meet Sassoonan," Boucher declared, picking Mallie up. They walked out of the palisade and to Boucher's canoe. Once on the eastern shore, they walked to another palisade. With every step, curious men, women, and children, Delaware and Shawnee, stuck to them like iron nails to a magnet, so that by the time they reached the chief's wigwam, they were encircled by a crowd.

"Chief Sassoonan is very fond of the white man," Boucher said. "He has a very good relationship with Governor Gordon."

The chief seemed indeed very happy to meet Maxkandep and Chipshkingwet. He had already been informed of how they had come to join Lone Bear's band and about the disastrous meeting with Ronald. *Gossip spreads in this Indian village as it does in Lisburn*, Blair thought, chuckling to himself.

"Tell the chief we heard he was in Philadelphia last month," Blair told Boucher, "when that shark entered all the way into the Delaware. We wish we could've seen it, but I was still recovering from my illness. What was it like?"

Sassoonan laughed and nodded, and with Boucher's help talked about watching the shark from the wharves. He was quiet for a moment before speaking again.

"He wishes to know if you're runaways."

It was all Blair could do to keep a blank expression. He glanced at Mallie. Fear flitted over her face for a second.

"No," Blair answered. Sassoonan smiled. They chatted for a while, and before the visitors left, the chief asked to see Mallie's eyes up close. Back on the canoe Blair was dying to ask Boucher: What would Sassoonan do if he discovered runaways hiding in Shamokin? For that matter, what would Boucher do? But he decided that, for the time being, it was best to keep his mouth shut.

"Do ye think they believed us?" Blair asked Mallie after Boucher had dropped them off at White Turkey's wigwam.

"Chief Sassoonan did. Remi didn't," she replied with confidence. "But he won't turn us in."

Although Blair trusted Mallie's instincts, he thought it best to leave as soon as she could walk to the trading post. Undoubtedly, they would be advertised as runaways in the

Pennsylvania Gazette or the *American Weekly Mercury,* or both. And according to what Boucher had said when they first met, he always managed to get recent issues. The Frenchman might not care if they were runaways, but he might well care that Blair was wanted for murder.

Red Leaf looked up from the basket she was weaving and smiled when she saw Mallie and Blair approaching. They waved and smiled back. Mallie sat on a log to watch the Delaware woman work. Blair went inside the wigwam. When he came out, he was not wearing the fox pelt and he was carrying a basket containing their dirty clothes. "I'm going tae the river tae wash this," he announced.

"I'll come with you," Mallie said, standing up.

"No. I wilna be long."

Ignoring him, she secured her walking stick under her armpit and followed after him.

"What a stubborn lass ye are," Blair grumbled.

They exited the palisade and walked along the island's shore. The view was absolutely stunning. Fluffy, white clouds made the sky glow like a polished sapphire. The Susquehanna stretched before their eyes, wide and pristine, its entire surface crimped with soft ripples, sparkling with sunlight, and dotted with a few canoes. All around them, the foliage was bursting in tones of ochre, mustard, and copper. The air was crystal clear, and the autumn sun was warm. He dumped the clothes on the grass, and Mallie removed her moccasins. "Lass, ye'll hurt yer arm and ankle," he said when Mallie removed her moccasins.

"I'm sure I can do this much," she insisted, rucking up her skirts and securing them with a knot. She took her petticoat in her right hand, limped into the water, and swished the petticoat around, her left hand stubbornly holding her shawl closed. Blair watched, arms crossed, until, with a pout, she gave up, marched out of the water, handed Blair her dripping petticoat, and plopped down on the grass.

"I dinna want tae get these wet," Blair said, pointing at his leggings. Mallie shrugged, but her pout disappeared. She gazed nonchalantly at the sky. After washing the petticoat, he dropped it in the basket and grabbed his shirt. He glanced at Mallie, who was staring at him. She quickly averted her eyes. Concentrating on the washing became much more difficult. Every time he stepped out of the river to retrieve another piece of clothing, the same thing happened: her cheeks blossomed pink as she guardedly studied him. He had finished wringing out their last item of clothing when three children in a small canoe caught his attention. The children—two boys manning the oars and a little girl—had skin quite darker than any other Indian he had ever seen, and their hair was curly instead of slick. The girl stood up and said something, pointing down at the water as she peeked over the side of the canoe. One of the boys stood up, upsetting the dugout, and the girl tumbled over and disappeared with a splash. Blair caught a figure running past him, and next thing he knew, Mallie had jumped into the river, having tossed her shawl onto the grass.

"Mallie!"

The girl's head surfaced, tilted back, mouth open, her hair plastered over her eyes. Both boys thrust their oars toward her, calling out, but she sank again. Swimming fast,

Mallie reached the spot where she had last seen the girl's head. She treaded water, frantically swiveling around. For a moment she thought she had spotted the girl, but it was one of the boys who had also jumped in. She submerged her head, eyes open. *There.* She swam to the girl, who was floating facedown, limp. Mallie turned her over and placed one hand behind the girl's head and another behind her upper back, trying to keep the girl's face above the water's edge while struggling to prevent her own head from going under. Two canoes had come closer, and she waited for one to reach her side. A man took hold of the girl and hung her upside down by the ankles. Water gushed from the girl's nose and mouth. She hacked violently and started to cry. A second man helped Mallie into the canoe. As soon as she was inside, she cradled the girl and sobbed uncontrollably.

From the shore, heart racing, Blair had watched, stunned. He ran to meet the incoming canoe, and froze for a split second at the sight of Mallie's back. When he finally reached Mallie, he and the two men in the canoe tried to coax her into releasing the girl, but it wasn't until the mother—a black woman—was brought over, in tears herself, that Mallie let the girl go. As soon as Mallie stepped off the canoe, she immediately clung to Blair, her torso freezing cold against his bare chest. He rubbed his hands over her back, his heart twisting at the feel of scarred tissue.

Wrapped in pelts, wearing a dry skirt, Mallie stared at the fire. At her side, Blair studied her red-rimmed eyes, troubled.

"I'm sorry I lost your moccasins," Mallie said to Red Leaf, pointing at her bare feet. Red Leaf waved a hand and said something in a soothing tone. Mallie's lips trembled, her eyes welled up, and she sobbed. This had happened time and time again since she had been brought back from the river: her crying petered out, her emotions settled for a few minutes, and then she started sobbing all over again.

"Lass, please tell me what ails ye, I'm begging ye."

Red Leaf discreetly left. Mallie wiped her cheeks with both hands. "I had a daughter. I *have* a daughter."

Blair's eyes popped.

"The father was my former master. He whipped me for having her and then gave her away or sold her, I don't know. I don't know where she is. She was my whole world, and I'll never see her again."

Blair hugged Mallie, her hot tears drenching his chest, her sobs gouging his heart. He had never seen her cry, and this was a veritable flood. After a very long time, her crying finally subsided. He took her face in his hands. "I'm so sorry, my darling, I'm so sorry."

When she finally spoke, her voice sounded steadier, although drained. "I'm tired."

They snuggled under furs on the bedstead, and Blair felt her body jolt a couple of times before her breathing deepened. His mind roiled. For the first time in his life, he truly wanted to kill someone—someone he did not even know. He had been aghast to discover Ronald had purposely killed a man. Now he understood. And then there was Mallie's daughter. If only they had not needed to run away, maybe there would have been a way to look for the girl. If only.

Blair and Mallie stood in awe in front of Looks to the East and Half Moon's new wigwam, amazed at how quickly Lone Bear's people had erected their new homes. The Delaware couple stood next to them, looking satisfied.

"Isna that the bairn ye saved?" Blair said. The little girl and her mother were approaching—accompanied by a Shawnee man. After greeting Half Moon and Looks to the East, the mother turned to Mallie.

"Please, take this," she said in English, draping on Mallie's shoulders a beaver fur shawl. The Shawnee said something, and the black woman interpreted. "We thank you for saving our daughter."

"Thank you," Mallie said, stroking the luxurious shawl. She leaned down, thrilled to see the girl fully recovered, pools of light in her black eyes, her plump lips a tawny peach. "You won't remember me when you grow up, but I'll never forget you." She took the girl's chubby hand and kissed it. She released it and straightened up, her eyes dry and her expression serene.

CHAPTER TWENTY-FOUR

Sometime during the night, Blair was awakened by the sounds of wood creaking and moans coming from the opposite side of the wigwam. Half Moon and Looks to the East were making love. Moonlight spilled through the smoke hole and chiseled the man's arms and shoulders as he propped himself up, a pelt draped over his buttocks and legs. When she hooked her legs around his lower back, Blair shut his eyes, wishing he could also shut his ears. He turned his back on the couple and discovered Mallie staring at the ceiling. She glanced at him at the same moment that the moans coming from the couple intensified. Desire rushed through Blair with a roar, but before he could even kiss Mallie, she had pulled the pelt over her head. *Damn my luck*, he thought as he felt a sharp pain in his groin. *It's going to be a long night.*

After a full morning spent repairing dugout canoes, Blair walked back to the palisade with Beaver Heart, Night Cat, and Looks to the East. The sight of Mallie, sitting outside the wigwam, humming as she stitched a moccasin, moved him. She had insisted on wearing her own clothes again, even though they lacked left sleeves, unlike himself, who had found the breechclout, leggings, and moccasins quite comfortable and had added only his own shirt to the ensemble. Half Moon paused from pounding corn in a mortar, looked up, and called out when she spotted the men. Mallie glanced up at him for a second, then immediately plunged back to the task at hand. Blair felt sad and awkward. Although Mallie had spent the previous night burrowed under pelts, he could tell she had been kept awake—just like him—by Half Moon and Looks to the East. Come morning, she had responded coldly to even his most innocuous remarks, until he had stopped talking to her altogether, and whereas she had previously detested letting him out of her sight, she had seemed relieved when the men took him away.

"Hullo," he ventured, sitting on a log across from her. She barely glanced up, throwing him a close-lipped smile before returning to her chore. Half Moon and the men went inside the wigwam and emerged a few minutes later. Half Moon had painted her eyelids red, and her cheeks were decorated with red circular spots; the men had white stripes on their faces. All around them, other Delawares—their faces also decorated—were gathering. Night Cat pointed at himself and the others and drew a rectangle in the air.

"I think they're going to that long dwelling," Mallie said.

Soon, they were all alone, surrounded by an unusual silence. Blair's eyelids drooped, and his chin dropped to his chest.

"You should go inside," Mallie suggested.

"Will ye come inside too?"

"I'm not sleepy."

"I'm no leaving ye out here all alone." He made to lie down directly on the ground, but she stopped him.

"Don't! You'll get your clothes covered in dirt."

"I said I'm no leaving ye alone."

"All right. I'll come inside." She turned brusquely, but Blair stepped in front of her and reached for her hands.

"Lass, yer hands are freezing! Are ye ill?"

"No."

"What's wrong?"

"Nothing," she replied weakly.

The realization that she was scared saddened him. "My darling, I wilna touch ye if ye dinna wish."

"You won't be upset?"

"No. I swear."

Her frown disappeared at once. He fell asleep almost as soon as he lay down, wrapped in a blanket of sheer contentment now that Mallie's tension had visibly evaporated.

Mallie woke up to sounds of drumming and singing carrying through the night air. Looks to the East and Half Moon had not returned yet. She watched the silvery light of the almost-full hunter's moon spill through the smoke hole and dust Blair's profile. She followed the line of his forehead, his straight nose, his lips, and his dimpled chin, his neck, the sculpted muscles in his chest and thighs. She slid her hand across his shoulders, and something stirred in her. She softly caressed his firm abdomen, and the feel of his hot skin quickened her breath. She tilted her head up and found him looking back. He did not blink, waiting for the remains of her fear to disperse, like smoke in the moonlight. She wriggled her way on top of him, her legs stretched over his, arms circling his head, and nestled her face in the angle between his shoulder and neck.

"Am I too heavy?" she asked, her voice muffled.

He laughed. "No."

He stopped laughing; she felt him growing hard. She brought her mouth to his, and he let her explore, lick and nibble and search, while at his sides his hands clutched at the pelts. She propped herself up on her hands and looked into his eyes. Then her hips swayed forward, pressing her pubic bone into him. He moaned and raised an eyebrow when an impish half smile drew on her face and her hips swayed—again and again—all the while their eyes locked.

"Mallie, I need tae touch ye," he said, his voice thick, grasping her buttocks over her shift. She kissed him and this time he kissed back, resisting the urge to bite into her soft lips. His hands peeled back her shift, desperate to feel her skin.

"Take it off," she said, and he helped her out of her shift and discarded his breechclout. Immobile as a mountain lion zeroing in on his prey, he remained paralyzed at the vision of her straddling him, moonlight splashing her shoulders, breasts, and legs. He stroked her thighs with eager hands.

"Please," he begged, "please, please, please…"

She brought herself up slightly onto her knees, took him in her hand, and guided him. She lowered herself slowly, every movement that brought their hips closer accompanied by a sharp gasp from her parted lips and a baritone groan from his throat. With one final, smooth motion and a soft grunt, she closed the gap between them. He took her by the shoulders and pulled her to him, her breasts cold on his chest. His hands wrapped around her hips and found their rhythm. She grasped his right shoulder with her left hand and hooked her right arm behind his neck, bracing herself as if she would fuse their skin. His hands caressed her from tailbone to neck, and inside she was all slick moisture and warmth. Spasms tugged at him, driving him mad with the need for release. He bit down on her shoulder, harder than he meant to, and she cried out in ecstasy. The clenching inside her and enveloping him was too much, and he could not hold back any longer. From the top of the crest they came crashing down, waves of pleasure rippling outward from the point of their union in hot pulses until they were lying in a heap of wilted limbs, gulping for air, drenched and blissful, and yet not satiated.

"Lass, it's time tae leave."

The breeze picked up, and a flurry of brilliant fall leaves swirled all around Mallie and Blair as they sat on a log on the southern tip of the island. Geese milled around them, pecking at the ground. It had been almost four weeks since their arrival, and twenty days since Night Cat had removed her stitches and applied sassafras oil to her scabs.

Mallie whimpered and shook her head. "I don't want to."

"We've asked too much of our hosts."

She was puzzled. With each passing day Blair had inexplicably seemed more and more anxious, whereas she felt safer and safer. And whenever Boucher visited them, Blair's anxiety seemed to spike.

"Don't you think Mr. Chisholm will look for us in Donegal and Pextang?" Mallie asked. "Surely he's advertised us and has offered a reward."

"My countrymen wouldna turn us in," Blair said, hoping he was right.

"Why can't we stay?" she asked wistfully. "Remi lives with the Shawnees."

"His wife is Shawnee, and they're his people now. The Delawares are no our people. And the men will be leaving soon tae their hunting grounds. It wouldna be right for me tae stay behind." Blair paused and pulled away.

"What is it?" she asked.

"I dinna ken..."

She followed his gaze. It seemed there was nothing. She blinked, and three Indians, wearing bandanas on their heads, were standing just a few feet away, like spirits that had jelled out of the air itself. They did not have the Delawares' friendly demeanor.

"Blair Eakins," one of them said. Although the man's expression was inscrutable, something in his voice put Mallie on guard. Blair gently slid her off his lap and stood up. With one hand she gripped the back of his leggings and timidly peeked out from behind him.

"I'm Blair Eakins. What do ye want?"

"I am We ipto. I think your brother kill my brother."

A cold chill spread through Mallie, and her hold tightened. She looked up at Blair, but his expression was blank.

"Who do ye think my brother is?"

"Ronald Eakins."

"Aye, that's my brother, but he wouldna kill anyone."

The man blinked, just once. He pointed at Mallie. "You and woman, guests of Lenape, no Shawnee."

With that, the three men disappeared just as suddenly as they had materialized. Blair took Mallie's hand and, in his haste, almost dragged her.

"What was that Indian talking about?" she demanded.

He didn't answer. They went straight to White Turkey's wigwam, where they found Red Leaf repairing leggings and White Turkey working on a bow.

"Remi Boucher," Blair said urgently. "I need tae talk tae Remi Boucher. Pextang. Ye wait here," he told Mallie when White Turkey stood up.

"No!" Her eyes flooded with frightened tears.

"Mallie." Blair's tone was as harsh as she had ever heard it. "*Wait here.*"

An impatient Blair stood next to Boucher outside Sassoonan's wigwam while the Frenchman spoke and the Delaware chief listened attentively. White Turkey had taken Blair on his canoe to the mainland and led him to the palisade where Boucher's in-laws lived. There, Blair had explained the situation to Boucher and had insisted he and Mallie needed to leave the following day. Boucher had thought for a moment and then suggested they go see Sassoonan first. A curious crowd was now gathered, eager to mop up this latest gossip. Sassoonan wanted to know: Could Blair identify the Shawnee?

"He said his name was Wisto, or Wepso, or something like that," Blair offered.

"We ipto!" a spectator exclaimed. Sassoonan and the man exchanged a few words, and the man slipped through the crowd.

"He's going to look for him," Boucher said. After a while half the spectators had melted away, and Blair's nerves felt like tight violin strings about to snap. A murmur rose from the remaining crowd. The man was back with We ipto himself.

"He's telling his side of the story," Boucher explained as the Shawnee talked to Sassoonan. Then, Sassoonan addressed the crowd. "He's reminding everyone of the Delawares' obligation to be good hosts," Boucher said. "He's asking everyone—the Shawnee included—that you be treated kindly as long as you're in Shamokin."

Blair's anxiety lifted somewhat. But then the Shawnee replied. When Boucher interpreted, he did not seem surprised. "He said the Delawares shouldn't shelter you and Mallie, because you're runaways."

Every single puff of air was at once sucked from Blair's lungs. The Shawnee must have been watching and listening before revealing themselves. All eyes turned to Blair.

"Sassoonan wishes to know if it's true."

"Aye," Blair said, choking on the word. "Chief, I'm sorry I lied tae ye. Our master is a bad man, and he wanted to hurt Mallie." We ipto looked at Blair with disdain, made one final statement, and was gone. "What, Remi? What did he say?"

"He's going to Philadelphia, to tell the authorities you're here."

Blair felt like he'd been punched in the stomach. "Please ask the chief tae stop him! We'll leave today."

"He can't do that."

Blair turned on his heels, panic clouding his senses. He would get Mallie and leave, even though the sun would be going down soon. Boucher grabbed him by the arm.

"Let me go!" Blair cried, and pulled away.

"The chief still has something to say."

Blair turned his head toward Sassoonan, but his entire body tugged against Boucher's grip.

"The Delawares won't turn you in," Sassoonan said through Boucher. "But if your master comes looking for you, we can't hide you."

Mallie tossed and turned on the platform inside White Turkey's wigwam. Blair had been gone almost three hours, and she was going out of her mind.

"Why did you take so long?" she almost screamed when the curtain over the door parted.

"Come with me."

Blair took her to a deserted corner of the palisade and sat her down on a stump next to the palisade wall. The cold wind blew a strand of her hair against her jaw, and she brushed it away angrily.

"The man who originally bought Ronald sold him later tae a Shawnee, who abused him terribly. Ye didna see it, but he's missing an entire ear, and his body is covered with burn scars."

Mallie gasped.

"The Shawnee who found us by the river is the Indian's brother. He was right. Ronald did kill the man."

Mallie's eyes grew wide, and understanding slowly filled her face. Blair told her about the meeting with Sassoonan, and that We ipto intended to turn them in.

"He'll return with Mr. Chisholm, then," she said, jumping to her feet.

Blair braced himself. "Mr. Chisholm is dead. I killed him."

"What?" The word sounded like a gunshot, and Mallie clasped her hand over her mouth. She stared at Blair, horrified, while Blair told her what Edward had reported to him.

"I swear it was an accident. I thought he was alive when I carried ye out. But if he had gotten up, and I hadn't seen any other way tae stop him...I would have killed him. I need ye tae ken that I'll do anything tae protect ye. Please dinna condemn me for it," he whispered, his words trembling.

She was heartbreakingly sad, not because he had revealed some dark side that repelled her, but because—although he believed in the fundamental righteousness of his actions— she knew he would carry this terrible thing on his conscience forever.

"You're the best man I've ever known, and I still can't believe you want me."

"My darling," he said with fathomless relief, "I dinna want anything else in the world." The gravity returned to his eyes. "Boucher says Sassoonan's friendship with Governor Gordon is very dear to him, as are the gifts of shirts, blankets, and other things he gets, like rum—especially rum. The last thing he'll want is for the governor to find out he's sheltering runaways."

"We should leave tomorrow, or even today."

"That's what I thought, but even if the Shawnee travels as fast as he can, it'll take him at least five days tae get tae

Philadelphia, and as many days tae come back. Can ye walk tae the trading post five days from now?"

"Yes."

———

The following morning Mallie and Half Moon had just stepped outside the wigwam with an empty kettle and a pile of cornhusks when an unfamiliar Indian approached. He handed Mallie a note and said something to Half Moon. Mallie read the note and looked up, stunned. Half Moon seemed puzzled and worried. The Delaware woman called out, and Looks to the East and Blair stepped out of the wigwam.

"Remi sent this," Mallie said, handing Blair the note. "We have to go—*now.*"

"What?" Blair's eyes darkened as he read the scrawled note. It was true: he and Mallie were to leave right that instant. Half Moon retrieved Mallie's cane and the bag containing Blair's clothes and shoes, Mallie's shawl and blanket. Inside the bag Alice had given them, Half Moon had packed dried meat and parched corn. Mallie, Blair, Half Moon, Looks to the East, and the man who had delivered Boucher's note headed to the palisade's entrance. Strangely, most of the village also seemed to be headed to the dugout landing area on the island's eastern shore, where they ran into Night Cat, Beaver Heart, Red Leaf, and White Turkey.

"Maybe they're going tae a council," Blair observed, pointing at Night Cat, who was carrying his bearskin. Mallie, Blair, Half Moon, and Looks to the East climbed into a dugout with Boucher's messenger. Night Cat, Beaver Heart, and other members of Lone Bear's band shared White Turkey's canoe. On the opposite shore, Boucher was waiting, looking troubled.

"Remi, where's everyone going?" Blair asked.

"Two Delawares who were in Philadelphia when the Iroquois were in council arrived last night with news about a new treaty. Everyone's gathering to hear about it."

To one side, Night Cat, Beaver Heart, White Turkey, Looks to the East, and Half Moon were talking, occasionally glancing at Blair and Mallie.

"But why do we have to leave?" Mallie asked.

"Your master is on his way, looking for you."

A wave of shock reverberated through Mallie and Blair, like a hammer striking cold iron on an anvil.

"But...but..." Blair stammered, "that's impossible...Who told ye this?"

"These same Delawares. They said that when the councils ended, some members of the chiefs' entourage went out to the streets and bought rum and got drunk. Several white men followed them, scolding them and saying it was time to return to their homes. One Iroquois replied saying he had seen a white couple traveling with a Delaware band on the Tulpehocken Path, so the whites should be more gracious hosts. One of the white men asked what the couple looked like. The Iroquois said the girl had strange eyes: one was brown and the other green. The white man then said those were his runaways, and that he would go secure them himself immediately."

Mallie tugged at Blair's shirt. "We should go."

"Aye." Blair looked around anxiously, half expecting Chisholm to appear at any moment. If the Delawares who had brought the news had arrived the previous night, how far behind could Chisholm be?

Night Cat, Beaver Heart, Looks to the East, Half Moon, Red Leaf, and White Turkey gathered around.

"May your moccasins always be dry, and your path free of logs and briars," Beaver Heart said, looking rueful.

"We'll be forever grateful to you all," Mallie said.

"Give our regards to Red Leaf's parents. Tell Lone Bear I'm sorry I dinna see him one last time," Blair said.

Night Cat draped his bearskin on Blair's shoulders. "You'll need this to keep warm. You lost a brother to try to help my people. I'm your brother now, and you will always have a fire burning in Shahëmokink."

CHAPTER TWENTY-FIVE

"Retrace the way we came," Boucher instructed. "You'll be on the Tulpehocken Path going south; your master will be coming north. When you cross the creek where we found your brother, the path will fork. Once you reach this fork and take the Pextang Path, you can't run into your master." He handed Mallie a tinderbox, which she put in her skirt pocket, and accompanied them for a mile before saying goodbye.

Thick, dark clouds covered the noon sky; Blair and Mallie protected themselves against the needling wind with their pelts. They walked in strained silence. Four miles later Blair was eyeing Shamokin Creek with weariness. Mallie looked inside her bag and took a linen handkerchief that Red Leaf had used to wrap some dried meat. She placed the tinderbox in the middle of the cloth, rolled it, and secured it around her neck with a knot. Blair folded the bearskin in half before placing it back on his shoulders so it wouldn't get wet. He held their bag atop his head with his left hand as he held a branch in his right to plumb the river. Mallie balanced the bag with food atop her head with one hand, and grabbed hold of Blair's jacket with the other. She gasped when she stepped into the frigid water. The current was much stronger than it had seemed when she had crossed on horseback.

They were less than halfway across when Blair stepped on some aquatic animal that slithered forcefully under his foot. Startled and thrown off balance, he lost his footing and splashed into the water. He heard Mallie scream his name before he felt himself being dragged under. He kicked desperately, fighting the urge to take a breath, until his head burst out of the water. He tried to paddle like a dog and pilot himself toward the far bank but sank again. When his feet hit bottom, he allowed himself to squat, and then pushed off with all his might. He had barely broken the surface when his head smacked into an overhanging tree branch. Stunned, he raised his right arm almost automatically, and his hand found another branch and clutched on.

Half a mile upstream, Mallie was pushing her way through the thick foliage, bare branches catching on her skirts. She had almost been dragged underwater herself before she released Blair's jacket. She recovered her footing only to watch helplessly as he sank. She had pressed on, feeling as if she were walking through the thickest of molasses, until she had reached the far bank, then dropped her bag and shawl and sprinted downstream. Around a bend she saw a figure on hands and knees, coughing up water in violent spasms. The relief of finding Blair alive was almost as jarring as if she had found his lifeless body. She knelt and slapped him on the shoulder, quite hard. "Don't you ever—!" she cried. "You careless—!" She covered her face with her hands and sobbed.

"I'm so-sorry, lass...I'm aw-ri-richt!" When he had some-what recovered, he rolled onto his back and she lay on top of him. Both trembled with cold, shaken but comforted in each other's presence.

"You need to dry off," she said at last. She gathered wood and started a fire. They undressed and wrung as much water as they could from their clothes before dressing again.

"I lost my moccasins and my bearskin," he said sadly, staring into the flames, a cloud of steam surrounding them both.

Mallie frowned at his bare feet and the abrasions on his face. She looped her left arm around his right and leaned her head on his shoulder.

"We should go back tae the path afore it grows dark," Blair said about an hour later. They had just started walking when he cried out, "Mallie, look!" Caught on a branch extending into the river was his bear pelt. He fished it out, grunting at the weight. They squeezed as much water out of it as they could manage, and he threw it over his shoulder.

"Where's my shawl and the bag?" Mallie said when they reached the spot where she had gotten out of the river. "I dropped them right here."

The items were nowhere to be found, and there was no time to search. They looked up apprehensively at a hill they would need to cross. It lay at the base of the creek, and its steepness was intimidating. If they should come tumbling down, they would end up in the creek.

They were completely out of breath when they reached the top, and rested for a moment before climbing down. Their limbs clamored for rest, but if darkness fell before they reached Mahanoy Creek, they would have to wait until morning to ford it. Four hours later they had crossed three more runs—puny puddles compared with Shamokin Creek.

Mahanoy Creek was at last before them. The sun was going down fast.

Drained and hungry, they drove themselves forward and reached the opposite bank with twilight to spare. They reached the fork and took the Pextang Path. When they felt they were a safe distance from the Tulpehocken Path, they stopped and made a fire and hunched close to it. Their heads were spinning; their stomachs growled and their hands shook, but they felt delivered. From this point forward they would not need to worry about chancing upon Chisholm, and for the time being, that knowledge was all the nourishment they needed.

The sound jolted them wide awake. It had been a sharp, regular, insistent sound. Barking—right next to their heads. They sat up with a start, and Blair watched in terror as a large dog brought his snout right up to Mallie's face. For a gut-wrenching second he thought the dog would snap its jaws on her. But the dog barked again in happy recognition and pushed its snout under her hand, its tail swishing back and forth. He breathed with relief and confusion, but Mallie looked as if they had been pounced upon by a mountain lion. She jumped to her feet, her voice choked with fear. "We need to go!"

Alarmed by her reaction, Blair jumped up too. Hearing dried leaves being crushed under heavy footing, he turned. A man on horseback was approaching, his long gun raised. Behind him, on another horse, was Chisholm, a long gun also in his hands, a smirk on his face and a scar running along the middle of his forehead. A dark, furry thing was draped on his left shoulder: Mallie's beaver shawl.

"My dog was confused there for a spell, following your scent," Chisholm said, dismounting and walking to Mallie. "We almost reached Shamokin. I don't know how we missed you at Shamokin Creek." Mallie yelped when he yanked her by her injured arm. Blair lunged at him.

"No!" Mallie cried as Chisholm smashed the butt of his gun into Blair's forehead. Hot blood trickled into his eyes. He stumbled to his knees, then fell forward onto his hands. Mallie tried to go to him, but Chisholm held her back.

"You ungrateful wench." He tied her hands behind her back with rope. "Would you accept that bearskin and this shawl as payment for your services?" he asked his companion.

"Aye, that would be acceptable."

Chisholm hoisted Mallie up and sat her in his saddle. Then he walked to Blair and kicked him hard in the ribs. "Stand up, you bastard," he snarled. "It's a long walk back to Philadelphia."

November 1, 1736

Mallie opened her eyes halfway and closed them again. *I must be dreaming*, she thought groggily, *because I'm in Newgate, but that was years ago.* The bone-splintering cold was the same, the dirty straw on the floor was the same, and a stinking bucket sat in the corner. There were other women in the cell, scrawny and pale and ragged, and one had two small children with her. Reality hit her like a club: it had been two days since she had last seen Blair, when they had arrived in Philadelphia. She was sick with worry, thinking about the gash on his forehead. The door creaked, and all heads turned, anticipating the morning rations.

"Malvina Ambrose," the gaoler said, "someone is here for you."

She stood up, her gut churning. Was she being released to Chisholm? As much as she hated being in jail, having to go back to the ropewalk would be much, much worse. The gaoler stepped aside, setting down a basket with bread and a water bucket, and a man Mallie did not recognize walked through the door.

"Mallie Ambrose," the stranger said, "when I saw the clerk writing your name, I had to come see if it was indeed you. My, how you've grown."

Mallie blinked, confused. Slowly, the man's features rekindled something in her memory. She knew who he was, but what was his name?

"Ah! Mister...Mister..."

"Mr. Wornell Bray."

"Mr. Bray!" Mallie's joy at seeing this man who had been so kind was quickly replaced by shame at having him discover her in jail, like a common criminal.

"Come sit," he said, walking to a table. "Tell me what happened."

Mallie sat with him, but hesitated to reply. Yes, Bray had been very generous, but that was years ago, and she had known him for only a few weeks. "I ran away from my master," was all she could bring herself to mutter.

"Why?"

How could she tell him? Simply thinking about putting in words what Chisholm had done made her feel filthy and ashamed, almost as if she herself were to blame.

"Mallie, look at me." She raised her eyes. "I swear I want to help. But in order to do that, I need to know everything."

She said nothing. She could not tell Bray that Blair had attacked Chisholm. What if this was taken as a confession? Bray sighed. He stood up and knocked on the door. "Gaoler!"

Bray left, and Mallie felt slapped by regret. Had she ruined their only chance? Just then, the door opened and Bray returned, holding a piece of paper. He sat down again, and read: "*On the petition of Nicholas Chisholm, setting forth that Malvina Ambrose and Blair Eakins his indentured servants did run away and absent themselves from his service for the space of thirty-seven days and that he had been at considerable expense in getting them apprehended and brought back, praying that the court would take the premises into consideration and allow him such additional time of their servitude as to them should seem reasonable and satisfactory. The court upon due consideration do order and adjudge that the said Malvina Ambrose and Blair Eakins serve their said master Nicholas Chisholm two hundred and fifteen days after the date of the expiration of the term of their servitude as limited by their indentures in compensation for his extraordinary expenses on their account and the loss of the said servants' time.*"

Mallie felt light-headed.

"Who is this Blair Eakins?"

"My sweetheart," she said, her voice breaking.

"Do you care for him?"

She nodded emphatically.

"He's been presented with assault."

The words went down like one of Bradnox's purgatives. "Am I being presented too?"

"No. In fact, you should have been back with your master already. I think he intends to teach you a lesson by keeping you here. Mallie, please talk to me."

"What will they do to Blair?"

"The punishment for assault is usually a fine. But given that Blair won't have money, they might add even more time to his indenture, or they might whip him, or—"

"No, no, no..."

Mallie told Bray what she knew, from the moment she had been given the laudanum to when she and Blair had been caught. Bray tapped a finger on the table, listening to every word.

"What can we do?" she asked.

"I'll represent Blair at trial. Would you be willing to testify?"

"Yes."

"I'll write a petition on your behalf, claiming ill treatment on the part of your master and requesting that he be ordered to release you from your indenture."

Mallie felt a surge of hope.

"Malvina Ambrose," the gaoler called through the grated window on the cell door, "you're being released."

Mallie looked at Bray. His grave expression made her realize he was thinking the same thing she was. She walked out the door, Bray right behind her.

Chisholm glared at Bray. "Who are you, and why were you talking to Mallie?"

The throbbing pain inside Blair's head muddied his thoughts. The cold stone floor pressed against his cheekbone and temple, and he shivered. His side hurt if he tried to take deep breaths. His feet were bruised and bloody and missing one toenail. He spat out wisps of straw, and as the blurry, huddled forms of other men slowly came into focus, his stupor sharpened into keen dejection. The additional three years that had been unfairly added to his original indenture would have ended in a month. Above anything else, what was driving him crazy was the thought of Mallie back at the ropewalk, at Chisholm's mercy. The door opened, sucking a frigid draft from the single grated window, stirring the cell's fetid air.

"Blair Eakins," the gaoler said, "you have a visitor."

Blair stood up, unsteady on his torn feet, brushing straw off himself. A well-dressed man grimaced at his appearance: Blair's entire face was covered in dried blood, his forehead wound was caked with dirt, and the left side of his face was black and blue.

"Blair," the man said, offering his hand, "my name is Wornell Bray, Esquire."

"Sir," Blair replied, showing the man his right palm, smeared with dirt and dried blood, "I dinna dare take yer hand."

"You're going to be my client; we must shake hands."

Blair looked at the man with suspicion. Only wealthy people could afford to have attorneys. This man was either mistaking him for someone else or was some sort of scoundrel. "I dinna have money."

"I'm not asking for money. I've spoken to Mallie—your Mallie—and I'm going to represent you both, free of charge."

"Why?"

"I owe her a great debt."

How could Blair trust that this man really knew Mallie? He remembered something she had told him that had happened on her way to Maryland. "What's her favorite fruit?"

Bray chuckled. "Well, she ate all my oranges once."

Satisfied, Blair shook Bray's hand. "How is she?"

"She's well. Now you and I need to talk."

They moved under the window. Weak rays of sunshine and the sounds of hooves and pedestrians on Third Street streamed through. When Blair finished narrating his version of events, the lawyer explained his plans. Blair nodded, his mind swirling.

"Could ye give Mallie a message for me?"

"Unfortunately, she was taken back to the ropewalk after we spoke."

"Oh no…"

"I offered to buy her, but your master refused. Now, listen: you'll be taken to court in a couple of hours. I won't be there, but all you have to do is plead not guilty. And I promise I'll see you the day past tomorrow for the trial. Mallie has agreed to testify on your behalf."

"But…wilna Mr. Chisholm retaliate against her?"

"We'll take this one step at a time. Trust me. I'll send a doctor to see to your wounds, and get you clothes for the trial."

"Mr. Bray, I appreciate yer willingness tae defend us for free, but my belongings are in the keeping of a gentleman called Lucius Groom. He left for New York during the smallpox outbreak, but he must've returned by now. If ye call on him, I can pay ye."

Bray's eyebrows rose and fell at the mention of Groom's name. "I know of the man," he said cryptically. "He didn't return to the city."

"Did he fall ill?"

"No, he's well. He simply didn't return."

Blair felt sick to his stomach. He had no choice now but to trust Bray and squash his own feelings of impotence. What a ghastly way to spend his birthday.

———

It was all Blair could do not to scream in outrage later in court when Chisholm, in front of the fourteen members of the grand jury, gave his self-serving version of their fight. Philadelphia was small enough that Blair recognized all the jurors' faces, even if he belonged to the "lower sort" and they were men of wealth. Most of them had at one time or another bought shoes from Craig. Blair was indicted for assault, and he pleaded not guilty. He was being escorted back to jail when a messenger came to inform the gaoler that Blair was being recalled to the courthouse. As soon as he was led back into the courtroom, he was startled to see Groom's stable boy. The boy had grown since Blair's first encounter with him, but his shifty eyes hadn't changed a bit. Magnus Lynn, the man who had once forgotten his snuffbox at Groom's house, was also there, stone faced. The stable boy, however, seemed delighted to see Blair, who was again made to take the oath.

"Blair Eakins," one of the justices said, "this young man has called you as his witness. He claims that Mr. Lynn made him drink too much and sodomized him this past month."

Blair was aghast. It was one thing for Lynn and Groom to be intimate, quite another for Lynn to force himself on someone else.

"He says," the justice continued, "that you were present once when Mr. Lynn bussed him and put his hand inside his breeches."

"That's a blatant lie, sir!" Blair exclaimed.

"Tell us what happened the night Magnus Lynn forgot his snuffbox at Lucius Groom's house."

"I found the snuffbox," Blair said, glancing at the stable boy with ill-concealed resentment. "Mr. Groom's maid said it belonged tae Mr. Lynn. I went out tae the stables, returned it, and went home."

"That's not the whole story!" the stable boy argued. "We both went inside the stables to return the snuffbox. That's when Mr. Lynn put his hand inside my breeches, and they both asked us to lie with them in the straw."

"That's not true!" Blair replied.

"Mr. Lynn offered him money," the boy said.

"Magnus Lynn," the justice asked, "did you offer Blair Eakins money?"

"Yes, but only as a reward for returning my snuffbox, and he didn't accept it," Lynn replied with dignified calm.

"Tell them what you saw through the window," the boy told Blair.

"Young man, do not speak again unless it's to answer one of my questions!" the justice said. The stable boy shrank a couple of inches.

"What did you see?" the justice asked Blair.

Although no one had been executed for sodomy since his arrival in Philadelphia, Blair knew that, by law, it was punishable by death. The fact that the stable boy's version of the night Lynn had forgotten his snuffbox was a complete fabrication made Blair certain that the rest was also a lie. So what if Lynn and Groom had kissed that night? Blair didn't want to say anything that might sway the justices against Lynn, but not saying what he had seen would be perjury. No one, however, would ever know. The stable boy himself had not been standing on the bale of hay when Blair had looked through the window; he did not know what Blair had or had not seen. Blair's reply to the justice's question would be a matter of what would weigh more on his conscience.

"I saw Mr. Groom and Mr. Lynn talking," Blair answered, with the most innocent expression he could manage. "That's all."

The stable boy fumed. Lynn's features visibly relaxed. The grand jury immediately issued their decision: *ignoramus.* They had refused to indict.

Two days later Blair was back in the courtroom, sitting on a bench with the other male prisoners. Behind them sat the women. He scratched at the bandage around his head. The justices' bench sat empty for the moment; below it, at a table, sat a clerk and Bray. Rain pounded on the roof, and gusts of wind slammed the windows. Bray put his quill down and approached Blair.

"How are you?" he asked.

"Nervous."

"I would be too." Bray thought for a moment. "The clerk said you were dragged in to testify for another case yesterday."

"Oh, aye," Blair said, rolling his eyes. "A waste o' time."

A loud rush came from the main courtroom door, which had been opened to allow the public in. Blair was mortified when he recognized Edward, William, and Susannah, but he kept his head high and met their gazes. Edward and William nodded at him; Susannah looked close to tears. When everyone had taken a seat, four men wearing powdered wigs and black robes made their way to the bench.

The bailiff stood up, struck his tipstaff on the floor three times, and recited in a clear, loud voice, "Oyez, oyez, oyez! All rise for His Lordship Mr. Andrew Hamilton, presiding justice. All present with concerns before the bench now draw near and give their attendance and they shall be heard." The courthouse's bell tolled.

The jurors took their benches. Seven sat to the left of where the accused would stand when tried, seven on the right. Blair hoped that the fact that most of them had heard him play in taverns would not now bias them against him, when oftentimes they had tipped him.

The foreman of the jury stood and read: "We the jurors present Lacy Hopkins for being delivered of a bastard child. We the jurors present George Goss, tailor, for that sometime in September past he abused Richard Thomson in his own house, and for swearing profane, contrary to the peace of our lord and lady, the king and queen, their crown and dignity. We the jurors present Blair Eakins for having assaulted his master, Nicholas Chisholm, on the nineteenth of September last. We the jurors…"

Once all charges were read, the first accused was brought forth. The woman confessed to giving birth without being married, and submitted to the court. The jurors went into a room to deliberate, and a few minutes later were back with the standard sentence for bastardy: twenty-one lashes. Because of the driving rain, the whipping would be carried out the following market day. The next accused related that, at the time of his "swearing profane," he was "much in drink and not sensible of what he did," and was fined five shillings.

Blair's stomach flipped when the clerk said, "Blair Eakins and Nicholas Chisholm, come forward."

At the witness box, right hand raised, left on the Bible, Chisholm took the oath to tell the truth.

"The prosecutor may proceed," Justice Hamilton said.

"My lord," Chisholm began, as the clerk put quill to paper, "on Sunday the nineteenth of September last, I was on my way out of the ropewalk grounds when I ran into Malvina Ambrose, looking pale and in great distress. I offered to bring medicine to her quarters. She agreed, and after drinking some laudanum, said she felt better. I asked if she wanted more, and she said yes. Shortly thereafter she fell into a peaceful sleep, and I got up to leave. I opened the door and found Blair Eakins standing there. He said he wished to see Mallie. I said she was indisposed, but he forced his way inside. I tried to compel him to leave, and he assaulted me. When I awoke, they were gone. I finally recovered them on the twenty-third of October."

A murmur rose from the spectators. Blair glared at Chisholm. *I dare ye tae look at me when ye speak, ye lying bastard.*

"Mr. Bray," Justice Hamilton said, "we will now hear you."

"Thank you, my lord. Yes, Blair Eakins and Malvina Ambrose ran away, but not from their indenture; they ran away to save Malvina from being abused at the hands of their master. Blair will tell the jury what really happened."

Blair took the oath, his voice steady. He spoke directly to the jury. "That Sunday I went looking for Mallie because one o' the cooks said she was feeling ill. I wanted tae ask if she wanted some food. When I opened the door, she was lying on her mat. She was"—he paused, blood rushing in his ears—"in a state of complete undress; she wasna even wearing her shift. Mr. Chisholm was on the floor by her side, one hand in her hair, shamelessly gawking at her."

"Oh, fie upon you!" Chisholm exclaimed, shaking his head and twisting his mouth, an indignant look in his eyes.

"I told him tae get his hands off her and get out. He told me tae leave. I refused, and he approached me in a menacing manner. We became entangled in a brawl, and I bested him."

Chisholm's fake, wounded expression was momentarily overtaken by one of genuine embarrassment.

"I dressed Mallie and carried her out," Blair continued.

"What was your intention?" Bray asked.

"Tae carry her tae safety, as far away from Mr. Chisholm as possible."

"I have a question for the witness," Justice Hamilton said. "Blair Eakins, why didn't you resort to the appropriate authorities?"

What could Blair reply? That the courts were unfair, and they overwhelmingly found in favor of masters? Did he dare alienate these privileged men? "I was afraid the word of a servant would be deemed less worthy than that of a master. I acted rashly, my lord; I only wanted tae protect Mallie."

"You may sit down."

When Blair was back on his bench, Bray said, "I call Malvina Ambrose."

Blair thought his heart would crack his ribs. This would be the first time seeing each other since having been brought back to the city. The sheriff stepped out into the hallway and came back with Mallie. She immediately searched the courtroom. When their eyes met, Blair felt twenty pounds lighter. She seemed nervous, but otherwise unscathed. If Chisholm had dared lay a hand on her, Blair would have seen it at once.

"Esquire Bray," Justice Hamilton said after Mallie had taken the oath, "I'd like to ask the witness some questions, if you don't mind."

Bray nodded graciously. Mallie faced the judge. Her eyes seemed larger than ever.

"Malvina Ambrose, did you willingly take the laudanum that your master offered?"

"Yes, sir."

"And you fell asleep?"

"Yes, sir."

"What's the last thing you remember before falling asleep?"

"Mr. Chisholm was in a chair."

"Were you aware of a brawl happening in your presence?"

"No."

"Where did you wake up?"

"In a room in a tavern in Hell Town. Blair was with me."

Justice Hamilton studied her carefully. "Why didn't you return to your master?"

"Why?" She blinked, flustered. "Because of what Blair told me he saw."

"You believed him?"

"Of course I believed him."

"Esquire Bray," Justice Hamilton said, "your witness."

"My lord, I believe you've asked all the questions I had in mind."

The justices conferred for a moment. "The witness is excused," Justice Hamilton said.

When the sheriff took Mallie by the arm and led her out, Blair felt as if she were drifting out to sea, all alone on a raft.

Justice Hamilton turned to Chisholm. "Does the prosecution have anything to add?"

"No, my lord."

"Do you have something to add, Esquire Bray?"

"Yes, my lord, thank you." Bray faced the jurors on the left. "Blair and Mallie's intention was to marry as soon as the law allowed. Keep in mind that Blair Eakins's indenture was expiring in a little under three months. Why would he risk the freedom that was so close at hand?" He turned to the jurors on the right. "Why would he drag Mallie to the most dangerous part of the city, then lead her on an uncertain journey, without money, without food? Why would he disregard the additional time *she* would get? Because he thought she was in legitimate peril, and he could do nothing else but protect her as best he knew how."

The jurors left the courtroom, and there was nothing left for Blair to do but wait for the verdict.

The jury had been gone for fifteen minutes now, an eternity. When they returned at last, the sound of rain pounding atop the roof was deafening. Blair stood up, Bray at his side.

"Upon our oath and affirmation," the foreman read, "we find that Blair Eakins, indentured servant to Nicholas Chisholm, the nineteenth day of September in the ninth year of the reign of our said George the Second King of Great Britain, France, and Ireland, defender of the Faith et cetera, at the City of Philadelphia aforesaid and within the jurisdiction of this Court—with force and arms, et cetera, in and upon Nicholas Chisholm in the peace of God and of our said Lord the King, then and there being an assault did make upon the same Nicholas then and there did beat wound and evilly intreat so that of his life it was greatly despaired, and other harms unto him did to the great damage of the said Nicholas and against the peace of our said Lord the King, his crown and dignity, et cetera."

Blair kept his head up, eyes steady.

"Blair Eakins," Justice Hamilton said, "the court assuming you don't have the means to pay a fine, sentences you to the pillory, to remain there for two hours. The sentence shall be carried out forthwith."

Thunder boomed, shaking the courthouse. Blair shook too; being sent to the pillory in weather like this was often as good as a death sentence.

———

The hinged, heavy pillory boards closed around Blair's neck and wrists, the lock closed with a metallic snap, and the gaoler ran for cover. Drenched and cold to the marrow, he shut his eyes against the sheets of rain. If only he could have been sentenced to the stocks instead: the idea of sitting on the ground with his ankles secured in the stock's boards seemed rather more appealing that this uncomfortable standing position, even if he would have had to sit in the mud. He shuddered violently and his teeth chattered. At least the weather was keeping away the usual market crowds, which would otherwise gawk and pelt him with mud and rotten vegetables, or worse. He sensed a presence and opened his eyes. Chisholm was standing in front of him, under an umbrella.

"I've been ordered to sell Mallie."

Blair's delight burst forth in a "Ha!"

"I'm going to deliver her to an agent who'll sell her outside the province, far, far away."

Blair's smile withered. His eyes bore into Chisholm's with such murderous rage that the man's bluster deflated a little.

"See you at the ropewalk." Chisholm rapped Blair's forehead with his knuckles before walking away, leaning into the roaring wind. Blair clenched his hands into fists and drowned a scream of fury. The rain subsided and a crowd gathered. A particularly biting shame stung him when he again spotted Edward and William. Why did they insist on witnessing his misery? A man next to Edward raised his arm, a clump of a suspicious-looking brown matter in his hand. Edward grabbed the man's wrist so hard that the man yelped and protested, but when he saw William on his other flank, glaring at him, he relented. Edward and William scanned the crowd, their eyes daring anyone else to try to throw anything, and several people scattered away. The two lingered for a while, but the rain soon returned, driving everyone off. Blair's muscles were in misery, tired from shivering nonstop.

It was as if awls were being driven into his feet. He opened and closed his fingers, bent one knee and then the other, but found no relief.

"Blair."

He opened his eyes and saw Susannah, carrying a small kettle. "I brought you lamb stew."

He looked at the stew with ravenous hunger, and for a split second considered refusing the generous gesture; as it was, it would not be long before he had no choice but to soil himself. His body's desperate need for food, however, annulled any other consideration, and he devoured the stew that Susannah spoon-fed him.

"Ye're an angel," he whispered, his words thin wafers of ice that crumbled as soon as they left his lips. When Susannah was gone, visions flickered in his mind, like snippets of strange dreams that made no sense. He was shocked back to reality by the muscles in his legs, which seemed to have grown fangs and were gnawing on his bones. He wheezed and groaned in pain, the sounds of his agony drowned out by the storm.

CHAPTER TWENTY-SIX

Mallie lay in the fetal position on her mat, sobbing. A hulking worker named Cole had been ordered to take her to the courthouse to testify, and to return her to the ropewalk the second she was finished. He was now standing guard outside the door. Clara and Lydia had been wonderful to her since her return and, in spite of Chisholm's orders to put her to work, had left her alone. A cold blast gave her goose bumps as the door opened.

"I'll teach that Clara to follow my orders," Chisholm snarled. "Get up and gather your things!"

Mallie glowered at him but did as she was told. "Where are you taking me?" she demanded.

"Speak again and I'll slap your mouth shut."

By the time they reached an inn on the south side of Walnut Street, next to Dock Creek, Mallie was soaked, Chisholm having refused her the shelter of his umbrella the entire way. Inside the inn's dining room, a man waited at a table.

"Mr. Fagan," Chisholm said, taking a seat while he made Mallie stand, "this is the girl I'm selling."

Mallie caught her breath. Bray had done it! She shuddered, more from the thrill of it than the cold.

"It should be easy to find a buyer, don't you think?" Chisholm asked.

"Not if she dies." Fagan called a barmaid over. "Elise, get a towel."

"Yes, sir."

"So," Fagan said, returning to the transaction at hand, "the schooner leaves next Sunday for South Carolina."

Mallie stared at the agent, her happiness curdling into alarm; she had thought she'd be sold to someone in Philadelphia. Elise returned with a towel, but Mallie was too dazed to take it.

"My dear," Chisholm said with soppiness as Elise took it upon herself to dry Mallie, "you'll love working on a rice plantation."

"You should eat something," Elise said, her big black eyes full of concern.

"I'm not hungry," Mallie muttered, curled up in the sawdust on the floor of the inn's basement.

"I made it myself. It's really good."

Something in Elise's kind voice made Mallie sit up. She accepted the beef stew that the girl offered and tried a spoonful. It was delicious.

"Your cooking is better than mine," Mallie said, meaning it. Elise smiled. "Can I ask you for a favor?"

Blair was practically hanging from the pillory, his legs no longer capable of holding him up. The drenched bandage around his forehead had slipped down over his eyes; the stitches on his wound were taut against his waterlogged skin. He felt a hand lift the bandage from his eyes. He blinked, failing to recognize the very nervous-looking girl who stood before him.

"Are you Blair?"

"Aye."

"Mallie sent me."

From the moment Elise began conveying Mallie's message until she finished, a scorching ire made Blair impervious to the cold. Chisholm had followed up on his threat. Elise spoke as fast as she could and immediately turned to leave.

"Come back!" Blair yelled. The girl kept walking. "Come back, please!" he yelled again, but the girl was gone. He remembered Samuel Shipboy's dejection on the ship when they were headed for Pennsylvania—how, once he had lost Christy, he had lost the will to live. He understood now.

He felt a dry blanket being draped on him. It was Bray, doing an appalling job of hiding how rattled he was by Blair's condition. A girl stepped forward and held a flask to Blair's lips; a warm, silky ribbon of hot cider glided down his throat.

"This is Lotte," Bray said, "my servant girl."

As soon as Blair had downed the entire flask, he blurted out, "Chisholm's sending Mallie to South Carolina!"

"South Carolina?" Bray asked, incredulous. "Why do you think this?"

"Mallie sent me a message with a servant girl from the inn she's being kept in."

"Here I was with the good news that the judges had ordered Chisholm to sell her. The merry-begotten scoundrel!" Bray pressed the heel of his palms against his temples. His defeated look did not give Blair any encouragement. "What inn is she in?" he finally asked. Blair told him, and Bray fell deep in thought.

"I need to get to Perth Amboy right away," Bray said.

"What?" Blair asked, confused.

"Don't worry. I'll find you as soon as I get back."

No sooner had Bray and his servant girl left than the clerk appeared and snatched the blanket off Blair.

"That's enough of people bringing you food and drink and blankets," the clerk said, holding down his cocked hat against the wind and throwing the blanket over his shoulder. Blair stared after the clerk as he made his way back into the courthouse. He looked around, feeling as if he were floating, everything out of focus. And for the first time since landing in Philadelphia, he cried. The dam burst and seven years came gushing forth, wave after wave of hopelessness tearing and slashing his heart and mind.

Blair reached for his forehead and felt a cool, damp cloth. "Where am I?"

"At the ropewalk," Edan said.

Blair sat up with a jolt. "But I'm soiled!" Immediately he was overtaken by a violent fit of coughing.

"That's a nice churchyard cough, that is," someone commented.

"Shut yer bone box, James," Edan said, and he gently laid Blair down. "I changed ye into clean clothes."

"Oh, Edan...I'm sorry..."

"It's awricht."

"I need tae see Mallie," Blair wheezed.

"It's nine o'clock, ye have a fever, and when ye breathe, it sounds like wagon wheels on gravel. Ye're no going anywhere."

"Tomorrow, then."

"Tomorrow, *maybe*." Edan removed the cloth—now hot—from Blair's forehead, and rinsed and wrung it before reapplying it.

The fever had worsened by morning, and Clara and Lydia took turns watching over Blair until it finally receded and he fell into a deep, dreamless sleep.

"I'm giving you one more day, and then I'm putting you back to work," Chisholm told him in the morning. "Cole will make sure you don't leave the grounds until Sunday."

Blair ground his teeth as Cole placed a chair next to the door and sat down. When Clara came in and set his breakfast on the floor next to him, Blair whispered, "Mallie is at the inn on Dock. Please go tell her I promise I'll be there at daybreak on Sunday." Clara said nothing, but Blair was sure she winked.

Clara stood nervously outside the inn on Dock. Knowing Mallie was somewhere inside, but not knowing how to reach her, was maddening. A side door opened up and a girl came out, holding a cat. She placed the cat on the ground, and the animal happily sauntered off.

"Good morning," Clara said, approaching the girl.

"Good morning."

"Can you help me? A friend of mine is in there, and I need to talk to her."

The girl looked at Clara for a moment, doubtful. "Mallie?"

"How did you know?"

"She's the only servant being kept here waiting to be taken away."

"Where is she being taken away?"

"South Carolina."

Cursed Chisholm, Clara thought.

"She asked me to take a message to someone at the pillory," the girl whispered. "I almost got caught by my master."

"I have a message from that same man. Can I see her, please?"

The girl shook her head. "I'm sorry; I really am. I'm afraid my master will paddle me if he catches us. But I'll give her your message."

Clara sighed. "Tell her Clara came, and Blair promises he'll come see her as soon as the sun rises on Sunday."

November 6, 1736

At a table in the inn's dining room, Mallie sat next to Chisholm and Fagan, who was drawing up some papers. Facing her was another man.

"Mr. Sweeting," Fagan said, "please sign here."

Mallie's heart pounded.

"Congratulations, sir," Chisholm said as he shook Sweeting's hand. "It's been a pleasure doing business with you. May strong winds tomorrow deliver you safely to Jamaica."

Jamaica? Mallie felt as if a heavy fist had landed between her shoulder blades.

"Goodbye, Mallie." Chisholm patted her head before walking out, but she hardly even noticed. She knew nothing of South Carolina, but the slaves in Maryland had talked about Jamaica like it was hell. Worse, she knew it was very, very far away.

"Mr. Sweeting," Fagan offered, "I can take her to the basement."

"That won't be necessary," Sweeting replied. "We're spending the night at an inn on King, close to the wharf where our ship is docked. I've arranged for a cart to take us there."

"No!"

Mallie's outburst startled both men. She looked from one to the other. Tell them the truth; tell them someone is coming to say farewell. But then she thought, Don't trust them; they'll tell Chisholm and he'll punish Clara and Blair, and Elise will also be in trouble. Again, she argued with herself. But I won't see him till 1739!

"What is it, Mallie?" Sweeting asked.

"Nothing." She forced her face into a blank expression.

She followed her new master out into the street and climbed into the box of the cart. As they made their way to the Delaware, she replayed in her mind the last time she had seen Blair in the courthouse. The image of him in shackles was not, however, how she wanted to remember him. So she erased that picture and thought of the time they had waded into the Schuylkill and he had found a baby turtle. He seemed to glow under the sun, and that glow had begun to rouse her from her despondency. She thought of his laughter, and those times after they had made love, when his wolfish hunger had been momentarily sated and he would turn into an almost fragile cub. If she never saw him again, that was how she would remember him: as the man who had taught her she was, after all, a creature worthy of being truly loved.

———

The early dawn light cast on the water mirror images of tanneries and breweries lining Dock Creek as it curled its way a few blocks into the city. Blair rested his hands on his knees as another fit of coughing roiled through him. His eyes watered and his face was red. He scanned the moored schooners and sloops, wondering which one would carry Mallie away. He heard voices, and several workers appeared from the alley adjacent to the inn.

"Elise!" he called out, crossing the street.

The girl stopped in her tracks, looking at Blair with apprehension.

"I'm here tae see Mallie."

"Oh! You're the man from the stocks. She was taken away last night."

Blair's knees went weak.

"He sold her." Elise pointed to Fagan, who was walking out the front door. Blair ran to meet the agent.

"Sir!"

"Are you here to take my baggage?"

"No. I'm looking for Malvina Ambrose."

"Ah, yes. She's not in my custody anymore."

"Where is she?"

"I'm not allowed to say."

Blair fell to his knees, right in the middle of the street. "Sir, I'm begging ye, Mallie is my whole life. Please."

Mortified, Fagan pulled Blair to his feet. "Young man, don't make a scene."

"*I am begging ye.*" Blair was halfway to his knees again when Fagan finally relented.

"She's being taken to Jamaica. The ship leaves this morning."

"Who bought her? What's the name of the ship?"

"The man is Scott Sweeting. The ship is the *Elizabeth and Ann.*"

Blair turned his frantic eyes to the dock.

"The ship is on the Delaware," Fagan said.

"What wharf?"

"I have no idea."

Blair took off. He leaped over dogs, dodged horses, zigzagged between pedestrians, and flew down the first set of stairs he found. People on the wharf stared at him with deep worry as he leaned on a barrel, hacking so violently it seemed he was convulsing. A man approached and asked if he needed help.

"*Elizabeth—and—Ann,*" Blair gasped, "tae Jamaica."

"That one's all the way down at the Arch Street Wharf. Walk leisurely, lad. Ye'll cough out a lung."

Blair took to his heels again. By the time he arrived at Arch Street Wharf, he felt as if he were drowning. He frantically scanned all moored ships; there was no *Elizabeth and Ann*. He looked out toward the anchored ships.

"What are ye looking for, lad?" a man asked.

"The Eliz—Elizabeth and—Ann." Hack, hack, hack. "Jamaica."

"Ye'll have tae take another ship; that one left an hour ago."

Blair crumpled on the wharf, unable to believe it, his chest and back aching, his face glistening with sweat. He lay on his back, despondent, until the rain drove him away. His indenture was shorter than hers, he thought as he slowly made his way to the ropewalk. He would finish his time and go looking for her. A fresh feeling of doom clawed at him when he saw Lotte—Bray's servant—and Clara waiting at the entrance to the men's quarters.

"Finally!" Clara exclaimed. He turned to Lotte, afraid to ask what dreadful news she might be bringing.

"Mr. Bray needs to see you immediately," the girl said.

Dear Blair,

Several weeks ago I sent you a letter, letting you know I was relocating from New York to Perth Amboy. Unbeknownst to me, you had run away. Wornell Bray, my friend, has come to inform me of the predicament you're in. I'm sending my secretary, Mr. Scott Sweeting, in an attempt to buy Mallie. If we succeed, she'll be under my care until you finish your time. Then I'll send her to Philadelphia. I'll

*be eagerly awaiting news, praying our plan comes
to fruition. Your belongings remain in my care, and
whenever you send word, I'll be glad to return them.*

With my eternal gratitude,
L. Gro.
Perth Amboy, New Jersey

Blair looked up, perfectly confused. "But the agent who
sold her said she was leaving for Jamaica."

"That's what Mr. Sweeting told Mr. Chisholm." Bray
beamed with satisfaction and raised a glass with brandy. "To
our success."

"I dinna ken what tae say. I'm afeared I'll wake up," Blair
said, wheezing.

"And I'm afraid you'll faint and *not* wake up, so do me
a favor and go lie down. And try to finish your time without
getting into any more trouble. If you need anything, anytime,
come find me."

Blair stepped into the muddy street. The clouds had
emptied themselves; the afternoon sun streamed down
onto his face and shoulders. The air had never seemed so
crystal clear, the sky so open. Every street, every building
shimmered with golden autumn light. He stumbled into
the empty ropewalk quarters. Now that there was no need
to run anywhere, from anyone, for any reason, the last scrap
of strength that had kept him going drained from his body.
He collapsed on his mat in a heap, rasping snores thrum-
ming in his chest, his mouth slack, his forehead smooth.

CHAPTER TWENTY-SEVEN

September 13, 1737

Blair tapped his fingers on the table and stared out the window of the tavern toward the intersection of Fourth Street and Vine. Inside his jacket was a letter from Sweeting, informing him of Mallie's departure from Perth Amboy three days prior. She would be arriving at this end of the York Road any moment. He had spent most of the day in the tavern, except at noon when—squirming with impatience—he had paced up and down the street until the sun chased him inside. He began to wonder if she was delayed and would arrive the following day.

During the remaining seven months of his indenture, he had not set foot in any tavern, determined not to give reason to have his term extended. He kept his head down at work, carrying out without complaint the most grueling tasks Chisholm threw at him. Without money, he could not write or receive letters. Sweeting had written to Bray a couple of times, mentioning how Mallie was doing. Those reports kept Blair sane. But they had also made those past months the longest of his life, as any small news he received made every fiber of his being cry out desperately for her. When he had finished his time six weeks before, he had immediately begun to play the fiddle again to earn some money and had finally written to Groom requesting his belongings and asking Mallie to wait so he could prepare things for her arrival.

He smoothed his sleeves, and for the umpteenth time felt the ribbon of his new clubbed wig to make sure the bow was just right. He ran his hand over his face, lamenting that the smoothness of his morning shave had been lost. He raised his gaze and stopped breathing; when he had last looked out the window, the corner of Fourth and Vine had been empty. Now, a wagon was stopped there. Mallie sat among other passengers, her face peeking out from under the hood of a black traveling cloak, her eyes searching. His heart thumped as he grabbed his cocked hat. He reached the wagon just as Mallie descended, her back to him.

"Miss Malvina Ambrose."

She froze for a second, then pushed back the hood of her cloak and turned slowly.

"Are ye going tae grow more and more beautiful as time passes by?"

The heat had flushed her cheeks and plumped her lips like ripe cherries. Her eyes appeared a richer brown and brighter green than ever before. She pushed the cape off her shoulders; white, green, and red floral patterns and butterflies decorated the gorgeous black fabric of her gown, and she wore white gloves. She looked nothing like a servant. *She's not a servant*, Blair reminded himself. *She never again will be.* He took her hand and kissed it, wishing he could sweep her up in his arms.

She looked him up and down, eyes a-glitter. "Is this a new suit of clothes?"

"Aye, ye're looking at my freedom dues. I also received an old suit o' clothes and a hoe."

"The hat and wig and shoes too?"

His eyes twinkled. "I bought the hat and wig. The shoes—no, I didna buy those."

They were not the most expensive hat and wig one could buy, but it was evident they were not secondhand. The driver handed Mallie a bag and gave Blair a violin case.

"Mr. Groom said he'll never play it as well as you," Mallie said.

The driver climbed back on the wagon and clucked his tongue, and the horses snorted and clopped off.

"Where are we going?" Mallie asked.

"Home."

Blair set the bag and violin case on a table, next to a dish with pears and a stack of newspapers. He hung his hat, jacket, waistcoat, and Mallie's cloak on a stand and opened the windows. She studied the room, empty but for the small table, the stand, a shoemaker's bench and tools, two chairs, two stools, and several shoes in different stages of construction. Two leather buckets with "EAKINS" painted on them hung from a wall.

"What do ye think?" he asked anxiously.

"It's wonderful…but how…?"

He wrapped her in his arms and kissed her. She clasped her fingers behind his neck, her every fear dissolving like snow falling on water. She nibbled his lip, and he pulled her closer still. He kissed her eyes and her forehead and whispered in her ear, "I need tae show ye something." He pulled the chairs in front of the fireplace and sat her down.

"Is it not warm enough for you?" she asked, removing her gloves and cap and fanning herself as he stoked the fire and hung a pot on a trammel over the flames. He worried a knife between two bricks on a wall until one came loose, and from the cavity took a black pillar candle and dropped it into the pot.

"Is that our supper?" Mallie asked, chuckling.

"Aye. And breakfast and dinner and rent, and my cordwainer tools."

She looked inside the pot; the candle was half melted. Mixed in with the melted wax were several coins: a collection of pounds and two guineas. Mallie looked up, eyes wide. "Where did that come from?"

"I've been saving it for years. I had another two candles like this one. They were with the things Mr. Groom was keeping." He stirred the tallow, and more coins were released from their fatty vault. He fished out the coins with a slotted spoon and placed them in a wooden dish. Mallie pulled out a handkerchief from her pocket and wiped her face.

"I dinna want ye melting too," Blair said. "We should go upstairs so ye can remove yer gown."

"I've something to tell you first," she said shyly, almost embarrassed.

"What?"

"Maybe it's silly…"

"Tell me."

"I decided that…today's my birthday."

He laughed. "I've a birthday gift for ye, then," he said, grabbing the violin case. When they reached the closed bedroom door on the second floor, he asked her to close her eyes. She heard the door creak softly and the floor squeak and felt his hand in hers.

"Take three steps. Open yer eyes."

She clapped her hands on her cheeks and squealed with delight. "A bed!" She sat on the edge and ran her hands on the bedspread. She might as well have unearthed a chest full of precious jewels. "I've never had my own bed." Something hanging on a wall caught her attention. "Where did you get that?"

A shadow flitted over Blair's face. "Ronald gave it to me," he said, taking the neck knife. "It was also with the things Mr. Groom kept for me." He pulled the knife out and offered her the sheath. She turned it over, appreciating the marvelous quillwork, stirred by the fact that Blair had hung it where he would be able to see it every morning when he woke up, and every night when he went to bed.

"It's beautiful," she said, handing it back. He returned it to the wall.

"Stand up and raise yer arms," he said. He took the bottom of her gown and peeled it off over her head, leaving her with her petticoats and stay.

"Ooh, that's much better," she exclaimed, and sat down again. He picked up the violin case from where he had left it on the floor, sat next to her on the bed, and opened the lid. Under the strings was a folded note with the words *For Blair Eakins* written on it.

"Will ye read it for me, Mallie?"

She took the note from him. "Esteemed Blair, although I would be very glad to hear you play this violin again someday, it is now yours to keep or sell. It's worth seventy pounds. L. Gro."

"*Seventy pounds?*" He closed the lid as if the violin were a sleeping child. He took a wig stand from a chair, hung his wig, placed both on the floor, and set the violin case on the chair. He looked at the bed, hands on his hips. "I havena slept in a bed since leaving Ireland. I've been dying tae try this."

"Haven't you been spending nights here?"

"Aye, but I've been sleeping on the floor. I was waiting for ye, my dear."

He removed his shoes, picked up her feet, and removed her shoes as well. He swung her legs onto the bed and jumped up, on all fours, catching her body between his arms and legs. She freed her arms, untied the cord holding his ponytail, and wove her fingers through his thick hair. He took the ends of the laces of her stay between his teeth and shook his head side to side, growling. She let her hands fall behind her head, giggling. A baby next door started to cry, a dog barked and a dozen more joined in, and a group of rowdy young men on their way to a tavern made a ruckus as they passed under the window—but neither Blair nor Mallie heard any of it.

ABOUT THE AUTHOR

INDRA ZUNO was born in Mexico, where she enjoyed a successful career as a performer in theater and television before turning to writing. She was a recipient of the 2017–2018 UCLA Claire Carmichael Scholarship in Novel Writing, and was subsequently nominated for the 2017 UCLA James Kirkwood Prize in Creative Writing and the 2018 UCLA Allegra Johnson Writing Prize. As part of her extensive research for her debut novel, *Freedom Dues*, Indra spent time in Northern Ireland, Pennsylvania, and two weeks aboard *The Lady Washington*, an eighteenth-century replica tall ship, washing decks and climbing masts. She met with the Master Cordwainer at Colonial Williamsburg and with a member of the Delaware tribe who is the Director of the Lenape Language Project. Immersing herself in her subject, she read over one hundred books on white servitude, the Delaware tribe, and Scots-Irish immigration, and reviewed original eighteenth-century court records at the Historical Society of Pennsylvania and the Philadelphia Archives. To learn more, visit her website IndraZuno.com, on Facebook @indrazunowriter, or follow her on Twitter @IndraZuno.

CPSIA information can be obtained
at www.ICGtesting.com
Printed in the USA
FSHW011726030820
72637FS

9 781734 165210